A CUPFUL
OF TEARS

A
CUPFUL
of
TEARS

Sixteen Victorian
Novelettes

Selected by

MARTIN SEYMOUR-SMITH

WOLFE PUBLISHING LTD
167 OXFORD STREET · LONDON W1

02352728

VL|UL

Printed in Great Britain by
Billing & Sons Limited, Guildford and London

Contents

To TERENCE HARDS

Foreword

If the occupation of writing books were simply an amusement, how pleasant the task might be made, by dwelling only upon pleasing themes —by describing human life as a scene of unclouded sunshine, and human nature as exempt from sorrow and sin!

But when the office of writer is undertaken as a duty, rather than as the glib pleasure of the trifler, the case assumes a widely different aspect. Human life must then be described, not as it might be, but as it is, in order that *truth* may be recognised under the garb of fiction—and that error of opinion may thus be traced out to its inevitable consequence—error of conduct!

Many of these stories from a former era point a moral; but the saddest of them is not without that tenderness of sympathy which must ultimately do much to avert those evils which have ever widely prevailed in our society, even to the extent of ruining homes—bodily depravity, drunkenness, addiction to games of chance, and, last but by no means least, the general weakness of character that can for one moment condone the abuses above enumerated. They are typical of the popular fiction of their time—roughly the latter half of the last century. The assiduous and attentive reader will note that they have not one, but two features, in common: while they bring a lump to the throat and tears to the eyes, they gently instruct us in the benign intentions of a power greater than ourselves. The editor and his publishers earnestly hope and trust that when this book has at last been put aside, the reader, flushed and tearful from his or her feast of sorrow, may also be purged of some of those sins within himself or herself to which all of us on this globe are prone.

Irene Iddesleigh is printed in all its splendid and not always orthodox grammatical entirety, but all the other stories have been somewhat abridged—but in no case have the author's words been substantially altered.

I should like to thank Mrs. W. Gardner, James Reeves and my father for their invaluable and generous help and advice during the compilation of this book.

MARTIN SEYMOUR-SMITH

Bexhill-on-sea
May, 1965

IRENE IDDESLEIGH

by

Mrs. AMANDA McKITTRICK ROS

CHAPTER I

SYMPATHISE with me, indeed! Ah, no! Cast your sympathy on the chill waves of troubled waters; fling it on the oases of futurity: dash it against the rock of gossip; or, better still, allow it to remain within the false and faithless bosom of buried scorn.

Such were a few remarks of Irene as she paced the beach of limited freedom, alone and unprotected. Sympathy can wound the breast of trodden patience—it hath no rival to insure the feelings we possess, save that of sorrow.

The gloomy mansion stands firmly within the ivy-covered, stoutly-built walls of Dunfern, vast in proportion and magnificent in display. It has been built over three hundred years, and its structure stands respectably distant from modern advancement, and in some degrees it could boast of architectural designs rarely, if ever, attempted since its construction.

The entrance to this beautiful home of Sir Hugh Dunfern, the present owner, is planned on most antique principles; nothing save an enormous iron gate meets the gaze of the visitor, who at first is inclined to think that all public rumours relative to its magnificence are only the utterances of the boastful and idle; nor until within its winding paths of finest pebble, studded here and there with huge stones of unpolished granite, could the mind for a moment conceive or entertain the faintest idea of its quaint grandeur.

Beautiful, however, as Dunfern mansion may seem to the anxious eye

A*   9

of the beholder, yet it is not altogether free from mystery. Whilst many of
its rooms, with walls of crystal, are gorgeously and profusely furnished,
others are locked incessantly against the foot of the cautious intruder,
having in them only a few traditional relics of no material consequence
whatever, or even interest, to any outside the ancestral line of its occupants.

It has often been the chief subject of comment amongst the few distinguished visitors welcomed within its spacious apartments, why seemingly
the finest rooms the mansion owned were always shut against their eager
and scrutinizing gaze: or why, when referred to by any of them, the
matter was always treated with silence.

All that can now be done is merely to allow the thought to dwindle
into bleak oblivion, until aroused to that standard of disclosure which
defies hindrance.

Within the venerable walls surrounding this erection of amazement and
wonder may be seen species of trees rarely, if ever, met with: yea, within
the beaded borders of this grand old mansion the eye of the privileged
beholds the magnificent lake, studded on every side with stone of costliest
cut and finish: the richest vineries, the most elegant ferns, the daintiest
conservatories, the flowers and plants of almost every clime in abundance,
the most fashionable walks, the most intricate windings that imagination
could possibly conceive or genius contrive. In fact, it has well been named
"The Eden of Luxury."

Dunfern mansion was handed down as an heirloom since its purchase
by Walter, third Earl of Dunfern, in 1674: and since then has been tenderly
cared for internally, and carefully guarded externally, by the skilful hands
of noted artisans. The present owner is only son of Sir John Dunfern, by
Irene, adopted daughter of Lord and Lady Dilworth, of Dilworth Castle,
County Kent.

CHAPTER II

THE December sun had hidden its dull rays behind the huge rocks
that rose monstrously high west of Dunfern mansion, and ceased
to gladden the superb apartment Sir John occupied most of the
day. They had withdrawn their faint reflection from within the mirrored
walls of this solitary chamber to brighten other homes with their never-
dying sheen.

As the dull, grey evening advanced to such a degree as to render a look
of brightness imperative to the surroundings of its sole occupant, Sir John
requested that his favourite apartment should be made bright as possible
by adding more fuel to the smouldering ashes within the glistening bars

which guarded their remains. This being done, three huge lamps were lighted, and placed at respectable distances from each other, when Sir John, with his accustomed grace, began to peruse some of his evening papers.

Though a man of forty summers, he never yet had entertained the thought of yielding up his bacheloric ideas to supplace them with others which eventually should coincide with those of a different sex: in fact, he never had bestowed a thought on changing his habits and manner of living, nor until fully realising his position of birthright, that had been treasured by his ancestors for such a lengthened period, and which, sooner or later, must pass into strangers' hands, did the thought ever occur to him of entering into the league of the blessed.

The clock had just chimed nine when a maid entered with a note, neatly laid on a trim little tray, which she placed on the table close beside her master, and then retired. It was rather unusual for him to receive letters so late in the evening, and until he was in full possession of its contents he could not form the faintest imagination of its worth.

Not far from Dunfern Mansion may be seen situated on a rising hill the beautiful Castle of Lord and Lady Dilworth, a prominent building commanding the finest view in the country. It had been remodelled by the present owner, after inheriting it from his late maternal uncle—Lord Leyburn; and, although equipped with all modern improvements and inventions necessary, yet there dwelt a lack of design and beauty about it that was possessed by Dunfern Mansion.

The bountiful owner of Dilworth Castle differed much in many respects from Sir John Dunfern. He was a nobleman of rare tact and capacities: a keen sportsman; a Turf frequenter; an ardent politician; and, in fact, a lover of everything which served to promote the interests of his extended and varied social circle in particular, and entire community in general.

Lady Dilworth, it may here be mentioned, was never of a very robust nature, and often had she felt the great strain of society press rather heavily on her weak frame, so much so, as to render the adoption of the subject of this book indispensable. Drawing his chair closer to the table, on which one of the great lamps stood, Sir John proceeded to peruse the contents of the note. It was an invitation from Lord and Lady Dilworth to attend a ball at Dilworth Castle on 22nd prox., given by them in honour of the marriage of Henry, fifth Marquis of Hill-Hall, with Ethel, Countess of Maidstone.

Lord Dilworth and the Marquis were personal friends of Sir John, and to accept this kind and courteous invitation would mean a step towards the summit of the matrimonial ladder, by meeting the majority of the fully-fledged belles in and around Canterbury, and especially Irene Iddesleigh, Lord Dilworth's adopted daughter, more generally known as "The Southern Beauty." He slept over the matter that night, with the result that next morning he wrote accepting the kind invitation, more through curiosity than desire.

Although he led a quiet and retired life, generally speaking, still he did not absent himself totally from a few social meetings occasionally, and if imagination painted his future in the manner so artfully designed by Lady Dilworth, no doubt this visit to Dilworth Castle might convert it into reality.

Arriving at the elegant castle, with its tower of modern fame, and spires of Gothic structure, Sir John was met in its great hall by the genial hostess, who conducted him to the brilliant reception-room, superbly laid out for the comfort of its guests; and being the first to arrive, was thus afforded a good opportunity of inspecting the many valuable relics and works of art that adorned its huge and velvety walls.

On the centre wall right opposite where he sat hung a painted portrait, life-size, an admirable production of the well-known artist, "Peto," and not knowing where such an original of perfection and beauty could be found, he resolved to inquire, when opportunity offered, whose portrait it might be.

At this stage the numerous guests began to assemble, including the majority of the leading gentry in and around Canterbury, as it was looked upon as the chief social event of the season. Mothers were most fidgety that their daughters should don their costliest gowns and brilliants, as rumour had it that the noble heir to Dunfern estate should honour the assembly with his august presence.

Report gained ground that Sir John, having quietly crept out of boy-hood for a lengthened period, would end his days harnessed singly, but idle gossip, flying at all times kite-high, soon gave place in the wavering minds of society belles to that of more serious consideration and welcome expectancy.

On being introduced to all those outside his present circle of acquaint-ance on this evening, and viewing the dazzling glow of splendour which shone, through spectacles of wonder, in all its glory, Sir John felt his past life but a dismal dream, brightened here and there with a crystal speck of sunshine that had partly hidden its gladdening rays of bright futurity until compelled to glitter with the daring effect they soon should produce. But there awaited his view another beam of life's bright rays, who, on entering, last of all, commanded the minute attention of every one present—this was the beautiful Irene Iddesleigh.

How the look of jealousy, combined with sarcasm, substituted those of love and bashfulness! How the titter of tainted mockery rang throughout the entire apartment, and could hardly fail to catch the ear of her whose queenly appearance occasioned it! These looks and taunts serving to con-vince Sir John of Nature's fragile cloak which covers too often the image of indignation and false show, and seals within the breasts of honour and equality resolutions of an iron mould. On being introduced to Irene, Sir John concluded instantly, without instituting further inquiry, that this must be the original of the portrait so warmly admired by him. There she stood, an image of perfection and divine beauty, attired in a robe of richest snowy tint, relieved here and there by a few tiny sprigs of the most dainty maidenhair fern, without any ornaments whatever, save a diamond necklet of famous sparkling lustre and priceless value.

As the evening rolled into the small hours of the morning, the numerous guests began to repair to their respective homes, none of the weaker sex having had the slightest advancement in the direction of their coveted intentions, save Irene, who was fortunate in securing the attention of Sir John Dunfern during the happy hours that fled so quickly.

Immediately before taking his departure he pressed firmly her snowy hand, and left the pretty-gilded area which surrounded his first hopes of matrimony to enter what he was beginning to believe the weary apartments of Dunfern Mansion, that previously had held him bound to them in hermit-like fashion.

CHAPTER III

AROUSE the seeming deadly creature to that standard of joy and gladness which should mark his noble path! Endow him with the dewdrops of affection, cast from him the pangs of the dull past, and stamp them for ever beneath the waves of trouble's waters; brighten his life as thou wouldst that of a faded flower; and when the hottest ray of that heavenly orb shall shoot its cheerful charge against the window panes of Dunfern Mansion, the worthy owner can receive it with true and profound thankfulness. Three weeks had scarcely passed ere Sir John was made the recipient of another invitation to Dilworth Castle. This second effusion of cordiality required neither anxious thought nor prolonged decision how to act, knowing as he did that it would again serve to bring his present thoughts into practice by affording him another opportunity of sharing in the loving looks of one for whom he feared there dwelt a strong inclination on his part to advance his affection.

Irene stood looking out on the lake beyond the richly draped window, ruminating on the days of her childhood, which lent a look of dullness to the beautiful face that beamed with delight as Sir John Dunfern entered. The evening was very pleasantly and quietly spent, Irene commanding the greater part of his time and attention, on account of Lady Dilworth being slightly ailing, whose health, generally speaking, at this period was not so robust as formerly, and consequently failed to warrant too many callers. As the clock struck eleven Sir John began to think of returning home, feeling quite happy, fancying his great affection was returned in full by Irene.

Being very domesticated, and having the stiff ideas of a bachelor of long standing so firmly imprinted in his nature, he felt very diffident in asking the object of his visit when next they should meet. But Lady Dilworth entering before taking his departure, saved him putting the shy question by placing herself in his position and demanding the required reply. Sir John promised without further ceremony to visit them more frequently in future, and left their midst with hasty step, lingering in the hall to cast another look at the lovely form which stood not far distant. Leisurely leaning back in his carriage, and burying himself in his great and costly cloak demanded by the night's icy aspect, he rolled along towards his home drowned in sweet thought of the beautiful girl whom he only recently knew, but his regard for her raged with such rambling anxiety as to convince him of the propriety of making her aware how he meant to play the part of lover.

Until now he was inclined to be prejudiced against the snares and allurements of women, but he strongly resolved to try gradually and abandon every unkind thought harboured in his mind against them, fearing lest all his conjured imaginations were both unjust and selfish; and determined to drown them for ever in the clashing gulf of fate, felt a prouder and happier mortal than before.

But time would solve the problem and heal the wound which penetrated so deeply his bosom. Yea, a short time he hoped would bring his creeping fever of endearment under the binding stay of appointed authority, and heal its weakening effects with the sacred salve of truth.

Not until the horses dashed up the winding avenue with increased alacrity was he shaken from his meditating attitude, to be ushered once more into his home of boundless wealth. The lonely stare of grave bewilderment took the place of happiness that formerly seemed built in abundance for him within its walls, as he entered the palatial and gorgeously equipped abode he principally inhabited, feeling the tinge of the dull past filling him with entire despair, whilst meditating on the happy future which presented itself to him. How in a trivial period this lonely spot, he thought, should prove the beacon of never-dying bliss, when once furnished with the most precious treasure on earth—a virtuous woman! Ah! the very thought of his embosomed and anticipated alliance made him nervously happy; and believing a bright and noble future lay in store for the lonely owner of Dunfern Estate, he resolved to indulge nature in a few hours of calm repose.

The days moved along more quickly Sir John believed than formerly; and possibly he may have imagined this was so, as he felt no longer fettered with fear of fighting with his inward friend—obstinacy, whose hand of drowsy bachelorism seemed for ever closed to his changing charity; he had at last thrown aside the garb of female dislike, and patronised that of a warm-hearted lover.

Irene did not lead Lady Dilworth to believe that she really cared for Sir John, and, when his name cropped up occasionally, she allowed herself always to keep the coast of conversation clear that would likely convict her views most, and managed cleverly thereby to deceive the friend who came not a day too soon to her rescue. Perhaps had Lady Dilworth proved less concerned about the orphan charge she freed from a life of toil, apparently, and instructed her more on the branches of integrity, then the lovely youthful Irene could have decided more honorably in all cases of questioning, and would have done justice, not alone to herself, but to all concerned; but, like many others similarly surrounded with lovers, battling in the war of extremes, and encompassed on all sides with apparent luxuries, she was confident she would some day come off victorious by acting the clever Corinthian.

CHAPTER IV

WHEN on the eve of glory, whilst brooding over the prospects of a bright and happy future, whilst meditating upon the risky right of justice, there we remain, wanderers on the cloudy surface of mental woe, disappointment and danger, inhabitants of the grim sphere of anticipated imagery, partakers of the poisonous dregs of concocted injustice. Yet such is life.

Sir John's visits began now to be numerous at Dilworth Castle, each visit serving further to strengthen the link of relationship, and bury, in the heaving breast of seeking solace, the dull delight of the weary past. As the weeks wore on, he reckoned them only as days, when comparing their loving length with those of the bleak years he tried to enjoy alone, before taking such steps—yes, serious steps—as those fancied by the would-be bachelor.

At first he was careless and indifferent to the flowery harangues of mothers who paid him periodical visits, with their daughters, of apology, and firmly retained the obstinate qualities of an autocratic ruler, until softened in the presence of one he found he was learning to steadily love. He believed now that the chief stripes, viz.—observation, inclination, advancement and accomplishment, in the well-spun web of matrimony, must harmonise with the groundwork of happiness, without which our lives are not worth an unstamped coin.

Love's path, on which Sir John was known now to tread with the step of intensity, seemed smooth as the ice of Inglewood. There were no obstacles in his way of which he was yet aware, save imagination; this, also, was chased from his mind by the evident and ample return of Irene's polished affection, the foul gloss of which he failed to notice, and whose pretentions were so cleverly carried out as to defy detection.

Irene was an accomplished and clever girl, and well able to sustain her hidden regard throughout for one who for years previous had been endeavouring to remove the great barrier of position which blocked his path of approach towards her affection. As yet her parentage was totally unknown to Sir John; still, he felt it must not have belonged to the rude and ridiculous, since she possessed all the qualities, outwardly, and features, of a highly refined race. And when only a girl of eleven summers, when the worthy hand of benevolence, friendship, and love clutched the tiny fingers of absolute want, there visibly seemed nothing lacking in appearance, manner, or education to solicit the pity or suspicion of her charitable guardian and protector.

Sir John Dunfern's many visits of late to Dilworth Castle had been creating quite a sensation throughout the quiet corners of costly curiosity, until an announcement appeared in *Mack's Society Journal* to the following effect:—

"A marriage is arranged to take place in August between Sir John Dunfern, of Dunfern Mansion, County Kent, and Irene Iddesleigh, adopted daughter of Lord and Lady Dilworth, of Dilworth Castle, in same county."

This notice, no doubt, caused the partakers in drawing-room *tête-à-têtes* to share in the pangs of jealousy, with silent resentment. Perplexity, a little, would find refuge within the homes of many who led Society by the string of superficial show and pompous importance; and during the interval that elapsed between such an announcement and its important celebration, many and infamous were the charges poured forth against Irene Iddesleigh.

The month preceding Irene's wedding was one of merriment at Dilworth Castle, Lord and Lady Dilworth extending the social hand of fashionable folly on four different occasions. They seemed drunk with delight that Irene, whom they looked upon as their own daughter, should carry off the palm of purity, whilst affluence, position, and title were for years waiting with restless pride to triumph at its grasp.

It was at the second of these social gatherings that the first seed of jealousy was sown within the breast of Sir John Dunfern, and which had a tendency to remain until it gradually grew to such a rapid state of maturity as to be rooted, if possible, for ever from its dusty bed of ambush.

Yes, when the merriment was at its height, and the heat too oppressive to allow much comfort to the corpulent, the espoused of Irene dropped unexpectedly out of the midst of the aristocratic throng, and being passionately an ardent admirer of the fairy-like fruits of the efforts of the horticulturist, directed his footsteps towards the well-filled conservatory at the south wing of the building.

The different-shaded lights which dangled from its roof bestowed a Indian exquisiteness on the many quaint and delicate productions of nature that rested daintily in their beds of terra-cotta tint.

But before leaving the room he vaguely scanned the throng to catch a glimpse of Irene, and failed to notice her amongst the many who danced so gaily to the well-timed tunes of the celebrated pianist, Charles Wohden, whose musical touch was always capable of melting the most hardened sinner into moods of mellow softness, or cheering the most downcast and raising their drooping look of sadness to that of highstrung hilarity.

Sir John wandered in and out through the numerous windings of sweetest fragrance, until arriving at the farthest corner, of rather darkened shade, and on a wire couch beheld the object of his pursuits, in closest conversation with her tutor, whose name he had altogether failed to remember, only having had the pleasure of his acquaintance a few hours before.

"Can it be possible?" exclaimed Sir John, in profound astonishment. "Why, I have been searching for you for some time past, and have accidentally found you at last!" Irene, rising to her feet in a second, was utterly dazed, and had the dim lights shewed her proud face to advantage, the ruddy glow of deepest crimson guilt would have manifested itself to a much greater degree. Making multitudinous apologies, etc., she at once joined Sir John, who led her back, in apparent triumph, to share the next waltz.

How the true heart beat with growing passion during the remainder of the merry festivity, and as the final announcement of separation was whispered from ear to ear, the gradual wane of Love's lofty right would fain have dwindled into pompous nothing as the thought kept tickling his warm enthusiasm with the nimble fingers of jealousy. That she whom he had ardently hoped should share his future with sheer and loving caresses of constant companionship and wifelike wisdom should be trapped in probably vowing to another her great devotion for him!

But better allow the sickening thought to die on the eve of insult rather than live in the breast of him who, at no distant date, would hear the merry peals of wedding bells ring with gladness, and naturally rejoice at the object of their origin.

CHAPTER V

OUR hopes when elevated to that standard of ambition which demands unison may fall asunder like an ancient ruin. They are no longer fit for construction unless on an approved principle. They smoulder away like the ashes of burnt embers, and are cast outwardly from their confined abode, never more to be found where once they existed only as smouldering serpents of scorned pride.

The little chat that Irene apparently enjoyed in the conservatory would gladly have become an act of forgetfulness on her part had not Sir John reminded her of its existence a few days afterwards. The spark of jealous passion had not fully died out after the incident referred to, and awaiting silently its decease, Sir John almost had grown a mourner to its imagined demise, following its undying remains so far as the village of Opportunity, when it was again to revive and shine as luminously as before.

It happened about three weeks preceding the day set apart for their holy union, on Sir John arriving at the castle, he was informed of Irene's recent exit, and gently turning away, he resolved to have a stroll in the tastefully laid-out gardens with the sole object of meeting her.

Walking leisurely along, and stopping to pick up some fallen fruit, he suddenly heard a faint sound issue from amongst the trees. Remaining breathless for a few seconds, lest he might be deceived by the rippling sounds of the adjacent waves, he again heard the same sweet strain, but of much longer duration than before, and quietly moving towards the spot whence it issued, another sound met his ear in the distance, which seemed to be the hasty tread of some one making good an escape, before he got time to view the object he would eagerly have pursued, but checking his desire somewhat, he allowed the matter to sink into silence. Boldly moving towards the spot whence the sound of music issued, how delightfully surprised was he to find a magnificently-constructed little summer-house, a charming pyramidal Gothic structure, robed internally with mossy mantles of nature, and brightened beyond conception with the instrument of humanity which gave origin to such pathetic and sweetened strains.

Politely offering an apology for intruding on the private little palace of Irene, who failed completely to hide her gross confusion from the keen gaze of her espoused, who never seemed to notice in the least the sudden change that swept so swiftly over her pallid cheeks at his unexpected visit, Sir John sat down.

Irene held in her snowy palms a roll of Italian music, which she earnestly endeavoured to conceal from his penetrating stare, probably on account of the words contained therein, which for ever would be unknown to his varied sphere of knowledge, and which would undoubtedly have betrayed her feelings, never dreaming that they should strike other ears than those for whom they practically were intended.

Perceiving her great excitement at the unexpected appearance of him, who ever afterwards kept his jealous thoughts in silent motion, he absolutely evaded making any inquiry whatever, or slightest allusion to the name and nature of the parchment she so firmly retained. Sir John chatted gaily until he gained good ground for delivering to her the message that instinct had so prompted him to utter.

"Irene, my beloved one," he began; "it is now only about a score of days until I hoped for ever to call you mine; a hope which unmercifully has haunted me since I fortunately gazed on your lovely face; a hope which I trusted should be fully appreciated by both you and me, and which, I now must own, can never be realised until the clearance of the barrier that since our engagement has been but too apparent."

"The sole object of my visit, my dear Irene"—here Sir John clasped her tender hand in his—"to-night is to elicit from you a matter that lately has cast a shadowy gloom over my anticipated bright and cheerful future. I am not one of those mortals who takes offence at trifles, neither am I a man of hasty temper or words—quite the contrary, I assure you; but it has, fortunately or unfortunately, been probably a failing amongst my ancestors to court sensitiveness in its minutest detail, and, I must acknowledge, I stray not from any of them in this particular point.

"I must acquaint you, though it pains me deeply to do so, that lately you have not treated me with such respect or attention as you certainly lavished upon me before the announcement of our engagement, and for what reason or reasons I now wish to be apprised. You seem when in company with others to ignore my remarks to you entirely, and treat them with proud disdain, as if shame took the place of pride at my wordy approach! I felt and do feel quite hurt, and am resolved that no such repetition shall take place in future. I promised to be at the castle last night, but unfortunately I felt indisposed, and only that I wished to have a thorough understanding relative to your recent conduct, and which has pained me acutely, I should not have ventured out of doors this evening either. I was, in consequence, obliged to write you last night, asking a written reply, which you failed to give! And this evening, instead of being doubly rejoiced at my presence, you, on the contrary, seem doubly annoyed! I therefore pray, my dearest Irene, that you will, and I am persuaded honestly, not hesitate to satisfy me regarding this unpleasantness, that should anything of which you are now aware cause your conduct to be changed towards me, do not allow it a lair within your breast, but confide in me as thou wouldst in a dearly-trusted and faithful lover."

At this stage Irene began to consider seriously the earnestness that accompanied the words of Sir John, knowing well she had been guilty, grossly guilty, of the charges with which he impeached her, and which were mixed with child-like simplicity, descriptive only of a world-famed bachelor. She pondered whether or not honesty should take the place of deceit—too often practised in women—and concluded to adopt the latter weapon of defence. Raising her hazel eyes to his, and clearing the weft of truth that had been mixing with the warp of falsehood to form an answer of plausible texture, fringed with different shades of love, she thus began:

"My dearest and much beloved, I assure you your remarks have astounded me not a little! Your words sting like a wasp, though, I am quite convinced, unintentionally. You are well aware that within a short period I will be marked out publicly as mistress of Dunfern mansion—an honour revered in every respect by me; an honour to which I at one time dared never aspire; an honour coveted by many much more worthy than I, whose parentage is as yet bathed in the ocean of oblivious ostentation, until some future day, when I trust it shall stand out boldly upon the brink of disclosure to dry its saturated form and watery wear with the heat of equality. You are about to place me in a position which cannot fail to wring from jealousy and covetousness their flaming torch of abuse. Yes, Sir John, on me you have not ceased to lavish every available treasure and token of your unbounded love. You have been to me not only a loyal admirer, but a thoroughly upright and estimable example of life's purest treasures. You have resolved to place me by your side as your equal, whilst wealth in boundless store is thirsting for your torch. You have elevated my unknown position to such a pitch as to defy taunt or jeer, and at any time if I may have, seemingly, ignored your advances, it was purely want of thought, and not through any underhand motive or scheme whatever.

"I assure you your allusion to my verbal answer last night is very pronounced, and may be overlooked on the ground of pure disappointment. Our time of singleness is now short, and begging your forgiveness for my seeming neglect or indifference, I hope the tide, which until now has flown so gently, may not be stayed on the eve of entering the harbour of harmony, peace, and love."

At the commencement of Irene's answer of lavishing praises and flimsy apologies, her affianced moved to the opposite corner of the rustic building to scan the features of her he wholly worshipped and reluctantly doubted. Every sentence the able and beautiful girl uttered caused Sir John to shift his apparently uncomfortable person nearer and nearer, watching at the same time minutely the divine picture of innocence, until at last, when her reply was ended, he found himself, altogether unconsciously, clasping her to his bosom, whilst the ruby rims which so recently proclaimed accusations and innocence met with unearthly sweetness, chasing every fault over the hills of doubt, until hidden in the hollow of immediate hate.

CHAPTER VI

THE silvery touch of fortune is too often gilt with betrayal: the meddling mouth of extravagance swallows every desire, and eats the heart of honesty with pickled pride: the imposury of position is petty, and ends, as it should commence, with stirring strife. But conversion of feminine opinions tries the touchy temper of opposition, and too seldom terminates victoriously.

"Great mercy! Only another week and I shall almost cease to be a free thinker! Just seven days more and what!—I shall openly have to confess to the world an untruth! Would there be any means of flight from the dangerous dragon that haunts me night and day? Could anything possible be done to save myself from false alliance? Too late!—too late!

"Only seven days and this beautiful boudoir shall own me no more, with its walls of purest white and gilded borders!

"Just seven days and I shall be fettered with chains of dragging dislike and disappointment! Only seven days and thus shall end my cherished hopes, my girlish pride, my most ardent wish, but, alas! not my love! Seven days more shall see my own darling Os"—— Suddenly Irene was aroused by the ringing of the breakfast bell, before she got time to finish the sentence that troubled her weary brain for months before. Dressing herself with frantic expertness, she dashed down the winding staircase with an alacrity better imagined than described, and rushing into the breakfast room where Lord and Lady Dilworth eagerly awaited her, presented the outward mocking appearance of being the happiest of mortals. Her beloved benefactors, who had been the prime movers in the matter of matrimony, saw plainly a saddened look about the lovely face, which Irene tried hard to suppress, and asking why it appeared at this gay time, was answered evasively. Indeed, Lord and Lady Dilworth were wholly ignorant of the present state of affairs, nor did Irene reveal at any time to Lady Dilworth her great hatred for Sir John, or her maddened desire to become the wife of a poor tutor.

Had she only taken into her confidence her whose wise counsel and motherly example were at all times a prompt step to decision; or had she only hinted to Lady Dilworth her manifest inability to return Sir John's great affection, matters would probably have reached another climax. But owing to the present precarious position in which Lord and Lady Dilworth stood, and as yet unknown to both Irene and other most intimate acquaintances, great was Lady Dilworth's desire to see Irene permanently settled, knowing as she did that ere the sun of another August day would flash its shimmering rays against the crystal stays of Dilworth Castle she would be beyond easy access to Irene either in time of rejoicing or sorrowing.

Preparations were at last completed for such an auspicious event. Invitations were issued numerously for the reception to be held at Dilworth Castle after Irene's marriage, but sparingly during the ceremony; all of which were mostly accepted. Costly, multiplying, and varied were the gifts received by Irene; enough to make a princess stare with startling bewilderment.

Amongst the many, none came from Irene's tutor, Oscar Otwell, And although he was the first to whom Lady Dilworth addressed an invitation, still there was no reply, much to the annoyance and astonishment of hostess on the one hand and knowledge of Irene on the other; as, verily, it was not known to Irene that absolute indifference to facts! seemingly of domestic importance, was a positive point in Oscar, and never better exemplified than in the present existing state of affairs, which, sickly as it proved to Irene, was deadly so to Oscar.

But future facts had to be solved, which undoubtedly would be treated with more comparative reverence than heretofore, by him who suffered severely—yea, acutely—from the blow struck him on the eve of aspiration and achievement. Love, alas! when smitten with the sword of indifference, dieth soon, but once struck on the tunnelled cheek of secrecy with the hand of pity there leaves a scar of indelible intolerance, until wiped out for ever with the curative balsam of battled freedom.

Sir John and Irene met in Dilworth Castle for the last time on the morning of the third day of August, being the day set apart for the celebration of their marriage. It commenced with the ringing of the village bells; the sun shone forth in all his universal glory; emblems of the approaching festivity did not fail to appear on the housetops of the humblest village peasant; gladness reigned throughout the household, and all hearts, save two, rejoiced with unabated activity.

It was a morning never to be forgotten by Lord and Lady Dilworth, who, on that day, would be robbed of the treasure held firm and fast by them for the lengthened period of nine years, and which they yielded up with hearts of sorrow, not because of the change in which Irene should have taken deep interest, but on account of the burthen of trouble which loaded them with leaden weights of which they could not possibly free themselves. The intense excitement that for weeks before had found such refuge within their cherished and much-loved home had not long now to live: it would die on the doorstep of apparent bereavement never more to appear within Dilworth Castle under similar circumstances. They knew well that the gnawing jaws of poverty, which for years had failed to expose their grinding power, had reached the last and only bite of sudden termination, and thereby stamped their marks of melancholy so impressively upon the noble brows of the worthy owners of Dilworth Castle, that time could never blot them from observation. As before stated few were those invited to be present at the wedding ceremony, which was to take place about twelve o'clock noon.

Sir John arrived at the Castle shortly before that time, looking charming indeed, whilst Irene, though departing from the rules laid down by Lady Dilworth, demanded from all present remarks bordering on similarity. She looked nervously pale, but queenly, and mastered thoroughly the exposure of the painful agony through which she was passing, knowing as she did and fully believed that "all is not gold that glitters."

It may interest some to know that Irene silently and secretly resolved not to array herself in white; she was reconciled that neither the marriage robe of purity nor the too beaming wedding face was to appear before such devout and reverential Church dignitaries as the Bishop of Barelegs and Canon Foot, with highly impressed and open falsehood, as that practised by her in the absence of labouring under such a solemn vow.

What must have been the breathless surprise of Lady Dilworth chiefly, and those present also, who, only the evening previous, had been pouring such praises over the magnificent duchesse satin gown, which eligible Parisian dressmakers pronounced their chief production of the season, when Irene appeared arrayed in an Irish poplin of the darkest visible shade of green, without either train or flower of distinction, not even a speck of ribbon or border of lace, and no ornament only the valued necklet which graced her pearly throat when first Sir John was tempted with her enhancing beauty to bestow upon her his choice collection of love's purest fragrance, which should cast the sweetest scent of mutual relationship throughout the dazzling apartments of the mansion she was to grace.

So thunderstruck and grievously horrified did Lady Dilworth seem at the vague departure of Irene from her orders, that she dare trust herself to offer her the first motherly embrace! Irene, perceiving the great embarrassment of her beloved Lady Dilworth, glided across the room, and sitting down to the right of her upon whom she had that day flung, in the face of devotion, the last dregs of defiance, "begged to offer an apology for such unruly conduct," and added "that all would be revealed at a future date when least expected."

In the very room where Sir John was first puzzled concerning the beautiful portrait, was he now made the recipient of the original. After the important ceremony was performed, and the register signed, Sir John and Lady Dunfern, when the usual congratulations were ended, left by the one o'clock train *en route* for the Continent. Thus were joined two hearts of widely different beat—one of intensive love, which hearsay never could shake; the other of dire dislike, which reason could never alter.

"Born under a lucky star," was the whispered echo throughout the distinguished guests who sat down to breakfast after the junction of opposites. Yea, this was a remark of truth visibly, and might have kept good during the remainder of their lives had not the tuitional click of bygone attachment kept moving with measured pace, until stopped after months, or it may be, small years of constant swinging.

Did Lady Dunfern ever dream that her apology for disobedience to Lady Dilworth's orders, in not arraying herself in the garb of glistening glory, could ever be accepted, even by the kind and loving Lady Dilworth?

Did she imagine for a moment that she, to whom she owed anything but disobedience, even in its simplest form, should be wrested from her arms of companionship ere her return to Dunfern Mansion? Did the thought ever flash through her mind that never again would she be able to pour into the ear of her trusted helper the secrets of the heart of deception, which, for the past seven months, had raged so furiously within her?

Better leave her to the freedom of a will that ere long would sink the ship of opulence in the sea of penury, and wring from her the words:— "Leave me now, deceptive demon of deluded mockery; lurk no more around the vale of vanity, like a vindictive viper; strike the lyre of living deception to the strains of dull deadness, despair and doubt; and bury on the brink of benevolence every false vow, every unkind thought, every trifle of selfishness and scathing dislike, occasioned by treachery in its mildest form!"

CHAPTER VII

DISTANT shores have great attractions and large expectations. They harbour around their beaches the exile and patriot, the king and peasant, the lawyer and artisan, the rising swindler and ruined prince. Spotted throughout the unclaimed area of bared soil may be seen the roughly-constructed huts and lofty homes of honest industry. Yes, and concealed therein are hearts yearning for the land of nativity and national freedom; hearts which sorrow after bygone days, and sink low when brooding over the future tide of fortune which already has stopped its gentle flow.

The reception on the evening of Irene's marriage was glorious and brilliant, as were all those given by Lord and Lady Dilworth, and, although attended by society's cream alone, there appeared a visible and unhidden vacancy in the absence of her who so often lent a glow of gaiety to the high-toned throng.

There seemed to be no rival now of buried lineage to mar their desire, or incur the jealousy of would-be opponents; no one to share sympathetically with the afflicted sister of equality and worth; nor was there any one present of such knightly and commanding dignity as he, who, not many hours previous, had taken upon him the sad duty of delivering up the keys of devotion to her who kept the door of ardent adoration locked against his approach.

It would probably be a long time ere such a scene of silly jealousy and ire would take place as that witnessed, in which the greater majority of those present were then partakers! And, further, it would surely be a much longer period before these guests would again share alike in the generosity so often extended them by Lord and Lady Dilworth.

Next day after Irene's marriage was a busy one at Dilworth Castle; hasty and numerous were the preparations for desolation and departure. Weeks preceding the joyful event, or what should have been, were leisurely devoted to the artistic arrangements in every room within the lordly manor. But, alas! so sudden now was joy's termination, that hours alone were the boundary of command.

It may be stated that Lord Dilworth owned three very extensive estates, namely—Dilworth, Ayrtown, and Howden. The first-mentioned extended around the castle of that name, encompassing a spacious tract of soil indeed, and might have done justice to moderation in its most expensive form. The Ayrtown Estate, which entirely covers the southern portion of Cheshire, owns a magnificent Hall, the residence of the Earl of Tukesham, and, although not considered so lucrative as Dilworth, may be estimated a handsome dowry for the son of any rising nobleman in the realm. The Howden Estate, on which are elegantly formed two buildings of note—namely, Blandford Castle and Lauderdale Lodge, both exquisite constructions of architecture and skilled workmanship, and occupied respectively by Sir Sydney Hector and Admiral Charles Depew —lies chiefly around the south-west of Yorkshire, and is not quite so desirable or adapted for agriculture as the two first mentioned, being mostly rented for grazing purposes by the numerous and varied owners of its rugged plots. These estates became so heavily mortgaged that prompt sale was indispensable, and, the matter being quietly arranged six months beforehand, the sixth day of August was the day set apart for the disposal of same.

Bidders were numerous and offers low. Eventually the purchasers were as follow:—The Marquis of Orland bought Dilworth Estate; Lord Henry Headen purchased Ayrtown Estate, whilst the lot of Howden fell upon Sir Rowland Joyce, the famous historian and national bard.

Thus were wrested from Lord and Lady Dilworth their luxurious living. They were driven from their nursery of rich and complicated comforts, their castle of indolence and ease. They were now thrown upon the shivering waters of want, without a word of sympathy in the dreadful hour of their great affliction, without home or friend to extend shelter or sustenance, and cast afloat upon the ocean of oscillating chance to speed across it as best they could.

Was Lord Dilworth therefore to be pitied? Were the torrents of gold which were bound to trickle from these enormous lands and dwellings, manufactories and villages, too trifling for his use? Not a morsel of pity was offered either him or Lady Dilworth as their circumstances became known in the homes of their associates, who so often fed on the fat of their folly and graced their well-lined tables always covered with dainties of deserving censure.

Could human mind contemplate that she who reigned supreme amongst society, she who gave the ball in honour of Irene Iddesleigh's marriage, should ere four days be a penniless pauper? Yet such was fact, not fiction.

The seventh day of August saw Lord and Lady Dilworth titled beggars, steering their course along the blue and slippery waves of the Atlantic, to be participators in the loathing poverty which always exists in homes sought after destruction, degradation, and reckless extravagance.

So soon may the house of gladness and mirth be turned into deepest grief! How the wealthiest, through sheer folly, are made to drink the very essence of poverty and affliction in its purest form! How the golden dust of luxury can be blown about with the wind of events, and is afterwards found buried in the fields of industry and thrift! Their names, which were as a household word, would now be heard no more, and should sink into abject silence and drowned renown, leaving them to battle against the raging war of ruin and hunger, and retire into secluded remorse.

On the return of Sir John and Lady Dunfern from their honeymoon, after four weeks' sojourn, what was her ladyship's consternation on perceiving Dilworth Castle in darkness as she and Sir John swept past its avenue on their way to their own brilliantly-lighted mansion? She was rather more taciturn on the night of her return than even during her stay in Florence, and it was only on her approaching her former place of temporary retreat and touchy remembrances that words began to fall from her ruby lips in torrents.

"Tell me, I implore of you, Sir John and husband, why the once blithe and cheerful spot of peace is now apparently a dismal dungeon on the night of our home-coming, when all should have been a mass of dazzling glow and splendour?

"Can it be that she who proffered such ecstasy for months before, on the eve of our return, is now no more? or can it be possible that we have crossed each other on the wide waters of tossing triumph or wanton woe?

"Speak at once, for pity's sake! and do not hide from me the answer of truth and honest knowledge? Oh, merciful heavens!"

Here Lady Dunfern drooped her head before Sir John got time to even answer a word, and drawing from his pocket a silver flask, proceeded to open its contents, when the horses suddenly stopped, and a gentle hand politely opened the carriage door to eagerly await the exit of his master and future mistress from its cushioned corners of costly comfort and ease.

"Tom," cried Sir John, in great and rending agony, "kindly wait for a few minutes, as her ladyship has been frightfully overcome only a short time ago by the blank appearance in and around Dilworth Castle. She fears something dreadful must surely have happened Lady Dilworth in her absence, since she has failed to make the occasion of our home-coming a merry torchlight of rejoicing." Tom, who had been in Sir John's service for the past twenty years, was about to testify to the truth of his remarks, when he was joined by other members of the household, who rushed to welcome their beloved master home once more, accompanied by his beautiful bride, of whom they all had heard so much.

Sir John saw that delay was dangerous, and helping to remove his darling Irene from the seat on which she unconsciously reclined, succeeded in placing her on a low couch in the very room he so often silently prayed for her presence. Bathing her highly-heated temples with a sprinkling of cooling liquid concealed in his flask, Sir John lost no time in summoning the village doctor, who, on arrival, pronounced Lady Dunfern to have slightly recovered, and giving the necessary orders left the room.

It was fully two hours ere she partly recovered from her ghastly swoon, to find herself the object of numerous onlookers of the household of which she was now future mistress.

Pale and death-like did she appear in the eyes of her husband, who was utterly overcome with grief at the sudden collapse of his wife under such a stroke of anticipated sorrow; and more grieved was he still when he found on inquiry that the removal of Lord and Lady Dilworth from their heightened haunt of high-born socialism must sooner or later be revealed to her, who, as yet, had only tasted partly of the bitter cup of divided intercourse and separated companionship.

Many, many were the questions asked by Lady Dunfern relative to Lady Dilworth when Dr. Corbett arrived next morning to pronounce her almost recovered, and, strange, yet true, that no one could possibly have humoured her in such a manner to warrant recovery as the village doctor, until she felt really strong enough to battle against the sorrowful tale of woe with which Sir John should shortly make her cognisant.

On learning from his lips, so soon as her ability occasioned, the real state of affairs concerning the emigrants who were now compelled to wander on the track of trouble, she received the truth with awe and smothered distress. The new sphere in which Lady Dunfern was about to move seemed to her strange; the binding duty which tied her firmly to honour and obedience was kept prominently in vague view; the staff of menials would probably find the rules of her husband more in accordance with their wishes than those which she was beginning to already arrange. She commenced her married life with falsehood, and she was fully determined to prove this feature more and more as the weeks and months rolled along. She was not afraid of the censure of one whose face she may never more behold, and who was the sole instigation of plunging her into a union she inwardly abhorred. Perhaps, had she never been trained under the loving guidance of Oscar Otwell, her revered tutor, she would only have been too eager to proclaim her ecstasy at her present position more vigorously. But all fetters of power were visibly broken which she wished should remain united, leaving her mother of her future premeditated movements.

As time moved on, Sir John and Lady Dunfern seemed to differ daily in many respects, which occasioned dislike in the breasts of both, and caused the once handsome, cheerful face of the much-respected owner of Dunfern to assume a look of seriousness.

These differences arose chiefly through his great disinclination to attend the numerous social gatherings which awaited them after their marriage. Sir John, finding it almost impossible to stare socialism in the face, seemed inclined rather to stick to the old rule of domestic enjoyment, never forgetting to share fully his cheerful conversation with his wife, when so desired, which, sorrowful to relate, was too seldom.

Now that Lady Dunfern was an acknowledged branch of society, her elegant presence would have been courted by all those who so often favoured Lady Dilworth with their distinguished patronage, but her social hopes being nipped in the bud by her retiring husband, she dare not resent, and determined, in consequence, to make herself an object of dislike in her home, and cherish her imprisoned thoughts until released, for good or evil.

CHAPTER VIII

A word of warning tends to great advantage when issued reverently from the lips of the estimable. It serves to allay the danger pending on reticence, and substantiates in a measure the confidence which has hitherto existed between the parties concerned. Again, a judicious advice, extended to the stubborn and self-willed, proves futile, and incurs the further malice and fiery indignation of the regardless, the reckless, and the uncharitable.

Lady Dunfern began now to grow both cross and careless, and seemed not to interest herself so much (since her propositions were so emphatically denounced by her husband) concerning the management of the household staff. She grew daily more retired, and often has her conduct been so preposterously strange as to cause alarm both to Sir John and all over whom he had immediate control.

Indeed, three months of married life scarcely elapsed until she cast a glow of despair within the breast which too often heaved for her with true piety and love. And what was meant by such strange conduct on her part, her husband often wondered. Only the mighty cessation of friendship caused by the flight of her beloved guardians, never attributing such silence and stubbornness to any fault he justly committed.

Yes, the duped husband, when being fished for with the rod of seeming simplicity and concealed character, and quickly caught on the hook of ingenuity, with deception for a bait, was altogether unable to fathom its shallowest meaning. Was he not, therefore, to be sympathised with, who so charitably extended the hand of honour and adoration to the offspring of unknown parents, and placed her in position equal to any lady of title and boasted parentage within the boundary of County Kent? Should Sir John Dunfern not have been almost worshipped by a wife whose binding duty it was to reverence her husband in all things pertaining to good? No doubt this would have been so had he gained the affections he imagined he possessed, but later on he would inevitably be made aware of matters which as yet only bordered on supposition.

Day after day Lady Dunfern pined like a prisoner in her boudoir, and scarcely ever shared a word with the great and good Sir John, who many times wished in former days that she had occupied his home and all its joys. She formed an inward resolution that if prohibited from enjoying life, to which she was accustomed at Dilworth Castle, she would make her husband, whom she knew too well made her his idol, feel the smart, by keeping herself aloof from his caresses as much as possible.

Often would he be found half asleep in deep thought, not having any friend of immediate intimacy in whom he could confide or trust, or to whom he could unbosom the conduct of his wife, whose actions now he was beginning to detest.

The thoughts of disappointment and shame were building for themselves a home of shelter within him—disappointment on account of cherished hopes which unmistakably were crushed to atoms beneath the feet of her who was the sole instigation of their origin; shame, in all probability, lest the love he sought and bought with the price of self might not be his after all! and may still be reserved against his right and kept for another much less worthy! The little jealous spark again revived and prompted him to renew its lustre, which had been hidden for a length of time behind the cloud of dread so silently awaiting the liberty of covering the hill of happiness.

Quietly ruminating over his wife's manner before marriage, about which he was compelled, through observation, to demand an explanation, and pondering carefully her strange and silent habits since it, he became resolved to probe the wound that had swollen so enormously as to demand immediate relief. Ringing furiously for a maid, he handed her a note, to be delivered without delay to Lady Dunfern, the nature of which might well be suspected. Be that as it may, its contents were instrumental in demanding immediate attention.

Soon after its delivery a slight tap was heard at the door of Sir John's study, this room being always his favourite haunt, where he sat beside a bright and glowing fire, engaged in sullen thought; and with an imperious "Come in" he still remained in the same thinking posture; nor was he aware, for fully five minutes or so, that his intruder was no other than she whom he so recently ordered into his presence!

Gazing up in a manner which startled the cold-hearted woman not a little, he requested her "to have a seat right opposite his," to which she instantly complied. At this moment the snow was wafting its flaky handfuls thickly against the barred enclosures of Dunfern Mansion, and chilly as nature appeared outside, it was similarly so indoors for the fond and far-famed husband of Lord Dilworth's charge.

Matters had appeared so unpleasant and altogether bewildering of late that Sir John formed a resolution to bring them to a crisis. Looking fully into the face that seemed so lovely just now, with the dainty spots of blazing ire enlivening the pale cheeks of creeping sin, Sir John began—

"Irene, if I may use such familiarity, I have summmoned you hither, it may be to undergo a stricter examination than your present condition probably permits; but knowing, as you should, my life must be miserable under this growing cloud of unfathomed dislike, I became resolved to end, if within my power, such contentious and unlady-like conduct as that practised by you towards me of late. It is now quite six months—yea, weary months—since I shielded you from open penury and insult, which were bound to follow you, as well as your much-loved protectors, who sheltered you from the pangs of penniless orphanage; and during these six months, which naturally should have been the pet period of nuptial harmony, it has proved the hideous period of howling dislike!

"I, as you see, am tinged with slightly snowy tufts, the result of stifled sorrow and care concerning you alone; and on the memorable day of our alliance, as you are well aware, the black and glossy locks of glistening glory crowned my brow. There dwelt then, just six months this day, no trace of sorrow or smothered woe—no variety of colour where it is and shall be so long as I exist—no furrows of grief could then be traced upon my visage. But, alas! now I feel so changed! And why?

"Because I have dastardly and doggedly been made a tool of treason in the hands of the traitoress and unworthy! I was enticed to believe that an angel was always hovering around my footsteps, when moodily engaged in resolving to acquaint you of my great love, and undying desire to place you upon the highest pinnacle possible of praise and purity within my power to bestow!

"I was led to believe that your unbounded joy and happiness were never at such a par as when sharing them with me. Was I falsely informed of your ways and worth? Was I duped to ascend the ladder of liberty, the hill of harmony, the tree of triumph, and the rock of regard, and when wildly manifesting my act of ascension, was I to be informed of treading still in the valley of defeat?

"Am I, who for nearly forty years was idolised by a mother of untainted and great Christian bearing, to be treated now like a slave? Why and for what am I thus dealt with?

"Am I to foster the opinion that you treat me thus on account of not sharing so fully in your confidence as it may be, another?

"Or is it, can it be, imaginative that you have reluctantly shared, only shared, with me that which I have bought and paid for fully?

"Can it be that your attention has ever been, or is still, attracted by another, who, by some artifice or other, had the audacity to steal your desire for me and hide it beneath his pillaged pillow of poverty, there to conceal it until demanded with my ransom?

"Speak! Irene! Wife! Woman! Do not sit in silence and allow the blood that now boils in my veins to ooze through cavities of unrestrained passion and trickle down to drench me with its crimson hue!

"Speak, I implore you, for my sake, and act no more the deceitful Duchess of Nanté, who, when taken to task by the great Napoleon for refusing to dance with him at a State ball, replied, 'You honoured me too highly'—acting the hypocrite to his very face. Are you doing likewise?" Here, Sir John, whose flushed face, swollen temples, and fiery looks were the image of indignation, restlessly awaited her reply.

Lady Dunfern began now to stare her position fully in the face. On this interview, she thought, largely depended her future welfare, if viewed properly. Should she make her husband cognisant of her inward feelings, matters were sure to end very unsatisfactorily. These she kept barred against his entrance in the past, and she was fully determined should remain so now, until forced from their home of refuge by spirited action.

Let it be thoroughly understood that Lady Dunfern was forced into a union she never honestly countenanced. She was almost compelled, through the glittering polish Lady Dilworth put on matters, to silently resign the hand of one whose adoration was amply returned, and enter into a contract which she could never properly complete. All she could now do was to plunge herself into the lake of evasion and answer him as best she could.

"Sir and husband," she said, with great nervousness at first, "you have summoned me hither to lash your rebuke unmercifully upon me, provoked, it may be, by underhand intercourse. You accordingly, in the course of your remarks, fail not to tamper with a character which as yet defies your scathing criticism. Only this week have I been made the recipient of news concerning my deceased parents, of whom I never before obtained the slightest clue, and armed with equality, I am in a position fit to treat some of your stingy remarks with the scorn they merit.

"You may not already be aware of the fact that I, whom you insinuate you wrested from beggary, am the only child of the late Colonel Iddesleigh, who fell a victim to a gunshot wound inflicted by the hand of his wife, who had fallen into the pit of intemperance. Yes, Earl Peden's daughter was his wife and my mother, and only that this vice so actuated her movements, I might still have lent to Society the object it dare not now claim, and thereby would have shunned the iron rule of being bound down to exist for months at a time within such a small space of the world's great bed.

"If my manner have changed in any way since our union, of it I am not aware, and fail to be persuaded of any existing difference, only what might be attributed to Lady Dilworth's sudden and unexpected removal from our midst, which occasioned me grief indeed.

"It behoves elderly men like you to rule their wives with jealous supervision, especially if the latter tread on the fields of youth. Such is often fictitious and unfounded altogether, and should be treated with marked silence.

"I may here say I was mistress, in a measure, of my movements whilst under the meek rule of Lady Dilworth; nor was I ever thwarted in any way from acting throughout her entire household as I best thought fit, and since I have taken upon me to hold the reins of similarity within these walls, I find they are much more difficult to manage. I, more than once, have given orders which were completely prohibited from being executed. By whom, might I ask, and why? Taking everything into consideration, I am quite justified in acquainting you that, instead of being the oppressor, I feel I am the oppressed.

"Relative to my affections, pray have those courted by me in the past aught to do with the present existing state of affairs? I am fully persuaded to answer, 'Nothing whatever.'

"You speak of your snowy tufts appearing where once there dwelt locks of glossy jet. Well, I am convinced they never originated through me, and must surely have been threatening to appear before taking the step which links me with their origin.

"I now wish to retire, feeling greatly fatigued, and trusting our relations shall remain friendly and mutual, I bid thee good-night."

Lady Dunfern swept out of the room, and hurrying to her own apartment, burst into an uncontrollable fit of grief.

She had surely been awaked from her reverie by Sir John, and felt sharply the sting of his remarks, which were truly applied, indeed. She now resolved to let matters move along as quietly as possible until after she should pass the most critical period of her existence. She was prepared to manifest her innocence throughout, without detection if possible. But amongst the household there moved a matron under whose hawk-like eye Lady Dunfern was almost inclined to shrink. She felt when in her presence to be facing an enemy of unbounded experience. She abhorred her stealing tread, but not without cause. It was to this dame she so often issued orders that never were carried out; and when intimating to Sir John the necessity of instantly dismissing such a tyrant, he quietly "rebelled," adding "that she had been almost twenty years in his service, and presently could not think of parting with such a valued and much-trusted friend."

This woman's name was Rachel Hyde, and proved the secret channel of intercourse between Sir John and Lady Dunfern, evidently paving the way for her ladyship's downfall; as Rachel, being mistress for such a period over Dunfern Mansion, could never step the fence leading to abolition of power, which she so unwillingly tried to mount since Sir John's marriage, and failing totally in her attempt, was lifted and thrown over by her mistress, an act she could never forget, and consequently carried all news, trivial or serious, concerning Lady Dunfern to her master, and delivered it in such an exaggerated form as to incur his wrath, which already had been slightly heated.

A few months elapsed again, during which time matters went on much as usual, until an event happened that should have chased the darkest cloud of doubt and infidelity from the noble brow of the mighty and revered master of Dunfern Mansion.

CHAPTER IX

THE thickest stroke of sadness can be effaced in an instant, and substituted with deeper traces of joy. The heart of honest ages, though blackened at times with domestic troubles, rejoices when those troubles are surmounted with blessings which proclaim future happiness.

On the tenth day of June, following Lady Dunfern's interview with her husband, she gave birth to a son and heir. This great event brought with it entire forgiveness on the part of Sir John of his wife's recent conduct. It served for a short time only, a trivial portion too, to stifle the alienation which existed between them, and to heal the sore of evident separation that marred their happiness for months before.

The glad and happy father was only too eager now to snatch a smile from his wife's face, and anxious was he to bury any little obstacle that may have existed in the past, and expel it for ever from its lurking corner

B

of tempting repose. He saw that Lady Dunfern's life was hanging by a flimsy hair, and who could, for an instant, depict the great despair of her husband when told that all hope must be abandoned!

The frantic father wrung his hands in a frenzy of momentary madness, and in spite of authoritative advice he timidly moved in the direction of the bed on which his beloved lay, and knelt beside it to fervently offer up a prayer "for the speedy recovery of her who was the chief object of his existence." Raising himself up and clasping his darling in his arms, he whispered in her ear a word of encouragement, and gently laying her highly-heated head on the silken pillow he again prayed, in deepest and gravest earnestness, "that she might be spared only a little longer."

No doubt his prayer was no sooner offered than answered, as she at this stage slightly rallied, and appeared somewhat strengthened. Day by day the still fond and loving husband sat by the bedside of the invalid until strong enough to battle fully against the weakening hand of her malady; and at the very time Sir John sat beside the bed of sickness, inwardly "showering blame upon himself for hindering his wife's social enjoyment, and for which he believed he acted wrongly;" she, on the contrary, was outwardly pouring rebuke on her own head "for ever entering into a league of life-long punishment by marrying a man she simply abhorred, and leaving her noble and well-learned tutor, Oscar Otwell, whom she yet loved, to wander in a world of blighted bliss!"

Ah! to be sure! It was during these days of unremitting attention that he was afforded an opportunity of storing up a multitude of touchy remarks uttered by his wife when the relapse of raging fever reached its defiant height! She never ceased to talk in a most gentle manner of "Oscar Otwell," "her darling and much-loved tutor." She even expressed sorrow, in the course of her broken remarks, "at the false step she had taken to satisfy, not herself by any means, but Lady Dilworth!" She strongly protested her "hatred for him" who sat listening, with grave intensity, to every word that escaped her lips! She even spoke of "a cavity in her jewel-case in which was safely deposited a ring, given her by Oscar during her happy period of instruction under his guidance," adding, in her painful discourse, that "she loved it as well as himself," etc., etc.

These rambling statements when ended, in an instant caused Sir John's resolutions, made by him so recently, to become worthless remarks; and if partly charged with jealousy before, he was doubly so now.

No onlooker could fail in the least to pity the sneered husband, whose livid countenance during the course of her remarks, rambling though they were, was a sight never to be forgotten. How he gazed with astonished indifference at the invalid so charged with deceit! She who acted the emblem of innocence at all times, and attempted to attach entire blame to her husband! She who partly promised peace in future to him who never again could enjoy it!

How his manner became so abrupt and his speech so scanty within such a short period was verily a proof of the belief he fostered relative to his wife's statements, which were yet to her unknown.

The doctors in attendance endeavoured strongly to imprint upon Sir John the fact that "such remarks as those uttered by his wife should be treated with silence and downright indifference," adding that "patients smitten with fever, of what kind soever, were no more responsible for their sayings than the most outrageous victim of insanity."

Sir John listened attentively to their statements, but failed to be altogether convinced as to their truth. Wondering what sin could be attached to an act he felt was his duty to perform, he moved softly to the bedside of his wife, and being in a sleepy mood, he resolved to sift some of her remarks to the very bottom.

Entering the room she so often occupied, and taking from a chink in her dressing-table a key of admittance to the jewel-case she spoke of, he lost no time in viewing its valuable contents; and the very spot in which she vowed dwelt her tutor's gift, there it lay! A golden band with pearl centre, and immediately underneath it there rested a note. At first he felt rather diffident about perusing its contents, but instinct so prompted his curiosity that he yielded to its tempting touch. It ran thus:—

> "Hedley,
> Berks,
> July 3rd.

"Ever beloved Irene,

"I am after reading your gentle yet sorrowful epistle. You cannot possibly retract the step you so publicly have taken without incurring the malice of Lord and Lady Dilworth, who have sheltered you from every sorrow and care with which you otherwise were bound to come in contact.

"They received you into their elegant home, and shielded you, by so doing, from the tyrannical rule of Miss Lamont of 'The Orphanage,' in which you were placed for a period of eight years. They failed not to give you a thorough and practical education, which in itself would enable you to achieve independence, if necessary, or so desired.

"This you received under one whose heart now beats with raging jealousy and vehement hatred towards the object of Lady Dilworth's choice, being well convinced, through your numerous letters to me lately, it never was yours.

"Dearest Irene, the thought of parting from you for ever is partly sustained with the hope of yet calling you mine! Through time you suggest an elopement, which as yet can only be viewed in the hazy distance; but it seems quite clear to me, dearest, and surely evident, that you abhor the very name of him who a month hence shall place you in a position considerably more elevated and lucrative than that which I now could bestow. But Irene, my beloved, my all! reluctantly I yield my precious treasure to him who, it may be this moment, is rejoicing at his capture.

"I shall ever remain forlorn, dejected, and ruined until such time as we suitably can accomplish the clearance of the cloud of dissatisfaction under which you are about to live. Please write by return.

"Ever your own

"Oscar.

"Miss Iddesleigh,
Dilworth Castle."

CHAPTER X

WHEN dreading the light of day contentment hath fled; imagination oftentimes proves a forerunner to reality; corners of horror shelter themselves within the castles of the queenly, the palaces of the powerful, the monuments of the mighty, and the cottages of the caretaker; but sunshine brings universal joy wherever its beams are wont to dazzle, and often allays the anxiety which precedes its appearance.

"Great heaven!" murmured Sir John, as the tutor's note fell from his nervous grasp, "Am I blind to touch or truth? Am I at last to labour under the fact that my wife loves another! she who only some months since protested her innocence in such strains as to cause the most doubtful to stay alarm. Here is the ring, and there lies the note—the note of him who claims to be not only her tutor but suitor. Why did she accept the former or cause the latter to be written?

"Then, the date! Just one month exactly before our marriage; and how I pined for it to elapse whilst another would eagerly have prolonged it. Oh, Irene!—false and low woman! Think you that any longer I can own you as wife or treat you with the respect a wife deserves!" Sir John, ever open to forgiveness, tried hard to master the dreadful spirit of jealousy which arrived at last at its highest point, if he could feel convinced that his wife's correspondence with her tutor ceased after her marriage, believing if still it continued that other proofs of their dastardly plots would be forthcoming. Thrusting his hand again into the aperture from which he took the two tributes of his wife's tutor, there appeared nothing to arouse further suspicion, save a Christmas card, written with the same bold hand. The lines were these—

"Accept my warmest greeting, friendship, love,
Thou art my charming Irene, pet and dove;
Although another claims thee for a time,

I trust to call you some day ever mine.
Oh! pray for parting soon with fettered chains,
To live and move regardless of those reins
That bind your Christmas sprigs of worldly woe
To him, whom you have hated long ago."

This was a second effusion of Otwell's, and must have been received by Lady Dunfern since her marriage; and, thought he who held it clutched in his trembling hand, Why did she deposit this card amongst her valuables—had she not held it as a treasure of priceless worth?

Nothing more was wanting now to convince the distracted husband of his wife's infidelity. Depositing the note, card, and ring in the drawer whence he had taken them, Sir John at once proceeded to Lady Dunfern's bedroom, and found her awake. Being a nobleman of sterling worth, and one on whose word the greatest dependence was always manifested, he could scarcely fail to inform her of the great and trying scene he had just come through. Struggling, however, manfully from mentioning anything that would serve to retard her recovery, he moved towards the bed on which she lay, and before a word was uttered by him he suddenly staggered and fell.

Who could then perceive the wan and haggard appearance of him who apparently lay lifeless without being totally terror-stricken—could she, whom he bathed in golden comfort, behold this outstretched form with calm silence? Surely not!

Instantly ordering a maid to send for Doctor Doherty, the false invalid lay back on her pillow, appearing not much concerned. On the doctor's arrival he applied restoratives, but without the desired effect. Then he ordered his instant removal to his bed-chamber, where every care and watchfulness was extended him by Rachel Hyde.

It was nearly two hours ere he manifested the remotest symptoms of animation, and on inquiry the doctor pronounced the sudden shock he had nervously sustained to be grave indeed. Sir John lay in an unconscious condition until next morning, when his first inquiry was relative to his son.

Gradually regaining strength, and venturing in the doctor's absence out of bed, he walked slowly into his wife's room to make personal his recovery. He looked pale, and much annoyed, and could only with difficulty refrain from acquainting her of what he had in store to communicate. Each day found both invalids, just and unjust, rapidly recovering, and a few weeks found both completely restored to health and strength.

Lady Dunfern could not help noticing the strange and frozen manner of her husband since the eve of his illness. At first she was inclined to fear his approach, but gradually she felt convinced he was slightly affected with a mild form of insanity; and making minute inquiries from the oldest inhabitants in the neighbourhood and adjoining village as to the accuracy of her fears, she was informed that "such never existed amongst his ancestors, so far as they knew or heard."

Was it strange that Sir John felt a changed man towards her who was so fully charged with deceit? Would it have been acting in accordance with his conscience to overlook her wily artifice? Could the once fond and loving husband, the brave and gallant knight, still trust in her whom he felt convinced would bring a world of disgrace, not alone upon himself, but upon one who in after years, he trusted, would proudly sustain the honourable reputation of his race?

Ah! no matter in what light he viewed her conduct now he was brought to loathe her very look, and was fully determined to shut her in from the gaze of an outside world, or the cunning tricks of a trifling tutor. He was resolved, so far as lay in his power, to treat her with the conduct she merited, and never again allow himself to be persuaded to postpone the visitation of his anger by her villainous pitiful appeals.

After serious thought, Sir John began to act; he was inclined to think delay would be dangerous, and on approaching his breakfast table one morning soon after his recovery, he hinted to his housekeeper that he "wished a private interview with her after his morning repast." This Rachel punctually obeyed.

Seeing her master's trembling hand twitch the tips of his beard, she feared something dreadful must surely be disturbing his peace of mind, and commanding her to "lock the door" lest they should be interrupted, he informed her of all that had happened.

Rachel, ever ready to sow doubt in the mind of her master regarding his wife, manifested her want of surprise by relating some incidents which occurred under her notice. Nothing, however monstrous, could astonish Sir John at this time regarding his wife's movements, and informing Rachel of his intention he ordered the key of one of the rooms that yet had been shut against the entrance of Lady Dunfern.

Hastening to fulfil her master's order, Rachel returned with the mighty key, and handed it to Sir John, who moved to the door, and thrusting the rusty key into its aperture, succeeded with great difficulty in effecting an entrance. Rachel followed, and both entered, locking the heavy-panelled oak door from within. "This," said Sir John, "is the room of correction, the room of death. It defies escape or secretion. It has been so long as I remember held in abhorrence by my late lamented parents, and, so far as I can understand, by many of my ancestors.

"First of all, the lady who shared its midst was a born imbecile, the eldest daughter of my great great grandfather—Sir Sydney Dunfern. She was nursed and tenderly cared for within these walls for a period of thirty-six years, and through the instantaneous insanity of her ward, was marked a victim for his murderous hand. Yes, it has been related that during midnight, when she was fast asleep, he drew from that drawer," here Sir John pointed to the wardrobe, "a weapon of warlike design, and severed her head almost from her body, causing instant death.

"It was not known until next day about noon that anything extraordinary had happened. It was first detected by Sir Sydney himself, who became alarmed at not having seen Wade—the ward's name was Hector Wade—as usual at ten o'clock, and tapping at the door, was surprised to hear some noise issue from within. Being of a hasty temper, he became indignant at the ward's indifference, and calling loudly, finally gained admittance.

"The murderer had her stretched on this floor, and every article capable of being removed piled upon her corpse. Horrified at such a sight, Sir Sydney became wild with grief, and at once handed the pitiful lunatic over to those in authority.

"The next inhabitant doomed to share in its dull delight was Kathleen, wife of my beloved grandfather, a beautiful woman, whose portrait you now see. She, I am sorry to relate, proved more an accomplice than the honoured wife of him who added so much to the welfare of those who now benefit by his great economy. The hand of death visited her here likewise with its separating touch.

"The last person inhabiting its cheerless enclosure was a distant relative of my mother, a gentleman named Rodney Rupert, who fell from the path of virtue and trod the field of vice, until confined within this prison of pathetic account, and who, in a moment of passion, ended his days with that pistol which hangs on yonder hook, and on that bed all these lay, and which shall again be made use of by a traitoress of no mean account either."

Sir John then proceeded to give orders to "have the room made as comfortable as its scanty furniture permitted," which consisted only of one small table, one chair, and an old-fashioned wardrobe, with several small drawers attached, one dressing-table and washstand, all of which were magnificently carved oak and richly panelled.

There was only one large window, made up of iron bars and a multitude of small panes of glass not larger than three inches square, all of equal dimensions, and inside this window were strong bars of iron looped on every side and firmly fastened.

The cocoa matting which served as a carpet, parts of which were grim with gore, was almost worn past recognition. These were all the articles this badly-lighted room contained, save several oil-paintings of enormous size. On the whole, it presented the appearance of a private prison.

An icy atmosphere pervaded throughout the room, damped with an odour of something inert, which Sir John believed would be rendered extinct in the presence of a fire.

Rachel, after receiving orders in confidence from her master, set matters to right by lighting a fire, dusting the old and much-worn furniture, airing the bed-clothes, etc., being strictly charged to admit, on no pretence whatever, now or at any time, any member of the household or visitor to the mansion.

When everything was in perfect readiness for the reception of its guest, Sir John directed Rachel to "bring her Ladyship into his presence." What could have astonished Lady Dunfern more on being ushered into a room which never before was open for her inspection? Nothing save the information her husband eagerly awaited her to receive. On being informed of her vast deception, which was proved beyond doubt, and to which she felt wholly incompetent to reply, she was absolutely dumb-stricken.

It required no further questioning now concerning her husband's recent strangeness of manner and rigid coolness with which he was forced to treat her whom he scorned to call wife.

"You, madam," said he, "have by your conduct, both before and after marriage, forced me to keep you a prisoner within these walls so long as you live or I exist.

"You have not failed to act the infamous by kissing me with the lips of a Judas! You have at last plunged me into deepest disgrace, not alone me, but him whom you should have been liberated to succour and chastise. Mocking wretch! your foul deeds shall have plenty of scope here for improvement, and a prisoner you shall be during the remainder of your life."

Sir John, without another word, glided from before the presence of her who once was treated as a goddess by him, and turning the great key that locked her for ever from his view, handed it to Rachel, who was to have sole admittance to, and full charge of, his wife.

When left to herself in the ghostly and spacious closet of crippled right, which until now she never dare approach, Lady Dunfern, instead of shewing signs of grief, which Sir John felt assured must burst from its midst, gloried in being aloof from the occasional rebukes to which she was subject whilst occupying the rooms free to her access. She would now have full opportunity of guiding her thoughts to self-advantage or disadvantage. She felt free to try and act as she in any case would have done, regarding very little the shame brought on her husband by her intrigue with the tutor, whom she simply idolized, never once casting a thought on her infant, knowing well it would be passionately cared for.

Oceans of thought took hold on her as she vacantly viewed the damp and darkened walls of her monstrous cell, now and then moving forward to inspect the many paintings of great and historic worth which hung from their lofty support, mostly all more or less resembling him who probably should ere long add to their number.

Lady Dunfern allowed the weeks and months to pass unheeded until afforded ample opportunity of resorting to some means that might not alone free her from such death-like surroundings, but snap the chain of obligation in two which presently connected her with a husband she cared not for.

She longed for the hour of flight from the dismal shelter under which she was doomed to dwell. She yearned for the days that had fled, and more so for her who had shared in their pleasure. She pined for him whom she so long lived to adore, and hesitated not to do so still.

Could she only acquaint him of her husband's cruelty, how he might assist her in effecting her release. What could be done, she frequently asked herself, to brighten her future only a little?

Could she possibly escape? She feared not.

Every two hours that villainous woman entered during the day since first she was snared in the net of revenge and compelled to remain within its enclosures of shivering fear. Still, she never lost hope of flight, and cheered with the thought of future stratagem, she tried to remain somewhat consoled.

CHAPTER XI

THE trickling tide of fortune sometimes ebbs slowly. It meets with occasional barriers of boisterous worth, and reaches its haven of intent too often with obstruction. Its waters drip on the proud and humble, the mighty and pitiful, the meek and unholy, and refuse to overlook even the weary and careworn confined in the cell. It ceases not to store within its water of wonder intricate windings of wealth and poverty, triumph and torture, joy and misery, and does not hesitate at any time to safely deposit its various burthens on the numerous beaches along which it must pass.

When almost a year of Lady Dunfern's private imprisonment was about drawing to a close, she was beginning to partly believe the truth of her husband's dogmatic remarks. She had strongly been endeavouring during this time to arrive at some possible means of communication with Marjory Mason, her much-loved maid, whose services Sir John still retained; but every endeavour she yet formed proved absolutely vain. She often thought had she been attended by any of the household staff, only her on whom she never could dream to rely, she might have made good her escape long since; but being watched and visited so regularly by Rachel Hyde, she felt her task much more difficult of performance than at first imagined. Sometimes she would bring her table close to the window and mount on its shaky leaf, then step into the great window-sill, pull out her handkerchief and rub the puny panes to try and catch a glimpse of nature and probably chance to see some of the servants pass.

B*

This heavily-barred window stood considerably high, and if viewed from a distance, or even from the ground adjacent, seemed small in consequence. It was, therefore, very difficult for her to recognise one menial from another, yet she often imagined she could not be mistaken in perceiving a form in the garden, right opposite, that surely strongly resembled her favourite maid.

What course was she, then, to adopt in order to discover the accuracy of her thoughts? How could she manage to be positive regarding Marjory's appearance? She felt it almost miraculous to identify her who trod so far beneath her heightened gaze. Each day she resolved to mount the window at the same hour, believing her constant watching might through time convince her who the object of her anxiety might be.

But the distance between them still remained the same, and ended with the same disappointing result. A thought at last crowned her precious efforts. She fancied if she could succeed in breaking one of the small window panes she could, with the aid of a telescope found in one of the drawers, define exactly who the maid might chance to be.

The same hour each day found the eager mistress and anxious maid in their respective places, the former mounted on the window-sill, the latter gazing pitifully towards the window of her mistress's hateful cell. But discernment was altogether impossible for Lady Dunfern, who was resolved not to be baffled much longer in ascertaining who the constant visitor was. Snapping from her finger an exquisite diamond ring, and studying which pane of glass would be least noticed, she arrived at the wise conclusion of extracting the lowest corner pane, which she cleverly and effectually succeeded in doing. Wondering, first of all, how she would hide the opening from the cute eye of her who proved her only visitor, she placed her fleecy wrap carelessly against it, and resuming her seat, was persuaded fully to believe she had successfully accomplished the first step to her freedom.

Rachel, arriving now with luncheon, failed to notice, or if noticed, to mention the article in the window. Next day, with great confidence, Lady Dunfern was found in her usual recess, and drawing forth the telescope, viewed keenly the object of her constant search, and to her wild delight she at once beheld Marjory Mason with grave face staring, she fancied, at her. At last, her Ladyship had achieved a mighty work, indeed, which she hoped would yet prove of more practical importance.

It may be mentioned that Marjory Mason visited the same plot of ground at the same hour every available morning since she was robbed of the pleasure of waiting on her mistress, merely to get a glimpse of the window she knew must belong to her Ladyship's haunt of hardship; and could honest Marjory have only seen the handkerchief that every day was pointed to its little transparent enclosures, how she would so gladly have waved hers in return. But other means had to be resorted to, through

Lady Dunfern's great perspicacity, to try and establish a line of communication with one she could trust. This being now arrived at cast a
world of grief from the mind of her who, under such a roof of suspense
as that beneath which she existed, felt if aid were not forthcoming, she
would shortly have to yield to the imperative command of the King of
Conquering Divines.

Who could now recognise the "Southern Beauty" of Dilworth Castle?
Who could visit the once beautiful bride of Dunfern Mansion without
naturally betraying signs of heartfelt sorrow? She who so often graced
the assemblies of the proud and famous; she who adorned society with
her majestic presence; she who, by her charming manner and elegant
bearing, failed not to steal the affection of him who treated her so, was
an object of abject commiseration where her conduct wasn't questioned.
She was no longer the cheerful associate, the bright converser, the lively,
robust Irene Iddesleigh. She, the pride of her guardians, the once adored
of her husband, the envied object of socialism, must bear to exist, though
by any means within her power, not where she existed presently. The next
part to be enacted was to attract Marjory's attention. This could easily
be tried, and tying her cambric square firmly round the top of a small
poker, she timidly sent it through the cavity, at the same time viewing
Marjory by means of her telescope. At first Marjory was seen to shade
her eyes with her hand, and move a little forward, then suddenly stop.
She would again move slightly nearer to the wafting emblem of despair,
and quickly advancing, until she neared the spot where best the snowy sign
could be seen, instantly concluded that she must be observed by her
ladyship.

When Lady Dunfern perceived that Marjory could by no means be
closer to her, she pulled the flag of victory back, leaving her maid in
breathless confusion, never for an instant flinching until she might again
have an opportunity of rendering her assistance whom she worshipped.

In less than five minutes another signal appeared through the open
space in the form of a small piece of paper, the meaning of which Marjory
knew well. It appeared to be making its way with wonderful alacrity
towards her, who now was in nervous despair lest she should be detected
by her master, or some of the other members of his staff. At last the missive
reached its destination, and, wildly grasping it, Marjory loosed the cord,
that was swiftly drawn back, and plainly written by her mistress's hand
were the words, "To Marjory, my trusted maid." Shrieking with delight,
she pushed the note into her pocket, and, speedily hastening to the mansion, entered her own room. Securing the door from within, she instantly
tore asunder the cover, and read with tearful eyes as follows:—

"Room No. 10.

"Dearest Marjory and Friend,

"You at last have proof of the confidence reposed in you by me. How

I have thought of you since I was severed from you no one knows. That you have been aware of my imprisonment I can no longer doubt. However, I shall not presently give you any particulars, but beg to say that if you could by any means you thought safe let me hear if you have ever received any letters for me from Oscar, I should ever feel grateful and reward you accordingly. My reason for such inquiry I shall explain further on. Dear Marjory, keep this dark. Might I suggest that you slip a note under my door this evening at five o'clock precisely. This you can do I believe at this hour with safety. Trusting you are keeping strong, and hoping soon to thank you personally for such secret kindness,

"Believe me,

"Sincerely yours,

"Irene.

"To Marjory."

This note was ample explanation of the confidence Lady Dunfern had in her maid. She well knew from previous experience how she could trust her, and felt assured she was not a victim to misplaced confidence. Marjory would sooner have suffered death than betray her whom she had served so long at Dilworth Castle, and so short a time at Dunfern Mansion, and, carefully folding the note she held in her hand, proceeded to reply.

Lady Dunfern, at the hour appointed, stood in agony behind the massive door, underneath which she soon felt sure of receiving news that would either increase or diminish her varied stock of fears. Nor was she disappointed. At the very hour referred to, the note appeared. Who could picture the ecstatic relief of Lady Dunfern as she paced her prison floor, whilst carefully scanning the contents of Marjory's note. In it she stated that her husband received all letters direct, not alone for himself, but for all his servants, and delivered them personally to each, this only happening since she was subject to his cruel treatment.

Lady Dunfern was a little surprised at not receiving through Marjory some news of Oscar. But when informed of her husband being the recipient of all letters, she felt confident his were amongst the many for his inspection, and would not therefore aid his aspect of matters much. Safely depositing the prayed-for epistle of Marjory in her drawer, she seemed to suddenly grow quite cheerful and animated, so much so that Rachel, on entering some short time afterwards, was so struck with the change as to acknowledge that her ladyship must surely appreciate the book she held in her hand to an extraordinary extent since it had altered her demeanour so.

Could this attendant only have known the true nature of Lady Dunfern's much-changed manner, how, with a conquering air, she would so soon have conveyed the tidings to Sir John. This, however, was not to be.

Lady Dunfern believed that such a line of intercourse as that which she had so artfully managed with one on whom she could ever place implicit confidence, must surely yet be the means of freeing her from the fetters of a fierce and prejudiced race.

Every morning, at the same hour, mistress and maid were at their respective posts, the former, with brightened eye, mounted on her favourite pedestal of triumphant account and gazing intently on the object of rescue; the latter, casting that grave and careworn look in the direction of the niched signboard of distress, stood firmly and faithfully until she received the watchword of action and warning.

CHAPTER XII

TORTURE trifleth not. It manifests in many instances the deserving censure imposed upon its stinging touch. It acts like the poisonous fangs of the serpent, unless extracted from its burning crypt of chastisement by hand of wily witchcraft. So frightened did Lady Dunfern become lest the eye of the straggler might chance more than once to catch the meaning of Marjory's loitering about the grounds immediately below her window, that she deemed it imperative to alter her arrangements, and, acquainting Marjory in the usual way, appointed an hour that would almost defy matters to be made conspicuous. This change made both of them more free to act, and proved a decided success.

Only some weeks elapsed since Lady Dunfern's first missive reached Marjory until word was forthcoming from Oscar Otwell. Her heart beat wildly with joy on reading the following, slipped to her in the usual way:—

"Hedley,
"Berks.

"Dearest Lady Dunfern,

"You may well guess my gross astonishment on receipt of your long looked-for note, and the dire news it contained. My heart bleeds for you, and believe me, no stone shall be left unturned until your release from that heathenish cell of woe shall be proclaimed. Often have I looked for an answer to my letters from you, but, alas! in vain. I began to be convinced that something must have driven your love for me into hate. I am further surprised that my uncle, who purchased Dilworth Estate, and who permanently resides at the castle with his wife and daughters, never alluded in any way in his letters to me to your retirement as it were from public life. His answers to my many questions concerning you he entirely evaded, and never having had an opportunity of a personal interview with him since I entered Chitworth College, I unfortunately have been debarred from rendering long since the aid you now seek.

"Your suggestion shall undoubtedly have my prompt attention, and I'll now say no more, until I rejoice in your freedom.

"Ever your loving

"OSCAR."

The mind of him who was in full possession of the facts regarding Lady Dunfern's present position became perfectly distracted, and on entering College next morning, after receiving her note, was so overcome with grief as to cause grave alarm amongst the many students who benefited so much by his strenuous efforts to insure success. Doctor O'Sullivan, the eminent President of the College, on seeing Oscar, whom he lately observed was labouring under some weight of sorrow, in such a state of despair, strongly advised a change of air, at the same time kindly offering him a substitute for four weeks, at the end of which time, if he still found himself unable to resume his tuitions, he would prolong his vacation by two weeks. This was the very thing Oscar wanted—absence from duty—and he gladly availed himself of the worthy president's generous offer.

How Oscar quitted the college on receiving the news which liberated him, not only for four weeks, but for ever!—how he sped along to his room in Upper Joy Street, and there wrote a few words to her who longed for his presence and aid, wondering how the clever trick, so ably concocted by Lady Dunfern, would be accomplished, or if attempted, would succeed!—better leave it to her who had so well managed to even reach the length of liberty which marked her heroism already.

Lady Dunfern was busily engaged, during her hours of uninterruption, in marking notes, with great caution and clearness, on paper for Marjory's use; and well guarded and guided must the steps be that should again lead her into the open field of freedom and health.

The heavy rain beat furiously against the darkened window of Lady Dunfern's confined and much-detested abode as Rachel approached her with supper on the night of 24th December.

As the next day brought many touching remembrances with it, Rachel, this iron-willed attendant, spoke in rather soothing strains to her whom more than once she tried to betray. Lady Dunfern, being so fully charged with thoughts edging on her flight, remained in perfect indifference to all her cunning remarks, never betraying the least outward symptom of the excitement that then raged so terribly within her; she was resolved that no word of any description whatever should be conveyed to him who so eagerly awaited Rachel's retracing footsteps outside the cell.

Prompted strongly by Sir John before entering, Rachel carried with her messages of a rather condoling character, to be delivered to her ladyship in such pitiful phrases as to twist from her remarks for the use of him who feared that something dreadful was about to happen owing to a miserable dream he had only a couple of nights before.

But Lady Dunfern was too watchful to allow even one word to escape her lips that might innocently convict her; and steadfastly guarding against the tongue of the treacherous maiden, remained in silence. The evil-intended Rachel lingered around the room fully fifteen minutes, thus affording Lady Dunfern every opportunity of saying something, but all of no avail; and angrily snatching up the large silver tray, bounced out of the room, banging the great door after her, probably in order to frighten her mistress, but not a nerve did the rude and audacious act disturb.

Turning the light very low, the confined woman slipped on tip-toe behind the defiant door, and heard faint sounds proceed from the adjoining corridor, the voices she well knew to be those of both her husband and Rachel. Her heart sank somewhat at the discourse that followed Rachel's recent visit, lest it might be concerning either herself or Marjory; or, worse still, she thought, relative to her intended flight within five hours, which she earnestly implored should not be prevented.

The voices, however, after a lengthy conversation, suddenly ceased, and gently moving to the fire, she sat quietly down to heat her icy limbs, that were almost benumbed with cold.

The thoughts which she allowed to disturb her anxious mind she found were very numerous, the principal one being that of flight, which she trusted strenuously should be fully accomplished within the time specified. The first hour slipped in, the second moved round too, likewise the third; and, gazing in wild despair in the direction of her dainty-jewelled watch, which she kept suspended from a trivial hook above the mantelpiece of richly carved oak, could scarcely refrain from tears.

The smallest hand of her little timekeeper could not fail to show that the hour of eleven had just been reached; this was precisely the time all the household retired, including Sir John, on whose part it was not a case of command, but option.

On this particular night the staff of servants was not so fully represented as usual. Marjory Mason had not been amongst the number who sought sleep, neither was it known by any one whether or not she was in her own room.

Immediately adjoining Marjory's room was Rachel Hyde's, both of which it was Marjory's duty always to keep in perfect order, thus affording the great friend of Lady Dunfern a daily opportunity of viewing the drawer in which the great key of her ladyship's room was at rest.

It was habit with Rachel to sleep with her bedroom door ajar, by order of her master, lest a fire might originate during the hours of repose, or burglars enter and carry with them some valuables of no slight worth or interest.

About ten o'clock, an hour before Marjory's usual time to retire, she ably feigned a very severe attack of indigestion, and, trying to look as dejected and sick as she could in consequence, requested that she might be permitted to go to her own room for the night; a request which Rachel readily granted, as Marjory and she always travelled by the express train of friendship. Rachel added that she would act in her stead by clearing her master's supper table herself.

No sooner had Rachel granted Marjory's request than she dashed up the many and winding steps of ascent until she reached the object of her premeditated scheme by boldly entering the housekeeper's room and taking therefrom the choicest treasure it contained—namely, the key which was so soon to prove the nature of the severe illness she so capitally assumed.

Rachel, on entering the room in which Sir John sat, was quickly asked where Marjory was; and after satisfying him as to her illness, she hastily removed the articles used at supper, and repaired to rest. When passing Marjory's door, Rachel tapped lightly, and failing to gain admission, called on her to admit her with a cup of hot milk. Still no reply came from within. Then, slowly turning the handle, she tried to admit herself without awaking Marjory, feeling sure that she must be sound asleep.

It was only during her third attempt to seek entrance that she found the door locked. Moving into her own room, she muttered something that did not distinctly reach the ear of her who was safely secreted underneath the housekeeper's bed. Divesting herself of her clothing, Rachel soon put herself in a position to guarantee slumber. She wrapped herself well within the fleecy folds of nature, and in less than ten minutes was safely sailing in the boat of dreamland.

Marjory, for it was she who lay stretched under the bed of her who never at any time doubted her word or actions, when fully convinced of Rachel's safe retirement, crept along the carpeted floor on hands and knees, carrying with her the key to victory. Proudly and much agitated did Marjory steal her way along the many winding corridors of carpeted comfort, until at last she came to the bottom of the ghost-like marble steps which led to her mistress; and swiftly running up the icy heights, until reaching the door of danger and blood-thirsty revenge, she, with the caution of a murderess, thrust with great and exceptional care the key into its much-used opening, and heroically succeeded in gaining admittance.

Behind the door lay Lady Dunfern, as if dead. With great presence of mind Marjory locked the door from within, struck a match, and tried to light the lamp, which had been extinguished not long before; this with difficulty she nervously did. Then, turning to her mistress, whose changed countenance was a sight Marjory never forgot until her dying day, she tried every effort to arouse her who so soon was likely to track the path of powerful pursuit. It was fully some minutes until she saw the faintest glimpse of animation, and gently raising the shadowy form in her strong arms, used every means in her power to quickly prepare her for the most trying part of all.

At last Marjory's efforts were completely baffled; and knowing it was approaching the time at which Oscar was to be in readiness at the gate farthest away from the mansion, that was seldom or never used, the poor trembling girl had now enough to bear. She believed the cup of sorrow had been drained to its last dregs; still she hoped on, never giving place to the remotest trace of doubt, being fully assured of achieving the top-most tier of triumph.

Lady Dunfern had, through pure fear of being caught in her adventure, stood an hour or so behind the door before Marjory's welcome steps were heard, and momentarily on hearing her trusted maid's nimble tread make such rapid strides towards her release was with overjoy so quickly stricken down, at a time when two-fold energy was most required, that she utterly failed to regain the slightest strength; and in this sad state her helper found her!

The moments were passing more quickly now than Marjory wished, and bestowing one final look at her ladyship's watch so firmly clutched in her fingers, was about to break down in despair, when she was suddenly roused by a dash of sandy pebble thrown against the window, which unmistakably announced the arrival of him who so soon was to shield the shaken form of her once lovely mistress from the snares of jealousy and intrigue.

Oscar, who stood at the gate appointed, was very uneasy, no doubt, as the hour slowly approached that should make him the recipient of the treasure he at first should have honestly secured, and fearing lest the escape might be detected in time for rescue, he was unable to remain any longer where he was. Mounting the iron gate, he soon flung himself over its speary top, and hurriedly making his way towards Lady Dunfern's window, where he perceived the dim light, he announced his arrival in the manner described.

Wringing her hands in wild despair, Marjory touchingly prayed for speedy release from such cruel torture, and opening the door for the last time she carried her mistress into the corridor, and there deposited her until again locking the giant block of oak, then she lightly tripped down the ashen steps, along the corridors, until at last she reached the open door of Rachel's room. Pausing for a moment lest the housekeeper might be awake, she satisfied herself this was not so. She then courageously entered and safely deposited the key in the exact spot whence she took it, retracing in a wonderfully quiet manner her shaking footsteps until arriving to convey her precious charge to a place of safety. Clasping Lady Dunfern once more in her arms, she crept down the chilly steps of fate along the well-padded paths of tapestry, down numerous flights of wiry-carpeted stairs, until finally reaching the lofty hall, where she paused for an instant, being a complete example of exhaustion, and dreading the least delay, approached the door with safety. She then deposited her lady-ship on a lounge that lay right behind it until she secured the key which from previous observation she noted, in case of emergency, hung on a silver hook not eight feet distant.

With the air of a duchess, Marjory dashed open the outer door, at the left wing of the building, and, with her liberated load of love, swept for ever from its touch. Blowing faintly a whistle she bought for the purpose, she soon was released of her charge by him who instantly appeared to shield them both from the breezy blast which bitterly swept that night o'er hill and dale.

Taking Lady Dunfern in his arms, Oscar paced the broad and pebbled walks, speedily arriving at the spot where stood a vehicle in readiness to convey them to their destiny. Not a word was spoken by Oscar, neither did Lady Dunfern betray the slightest symptoms of recovery until safely driven to the pretty home Oscar had previously arranged for her rescue, some twenty miles distant from Dunfern Mansion.

It was situated nearly in the centre of Dilworth Park, and generously handed over to Oscar as a conditional gift from his uncle, the Marquis of Orland, who owned its many acres. Marjory's joy at this stage fully balanced her previous hours of sorrowful and dangerous adventure. She could hardly refrain from tears as she viewed the weary night before through the telescope of trickery. She seemed confident of having per-formed a great and good work by liberating from the pangs of emotional imprisonment the weak and forlorn, who so soon would have been ordered to separate herself from a closet of chastisement to enter the home of joy everlasting, which ever has its door of gladness open to the ring of the repentant and contrite.

After leaving Lady Dunfern in the careful charge of Marjory, Oscar proceeded to handsomely reward his uncle's coachman, who drove them so quickly from Dunfern Mansion to Audley Hall, requesting him at the same time to treat the matter with profound silence.

The rescued form now opened her eyes, and suddenly a convulsive twitch shook her feeble frame. Casting her heavily-laden orbs of blinded brilliancy around the cosy well-lighted room, had not to be informed by any one what happened; she gasped, "Thank Heaven, I'm safe!"

Oscar, tenderly bidding Lady Dunfern "Good night," instructed Marjory to carefully administer to her wants until daybreak.

CHAPTER XIII

I T is astounding to view the smallest article through a magnifying glass;
how large and lustrous an atom of silver appears; how fat and fair the
withered finger seems; how monstrously mighty an orange; how im-
measurably great the football of youth; but these are as nought when the
naked eye behold the boulder of barred strength—a mountain of mystery.

The usual hour for arousing the inmates of Dunfern Mansion was
designated by the ringing of a bell, constructed at the back part of the
building, and connected by means of a wire with the room of the footman,
whose duty it was to ring fully three minutes every morning at the hour
of seven o'clock in winter and six in summer.

On Christmas morning, only a short time after Lady Dunfern's escape
was effected, it rang somewhat later, arousing from sleep all the servants,
with the exception of Marjory Mason, who failed entirely to put in an
appearance, even when called thrice by Rachel. However, believing that
she was still fast asleep. Rachel ceased to further call on her until after
serving her ladyship's breakfast.

On this festive day the breakfast served in the servants' spacious hall
was a sumptuous repast, truly, and required longer time to prepare than
was customary. This being so, evidently delayed the housekeeper a considerable time in attending to the wants of her mistress, whose breakfast
was always punctually served at nine o'clock. This rule was violated to
the extent of about half an hour on the memorable morning of Lady
Dunfern's flight.

Sir John breakfasted at fifteen minutes after nine, and looked both
careworn and sad, intimating to Rachel his inability to sleep the previous
night. Ordering her to prepare a dainty dish for Lady Dunfern, he proceeded to read the daily paper, that had been so customary for years.
Rachel, hastily executing her master's orders, and having all in readiness
for her mistress, hurried to her room for the key. Sharply telling the usual
maid to follow her with the tray, she wended her way towards the door
that twice had been locked since her last visit. Unlocking it, turning the
handle and pushing it open, she took from the servant the tray, as was
her custom, by strict orders of her master, never allowing the maid further
than the door.

Depositing it upon the table, she swiftly turned to the door, and locking
it from within, began to gaze around for Lady Dunfern, who sometimes
breakfasted in bed. Moving in its direction with tray in hand, no Lady
Dunfern appeared! The bed remained unused since she settled it the

previous day. Wildly shouting with momentary pain, Rachel let fall the tray, smashing the china, &c., and thickly spotting the matting in some places with its contents. In deep despair she cast one delirious stare around the room, but all to no effect. Heaven help me! has she fled? Oh, what! —what shall I do? Thinking that she might have hidden under the couch of rest, she threw herself on the floor to try and catch only a glance of her hidden form, but was disappointed once more.

Running to the door and frantically opening it, she ran to Marjory's room. Failing to be admitted, she hurried down to acquaint some of the men, who attempted to open Marjory's door, but all their masculine efforts to arouse her were futile. What was there left to be done, save to acquaint Sir John of the matter. Agitated did Rachel enter without signifying her approach to her master, who sat in silence. "Oh, sir," cried she, drowned in tears, and uttered in broken accents the words, "Your wife has escaped —she is not in her room!" "What!" gasped Sir John. "It cannot be!"

Following Rachel to the room of terror he found her information too true. "How on earth has this happened?" asked the horrified husband. "Had you the key?" he fiercely asked of Rachel. Ever ready to substitute the truth with a lie, where the former especially would convict her, she replied, with a stamp of her foot, "that it never was out of her drawer of safe deposit." Thinking probably she may have trifled with the window, Sir John moved forward, and the wrap never being removed, he thought it had not in any way been tampered with until Rachel espied the corner pane. "Ah!" said she, "this is the clue to her cursed craft. This must have had something to do with her escape." Then the thought of Marjory's room being still closed to view she fancied might have something also to do with the mysterious and marvellous mark of ingenious intrigue.

Both Sir John and Rachel tottered to Marjory's door, and demanding it to broken open, Sir John entered to be further astonished at her absence, to be sure. On her bed she cannot have lain the previous night, which was proof positive that she was an announced accomplice. But the mystery had yet to be solved as to the action of their flight. Guilt took strong hold on Rachel. She knew the key was always kept in a drawer in her own room, which drawer was constantly kept locked by her and the key hidden inside the little clock that ticked so gently on the mantelpiece in her room; but on second thought, she was so busily engaged during the Christmas season that actually she forgot to lock the drawer the whole week. Never dreaming that this overlook on her part was so cleverly taken notice of by her who not alone committed the ruffianous act, but caused all the blame to be thrown on the party in charge. The housekeeper, who felt sadly and very much annoyed about the affair, grasped the whole thing—first, she thought of Marjory's professed illness the evening previous, then how she tried her door before going to bed, and in this attempt to enter was unsuccessful, and that very morning there was no answer, and, finally, she was missing as well as Lady Dunfern. The well-arranged plot pictured itself in a most vivid manner to her who in one respect, regarding the key's safety, was entirely to blame.

Sir John, summoning all his men, ordered them to go at once and intimate to the officers of the law the sudden flight of the miscreants, and to try and find out their whereabouts; but no trace of them was as yet nigh at hand.

The deceived husband appeared greatly crushed under such a weight of sorrow, and wondering whether or not they could be found, or if Oscar Otwell, he who so often wrote to his wife during her period of imprisonment, had ought to do with her daring adventure, aided by Marjory Mason! It is no longer an unsolved problem that Oscar Otwell was from first to last the chief irritating item of Sir John Dunfern's unhappiness, and whose supposed underhand communications with Lady Dunfern were the principal features depicted in this escape.

These letters of Otwell's Sir John still retained, never reaching her for whom they were intended. Opening his large Davenport that stood close by, he extracted therefrom all the letters of the vaguish tutor, and coming to the one received lastly, found it bore the address, "Chitworth College, Hedley, Berks." This was so much information regarding the rascal who was the sole means of separating Sir John Dunfern and his wife.

The husband, paralysed with sorrow, instantly wrote to Doctor O'Sullivan, the President of the College, who in youthful years was his most intimate acquaintance, and whose name appeared so often in Oscar's letters, making the necessary inquiries relative to one of the teaching staff named "Oscar Otwell".

After two days' rending suspense, he received the following reply:—

"Chitworth College,
Berks.

"Dear Sir John,

"I am very sorry to inform you that, owing to a grave despondency which of late troubled Oscar Otwell, one of my able and talented assistants, I was compelled, though reluctantly, to allow him either one month's leave of absence or six weeks' if he so desired, in order to recruit him somewhat. I strongly advised him to seek a change of air, which I believe he did. I myself, on receipt of your note, visited his lodgings to ascertain from his landlady when he was likely to return. She informs me she has never heard from him since he left, and cannot give the least clue as to his present quarters. She adds that he took all his belongings with him. —Trusting you enjoy good health.

"Believe me,
"Very sincerely yours,
"D. O'SULLIVAN,
Pres."

"Merciful Father!" exclaimed Sir John, as he finished reading the President's note, which he laid on the table. "God strengthen me to bear this unChristian-like calamity. Oh, my son, my son! What disgrace shall this not bring upon you, my child, my all!"

Pacing the floor in profound agony, Sir John rang for his housekeeper to convey the tidings he had just received. Rachel suspected this beforehand, but dare not even hint at such a thing to him, who had already enough to bear. Speaking in terms which shewed manifest symptoms of sorrow, combined with rage and perplexity, he ordered her for ever from his service. "You," said he, "are solely to blame. Of this I am positively convinced, and through that door march, as I never wish again to set eyes on such a worthless woman." Here Rachel, who was grievously affected, passed for ever from the presence of him who dared to be questioned.

Next of all, he ordered the footman, Tom Hepworth, into his room. "You," said he, "are well aware of my present calamity, and might I ask of you how my wife and Marjory Mason effected their escape from below? Had you not the hall doors locked and likewise all the others?" Replying in the affirmative, the footman shook like a poplar, knowing well that instead of having in his room during the hours of repose all the keys of the various doors which led to the outside, he allowed them to remain where they were during the day. "Had you all those keys in your own room at night, according to my orders since Lady Dunfern was obliged to be dealt with in the manner already described?" demanded Sir John angrily. The honest-hearted footman, being trapped, frankly acknowledged he had not.

"Go, then," said his master, "and seek employment elsewhere. You are no longer fit to be here. You have neglected to carry out my orders, therefore you must go." So saying, the sturdy footman bowed and retired.

It no doubt caused Sir John a vast amount of pain to part with two such helps as Rachel Hyde and Tom Hepworth; but once he formed a resolution, nothing save death itself would break it.

Terror seized every dependant in the mansion lest Sir John would visit his anger on each and all in like manner. However, this was not so, as Rachel and Tom, being longer in his service than any of the others, caused him to intrust them with the chief care of matters of importance in preference. And when he found out that they had so carelessly disobeyed his injunctions they were then compelled to reap the result.

Tom and Rachel, in less than an hour after their master issued his words of censure and dismissal, left the beautiful home, of such lengthy shelter, in which they had shared their help so willingly, to plough the field of adventure on which they now might wander.

CHAPTER XIV

THE affections of youth never die. They live sometimes to lift the drooping head, and help to chase sorrow from the heart of the oppressed. If fostered unduly they generally prove to be more closely interwoven than if retained through honesty alone, and fight the battle of union with cannon strength until gained for good or evil.

Awaking from the deep sleep she so much enjoyed after her troublesome adventures in the past, Christmas Day seemed wreathed with flowers of heavenly fragrance for the once fair bride of Dunfern Mansion. She now felt free to act as she thought best without undergoing an examination which demanded answers of evasive tact—free from the hovering cloud of dislike under which she so solemnly moved since her marriage day—free from the wild gaze of that detestable of mortals, Rachel Hyde, who proved as false as she was foul—free from reposing on the suicidal couch of distrust and distress—free from the surveillance of a so-called philanthropist; and free from the traps of tyrannical power.

She had no longer to fear the opening door of creaking custody or crushed hopes, and well might she now enjoy her Christmas dinner with rural relish and savoury zest. She found in Audley Hall every simple and inexpensive comfort, and rejoiced once more to be under the gentle rule of him whom she would have died to serve. She seemed now to have reached joy's greatest height, and never hoped that she should again be dashed into the dam of denounced riches, where love was an absenter to its silvery depth; since she had aspired to and achieved the greatest aim of her ambition.

Oscar Otwell's happiness knew no bounds. The trusted tutor had at last secured the only hope he ever wished realised, although gained with daring enterprise and false advances. He believed that life at last possessed some charms for him, viewing matters lightly. But behind the silvery rock of fortune there lies a hollow filled with darkened traces of fate.

The love-dream of youth had hardly time to be told until the future dream of wonder and dread was about to be prophesied. A couple of months or so after Lady Dunfern took up her residence at Audley Hall found her more a dependant than a patroness. She had recently fled from a dungeon, still it was not one of either starvation or poverty. Whilst occupying its darkened midst she never had any cause for complaint regarding food or attendance, both of which could not possibly have been excelled. It was only when staring her lover's scanty table fully that thoughts of any nature, save cruelty, haunted her and caused a sad expression to appear which before seemed invisible.

Oscar, who had no means whatever of a private nature, soon commenced to feel the touch of want as well as Lady Dunfern. He had no situation, neither had he the means to afford the homeliest fare, and although made owner of his present habitation, yet it was only conditionally he obtained it from his uncle. Must not the great love they naturally had for each other have been of very superlative strength, since it bade adieu to boundless wealth on the one hand and a comfortable allowance on the other, to face the future with penniless pride!

Advertisements were often seen in the leading journals for a situation, and once the name "Oscar Otwell" appeared below. It was treated with muffled silence, so much so that after a month's daily appealing to a praiseworthy public, the result proved a decided failure.

Did he imagine his conduct in robbing Sir John Dunfern of his youthful wife would be appreciated by a public band of critics? Did he by his various attempts to enter the minds of the needy ever think to solicit their assistance or gain their confidence by tearing asunder the lawful bond of superficial union and right, casting it upon the sieve of shattered shelter to separate the corn of crowded comfort from the chaff of crafty want?

Oscar Otwell, whose literary abilities were proved beyond doubt, and which were the sole source of his existence, was, by his conduct and craving desire, driven into the pit of trifling tenure and allowed to lie dormant until again aroused in a clime to which he soon must wend his wasted way.

It was now that the heated passion of youth's folly became abated as Oscar was beginning to near his purse's wrinkled bottom, and failing in his strenuous efforts to secure a tutorship, was smartly made to feel that he must visit a land of strangers, where height of ability and depth of character were alike unquestioned. It was at this stage, too, that Lady Dunfern was made to taste of the dish of fanciful wish in which she often dipped her slender fingers to sprinkle her body of dishonesty. She got time now to brood over her actions of silly execution and hatch them with heated hunger. The orphan, the pampered, the honoured was at this period the deluded, the mocked, the hungered.

This was only the beginning of what must follow; and where did the blame attachable rest? But on the shoulders of her who had edged the road of unreasonable revenge, and stripped herself of the covering of coveted cost to array herself in linen of loose lore and lengthy wear, and die, it may be, on the wayside of want.

The shaft of poverty still kept striking the inmates of Audley Hall, until forced to withdraw its clumsy blow. There was evidently now plenty of scope for the talent of the learned Oscar to develop; he must plan how to arrive at an idea that would bring to the occupants of his temporary home the necessaries of which they stood immediately in need. Failing in his efforts to gain one step towards relief, Lady Dunfern advised the disposal of Audley Hall privately, which, she strongly hinted to Oscar, was their only path of safety from the door of starvation. To this suggestion she succeeded in gaining his consent.

He accordingly, acting upon her advice, wrote to Doctor O'Sullivan, President of Chitworth College, intimating to him his present circumstances and intention, and begged of him to use his best efforts in sending him a purchaser, the sale to be kept strictly private for reasons which, presently, he felt too delicate to explain.

In a week or so after, a gentleman was seen approach the door of Oscar's home, and making the necessary inquiries regarding the price Oscar meant to accept for it, offered the sum of one thousand pounds, which, needless to say, was gladly accepted.

The purchaser was rather an elderly gentleman, with chiselled features, tall and straight, and seemed to have borne the melting heat of a far-off clime to a large extent. He informed Oscar that being a retired army pensioner, named Major Iddesleigh, he chose to leave the foreign land in which he sojourned for upwards of thirty-five years and reside in his native county, adding that he was a widower, having had two sons, both of whom predeceased him, and preferred a home of his own rather than take up quarters he could not solely claim.

He went on to say he had an only brother, a colonel, who formerly resided at Flixton, a quaint little town on the east coast of Kent. He had not heard from him for many years, and was resolved on arriving in England to lose no time in finding out his whereabouts, and, much to his grave disappointment and vexation, he was informed, whilst staying for a few days with President O'Sullivan, that he and his wife had long since been dead, leaving an only daughter, of whom he was now in earnest pursuit. Oscar's deadly countenance during the latter part of Major Iddesleigh's remarks filled the mind of the purchaser of Audley Hall with thoughts of wonder, and on casting a sharp and penetrating stare at her who passed as Oscar's wife, he was similarly struck with intense awe at the sudden change that swept over her handsome face.

Her brain whirled with dire excitement on being at last informed of him who for years previous she considered had been a member of the missing majority.

"Great and Merciful Forgiver!" thought Lady Dunfern, "am I at last face to face with Major Iddesleigh, whose name has been so often the subject of conversation with both Lord and Lady Dilworth?" Gathering her thoughts and submitting them to subjection, she tried to subdue her shattered nerves and lock them under proper restraint, until her uncle should safely be out of sight on his way back to the home of the kind-hearted President of Chitworth College.

She had not, however, the slightest thought of making him cognisant of the fact that she was the proud and lovely daughter of his brother, the late Colonel Iddesleigh—the once-adored wife of the widely respected and generous owner of Dunfern Estate, and now the tempted tool of emigration.

She prayed in her bewilderment that she might escape unknown to him, rather than make him aware of the disgrace into which her past conduct had unmistakably plunged her. Bidding Oscar and her "Adieu," Major Iddesleigh left what was to be his future home, and returned to Doctor O'Sullivan to acquaint him of his purchase.

Before he had even reached the College on his way from Audley Hall, Oscar Otwell, Lady Dunfern, and Marjory had booked for New York, on board the "Delwyn," and when the worthy President was informed of the purchase, the dashing waves of Atlantic waters were raising themselves to a considerable height before the eyes of the fugitives, who nervously paced the deck of danger in despair and deepest thought of their foul transaction and Major Iddesleigh, lest before they reached their destiny he would be made possessor of his niece's conduct, and, with the warlike will of a soldier of strength, follow her, and bring her back to Audley Hall to administer to his many wants and comforts, and bequeath to her all he possessed.

Nor did Oscar Otwell, whose nerves were reaching their shaky height, feel free until safely ensconced in a trim little cottage on the outskirts of Dobbs Ferry, some miles distant from the suburbs of New York. Oscar's first thought, after being quietly settled in his new home, was to bind himself for life to be the husband of her who had risked so much to bring him the joy he long sought after; and within one month after their safe arrival in New York borders, the pretty little church, situated at the east end of Dobbs Ferry, was the scene of a charming group of wealthy sight-seers and warm admirers of the handsome bride of Oscar Otwell, who had lately regained some of her former spirits, which enlivened her to a pleasing extent, and manifested signs of joy where lines of sorrow so lately lived.

It was for this celebration that Lady Dunfern arrayed herself in the gorgeous gown of purest duchesse satin, which bore such a train of past remembrances. Why its puffs of pearly wealth surrounded her well-formed figure on the celebration of her marriage with him who long ago should have claimed its shining folds, may be considered mysterious. But in this, as well as in many other instances, the busy brain of Marjory Mason was prime mover.

During Lady Dunfern's confinement in the mansion over which she unjustly was appointed mistress, Sir John Dunfern, never suspecting the maid of her on whom he was driven to lavish correction, appointed Marjory mistress of her ladyship's wardrobe, and it was during her term of office that she stole from its midst the box containing the beautiful Parisian outfit which failed to put in an appearance on Lady Dunfern's previous wedding-day. This Marjory kept, until safe in the shady cot of comfort which encompassed within its wooden walls the trio of adventure. Lady Dunfern resolved that this gown should be kept a prisoner until either worn with a face of happiness and prided ambition or never worn at all.

On entering the church on the morning of her marriage with Oscar, how every eye was turned towards the beautiful woman whose radiant smile gained the hearts of each and all of its occupants. There she stood before the holy altar with calm resolution and undaunted fear, and her elegant bearing and manner throughout the trying ceremony were thoroughly appreciated by the assembly.

Oscar bore slight traces of nervousness throughout the oratorical ordeal, and was rejoiced indeed as he turned to leave the scene of such outbursts of praise, taking with him her who was to be his coveted partner for life; her, whose footsteps he so often worshipped in days gone by; her, who entered into treaty legally with a man she never could learn to love; her, whom he now claimed as his own, and for whom he stumbled over many an awkward and winding stile, until at last his footsteps had reached the path of level tread, on which he hoped to travel until his journey would be ended to that distant land where strife is a stranger.

CHAPTER XV

THE wealthy, the haughty, the noble must alike taste of disappointment. They court ideas whilst surrounded with bountiful store to be fostered and fed with heaven-bordered hopes which nothing save denial could thwart. The meek, the humble, the poor share equally in its visitation, and learn not to frown at its unwelcome intrusion while they bear the load of blighted hopes with unshrinking modesty.

At Dunfern Mansion matters seemed at a standstill, since that Christmas Day which began with such sunshine and ended with such misery. Energy had fled from the able-bodied staff of servants who occupied its rooms of plentiful repast. Each and all of them seemed as if death had entered their midst and snapped from amongst them their sole support.

Was it because of Rachel Hyde's hasty departure? No! They had now no domineering inflicter of petticoat power to check their honest actions or words; no eyes of dreaded terror viewing through spectacles of sin their little faults, and submitting them, in exaggerated form, to the ear of him who now lay so dangerously ill; no false face masked in brasen mould, nor tongue of touchy cut to divide their friendship. Rachel Hyde, whose word, nay, look, was law, was driven from the presence of him who too long was blind to her false approaches, and who always treated her with more leniency and consideration than she really deserved, never again to mount a pinnacle of trust and truth, or share in the confidence of such a just and true specimen of humanity as Sir John Dunfern. She had been made to reap the crops of cunning falsehood, sown so oft in the fields of honour and true worth, and pocket the result of their flimsy income. She, by her long service of artifice, had scattered the seeds of scepticism so thickly around the corners of harmony, goodwill, and peace as to almost defy their speedy removal; but time would swamp their silent growth and supplant in their stead roots of integrity, justice, and benevolence. She had at last been cast on the mercy of a world of icy indifference to facts of long standing, and made to taste of the stagnant waters of pity, which flung their muddy drops of rancid rascality on the face of dogmatic dread, until crushed beneath their constant clash she yielded her paltry right to Him Whose order must never be disobeyed.

Tom Hopworth, whose absence was partly the cause of sorrow within the breasts of his fellow-workers in Dunfern Mansion, was much to be pitied; he was the very soul of honour, and was highly respected by all who knew him. In his presence every care vanished like snow in sunshine; the pitiful look that shot from the eye of the down-trodden in Rachel Hyde's presence was thrown aside when Tom appeared. He acted as a father and friend on all occasions where trouble reigned supreme, and never failed to hear the light laugh of youth proceed from its hidden bed, where it too often reposed untouched.

Tom Hepworth, whose race was nearly run, when leaving Dunfern Mansion took refuge in the home of Mrs. Durand, his sister, who lived only a short distance from where he had spent more than a third part of his existence. A few months only elapsed whilst under her roof when he was seized with a fit of apoplexy, terminating in a few hours a life of usefulness and blameless bearing. The shock of his sudden demise, when conveyed to his master, whom he revered, brought on a severe attack of haemorrhage, under which Sir John Dunfern now lay prostrate.

Not a week passed after Lady Dunfern took up residence at Audley Hall until Sir John was informed of her whereabouts. Had her escape been effected unknown to Oscar Otwell, it would scarcely have taken such hold on the mind of him who, unfortunately, claimed her as his wife; but to think he had again been duped by a rascally pauper tutor was a pill too difficult to swallow without being moderately reduced. The troubles that visit the just are many, and of these Sir John had ample share. He knew, when too late, that he had jumped the drain of devotion with too much intensity to gain a worthless reward.

He was tempted to invest in the polluted stocks of magnified extension, and when their banks seemed swollen with rotten gear, gathered too often from the winds of wilful wrong, how the misty dust blinded his sense of sight and drove him through the field of fashion and feeble effeminacy, which he once never meant to tread, landing him on the slippery rock of smutty touch, to wander into its hidden cavities of ancient fame, there to remain a blinded son of injustice and unparallelled wrong! All these thoughts seized the blighted protector of the late Colonel Iddesleigh's orphan daughter; and being gradually augmented by many others of private and public importance, rose, like a tumour of superfluous matter, and burst asunder on receiving the last blow relative to poor old Tom Hepworth.

Sir John in a few weeks gradually grew stronger, until finally he baffled his severe illness with Christian bravery, and was again able to keep the ball of industry moving in the direction indicated during his years of singleness, on which he now looked back, alas! not with sorrow, but pride.

During all this trying time, however, it must be admitted there shone one bright star of filial attraction which seemed to shoot its reflected lines of loving brightness towards him, whose face always beamed with delight in return. Yes, his little son Hugh, who had been placed under the care of Madam Fulham, since Lady Dunfern, by her conduct, could no longer fill the post of mother, had grown to be a bright child, able to totter around his nursery toys of cost and variety. He always seemed a cheerful, intelligent boy, and extremely beautiful, but inclined to be slightly self-willed, a trait which developed itself more and more as years rolled on.

At the age of six, Sir John, abhorring the advice of his many friends to procure for him a tutor, had him sent to Canterbury High School, where he remained for a period of five years as boarder, under the careful charge of Professor Smeath, a man of the highest literary attainments, and whose exemplary training of the many youths placed under his august rule was so pronounced as to leave no room for doubt in the minds of the many parents who intrusted their respective charges to him. Each week during this period found Sir John a visitor at Canterbury; he gave every instruction necessary to Professor Smeath that would serve to interest his son in any way, and strictly prohibited him from allowing any outsider whatever, male or female, an interview with his boy, always treating with dread the wily ways of her who claimed to be once his partner, and who had brought a shower of everlasting shame upon himself and child. This order had only to be issued once to the stern professor carrying out on all possible occasions any instructions received from the parents of the pupils under his control with unflinching and undeniable reliance.

During these five years of Hugh Dunfern's instruction at Canterbury, Sir John was seen to gradually grow careless and despondent. The healthy glow of youth disappeared daily since domestic affliction entered his home, and wrote its living lines of disgust with steady hand on the brow which was now thickly marked with them. He got too much time to meditate on the immediate past, which was considerably augmented by the absence of his son.

He was known to sit for hours at a time in deep and painful thought, and it was only when aroused by Madam Fulham that he ever cared to stir from his much-frequented couch of rest; she whom he appointed housekeeper in Rachel Hyde's stead, and who acted as well mother to his little son until removed to school—she extended him every attention, of which he stood in great need, after his severe attack of illness and trial, bodily and mentally.

Time rolled along until his son's return from Canterbury, whose very presence should have healed the gaping wounds his absence inflicted, and chased away all gloomy cavities from the mind of Sir John. On the day of Hugh's home-coming, after five years' training under Professor Smeath, which should have been a day of gladness and rejoicing throughout Dunfern Mansion, it was only one of sadness for the heart-broken father.

Bouncing into the room with boyish pride, Hugh ran and proudly embraced him, who, in return, stood face to face with the very image of her whom he could never again own.

There were the rounded forehead, the aquiline nose, the hazel eyes, the nut-brown hair, the ruby lips, the pearly teeth, the dimpled cheeks and tiny chin of his mother, who probably was grappling at the crumbs of pauperism! However, Sir John manfully tried to hide from his boy the source of his grave looks, until some day of revelation would demand their blackened origin to be boldly announced to him who as yet was solely ignorant of his mother being alive.

Six weeks' holiday passed too quickly, Hugh thought, until he would another time be compelled to quit his home of unbounded luxury and enter Chitworth College, Berks, for a further period of instruction, the length of which events alone would define.

Although the very name of Chitworth College brought reminiscences of dislike to him who suffered so much from one of its former staff, yet those days had fled, and with them the footsteps of flaming stratagem.

Being a personal friend of Professor O'Sullivan, Sir John preferred his son to reside with him, and receive under his able control all the necessary acquirements devolving upon a son of such a proud and distinguished race. The morning at last arrived for Hugh to start on his college career, and, accompanied by his father, was not long in completing the journey.

The interview between Sir John and his attached friend, Doctor O'Sullivan, was affecting in the extreme, so much so that Hugh, being an entire stranger to such outbursts of grief, and not being prepared for such sudden emotional and silent greeting as that now witnessed by him, began to feel it impossible to refrain from joining in their sorrow.

Throwing his youthful arms around his father's neck, he sobbed hysterically, and could only be quieted when his father again appeared cheerful.

Leaving his son in charge of Doctor O'Sullivan, the latter retired from duty that day, and begged Sir John to remain over-night, adding that he would so much like to have a chat with him over matters he had known, and was persuaded to believe caused heartfelt pity to be secreted where once there dwelt heartfelt pride. To this proposal Sir John consented willingly, not caring to leave his gentle and much-loved boy so soon after such a trying meeting as that which he not alone witnessed between friends of old standing, but in which he modestly and sympathetically joined.

All the past gravity which marred Sir John Dunfern's mirth and usefulness, and which he kept attracted to one common centre, crept from its crazy cell on this evening. So soon as dinner was over the President and Sir John retired to a room of seclusion, and the intense relief it gave the trodden and blighted messenger of manhood to at last have a friend in whom he could confide no one could half imagine!

For fully five hours both sat talking confidentially to each other and sympathising when necessary, and it was only during this conversation that Sir John was first made acquaint either of his wife's marriage with Oscar or her present abode, neither of which, in the President's estimation, moved the husband of treachery in its most mischievous form much.

The news of his wife being Mrs. Otwell, instead of the honourable name her conduct ordered her to bury, only served to cast for ever the gentle words of practical remembrance Sir John had in his last will and testament concerning her into an unknown chasm. Until now the forgiving husband, the meek adviser, the patient sufferer, the wounded knight, the once attached partner, the loving father, and the son of justice, gratitude, and chastity was ready to share a little of his ransom with her whom he thought he may have probably wronged by too rigorous punishment. But President O'Sullivan, whose well-guided words and fatherly advice had on this evening so sealed the mind of forgiveness with the wax of disinterested intent that Sir John, on his arrival home, at once sent for his solicitors, Messrs Hutchinson & Harper, and ordering his will to be produced, demanded there and then that the pen of persuasion be dipped into the ink of revenge and spread thickly along the paragraph of blood-related charity to blank the intolerable words that referred to the woman he was now convinced, beyond doubt, had braved the bridge of bigamy. Some slight alterations, in consequence, were necessary to be made, and these being righted, the will of Sir John Dunfern remained a prisoner until released on the day of execution, which as yet could not possibly be named.

CHAPTER XVI

H ARK! The bell tolled its death-like strains, faint as the far-off fatherland, steady as the starlight, and sweet as the scent of the blooming woodbine. The hour of departure is sure and settled, the loss is sharply felt, the gain completed, and vigorous attempts to retain both are oftentimes multiplying on the exertions of the benefited.

During all these years of revolution the wheel of action rounded its roads of revelling, riot, and separation. Shandon Cottage, the little house of Oscar Otwell, where he took up residence when first a visitor to the land of laudable ingenuity, was a pretty structure, and would doubtless have proved a little palace of peace to two such lovers had the means been forthcoming to keep the glare of poverty within its bed of stillness, and prohibit its visitation where least desired.

Oscar, who, during his English career, never was possessor of aught but a slight pittance derived from the sources of his mental labours, and who courted the vain idea, on being made the recipient of £1,000, which he pocketed under false pretences by the underhand sale of Audley Hall, that he was a man of wealth for life, and when safely settled in his trim little cottage, squandered his trifle in a very short time, leaving himself and wife on the mercy of strangers' sympathy, which more or less presents an icy aspect to the eye of the needy.

Marjory Mason, who just spent twelve months under Oscar's roof, was fortunate in securing a husband, whose calling kept her during her short lifetime aloof from the imaginative pinches of the uncertain future.

It was only when Oscar was forced to evade starvation that he deemed it imperative to accept an appointment in a public school, at the yearly income of one thousand dollars, an office he retained until compelled to resign through courting too great love for the all-powerful monster of mangled might—Intemperance. After a number of years the partaker of maddened love was the imparter of maddened might.

With beastly force did Oscar Otwell enter Shandon Cottage on the night of his open dismissal from Waketown Public School, and arousing from sleep his wife, with monster oaths inflicted upon her strokes of abuse which time could never efface.

Ah! it was now the actions of youthful frivolity stood before her mountain high and baffled her sickly retort. It was now she pored over her journal of events, which seemed a burthen unbearable for such a fragile frame, and begged the credit side to be for ever closed to her view, whilst she prayed that the debit be left open until she would enter therein all her past debts to him whom she deceived, deluded, denounced, and despised.

Next morning mended matters little for Oscar Otwell's wife. Still raging with drunken horror, he lavished upon her torrents of insinuations, which she found impossible to overlook, and which forced her to take refuge in the house of the Reverend Bertram Edgar, near by. This man of true piety, at whose church she had occasionally worshipped, extended the refuge she presently implored, and proved instrumental in securing for her the position of governess in a nobleman's family some miles distant.

Disposing of all the household effects, Oscar pocketed their dainty worth, and left Shandon Cottage in earnest pursuit of his wife, intending to again return to their native county in England.

His various inquiries regarding her whereabouts proved vain as the vanishing shadow of Venus, and finally, when completely overcome with sober thoughts of his riotous conduct towards the loving and faithful object of his choice, who had risked so much for him, he cursed his very existence.

A few weeks found him in utter destitution, without either house or chattels to illegally dispose of in case of emergency, and line his pockets of pauperism with coin of dishonest stamp and flashing forgery. Unsuccessful in his worthless attempts to further manifest a standing in the literary world, and being driven almost crazy in his eager efforts to ascertain whither his wife had bent her footsteps, he, in a moment of madness, resolved to resign himself to that ever-anxious defender of Satanic rights who prowls about in ambush until safely securing his prey with the crooked claws of callous craft.

Walking along in the moonlight in the direction of Afton Lake, which sometimes offers its deep waters too freely to victims of sin and suffering, Oscar Otwell resolved to bathe his body of perilous adventure in its darkened waters of deepest death, never more to face the troubles and trials of weak man and share them with weaker woman—never again to approach the wife of his bosom with language of lowest type or lift to her the hand which he so often had sworn should extend her the aid she now must seek.

Arriving at the water's edge, Oscar Otwell divested himself of his scanty attire, and in another moment was struggling in the freezing element which soon should shroud his future with robe of blackest doubt.

Dunraven Hall was situated only a mile from Afton Lake, and was inhabited by the Honourable Eric Eustace, a nobleman of unbounded wealth, whose extension of charity was both wide and varied. It was in this family that Mrs. Otwell was fortunate enough in securing the position before referred to through the instrumentality of her spiritual adviser.

On the night that Oscar Otwell resigned his worldly career, there beat one heart in Dunraven Hall with wild emotion. Mrs. Otwell, retiring to

C

bed as usual, found sleep had altogether fled, and rising from her springy structure of restlessness, dressed herself and paced the bedroom floor enveloped in dread. She was convinced something was about to happen, and struggling in her great efforts to baffle the fear that haunted her night and day lately, she resolved, so soon as daybreak peeped its cheerful face through her window, to take a walk along the road in order to cast her fears upon the highway of forgetfulness.

Wrapping herself in her warmest cloak, she soon was found walking rapidly along in silence on the road that swept round Afton Lake. She had not gone far when people were seen to mount the fence that conducted them to the nearest point of its watery expanse, which lay about fifty perches from the main road.

Courting her curiosity with nervous fear, she walked along, wondering what had happened to attract such crowds. And finding it rather difficult to refrain from making inquiry from some of the gathering, who by this time had hurriedly been retracing their flighty footsteps from the imaginative scene of death, Mrs. Otwell, modestly approaching a female who swiftly hopped over the fence in tears, asked what had happened.

"Oh, madam," cried the woman, "the clothing of a gentleman was seen early this morning as David Gillespie, a labourer, was engaged at a drain hard by. It was neatly folded and deposited on the brink. Surely some one must have been demented and drowned himself in Afton Lake. The authorities are now on the spot and refuse to mention who the gentleman is."

Thanking her for kindly informing her of what she had both seen and heard, Mrs. Otwell hurried back to Dunraven Hall in nervous astonishment, and hastily proceeded to her bedroom to prepare herself for what soon must follow.

The breakfast being shortly afterwards announced, Mrs. Otwell, pale as death, entered the room, and taking her accustomed seat to partake of it as best she could. She had scarcely got properly seated ere two officers of the law were seen approach Dunraven Hall. Ringing furiously, they demanded an interview with the Hon. Eric Eustace.

Satisfied as to the name of his present governess, they wished to be allowed to see her, which request was willingly granted. Being told that morning by the gardener at Dunraven Hall, who ran to the spot on hearing the news, that a lady named Mrs. Otwell permanently resided at the Hall as governess, the authorities immediately grasped the fact that she might be the unfortunate widow, and on putting the usual questions to her concerning her husband, they were still further convinced as to her identity. Drawing from his pocket a parcel containing Oscar's card, photo, and a letter addressed to Mrs. Oscar Otwell, the officer in charge asked her to read it aloud, which she did in a rather trembling voice, without betraying such signs of grief as anticipated. The letter ran thus:—

"Dobbs' Ferry,
Friday Night, 11 p.m.

"Dearest Irene and Wife,—

"Should ever this reach your length, I trust you will pardon me for the rash act I am about to commit.

"Since the morning you left me at Shandon Cottage my sorrow has been greater than my present frame of mind can well support. I, therefore, have decided on ending my days of starvation by hiding for ever beneath the glassy surface of Afton Lake to shield my wicked body from further inflicting upon you the wrongs I have perpetrated in the past, and for which I am grievously tormented.

"Dearest Irene, I hope you, in your past great warmth of devotion for me (your poor tutor and husband), will forgive my late ungentlemanly conduct in striking you so cowardly on the eve of my downfall, and thereby breaking the confidence you reposed in me for such a lengthened period of our existence.

"From what I know of your noble character, I have every faith in your forgiveness, and rest assured, I never mean to face death without imploring you to rectify, if ever in your power, the wrong you accomplished, partly at my request, in breaking the holy cord of union which bound you during your natural existence to Sir John Dunfern, and again uniting it under foul auspices.

"Had I been so fortunate as to secure you first of all, my conscience, certainly, would at this moment be both clear and unclouded. But feeling persuaded I have robbed that nobleman who now possibly is pining for separation from a world of shame and sorrow underneath the lordly roof of Dunfern Mansion, I am positively convinced, under such dangling dishonour, that never more can this world of sin extend to me the comfort I in vain have tried to seek.

"Awake, then, my beloved, to whom I attach not the slightest blame, to a sense of feeling and justice, and go, I implore of you, and cast yourself at the feet of him and beg his forgiveness, who loved you with a love unspeakable—who severed nearly all his self-indulgence with the instrument of intensity and hesitated not to lavish it upon the head of her to whom I offer my last advice. Then shall you meet the messenger—death—not with shrinking fear (like me), but daring bravery.

"Of your present position or abode I am totally unaware, but, dearest wife, I trust your race of penury is almost run, and that your latter years may be crowned with Christian fortitude and ease, and freed from the thorny dart of the wicked, in whose grave I must soon lie unwept.

"Good bye, for ever!

From your affectionate

"Oscar.

"Mrs. Oscar Otwell
    (Address unknown)."

Folding the letter, and handing it to the officers, together with Oscar's card and photograph—all of which would prove indispensable for their future use—Mrs. Otwell quietly moved again to the breakfast room, and, strange to say, finished her meal in silence.

Then turning to him in whose service she was, intimated her intention to sail for England when the missing body would be recovered, which she meant to bury in Greenwood Cemetery. She lingered on in eager expectation of casting one final look at her husband, but week after week died away without any sign of it being forthcoming, and all hope being fled, Mrs. Otwell resolved to lose no further time in returning to her home of nativity, in order to obey the last instructions from the hand of Oscar Otwell, from whom she was reluctantly obliged to part in the manner described.

Another side the picture of futurity presented for the anxious mother, and that was to try and obtain an interview with her son, who at this period must be a boy of some fifteen summers. Having everything in readiness for her journey to her native land, Mrs. Otwell left Dunraven Hall amidst torrents of sympathy and warm expressions from every member of the family; and it was when driving past Afton Lake for the last time on her way to the deck of the "Delwyn" that the crushed widow of Oscar Otwell and legal wife of Sir John Dunfern was made to taste of the unlimited sorrow of her sad career.

There she was, a stranger in a foreign land—an outcast to the society she shone so brilliantly amongst during years that were now no more, the fostered orphan, the adopted daughter of heiressed nothing, the wife of devotional distinction, the illegal partner of crutchy poverty, and the penniless widow of undeniable woe.

She was not even granted the ghostly pleasure of viewing her lover's lifeless body, that would have ended her thoughts relative to him, at least for a time, but as matters stood encircled in doubt, there was nothing left save trouble and anxiety for her whose futurity must ever be shaded.

On approaching the harbour of New York, her attention was attracted by a tall gentleman standing not many yards distant, and being so long familiar with his appearance, she found the object of attraction to be no other than Lord Dilworth. Ordering the cabman to a standstill, she popped her head out in utter astonishment, and shouted in such a strain as to instantly attract his attention. Alighting with ardent enthusiasm in the very midst of her troubles, she soon found herself in the arms of Lord Dilworth, who appeared utterly dazed.

"Protector of Powers! can it be Irene? Lady Dunfern, I mean?" gasped he in bewilderment. To which she bowed, blinded in tears, and in as few words as possible, he related a short narrative concerning both himself and Lady Dilworth, who had long since been dead. On hearing of the death of the once noble mistress of Dilworth Castle, Mrs. Otwell seemed as lifeless as a marble statue, and trying vigorously to regain strength after such a sudden shock, she, in a few broken snatches, related her plotted career; but misery having likewise carpeted Lord Dilworth's floors of fate so much of late, he consequently did not seem so astonished as imagined.

Leaving Mrs. Otwell so far as his time permitted, he pathetically took his final farewell, and shortly after was busy pouring over his books in Franklin Street, office No. 715, where he was employed as a clerk at five hundred dollars a year.

On the other hand, the mighty ocean palace was steering firmly against the clashing breakers with unobstructed speed, acting as protector and friend to all those who entrusted themselves to its unsettled shelter.

CHAPTER XVII

THE mighty orb of gladness spreads its divine halo over many a harrowed home—it encircles the great expanse of foreign adventure and home-hoarded enterprise, and wields its awakening influence against the burthened boroughs of bigotry and lightened land of liberty to a sense of gilded surprise.

The laurels of separation were twining their oily leaves and speedily constructing a crown for the brow of Sir John Dunfern. After returning from Chitworth College, and ordering the last few finishing touches to be made in his will, he grew more drooped and heartless every year, and seemed almost indifferent to life's ploughing changes.

He felt acutely the information imparted to him by President O'Sullivan regarding the wife he now for ever despised, and who unlawfully belonged to Oscar Otwell. He even felt more severely the effect of such on account of his beloved boy, who was steadily endeavouring to increase his slight store of knowledge under the watchful eye of the most scholarly personage of the day.

He knew ere long—owing to his present state of health, brought to such a low ebb by the mother of his son—that he would be obliged to open to Hugh the book of nature as it stood past and present, and instruct him in its disagreeable pages.

The thought of opening up the past, with its stains of dissipation, perhaps acted on the mind of Sir John more severely than the reality. Yet he must brave himself for the trial when opportunity offered, lest it might be too late.

The time for Hugh Dunfern's fourth summer vacation was close at hand. The boy's genial manner, affability, and frankness, gained for him hosts of friends at Chitworth College, and equally numerous were the sharers in his sorrow on receiving a telegram a very short time before his summer holidays commenced to the effect that his father had taken suddenly ill, and asking him to delay as little as he possibly could during his journey to Dunfern Mansion, which must commence immediately.

The poor, sorrow-stricken boy, who was deeply attached to his father, was quite overcome with grief. Bidding "Good bye" to all his college companions, and taking affectionate leave of his masters and President O'Sullivan, he left the much-loved seat of learning, never more to compete in its classes of clever instruction and high moral bearing—never again to watch with craving eye the distribution of letters, and rejoice on observing his father's crested envelope being gently reached him by the President; and no more to share in the many innocent games of youth, at some of which he was an unequalled expert.

The dull hum of voices in the hall of his home met his anxious ear on the eve of his home-coming, and told a tale without further inquiry. Meeting the three most eminent London physicians—namely, Doctors Killen, Crombie, and Smiley, in the library, where they held a long consultation, Hugh was nerved somewhat before entering the chamber of death with words of truth regarding his father's hopeless condition; and, on moving quietly to his father's bed, how the lad of tender years was struck with awe at the bleached resemblance of what used to be a rosy, healthy father!

Perceiving his son's bent and weeping form hang over him with meekest resignation, Sir John cast aside the bedclothes, and, extending his hand, caught firm hold of his son's. Hugh spoke not a word, by order of the doctors, lest his father, who was now bereft of speech, would feel the pain of not being able to reply in return.

The suffering patient lingered on in this dumb condition for six weeks, when suddenly he regained speech partly, but only for some hours—a great dispensation of the Almighty, no doubt, in answer to the silent prayers of the invalid. It was first noticed by Madam Fulham, who proved a mighty help to Sir John since his wife's flight.

On entering the chamber of sickness one morning with a new bottle of medicine, sent direct from London, Sir John raised himself slightly on his left elbow and made inquiry about his son.

With hurried and gladdened step was Madam Fulham seen to glide from the presence of her master, and hasten to find Hugh, who was noticed to pace the topmost corridor in agony.

On observing his father had regained speech after his paralytic attack had somewhat abated, how great was his son's delight! Drawing forth a chair to the bedside of the august patient, Hugh, quite unprepared, received the awful intelligence of his mother's conduct and life from the lips of the afflicted, who, in broken accents, related the tale of trouble which for years had kept him a prisoner to its influence.

Taking his son's hand in his, Sir John Dunfern, after audibly, yet a little indistinctly, offering up a prayer of thanks to Him Who never overlooks the words of the just, for His great mercy in again enabling him to regain his sense of speech, of which he so lately had been deprived, began:—

"My much-loved and faithful son, I, your father, am now stricken down in the middle almost of manhood, and am sensitive to the fact that a short space of time—yea, a short space too—must inevitably elapse until I shall be ordered from this temporary abode, which now to me seems only a floating speck of shelter in the great ocean of time. I am more than thankful that recovery of speech has been granted me for many reasons, which, I fear, my strength cannot permit to be fully explained. However, my great wish to acquaint you of my miserable married career shall, I trust, not be barred from your knowledge by any further visitation of Kingly Power.

"You are aware, my son, that this mansion which soon shall own me no more has been the scene of my frolicking boyhood, my joyful manhood, and, I must now tell you, the undying trouble of a blighted married life.

"Your mother's name was Irene Iddesleigh, the orphan daughter, I understand, of one Colonel Iddesleigh, of Flixton, in this county. Her father and mother both died about the same time, leaving their daughter absolutely unprovided for. She was taken to an orphanage at the early age of three years, and there remained for a period of eight more, when, through the kindness of one Lord Dilworth, of Dilworth Castle, of whose existence I have already acquainted you, she was brought under his charge, and remained as his adopted daughter until, unfortunately, I brought her here as my wife.

"I cannot help informing you that she was the most beautiful and prepossessing young lady I ever met, and, on making her acquaintance at a ball given by Lord and Lady Dilworth, at Dilworth Castle, not far distant, as you know, I became so intoxicated with her looks of refinement and undoubted beauty that I never regained sobriety until she promised to become my wife!

"The beginning of our married career was bright enough, I dare say, for some weeks only, when she grew very strange in her manner towards me. So remarkably strange, that I was reluctantly compelled to demand an explanation. Being satisfied with her false apologies, used as a way out of her difficulty, I remained content. She still continued nevertheless to maintain the same cold indifference towards me until your birth.

"Knowing that a son was born to me, who, if spared, would still keep up the good old name of Dunfern, I became altogether a foreigner to her past conduct, and it was only when recovering from her illness, after your birth, that I caught hold of the trap of deception she had laid since long before our marriage.

"She was found out to be the idolised of one man named Oscar Otwell, who occupied the position of tutor to her during her years of adoption; and not even did her love in return for him cease when I claimed her as my lawful wife, but continued, so far as I know, until now!

"I was therefore obliged through her malpractices to shut her in from the gaze of outsiders, and also from my own. I chose Room No. 10 of this building as her confined apartment. You were only a child then of some two months, and, since, I have never beheld her face, which was false as it was lovely.

"My rage was boundless on the day I ordered her into my presence in that room, and, labouring under the passion of a jealous husband, I told her I would confine her within its walls so long as she existed.

"Over a year passed along, every month of which I grew more and more repentant, until the second Christmas of her seclusion, when I fully resolved to free her once more; at the same time, never again to share in my society or companionship.

"But, behold! the mischievous hand of her maid, Marjory Mason, whose services I retained after her imprisonment, was busy working its way for her escape, which she nimbly succeeded in effecting, exactly on the morning of Christmas Day, by stealing from the room of Rachel Hyde, Madam Fulham's predecessor, the key of her door, and thereby released your mother. Ah! my son, from that hour my life has been a worthless coin, the harp of hideous helplessness struck forth its tunes of turmoil, trouble, and trial, and poured its mixed strains of life and death so vividly in my ear, that since I have, in a measure, been only a wanderer between their striking sounds of extremes.

"I shortly afterwards learned she took refuge in Audley Hall, a residence on the estate of its present owner—the Marquis of Orland, and situated some twenty miles distant, and, horrifying to relate, had been living with Oscar Otwell!

"The dreadful news of her conduct irritated me so that I only, in my last will and testament, bequeathed to her what would grant the ordinary comforts of life, provided I predeceased her. This reference to her remained until I accompanied you to Chitworth College, when President O'Sullivan revealed to me in silent friendship the fact of which I was wholly unaware, viz.—that she had long since sailed for America, at the same time handing me a *New York Herald* sent him by Otwell, and there I beheld the announcement of her marriage with him who ruined my life, and who has been the means of driving me into the pit of tearful tremor, out of which I never more shall climb.

"On returning home from Chitworth College I at once blanked the reference to her in my will, and never more wished to behold the face that swore to me such vows of villainy; the face that blasted my happiness for life; the mother of you, whom I now earnestly implore never to acknowledge, and who possesses every feature she outwardly bore.

"It may be yours to meet her face to face ere she leave this tabernacle of torment; but, my child, for my sake avoid her cunning ways and works, and never allow her shelter underneath this roof she dishonoured and despised. And I trust God in His great mercy shall forgive her errors, and grant you the blessing of a Father of Love."

Sir John Dunfern now lay back exhausted on his pillow, and muttered quietly "Thank God."

Next morning the Angel of Death was seen to spread its snowy wings over his wasted form, and convey the departed spirit into that region of bliss where sorrow, sighing, sin, and suffering are cast for ever from its rooms of glory.

Thus passed away another link of a worthy ancestral chain, who, during his tender years of training, had been guided by the charitable Christian example of a mother of devotion, and who was, during the brighter battle of her son's creeping years of care and caution, summoned before the Invisible Throne of purity, peace, and praise everlasting, shrouded in hopes of sunshine concerning his future happiness, which, never after his marriage, was known to twinkle in Dunfern Mansion.

CHAPTER XVIII

MOCKING Angel! The trials of a tortured throng are naught when weighed in the balance of future anticipations. The living sometimes learn the touchy tricks of the traitor, the tardy, and the tempted; the dead have evaded the flighty earthly future, and form to swell the retinue of retired rights, the righteous school of the invisible, and the rebellious roar of raging nothing.

The night was dark and tempestuous; the hill rather inclined to be steep; the clouds were bathed in wrinkled furrows of vapoury smoke; the traffic on the quiet and lonely roads surrounding Dunfern Mansion was utterly stopped, and nature seemed a block of obstruction to the eye of the foreigner who drudged so wearily up the slope that led to the home of Mrs. Durand, who had been confined to bed for the past three years, sufferer from rheumatism.

Perceiving the faint flicker of light that occasionally flung its feeble rays against the dim fanlight of faithful Fanny's home—the aged sister

C*

of the late Tom Hepworth—the two-fold widowed wanderer, with trembling step, faltered to the door of uncertain refuge, and, tapping against it with fingers cold and stiff, on such a night of howling wind and beating rain, asked, in weakened accents, the woman who opened to her the door, "If she could be allowed to remain for the night?"—a request that was granted through charity alone. After relieving herself of some outer garments, and partaking of the slight homely fare kindly ordered by Mrs. Durand, the widow of Oscar Otwell and Sir John Dunfern warmed herself and dried her saturated clothing before going to bed. She had just arrived the day previous, and hastened to take up her abode as near her former home of exquisiteness as she could, without detection.

On extinguishing the light before retiring, and casting one glance in the direction of the little window, the innumerable recollections of the abundant past swept across the mind of the snowy-haired widow, and were further augmented by the different starlike lights which shone from the numerous windows in Dunfern Mansion, directly opposite where she lay.

A couple of days found her almost rested after such a trying night as that on which she arrived, and observing the sharpest reticence lest she might be known, she nerved herself to appear next day at Dunfern Mansion, to accomplish the last wish of her late lover and husband, for whom she ventured so much and gained so little, and particularly to try and see her son.

The morning was warm and fine; numerous birds kept chirping outside the little cottage of Mrs. Durand. The widow, with swollen eyes and face of faded fear, prepared herself for the trying moment, which she was certain of achieving. Partaking of a very slight breakfast, she told Mrs. Durand not to expect her for dinner.

Marching down the hill's face, she soon set foot on the main road that led direct to Dunfern Mansion. Being admitted by Nancy Bennet, a prim old dame, who had been in charge of the lodge for the last eighteen years, the forlorn widow, whose heart sank in despair as she slowly walked up the great and winding avenue she once claimed, reached the huge door through which she had been unconsciously carried by Marjory Mason a good many years ago.

Gently ringing the bell, the door was attended by a strange face. Reverently asking to have an interview with Sir John Dunfern, how the death-like glare fell over the eyes of the disappointed as the footman informed her of his demise! "Madam, if you cast your eyes thence— [here the sturdy footman pointed to the family graveyard, lying quite adjacent, and in which the offcast of effrontery had oftentimes trodden]— you can with ease behold the rising symbol of death which the young nobleman, Sir Hugh Dunfern, has lavishly and unscrupulously erected to his fond memory."

The crushed hopes of an interview with the man she brought with head of bowed and battered bruises, of blasted untruths and astounding actions, to a grave of premature solitude were further crumbled to atoms in an instant. They were driven beyond retention, never again to be fostered with feverish fancy. After the deplorable news of her rightful husband's death had been conveyed to the sly and shameless questioner, who tried hard to balance her faintish frame unobserved, she asked an interview with Sir Hugh Dunfern. This also was denied, on the ground of absence from home.

Heavily laden with the garb of disappointment did the wandering woman of wayward wrong retrace her footsteps from the door for ever, and leisurely walked down the artistic avenue of carpeted care, never more to face the furrowed frowns of friends who, in years gone by, bestowed on her the praises of poetic powers. Forgetful almost of her present movements, the dangerous signal of widowhood was seen to float along the family graveyard of the Dunferns.

Being beforehand acquaint with the numerous and costly tombstones erected individually, regardless of price, the wearied and sickly woman of former healthy tread was not long in observing the latest tablet, of towering height, at the north-east end of the sacred plot.

There seemed a touchy stream of gilded letters carefully cut on its marble face, and on reading them with watery eye and stooping form, was it anything remarkable that a flood of tears bathed the verdure that peeped above the soil?

The lines were these:—

I.

The hand of death hath once more brought
   The lifeless body here to lie,
Until aroused with angels' voice,
   Which calls it forth, no more to die.

II.

This man, of health and honest mind,
   Had troubles great to bear whilst here,
Which cut him off, in manhood's bloom,
   To where there's neither frown nor tear.

III.

His life was lined with works of good
   For all who sought his affluent aid;
His life-long acts of charity
   Are sure to never pass unpaid.

IV.

Sir John Dunfern, whose noble name
    Is heard to echo, far and wide;
In homes of honour, truth, and right,
    With which he here lies side by side.

V.

The wings of love and lasting strength
    Shall flap above his hollow bed;
Angelic sounds of sweetest strain
    Have chased away all tears he shed.

VI.

Then, when the glorious morn shall wake
    Each member in this dust of ours,
To give to each the sentence sure
    Of everlasting Princely Power—

VII.

He shall not fail to gain a seat
    Upon the bench of gloried right,
To don the crown of golden worth
    Secured whilst braving Nature's fight.

After carefully reading these lines the figure of melting woe sat for a long time in silence until a footstep came up from behind, which alarmed her not a little. Looking up she beheld the face of a youth whose expression was very mournful, and asking after her mission, was informed she had been casting one last look on the monument of her lamented husband.

"Mighty Heavens!" exclaimed Sir Hugh Dunfern, "are you the vagrant who ruined the very existence of him whom you now profess to have loved? You, the wretch of wicked and wilful treachery, and formerly the wife of him before whose very bones you falsely kneel! Are you the confirmed traitoress of the trust reposed in you by my late lamented, dearest, and most noble of fathers? Are you aware that the hypocrisy you manifested once has been handed down to me as an heirloom of polluted possession, and stored within this breast of mine, an indelible stain for life, or, I might say, during your known and hated existence?

"False woman! Wicked wife! Detested mother! Bereft widow!

"How darest thou set foot on the premises your chastity should have protected and secured! What wind of transparent touch must have blown its blasts of boldest bravery around your poisoned person and guided you within miles of the mansion I proudly own?

"What spirit but that of evil used its influence upon you to dare to bend footsteps of foreign tread towards the door through which they once stole unknown? Ah, woman of sin and stray companion of tutorism, arise, I demand you, and strike across that grassy centre as quickly as you can, and never more make your hated face appear within these mighty walls. I can never own you; I can never call you mother; I cannot extend the assistance your poor, poverty-stricken attire of false don silently requests; neither can I ever meet you on this side of the grave, before which you so pityingly kneel!"

Speechless and dogged did the dishonoured mother steal for ever from the presence of her son, but not before bestowing one final look at the brightened eye and angry countenance of him who loaded on her his lordly abuse. The bowed form of former stateliness left for ever the grounds she might have owned without even daring to offer one word of repentance or explanation to her son.

Walking leisurely along the road that reached Dilworth Castle, how the trying moments told upon her who shared in pangs of insult and poverty!—how the thoughts of pleasant days piled themselves with parched power upon the hilltop of remembrance and died away in the distance! The whirling brain became more staid as she heard the approach of horses' feet, and stopping to act the part of Lot's wife, gave such a haggard stare at the driver of the vehicle as caused him to make a sudden halt. Asking her to have a seat, the weary woman gladly mounted upon its cushion with thankfulness, and alighted on reaching its journey's end, about three miles from Audley Hall. The drive was a long one, and helped to rest the tired body of temptation.

Returning thanks to the obliging driver, she marched wearily along until she reached the home of her first refuge after flight.

Perceiving the yellow shutters firmly bolted against the light admitters of Audley Hall, she feared disappointment was also awaiting her. Knocking loudly twice before any attempt was made to open the door, there came at last an aged man with halting step and shaking limb.

"Is Major Iddesleigh at home?" asked the saddened widow. "Oh, madam, he has been dead almost twelve years, and since then no one has occupied this Hall save myself, who am caretaker. The Marquis of Orland was deceived by his nephew, who sold it in an underhand manner to the major, and he resolved that never again would he allow it to be occupied since the major's death by any outsider."

"You are rather lonely," said the widow. "Yes, yes," replied he; "but I have always been accustomed living alone, being an old bachelor, and wish to remain so. It is better to live a life of singleness than torture both body and soul by marrying a woman who doesn't love you, like the good Sir John Dunfern—a nobleman who lived only some miles from this, and who died lately broken-hearted—who became so infatuated with an upstart of unknown parentage, who lived in Dilworth Castle, with one Lorp

Dilworth, the previous owner, that he married her oft hand, and, what was the result, my good woman?—why she eventually ran off with a poor tutor!—and brought the hairs of hoary whiteness of Sir John Dunfern to the grave much sooner than in all probability they would have, had he remained like me."

Facing fumes of insult again, thought the listener. And asking after Major Iddesleigh's will, eagerly awaited his reply.

Placing one hand upon her shoulder, and pointing with the other, "Behold," said he, "yonder church? that was his last will—Iddesleigh Church. It was only when the jaws of death gaped for their prey that the major was forced to alter his will, having had it previously prepared in favour of his niece, whose whereabouts could never be traced until after his death." "Enough—enough, I must go," said the painful listener, and thanking the old man for his information, which, like her son's, had screwed its bolts of deadly weight more deeply down on the lid of abstract need, turned her back on Audley Hall for ever.

CHAPTER XIX

HOPE sinks a world of imagination. It in almost every instance never fails to arm the opponents of justice with weapons of friendly defence, and gains their final fight with peaceful submission. Life is too often stripped of its pleasantness by the steps of false assumption, marring the true path of life-long happiness which should be pebbled with principle, piety, purity, and peace.

Next morning, after the trying adventure of the lonely outcast, was the scene of wonder at Dilworth Castle. Henry Hawkes, the head gardener under the Marquis of Orland, on approaching the little summerhouse in which Irene Iddesleigh so often sat in days of youth, was horrified to find the dead body of a woman, apparently a widow, lying prostrate inside its mossy walls. "Lord, protect me!" shouted poor Hawkes, half distractedly, and hurried to Dilworth Castle to inform the inmates of what he had just seen.

They all rushed towards the little rustic building to verify the certainty of the gardener's remarks. There she lay, cold, stiff, and lifeless as Nero, and must have been dead for hours. They advised the authorities, who were soon on the spot.

What stinging looks of shame the Marquis cast upon her corpse on being told that it was that of the once beautiful Lady Dunfern—mother of the present heir to Dunfern estate!

Lying close at hand was an old and soiled card, with the words almost beyond distinction, "Irene Iddesleigh." In an instant her whole history flashed before the unforgiving mind of the Marquis, and being a sharer in her devices, through his nephew Oscar Otwell, ordered her body to be conveyed to the morgue, at the same time intimating to Sir Hugh Dunfern her demise.

It transpired at the inquest, held next day, that she was admitted the previous night to the grounds of Dilworth Castle by the porter at the lodge, giving her name as "Irene Iddesleigh."

She must have taken refuge in the little construction planned under her personal supervision whilst inhabiting Dilworth Castle during her girlhood, and, haunted with the never-dying desire to visit once more its lovely grounds, wandered there to die of starvation.

No notice whatever was taken of her death by her son, who obeyed to the last letter his father's instructions, and carried them out with tearless pride.

The little narrow bed at the lowest corner on the west side of Seaforde graveyard was the spot chosen for her remains. Thus were laid to rest the orphan of Colonel Iddesleigh, the adopted daughter and imagined heiress of Lord and Lady Dilworth, what might have been the proud wife of Sir John Dunfern, the unlawful wife of Oscar Otwell, the suicidal outcast, and the despised and rejected mother.

She who might have swayed society's circle with the sceptre of nobleness—she who might still have shared in the greatness of her position and defied the crooked stream of poverty in which she so long sailed—had she only been, first of all, true to self, then the honourable name of Sir John Dunfern would have maintained its standard of pure and noble distinction, without being spotted here and there with heathenish remarks inflicted by a sarcastic public on the administerer of proper punishment; then the dignified knight of proud and upright ancestry would have been spared the pains of incessant insult, the mockery of equals, the haunted diseases of mental trials, the erring eye of harshness, and the throbbing twitch of constant criticism.

It was only the lapse of a few minutes after the widowed waif left Dunfern Mansion until the arrival of her son from London, who, after bidding his mother quit the grounds owned by him, blotted her name for ever from his book of memory; and being strongly prejudiced by a father of faultless bearing, resolved that the sharers of beauty, youth, and false love should never have the slightest catch on his affections.

HUMPTY-DUMPTY

by

AN UNKNOWN AUTHOR

"GET down from that wall, Humpty, or you will have a great fall, like the real Humpty Dumpty. You are just as fat, you know."

The child addressed looked down from her exalted height upon the saucy upturned face of her brother Egbert, and her eyes flashed fire; nevertheless, she answered in a measured unchildlike voice—"Go away, Egbert. I shall not come down for you, so you needn't think it."

"Humpty is cross; what fun!" shouted the boy, with glee. "Girls, come and look at her Royal Highness Humpty Dumpty sitting on her throne."

Two little girls came slowly up the garden; they were pretty, fair-haired children, and no one would have known the child on the wall to be their sister.

They surveyed Humpty with looks of scorn; and indeed, she did look an unpleasant sight, for her face was puckered into a frown, and the expression of her mouth was hard and unchildlike.

"You are always on that wall, Lillian. I heard mamma saying yesterday that you were not a bit like other children."

"I don't want to be like other children," retorted the child, with equal scorn. "I mean to be an uncommon woman, Geraldine, like—like,"—the child hesitated a moment, and looked down at the book that lay in her lap—"like Florence Nightingale," she said at last, with a proud ring in her voice. The children shouted at this more than ever, and presently left her alone, all agreeing that she was a great goose.

The child still kept her seat on the wall, and as her brothers and sisters went off, a softer expression came to the strong little face.

"I wish I was good," she murmured earnestly, "then perhaps people would forget that I am ugly and bad-tempered.

Lillian's parents were well-to-do, kind-hearted people, who liked their children to be happy, and to look bright and pretty. Lillian's plainness was a disappointment to them. In the nursery, from her youngest days, she had been overlooked in favour of her more attractive sisters and brothers. Her nickname, too, which her brothers had given her when a little tot of three or four, on account of her plumpness, had caused her an amount of pain no one would have believed possible. Lillian was, I must own, not an easy child to understand: she had a strangely morbid temperament, and was also very highly nervous. She had great faults, and also great virtues. It is often the case that our troublesome, restless, misunderstood little ones possess the noblest, deepest, most generous natures—but love and wisdom must train them, or these "might-be blessings" will prove a failure, all the greater that it might have been otherwise.

One day Geraldine was slightly ailing: she could not eat, and complained of headache and sore throat. Her parents were frightened, and sent at once for the doctor, who proclaimed it a bad kind of scarlet fever. The other children were ordered to the west end of the large rambling house, to be out of danger from infection; and the anxious mother kept entirely to the sick-room. The nurses had strict orders to keep the children confined to the left wing of the house; and as this would cause a great deal of watchfulness and trouble on their part, they hit upon an easy yet effectual way of keeping them within bounds. They told such terrible tales of the suffering and appearance of their sister, and of the awfulness of the illness, that the children were so scared that they hardly dared to venture beyond the nursery unless an older person were with them.

Geraldine was very ill, 'tis true, but her illness partook of none of the hideousness pictured by the maids. Lillian thought of her sister lying in pain and misery on her bed, and pity filled her heart. She wished she were a grown-up woman, and a nurse like Florence Nightingale, who was not afraid to see the soldiers' legs and arms cut off; if she wanted to be brave also, she must not be afraid of anything either.

An idea crept into her mind. *She* would nurse Geraldine. They would not let her go to her: she felt sure of that; but one night, when they were all asleep, Lillian made up her mind to go quietly to her sister's room.

That night Lillian lay trembling with nervous excitement in her bed. The thought of the long lonely passages was terrifying to her, and she asked herself if she possibly could do it; she almost decided to give up her intention altogether; and yet she wanted to be a great and brave woman, like her favourite heroine.

With beating heart she put on her little dressing-gown and slippers, and went quietly from the room. All was hushed and still; the moon shone in through the passage windows with a weird effect that made poor Lillian's heart beat; but on she went, until at last she reached the door of the green room, where she knew Geraldine was lying. She listened breathlessly at the door. No screams of agony, as she expected, rent the air; all was quiet as the grave. Could Geraldine be dead? An awful fear filled her heart almost to bursting, and an almost uncontrollable impulse nearly made her run back the way she had come. But no! with resolution she pushed open the door and looked into the room. On the bed lay Geraldine fast asleep, and looking, to Lillian's inexperienced eyes, as well as ever she had been. The nurse was lying back in an arm-chair, fast asleep also, and the little would-be Florence Nightingale felt a lump rise in her throat with disappointment. She bent over her sleeping sister for a minute or two, and as she felt her hot breath she decided that Geraldine *was* very hot, but she could not be really ill with such rosy cheeks; all the sick people she had ever seen looked, oh, so pale! No, it was all no use, and she was not wanted. The woman on the chair would scold if she awoke and found her, so with reluctant feet she wended her way back through the passages, and got into her own little bed again.

It was long before she fell asleep, and when she did so, she dreamt that Geraldine, with very red cheeks, was chasing her with a broomstick.

All went on as usual for a few days. The children got more accustomed to being shut off in the left wing of the house, and played together happily as before. Lillian would turn over and over in her busy little brain why Geraldine was kept so long away, and why mother did not come and see them every day as she used to do. The child was feeling languid and unwell, but, with her usual reserve, said nothing. There was no loving mother to notice the child's weary, drooping eyes, and the servants were never disposed to pay much attention to "Miss Lillian," so she was turned out with the rest one hot summer day to play in the garden, though she begged to be allowed to remain in the cool nursery.

The children laughed and shouted in their play, and the aching head of Lillian throbbed painfully at the sound. She walked heavily round to her favourite wall, and clambered up with an effort to the top. She sat there some time, but the sun was very hot, and she felt sick and faint, so moved to get down again. It was a dangerous thing to do under the circumstances: her foot slipped, and, with a cry, she fell to the ground. It was not far to fall —only about six feet—and the children who saw it did not seem frightened, for they had fallen sometimes from there themselves. They came running up with the cry of, "Humpty Dumpty sat on a wall; Humpty Dumpty had a great fall;" but they hushed their voices, and stood frightened and surprised, looking down on their sister, who lay with closed eyes upon the grass.

They ran in haste to the nurses, who sat chatting on a seat some distance away; and when they came, Lillian aroused a little from her faint, and they carried her into the house, and sent for the doctor. He found only a few slight bruises on her, but, to their surprise and alarm, told them that Lillian was sickening for the fever, and that the shock of the fall was likely to aggravate the case greatly. No one could account for her having caught it, for she had not been near her sister Geraldine, so they thought; and with wonder and perplexity Lillian was carried into the left wing of the house, to be nursed back to health again by careful mother and nurse. But as one child grew better, the other grew rapidly worse; and before night anxious parents were watching round Lillian's bed, where she tossed in high delirium and fever. In this time of trouble and suspense the parents found that the misunderstood child was very dear to them, and that they could not spare her from their midst. When, in her wanderings, they heard her lamenting that no one loved her, and heard her longings to be pretty like Clara and Geraldine, they understood better the sensitive and loving nature of their child; and when, with flushed face, she would raise herself in the bed, and beg them to let her go and "nurse poor Geraldine, for she must be brave, like Florence Nightingale," they could not restrain their tears.

Once she tried to get over the side of her bed, and when held back, cried in imploring tones—

"Oh mother! let me go to Geraldine. The servants say she—— Oh, mother! poor pretty Geraldine! She will die. I *will* go—I *will* go to her!"

Then she let them place her back upon the pillows, where her little life seemed beating out in laboured breaths.

"If it were only me," she murmured, "it would not matter; but poor, pretty Geraldine!"

The mother leant in agony over the child.

"Hush, darling!" she said hoarsely; "we cannot lose you. You must get well, and we will love you. Yes, my darling, we will love you."

On the fourth day the crisis came, and Lillian awoke to perfect consciousness once more; but, alas! it was only the flicker of life that so often comes before death. The weary little eyes looked imploringly up at her mother, who was bending anxiously over her.

"I wanted to be a good girl, mamma," she whispered, speaking with difficulty from the sore little throat.

"Yes, dear, we know that; and now you must get well, and play with Geraldine. She is longing to have you."

A sweet smile shone on the face of the child, and she shook her head.

"Tell the children I am sorry that I got angry when they called me 'Humpty Dumpty.'"

Her voice grew fainter. She lay back wearily on her pillow; and with one sigh little Lillian had passed away to the land where she would be a greater than Florence Nightingale.

And when, ever after, the children came across the old nursery rhyme of "Humpty Dumpty," tears would come into their eyes, and they thought with remorse of the little girl whom

"*All the king's horses and all the king's men*
Couldn't put together again."

THY CLOKE ALSO

by

ALBERT E. HOOPER

"Christes love, and His apostles twelve,
He taught but first He folwed it him selve."—CHAUCER.

CHAPTER I

THE CURATE MAKES A DISCOVERY

THE Rev. Sydney Clare laid down his pen and leant back in his chair, waiting for his visitor to speak.

He was not kept waiting long.

"Is it permitted that the sheep speak their mind to the shepherd?"

Young Godfrey spoke in a loud, clear voice, and his eyes twinkled as he flicked with his riding-whip the booted leg which he had carelessly flung across its fellow.

The curate nodded, and smiled.

"Fire away, Austen," he said. "You will listen to me to-morrow, so you had better take your turn to-day."

The week-day preacher planted himself upon the hearthrug. Fair and blue-eyed, with his handsome head flung back, and his figure drawn to its full height, Austen Godfrey was a specimen of young English manhood well worth looking at; and in his scarlet racing jacket he was seen at his best. It would have been hard to find a greater contrast than existed between him and his friend the curate. Clare was pale and narrow of chest, and there was

85

already a stoop in his shoulders; indeed, he would have looked altogether commonplace but for his eyes. They were small, and dark, and deepset, and, though they possessed none of Austen's frank open brightness, they burned with a strange inward fire which marked him out as an enthusiast.

The preacher from the hearthrug flourished his whip and began—

"For the maintenance of a sound mind, a man requires a sound body. The remark is not original, but I believe it is beyond dispute. My dear Sydney, why were you not on the course this morning?"

"Too busy."

"Nobody ought to be too busy to give his brain an airing; and a parson has less excuse than anybody else."

"Well, you see, I get my exercise in another way—the parish is wide. Besides, you know, I have views about horse-racing which we won't enter upon. They are as contemptible to you as—as—well, to be frank, Austen, as contemptible as yours are to me. It's a question of mind and morals. You think the one weak in me, I think the other weak in you, and we are not likely to agree."

"The vicar was there," Godfrey said, "and so was Miss Nelly. What an uncomfortable thing a man's religion must be when it brings him to loggerheads with his own vicar and with his wife-who-is-to-be."

A look of pain passed across Clare's pale face.

"Nelly is very young," he said, "and I don't quarrel either with you or the vicar for not agreeing with me. If I did, I should have to quarrel with my two best friends."

"You're a good fellow, Clare!" cried Austen. "I only wish you could be a little more practical."

"Explain yourself," said the curate. "Tell me why you think me unpractical."

"If I wanted an illustration, I don't expect I should have to look far." said Godfrey. "I expect that sermon of yours would furnish an example. What is it all about?"

He turned over the pages of his manuscript, and Godfrey, looking over his shoulders, read the words written at the top of the first sheet:—

"Whosoever smiteth thee on thy right cheek, turn to him the other also. And if any man would go to law with thee, and take away thy coat, let him have thy cloke also. And whosoever shall compel thee to go one mile, go with him twain. Give to him that asketh thee, and from him that would borrow of thee turn not thou away."

"Do you mean to say that you are actually going to preach from that text?" he asked.

"Yes. Why not?"

"Well, I grant that the proceeding is practical enough in one sense. If you believe it, you must preach it; but how can you believe it? The saying itself is about the most unpractical that was ever uttered."

"I am going to preach about it because I hope to prove the contrary," said Clare.

"Oh, yes—preaching and proving!" cried Godfrey, with a slight accent of scorn in his tones. "Anybody can preach and prove anything. The question is—Can it be *done*?"

"*He* did it."

"Who? Oh!—well, yes, I suppose He did; and we all know what came of it. Much the same thing would happen to anybody who followed His advice to-day."

"Well?" said Clare.

"Well?" repeated Godfrey, half-angrily. "The world can't afford to lose its heroes."

"I quite agree with you," answered the curate; "but the world never really has its heroes until it has crucified them."

Austen Godfrey did not answer, but strolled to the window, and looked down into the vicarage garden.

"See here, Clare!" he cried. "While we are talking, the vicar is still airing his brain. And there is Miss Nelly among her flowers.

The curate rose and approached the window. Over Godfrey's shoulder he caught sight of Nelly Chester's smiling face. She was still dressed in her riding habit, and, looking up from her flowers, she gaily waved her little gauntleted hand to the man in the racing jacket.

Godfrey made way for Clare, and the curate's black coat became visible at the window, side by side with the scarlet. Then Clare felt a great pain at his heart, as if it had been seized and suddenly compressed in a hand of iron; for, looking out of the window, he saw the light of gladness ebb from Nelly's face.

The two men turned and looked at each other, and each was troubled by what he saw. The curate saw an expression in Godfrey's eyes which he could not mistake, and Godfrey saw that his friend was pale with pain.

Godfrey's cheeks flamed scarlet as he met Clare's earnest gaze.

"I must be going, Sydney," he said, holding out his hand.

The curate took it in silence, and in silence he followed his friend down the stairs. Then, when his friend had ridden off, with the same dull pain at his heart, he made his way to the garden at the back of the vicarage.

CHAPTER II

IN THE SUMMER HOUSE

THE Rev. Adolphus Chester was walking up and down his trimly kep garden-path with his hands clasped behind his back. His figure was portly and his step firm; and, as he greeted his pale, narrow-chested curate, he looked the picture of good health and good humour.

"Ah, Clare, my boy!" he cried heartily. "So your conscience wouldn't let you come on the course this morning? If you'll take my word for it, that conscience of yours has been quarrelling with your liver, and it's out of temper. Why, bless my soul, boy! I made a better sermon in the saddle this morning than I ever made at my desk. And now go and make your peace with the little girl," he added. "She's mightily offended because you were not out to see her ride to-day. There, go away; you needn't mind me—I'm going in to jot down the heads of my sermon before I forget them."

Mr. Chester turned away, and when he had gone into the house Clare walked on down the path towards Nelly.

She came to meet him, and she held out to him a single rose. Clare snatched at it and caught it before it reached the ground; but he was too hasty, and he only grasped the stalk—the delicate petals fell in a fragrant shower upon the path at his feet.

"I'm so sorry!" he blurted out in his distress.

"How could you be so clumsy?" she cried petulantly.

"I don't know," he answered rather absently, and, looking into her face, which Austen had called "the sunniest and brightest" flower, he added, as if talking to himself, "It seems a pity to destroy anything so lovely."

"Of course, it does," answered Nelly. "What are you talking about, Sydney? Why do you look at me so strangely?"

"I want to talk to you, Nelly," he said. "Can you spare me a few minutes now?"

"I suppose so: but I hope you're not going to be dreadfully serious. It's not about the race, is it? I've had such a beautiful morning, and it will be very unkind of you if you spoil it all by telling me dreadful tales about gambling."

Nelly's face was flushed, and she spoke quickly.

"It isn't about the race," said Clare. "Let us go into the summer-house; it is rather hot out here."

Now for the first time Nelly looked up into his pale face, and what she saw there made her open her eyes wider and feel a little frightened.

"You are not ill, are you, Sydney?" she asked anxiously, laying her hand on his arm.

"Oh no, not at all; only a little troubled, Nelly. Will you come with me?"

Sydney Clare folded his arms tightly across his breast, trying to deaden the bitter pain at his heart. Twice he cleared his throat to speak, and twice his dry tongue refused to obey his will. At the third trial the words came; but it seemed to him that his own voice sounded far away, hard and mechanical, as if it belonged to somebody else in whom he was not in the least interested.

"I want to tell you about a discovery I have made, Nelly," he said. "It is something you may not know yet. If it has ever crossed your mind, you have put it away at once, because you have meant to be quite true and faithful to me. But it will not do, Nelly dear, to stifle the inner voices which try to tell what is going on within us. They can never be silenced for long, and if they speak too late their voices are very loud and full of terror."

"Sydney, tell me what you mean?" whispered Nelly, clasping her hands tightly and beginning to tremble.

"Nelly, we have both made a great, a terrible, mistake," said Clare; "we ought never to have promised to marry each other."

"Do you mean that you don't love me any longer?" she asked.

"No; I don't mean that. Think, Nelly, and you will know what I mean."

"You mean? Oh, Sydney! how can you think I don't love you? You are so good—so noble—so wise!"

"God forgive me, Nelly, for liking to know you believe what isn't true. I am neither good, nor noble, nor wise. Such things may well belong to a curate—or a brother, Nelly; but I am talking about a husband."

"Are you angry with me? Have I done anything to vex you?" she asked.

"No, dear; there is no room for anger. Don't you see it is all a miserable mistake? It is just like that beautiful rose. I did not mean to crush it, but I took hold of it wrongly and it was spoilt: and in the same way your fair, beautiful young life would be spoilt if I had it in my keeping—I see it all now. Try not to feel too sad about it. Let us resolve to put our mistake right before it is too late."

Nelly was weeping quietly to herself. Every word the curate spoke roused in her heart an echo of its truth. A sudden revelation broke upon her, and in its light she saw the meaning of the strange discontent which had lately oppressed her. In the midst of her grief a great load seemed to be lifted from her heart, and she began to feel for Sydney Clare a love deeper and different from anything she had felt for him before. Good, wise, noble! —yes, he was all that; but how glad she was that he would never be her husband; and yet how cruel and heartless it was to be glad when she was causing his true heart such pain. Something told Nelly that the mistake had been all on her side, and none of it on his. She knew that he would never cease to love her. She thought of the dull and lonely life he would live without her, and she was almost impelled to say the words which would bind her to him for ever.

But, before she could speak, Clare's voice broke the silence.

"Don't think me unkind, Nelly, if I say one thing more. It is on my heart, and I must say it."

He paused a moment, and then continued:

"Some day the right man will come to you——"

"Oh, Sydney! don't—please don't speak of such a thing!" cried Nelly, raising her head and looking at him with tearful eyes.

"I must say it—the right man will surely come—I don't think it will be very long."

The hot blood burned in Nelly's cheeks; she knew what he meant, and a second revelation flashed upon her, dazzling her with its brightness. The pressure at Clare's heart grew tighter; but he went on quite calmly—

"Don't let the remembrance of our mistake close your heart against the right man when he comes. He will be a good man. Nelly; listen to me, and remember my words as if they were the words of a brother who loves you. He will be a better son to your father than ever I could have been."

Nelly's burning face was buried in her hands, but she heard every word Clare said. When she looked up once more he was gone. She listened until she could hear the sound of his retreating footsteps no more, and then she began to cry again—not bitter, passionate, or painful tears, but tears which flowed gently and comforted her heart, as warm summer showers refresh the thirsty earth.

CHAPTER III

"THY CLOKE ALSO"

WHILE the vicar was reading his paper and eating his lunch, his curate was walking swiftly away over the common. The day was hot, but the curate shivered; it seemed that he had stripped from his soul its warmest garment, and, as yet, he had not grown accustomed to the feeling of nakedness. Nay, just now, it seemed more than the chill of nakedness; the "lordly pleasure-house" which he had built for his soul's delight was in ruins, and, though his own hands had wrought the destruction, the sense of homelessness almost terrified him. Doubtless the Ark still sailed in safety somewhere upon the Flood; but there was a mist over the face of the waters, and he could not see it.

Sydney Clare walked on across the common, oblivious of the blinding glare of the sun, heedless of everything in his desire to get away. Leaving the common at length, the curate wandered along the bank of the stream which flowed through Squire Godfrey's meadows; and presently he entered the little belt of wood which divided the meadow-land from the park. It was when he reached the edge of this wood, and, looking across the stretch of velvety turf, caught the glimmer of the White House in the distance, that Clare at last paused. He leaned upon the park railings, and allowed his eyes to wander lingeringly over the green expanse, the swelling outline of foliage which marked the avenue, and upon the shining windows of the White House itself. It looked a lovely picture as it lay in the warm golden sunshine; the gilded vanes on the outbuildings twinkled brightly, the pigeons flew round in shining circles, and there was a cheery note in the stable clock as it chimed the hour. Then he took one step backward into the wood, and, allowing the foliage to close like a screen around him, fell upon his knees.

Not only for one brief moment did he kneel in the shadow; not only to utter a word or two of passionate ejaculation did his lips move in prayer. The voice of Science, preaching its sermon of inviolable law, was well known to him, and his mind appreciated its message; but there was something within him which still sent out a cry into the vast Unseen; and from the vast Unseen "a sound of gentle stillness" seemed to fall upon his spirit like the morning dew. In time, around the craters of extinct volcanoes the flowers bloom again; and slowly the fire died down in the curate's heart, and gave place to a holy calm, out of which new thoughts arose—the blossoming of heart's ease. The stable clock chimed four quarters, and Sydney Clare still knelt and prayed.

When at last he was aroused, it was by the sound of a voice speaking close beside him.

"Business is business, Mr. Austen Godfrey," said the voice; "and I don't mean to wait for my money much longer."

It was a hard and bitter voice, but the curate recognised it at once, although he had not heard it since his college days. Many a time had he pleaded against its hardness and bitterness for mercy to his friends; and he had always pleaded in vain. It was the voice of Mr. Isaacson, a rich Jew, who did much business at the universities. An hour ago the knowledge that Austen Godfrey was in Isaacson's clutches might have roused a demon in the heart of the curate; but now, the strength of old friendship had asserted itself, and the discovery came upon him with a shock of distress. Then came the thought, What should he do? The slightest movement would betray his presence to the speakers; he could not force his way through the thick undergrowth, and escape unseen into the wood; and if he stepped out into the pathway Austen must know that his secret had been overheard. While he was debating with himself what to do, young Godfrey spoke; and the curate remained in his concealment, with tingling cheeks, a shamefaced listener to the conversation.

"Why can't you wait till I come of age?" said Austen. "My uncle will increase my allowance, and I shall be able to settle up."

"It's rather too risky," returned Isaacson. "If there is any truth in reports, the old gentleman is thinking better of it, and means to bring a young wife to the White House."

"Nonsense!" cried Austen sharply. "My uncle hasn't the least thought of being married."

"Maybe no, maybe yes. Stranger things have happened, young sir; I can't risk my money on the chances of Mr. Godfrey keeping single. If I go to him now, and tell him the whole story, he'll be feeling a bit soft about the disappointment he has in store for you. If I go later, when the deed's done, he'll be harder, and I may whistle for my money. It's my business to study character, and I don't want anybody to tell me when the iron's hot, or how soon it'll get cold. Of course, if you like to manage the business yourself, I'm willing to settle things comfortably. Bring me the thousand pounds in a month's time, or——"

"I tell you, I can't ask my uncle for fifty pounds, let alone a thousand," said Austen. "He made me a liberal allowance when I was at college, and if he finds I exceeded it, I may as well say good-bye to the White House. He has always vowed that he will never leave the place to a spendthrift; and I could never persuade him that I did not spend the money on my own pleasure."

"No, I dessay not," returned Isaacson, with a sneer. "Men of the world find it hard to believe that youngsters help their unlucky friends to the tune of a thousand pounds, and go in debt for it, into the bargain. The yarn's too tall for a man of business, my boy."

"Keep a civil tongue unless you wish me to knock you down," said Austen quietly; and Clare could hear that his voice was shaking with passion. Then he added: "Get out of my sight before I am tempted to kick you. You shall have the money within a month."

"I thought I should teach you business, Mr. Austen. Be punctual, of——"

The hard, bitter voice of the money-lender ceased, and the sound of hasty footsteps fell upon Clare's ears. The curate peered cautiously over the bushes, just in time to see the fat figure of Mr. Isaacson in full flight down the pathway, and Austen Godfrey, shaking with laughter, following leisurely behind.

When they had both disappeared, Sydney Clare rose from his knees and returned to his old place at the park palings. Suddenly he thought of a clause of the text of tomorrow's sermon—"*Give him thy cloke also!*"

Sydney Clare believed that a means of communication had been opened between him and the Unseen. Not only were the words of the text explicit, but their meaning—which might have been obscure to some men—was to him quite plain and unmistakable.

Instantly the whole man became transfigured. His face flushed, and his eyes brightened; his stooping shoulders grew straight; and, turning on his heel, the curate walked with a firm tread and a swinging pace through the wood and out into the high-road.

Soon Clare found himself in the little market-town of Newborough, facing a little green door ornamented by a shining plate of brass, bearing the name of "*Jasper Greed, Solicitor*."

In answer to Clare's ring, the door was opened by an old gentleman with a pair of kindly blue eyes.

"Ha, Sydney, my boy, I'm glad to see you! Another minute, and I should have been gone. Come in, come in!"

The old man drew him into a dusty little office, and pushed him into a seat. He then sat down in his own chair, and prepared himself to listen.

"You won't like what I am going to say," continued Clare; "so it will save time to tell you that I have quite made up my mind. The fact is, I want to lend some money."

"May I ask if the securities are good—as a matter of curiosity, I mean?"

"Well, yes, they are good enough for me. They are moral securities."

The old lawyer sniffed.

"And the amount?" he asked.

"A thousand pounds."

"Just about the amount your shares will sell out at. You mean to depend entirely upon your curacy in future."

" Yes."

"And you are going to be married, I believe?"

"No, I am not," answered Clare quickly. "I want this money paid over to a Mr. Isaacson in the name of Mr. Austen Godfrey. Tell me, Mr. Greed, is it possible for you to arrange matters so that Austen does not know who has paid the money?"

The lawyer leant back in his chair, speechless. Seeing that some explanation was necessary before the legal mind would get into working order again, Clare gave the old man a brief account of the discovery he had made in the wood. While he listened, the lawyer's face became the scene of a curious battle. The firmness of his mouth fought desperately to overcome the kindly expression of his eyes; but by the time Clare had finished, the tight lips had relaxed, and the blue eyes were beaming mild victory.

"You have quite made up your mind, my boy?"

"Quite."

"Then I will settle the matter for you."

The old man's eyes glistened; but to cover their weakness, his mouth suddenly snapped like a steel-trap.

"When you want to join the Mormons, or indulge in any other little freak of enthusiasm, I hope you will come to me," he said. "I assure you it's quite impossible for you to surprise me."

Clare rose laughing, and grasped the lawyer's hand.

The sun had sunk by the time the curate reached the vicarage; and, finding his way unnoticed up to his study, he sat late into the night writing his sermon.

CHAPTER IV

THE SERMON—AND AFTER

I T was Sunday evening; the last notes of the hymn still echoed in the roof of the church, and the Rev. Sydney Clare stood in the pulpit facing his congregation. He read his text, and stretched out his hand towards the sermon-case which lay on the desk before him. Then a sudden impulse made him push the sermon case aside unopened; and, for the first time in his life, he began to preach without his manuscript.

" '*Whosoever smiteth thee on thy right cheek, turn to him the other also.*' Practical maxims fly farthest when they are winged with hyperbole." Clare began by showing that the essence of his text was a doctrine so well known and generally approved that it has become a neglected truism. Never retaliate; be generous, having a disposition to exceed the most exacting demands; kill evil with goodness; drive away darkness with light. To-day, whether consciously or not, the Sermon on the Mount is being ratified by the signature of Science. Clare here gave a graphic description of the working of the Elmira Reformatory of New York. Here criminals, who have for years been borrowing from society, robbing society, and smiting the cheek of society, are receiving larger loans and the "*cloke also*" at the hands of society: society is turning the other cheek to the smiter; and the criminals, treated carefully as moral invalids, are becoming honest men. Then, having painted his picture upon the imaginations of his hearers, Clare left the object-lesson, and began to call the long muster-roll of the world's heroes, bidding them one by one stand forth and attest the truth of his text. "The true kings of the world march through all history in royal progress—a procession of heavy-laden men bearing their own crosses; and the Lord Christ walks at their head. The throne of humanity is set for evermore in the Place of the Skull." With a few earnest words of personal application, hinting at the Gethsemane and the Calvary which await every true soul, and calling his hearers to accept at once the law of sacrifice under which, be it soon or late, all the children of men must bow, Sydney Clare ceased; and he knew that he had preached his last sermon in Mr. Chester's church.

As the vicar sat in his cosy study, smoking his after-supper cigar that night, there came a knock at his door.

"Come in," said Mr. Chester, rousing himself from his contemplation of the smoke spirals which floated above his head.

"Sit down, Sydney, sit down!" cried the vicar heartily. "Why didn't you come in to supper? A bit knocked up after preaching, eh? That was a remarkable sermon of yours, my boy—perhaps a trifle too exalted, if I may say so—most of us are commonplace people, and we can't bear too much mountain-air, you know; but you can preach, Sydney, you can preach. I can tell you, I felt proud of you to-night, my boy; and Nelly was proud of you too—the excitement has quite upset her, poor child!"

Clare knew from experience that it was useless to interrupt the vicar, so he stood leaning against the chimney-piece, while the old man rambled on. At the first pause he said:—

"It was about Nelly I came to speak to you."

"You have been having a difference of opinion, I suppose?" broke in the vicar. "What of that?"

"This cannot be easily settled," said Clare gravely; and Nelly and I have decided that our engagement had better come to an end."

"Nonsense!" cried Mr. Chester, his rosy cheeks suddenly deepening into purple. "You will settle matters comfortably in a few days. I'm ashamed of you, Sydney—a clergyman, fresh from preaching a sermon like that, how can you dare to indulge in such an unforgiving spirit? She'll be sorry enough directly; and, if you're the man I take you for, you won't be hard on her."

"Hard on Nelly!" said Clare, with a sad smile. "Who could be hard on Nelly? I allowed Nelly to engage herself to me before she properly knew her own mind. She knows it now, and she must be free to love where she can.

The curate bent down, and added something in a low voice.

The vicar started.

"Austen!" he exclaimed. "Are you sure of what you say, Sydney?"

"Quite; I could not be mistaken. No man could make Nelly a better husband; she will be very happy."

"And you, Sydney?"

"I have thought about the matter carefully; and I must go away. It will be better for us all. I have decided to go to Africa."

"As a missionary !"

"Yes," said Clare; "and I want your influence in the right quarter, so that I can go soon."

For once the vicar was at a loss for words. It cannot be said that the prospect of Austen Godfrey for a son-in-law was unpleasant; and the thought of Nelly as the future mistress of the White House was, on the whole, most satisfactory; but Mr. Chester felt uncomfortable. The presence of this grave young curate, with the pale face and deep, bright eyes, was a rebuke to all his thoughts of worldly advantage. This man was not only giving up his wife, but the snug living as well; for the living was in Mr. Chester's gift; and only a week ago he had told his curate to prepare for its acceptance on his wedding-day.

"Nothing that I can say will alter your resolve?" said Mr. Chester.

"No, I think not. That you will add to your past kindness by helping me to get away soon is all I ask."

"That's easily managed," returned the vicar gloomily. "They always want money as well as men; and, as I suppose you mean to embark your money in the scheme, they will naturally give you advantages."

"I think we must leave the money out of the question," said Clare.

The vicar glanced at him sharply, but did not question him.

After this the two men began to talk over the details of the arrangement; and an hour slipped away before Clare rose to go.

Mr. Chester followed him to the door, and grasped him warmly by the hand.

"My boy," he said, "you should have stayed with us longer. We shall not know what we have lost until you are gone."

To Clare the words were more than mere words of kindness; and he passed out with the warm glow of friendship in his heart.

And the vicar returned to his seat and sat on in deep thought.

And as he thought his eyes rested upon the picture of the thorn-crowned Man of Sorrows which hung on the opposite wall—

"Ecce Homo."

CHAPTER V

"SUNSET AND EVENING STAR"

TEN years later.

It was evening in Africa—one of those bright and glorious evenings so common in the tropics, when it seems as if the great sun itself must have burst in the western sky, spilling its golden splendour all over the world. The river lay like a plate of pure gold, burnished to a dazzling brilliancy.

In the creek of the river a little steamer was moored, and on the shore, clustering down to the water's edge, were hundreds of native huts which looked like monster bee-hives of bright gold.

In the midst of the huts there stood a large, barn-like building, with a sloping roof, surmounted by a tiny bell-tower.

There was little movement to be seen in the village and but for the flitting to and fro of a few dark-skinned figures on the river's bank, and the slow-pacing form of a man dressed in white on the steamer, it might have been a village of the dead.

But, stay! from out of the grove of palm-trees another figure stepped—

the figure of a man hastening down the slope towards the creek—a magnificent-looking man, sunburnt and brown-bearded.

As he neared the river, the man on the steamer saw him, and, springing ashore, went to meet him.

A look of disappointment sprang into the traveller's blue eyes as he took the hand which was outstretched towards him.

The man in the white linen suit was young, and he scanned the stranger's face eagerly.

"Welcome, whoever you are!" he cried, and then added, with a sigh hastily checked, "It is good to see a white face."

"Yes."

"Can you tell me if Sydney Clare is here? I was directed to this station."

A shadow fell upon the missionary's face.

"Are you a friend of Clare's?" he asked.

"Yes—is he here? Tell me—is anything wrong? You don't mean——"

"No, he is with us at present; but——"

"You mean, that he is ill—dying?"

The missionary laid his hand on the stranger's arm.

"I will take you to him," he said; and then, as he led the way among the native huts, he continued: 'Sir, your friend is a noble man. You will be proud of him when you know his story."

"I know—I know," answered the other. "Is it fever?"

"No," said the missionary—"it is murder! But here is the place—you would like to see him at once?"

As he spoke he lifted the mat which hung before the entrance of a large hut, and signed to his companion to enter.

The stranger obeyed, and by the light which poured in a golden stream through an opening in the roof, he saw another figure in white kneeling beside a mat couch, supporting on his arm the head of a dying man; and at a distance an old native woman sat upon the floor rocking herself backwards and forwards, moaning piteously.

At the sound of footsteps the dying man opened his eyes. He gave no start of surprise, but his bright eyes grew brighter still, and he cried—

"Austen!"

"Sydney!" exclaimed the stranger, and, pushing his rifle into his companion's hand, he swiftly crossed the floor of the hut, and fell upon his knees beside the couch.

"You will give him up to me, won't you?" he said to the kneeling missionary; and in another instant Clare's head was resting upon his shoulder.

"It was good of you to come, Austen."

"How could I stay away, Sydney? I started to come to you directly I knew the truth. Mr. Greed is dead, and before he died he sent for me and told me that it was you who helped me in my greatest need."

"It was nothing: I was only obeying orders: and you had brought your-

D

self into the need by doing the same thing," said Sydney. "But don't let us talk about it now; there is no time, and I want to know about Nelly."

"She is well," said Godfrey; "and she sent her dear love to you. She would have come herself if it had not been——"

"Yes, yes," cried Clare eagerly; "you have children. Tell me about them, Austen."

"A son and a daughter," said Godfrey, with a touch of pride in his tones. "We have called our boy Sydney, and our girl is named Clare."

A deep flush of pleasure came into Clare's pale cheeks. He closed his eyes, and his lips moved; and Godfrey knew that he was praying for the children.

Presently Godfrey said, "The children hear a great deal about you, Sydney; and I came hoping that I might persuade you to come back with me. Oh, Sydney!" he cried passionately, "why have you sacrificed your life among these savages?"

"God grant that I have opened eyes which were too blind," said Clare faintly, in reply.

After this he did not speak much more. He sent his love to his friends in England, and then he lay still in Austen's arms; and, while the square of gold in the roof gradually paled, his life slowly ebbed away. When the sun sank he died.

"Hark!" said the elder of the missionaries. "It is well said 'The blood of the martyrs is the seed of the Church.' For nearly ten years Clare has been labouring to break the power of idolatry in this place, and by his life he only succeeded in making the people angry enough to kill him. Now he is dead they begin to know him."

Then Godfrey remembered some words of Sydney Clare's spoken to him long ago—"*The world never really has its heroes until it has crucified them.*" And the sudden twilight of the tropics fell upon them like the downrush of a purple curtain veiling the golden afterglow of the sunset; flashing hosts of worlds became visible in the deep spaces of the night, and the death of the day was forgotten in the glory which followed it.

THE PRODIGAL'S RETURN

by

HENRY SETON MERRIMAN

"YES, mother, he will come. Of course he will come!" And the girl turned her drawn and anxious young face towards the cottage door, just as if her blind mother could see the action.

It is probable that the old woman divined the longing glance from the change in the girl's tone, for she, too, half turned towards the door. It was a habit these two women had acquired. They constantly looked towards the door for the arrival of one who never came, through the long summer days, through the quiet winter evenings; moreover, they rarely spoke of other things, this arrival was the topic of their lives. And now the old woman's life was drawing to a close, as some lives do, without its object. She herself felt it, and her daughter knew it.

There was in both of them a subtle sense of clinging. It was hard to die without touching the reward of a wondrous patience. It was cruel to deprive the girl of this burden, for in most burdens there is a safeguard, in all a duty, and in some the greatest happiness allotted to human existence.

It was no new thing, this waiting for the scapegrace son; the girl had grown up to it, for she would not know her brother should she meet him in the street. Since sight had left the old mother's eyes, she had fed her heart upon this hope.

He had left them eighteen years before in a fit of passionate resentment against his father, whose only fault had been too great an indulgence for the son of his old age. Nothing had been too good for dear Stephen—hardly anything had been good enough. Educated at a charity school himself, the simple old clergyman held the mistaken view that no man can be educated above his station.

There are some people who hold this view still, but they cannot do so much longer. Strikes, labour troubles, and the difficulties of domestic service, so-called gentleman farmers, gentleman shopkeepers and lady milliners—above all, a few colonies peopled by University failures, will teach us in time that to educate our sons above their station is to handicap them cruelly in the race of life.

Stephen Leach was one of the early victims to this craze. His father, having risen by the force of his own will and the capabilities of his own mind from the People to the Church, held, as such men do, that he had only to give his son a good education to ensure his career in life. So everything—even to the old parson's sense of right and wrong—was sacrificed to the education of Stephen Leach at public school and University. Here he met and selected for his friends youths whose futures were ensured, and who were only passing through the formula of an education so that no one could say they were unfit for the snug Government appointment, living, or inheritance of a more substantial sort, that might be waiting for them. Stephen acquired their ways of life without possessing their advantages, and the consequence was something very nearly approaching to ruin for the little country rectory. Not having been a University man himself, the rector did not know that at Oxford or Cambridge, as in the army, one may live according to one's taste. Stephen Leach had expensive tastes, and he unscrupulously traded on his father's ignorance. He was good-looking, and had a certain brilliance of manner which "goes down" well at the 'Varsity. Everything was against him, and at last the end came. At last the rector's eyes were opened, and when a narrow-minded man's eyes are once opened he usually becomes stony at heart.

Stephen Leach left England, and before he landed in America his father had departed on a longer journey. The ne'er-do-well had the good grace to send back the little sums of money saved by his mother in her widowhood, and gradually his letters ceased. It was known that he was in Chili, and there was war going on there, and yet the good old lady's faith never wavered.

"He will come, Joyce," she would say; "he will surely come."

And somehow it came to be an understood thing that he was to come in the afternoon when they were all ready for him—when Joyce had clad her pretty young form in a dark dress, and when the old lady was up and seated in her chair by the fire in winter, by the door in summer. They had never imagined his arrival at another time. It would not be quite the same should he make a mistake and come in the morning, before Joyce had got the house put right.

Yet, he never came. A greater infirmity came instead, and at last Joyce suggested that her mother should not get up in bad weather. They both knew what this meant, but the episode passed as others do, and Mrs. Leach was bedridden. Still she said—

"He will come, Joyce! He will surely come."

And the girl would go to the window and draw aside the curtain, looking down the quiet country road towards the village.

"Yes, mother, he will come!" was her usual answer; and one day she gave a little exclamation of surprise and almost of fear.

"Mother," she exclaimed, "there is some one coming along the road."

The old lady was already sitting up in bed, staring with her sightless orbs towards the window.

Thus they waited. The man stopped opposite the cottage, and the two women heard the latch of the gate. Then Joyce, turning, saw that her mother fainted. But it was only momentary. By the time she reached the bed her mother had recovered consciousness.

"Go," said the old lady, breathlessly; "go and let him in yourself."

Downstairs, on the doorstep, the girl found a tall man of thirty or thereabouts with a browner face than English suns could account for. He looked down into her eager eyes with a strange questioning wonder.

"Am I too late?" he asked in a voice which almost seemed to indicate a hope that it might be so.

"No, Stephen," she answered. "But mother cannot live much longer. You are just in time."

The young man made a hesitating little movement with his right hand and shuffled uneasily on the clean stone step. He was like an actor called suddenly upon the stage having no knowledge of his part. The return of this prodigal was not a dramatic success. No one seemed desirous of learning whether he had lived upon husks or otherwise and with whom he had eaten. The quiet dignity of the girl, who had remained behind to do all the work and bear all the burden, seemed in some subtle manner to deprive him of any romance that might have attached itself to him. She ignored his half-proffered hand, and turning into the little passage, led the way upstairs.

Stephen Leach followed silently. He was rather large for the house, and especially for the stairs; moreover, he had a certain burliness of walk, such as is acquired by men living constantly in the open. There was a vaguely pained look in his blue eyes, as if they had suddenly been opened to his own shortcomings. His attitude towards Joyce was distinctly apologetic.

When he followed the girl across the threshold of their mother's bedroom the old lady was sitting up in bed, holding out trembling arms towards the door.

Here Stephen Leach seemed to know better what to do. He held his mother in his arms while she sobbed and murmured out her joy. He had no words, but his arms meant more than his lips could ever have told.

It would seem that the best part of happiness is the sharing of it with some one else.

"Joyce," was the first distinct word the old lady spoke, "Joyce, he has come at last. He has come! Come here, dear. Kiss your brother. This is my firstborn—my little Steve."

The young man had sunk upon his knees at the bedside, probably because it was the most convenient position. He did not second his mother's proposal with much enthusiasm. Altogether he did not seem to have discovered much sympathy with the sister whom he had left in her cradle.

Joyce came forward and leaned over the bed to kiss her brother while the old lady's hands joined theirs. Just as her fresh young lips came within reach he turned his face aside, so that the kiss fell on barren ground on his tanned cheek.

"Joyce," continued the old lady, feverishly, "I am not afraid to die now, for Stephen is here. Your brother will take care of you, dear, when I am gone."

It was strange that Stephen had not spoken yet; and it was perhaps just as well, because there are occasions in life when men do wisely to keep silent.

"He is strong," the proud mother went on. "I can feel it. His hands are large and steady and quiet, and his arms are big and very hard."

The young man knelt upright and submitted gravely to this maternal inventory.

"Yes," she said, "I knew he would grow to be a big man. His little fingers were so strong—he hurt me sometimes. What a great moustache! I knew you had been a soldier. And the skin of your face is brown and a little rough. What is this? what is this, Stephen dear? Is this a wound?"

"Yes," answered the Prodigal, speaking for the first time. "That is a sword cut. I got that in the last war. I am a colonel in the Chilian army, or was, before I resigned."

The old lady's sightless eyes were fixed on his face, as if listening for the echo of another voice in his deep quiet tones.

"Your voice is deeper than your father's ever was," she said; and all the while her trembling fingers moved lovingly over his face, touching the deep cut from cheek-bone to jaw with soft inquiry. "This must have been very near your eye, Stephen. Promise me, dear, no more soldiering."

"I promise that," he replied, without raising his eyes.

Such was the home-coming of the Prodigal. After all, he arrived at the right moment in the afternoon, when the house was ready. It sometimes does happen so in real life, and not only in books. There is a great deal that might be altered in this world, but sometimes, by a mere chance, things come about rightly. And yet there was something wrong, something subtle, which the dying woman's duller senses failed to detect. Her son, her Stephen, was quiet, and had not much to say for himself. He apparently had the habit of taking things as they came. There was no enthusiasm, but rather a restraint in his manner, more especially towards Joyce.

The girl noticed it, but even her small experience of human kind had taught her that large, fair-skinned men are often thus. They are not "de ceux qui s'expliquent," but go through life placidly, leaving unsaid and undone many things which some think they ought to say and do.

After the first excitement of the return was over it became glaringly apparent that Stephen had arrived just in time. His mother fell into a happy sleep before sunset; and when the active young doctor came a little later in the evening he shook his head.

"Yes," he said, "I see that she is asleep and quiet—too quiet. It is a foretaste of a longer sleep; some old people have it."

For the first time Joyce's courage seemed to give way. When she had been alone she was brave enough, but now that her brother was there, woman-like, she seemed to turn to him with a sudden fear. They stood side by side near the bed, and the young doctor involuntarily watched them. Stephen had taken her hand in his with that silent sympathy which was so natural and so eloquent. He said nothing, this big, sun-tanned youth; he did not even glance down at his sister, who stood small, soft-eyed, and gentle at his side.

The doctor knew something of the history of the small family thus momentarily united, and he had always feared that if Stephen Leach did return it would only kill his mother. This, indeed, seemed to be the result about to follow.

Presently the doctor took his leave. He was a young man engaged in getting together a good practice, and in his own interest he had been forced to give up waiting for his patients to finish dying.

"I am glad you are here," he said to Stephen, who accompanied him to the door. "It would not do for your sister to be alone; this may go on for a couple of days."

It did not go on for a couple of days, but Mrs. Leach lived through that night in the same semi-comatose state. The two watchers sat in her room until supper-time, when they left their mother in charge of a hired nurse, whose services Joyce had been forced to seek.

After supper Stephen Leach seemed at last to find his tongue, and he talked in his quiet, almost gentle voice, such as some big men possess, not about himself or the past, but about Joyce and the future. In a deliberate business-like way, he proceeded to investigate the affairs of the dying woman and the prospects of her daughter; in a word, he asserted his authority as a brother, and Joyce was relieved and happy to obey him.

It is not in times of gaiety that friendships are formed, but in sorrow or suspense. During that long evening this brother and sister suddenly became intimate, more so than months of prosperous intercourse could have made them. At ten o'clock Stephen quietly insisted that Joyce should go to bed while he lay down, all dressed, on the sofa in the dining-room.

"I shall sleep perfectly; it is not the first time I have slept in my clothes," he said simply.

They went up stairs together and told the nurse of this arrangement. Joyce remained for some moments by the bedside watching her mother's peaceful sleep, and when she turned she found that Stephen had quietly slipped away. Wondering vaguely whether he had intentionally solved her difficulty as to the fraternal good-night, she went to her own room.

The next morning Mrs. Leach was fully conscious, and appeared to be stronger; nevertheless, she knew that the end was near. She called her two children to her bedside, and, turning her blind eyes towards them, spoke in broken sentences.

"I am ready now—I am ready," she said. "Dears, I am going to your father—and . . . thank God, I can tell him that I have left you together. I always knew Stephen would come back. I found it written everywhere in the Bible. Stephen—kiss me, dear!"

The man leant over the bed and kissed her.

"Ah!" she sighed, "how I wish I could see you—just once before I die. Joyce!" she added, suddenly turning to her daughter, who stood at the other side of the bed, "tell me what he is like. But—I know . . . I *know*—I feel it. Listen! He is tall and spare, like his father. His hair is black, like—like his father's—it was black before he went away. His eyes, I know, are dark—almost black. He is pale—like a Spaniard!" . . .

Joyce, looking across the bed with slow horror dawning in her face, looked into a pair of blue eyes beneath tawny hair, cut short as a soldier's hair should be. She looked upon a man big, broad, fair—English from crown to toe—and the quiet command of his lips and eyes made her say—

"Yes, mother, yes."

For some moments there was silence. Joyce stood pale and breathless, wondering what this might mean. Then the dying woman spoke again.

"Kiss me," she said. "I . . . am going. Stephen first—my firstborn! And now, Joyce . . . and now kiss each other—across the bed! I want to hear it . . . I want . . . to tell . . . your . . . father."

With a last effort she raised her hands, seeking their heads. At first Joyce hesitated, then she leant forward, and the old woman's chilled fingers pressed their lips together. That was the end.

Half an hour afterwards Joyce and this man stood facing each other in the little dining-room. He began his explanation at once.

"Stephen," he said, "was shot—out there—as a traitor. I could not tell her that! I did not mean to do this, but what else could I do?"

He paused, moved towards the door with that same strange hesitation which she had noticed on his arrival. At the door he turned, to justify himself.

"I still think," he said gravely, "that it was the best thing to do."

Joyce made no answer. The tears stood in her eyes. There was something very pathetic in the distress of this strong man, facing, as it were, an emergency of which he felt the delicacy to be beyond his cleverness to handle.

"Last night," he went on, "I made all the necessary arrangements for your future—just as Stephen would have made them—as a brother might have done. I . . . he and I were brother officers in a very wild army. Your brother—was not a good man. None of us were." His hand was on the door. "He asked me to come and tell you," he added. "I shall go back now. . . ."

They stood thus: he watching her face with his honest soft blue eyes, she failing to meet his glance.

"May I come back again?" he asked suddenly.

She gave a little gasp, but made no answer.

"I will come back in six months," he announced quietly, and then he closed the door behind him.

D*

"*You shall tell me another time*"

CHRIS

by

MARY
BRADFORD-
WHITING

CHAPTER I

RAIN was falling: it had been falling all day, and now that darkness was drawing on, the wind had risen, and was dashing the drops against the window-panes with ceaseless fury.

It was a dreary outlook, and inside the room where Mrs. Winton and her little boy were sitting it did not seem much brighter. The fire was getting low, but it gave a feeble gleam now and then, which showed up the worn patches on the hearthrug and the bare look of the whole place. Mrs. Winton had fallen asleep in the one arm-chair the room boasted. It was not a very comfortable seat, for the springs had long ago been broken, and the cushions were old and thin, but she was tired-out with her day's work, and slept as peacefully as though it were the most luxuriously padded resting-place.

Chris was lying on the rug, gazing thoughtfully at the glowing embers, his chin propped up in his hands. He was an imaginative child, but at this moment his thoughts were practical. "It's getting very cold," he muttered to himself, "and mother was coughing before she went to sleep."

He waited for a minute and then got up cautiously. Chris stooped over the coal-scuttle to see what he could find. There were only a few pieces of coal at the bottom, and he scraped them up carefully with his hands and put them on the fire, which gave out a grateful little blaze.

A new idea darted into his mind. "I'll get the tea," he thought; "and then mother can have it as soon as she wakes up."

When tea was made he went to the door, and tried to turn the handle quietly that he might go and fetch the kettle from the kitchen, but it slipped back with a click, and Mrs. Winton opened her eyes. "Is that you, Chris?" she asked.

At the first sound of her voice Chris darted towards her, and, jumping on her knee, covered her face with kisses. "I didn't mean to wake you," he said, "but it's struck five, and I've been getting tea."

Chris' father had been dead three years, but though the little boy could not remember much about him, there was one thing that he had never forgotten. He had been brought up and put upon the bed on the day that his father died.

"Chris," he said faintly, "I am going away; but I shall see you again some day, and till then you must take care of mother for me." And Chris, though he could not understand it all, remembered one thing—that he must always take care of mother.

Mrs. Winton had had many troubles to bear since that day. Poverty and ill-health had worn her down, and she had had to leave her pleasant house for a four-roomed cottage, but through it all she had had one great consolation: and that was the love of her boy.

Chris was eight years old now, and liked to consider himself as the man of the house. He always locked up the house himself after it got dark, and strongly resented being sent to bed while his mother was still sitting up. Just as he was going up on the evening in question, however, a ring came at the bell, and he darted back to the parlour.

"There, mother!" he cried, "I'll have to wait now to answer the door," and before she could reply he had run out into the passage again.

"Who was it?" she asked, when he came back.

"I think it was Mr. Grant," said Chris; "but he gave me this letter, and went away in such a hurry I could hardly see."

Mrs. Winton sat some time with the unopened letter in her hand after the little boy had finally disappeared. She was not in much doubt as to its contents. Mr. Grant was the vicar's brother-in-law, a rich man, who owned a place called Courthope, a few miles off. He had remained a bachelor so long that people were tired of prophesying his marriage, but as soon as he saw Mrs. Winton he knew that his time was come. He was some years older than she was, but his natural buoyancy of manner made him seem almost younger, and she often wondered what it was that attracted him to her. Much as she liked him, she was not at all sure what her answer would be. She felt convinced that Chris would set himself against the marriage with all the force of his childish nature, and she did not know how to inflict such a wound upon him. Yet, after all, might it not be the best thing for him? She understood Richard Grant well enough to know that he would care for the boy as though he were his own.

She sighed as she opened the envelope at last, but the sigh was succeeded by a smile. It was not possible to read that outpouring of love without being touched by it, and as she read, her doubts and fears vanished away.

"I should have come to you," he wrote, "to have your answer from your own lips, but I am unexpectedly called away. Write to me at once to the enclosed address, and if I may come to you, I will be with you as soon as possible."

Mrs. Winton looked at the clock; it was already nearly post time. Three words would suffice, and she did not hesitate long; fetching paper and ink, she wrote her brief note, and hastened out to post it. At present she hardly realised what she had done, but when she came back, she stole up to Chris's room. He was lying quietly, his curly hair tumbled on the pillow. She knelt down by the bed, and put her arm gently over him.

The child stirred, lifted his heavy lids, and put up his face to kiss her; she waited till he was quiet again, and then crept out of the room, and Chris slept that night with his mother's warm tears lying on his cheek.

CHAPTER II

THE next day passed like a dream to Mrs. Winton, but on the following morning a letter came for her from Mr. Grant, to say that he should be at the vicarage in the evening, and that he would fetch her to tea by his sister's request. It was evident, then, that the vicar and his wife knew all that was going on; and soon after breakfast Mrs. Milman herself arrived, and an hour's talk with her convinced Mrs. Winton that she need have no fears about her reception.

But there was still something before her that she dreaded. Chris was to go with her to the vicarage, and she was determined that he should not meet his future father-in-law until he knew all about it. But though she had made up her mind to tell him, it was not an easy thing to do, and she felt strangely nervous when he came running in at dinner-time from his play.

"I have something to tell you, Chris," she said: "something that will be a great surprise to you. I think the time will soon come when we shall not have to be so very careful as we are now."

"But, mother, that's just what I told you yesterday!" exclaimed the boy. "I told you I should soon be big enough to take care of you, and earn lots of money, and you only laughed at me!"

The last words were uttered rather unsteadily, and Mrs. Winton held out her arms to him. "You must forgive me if I made you unhappy, but you know, Chris, you are only a little boy yet, and it will be a long time before you can earn money for me. And so, dear, you must try and listen. Mr. Grant has asked if he may take care of you and me, and I have told him yes."

Her voice had been getting lower, and now she stopped altogether. "I don't quite understand," said Chris, in a doubtful voice.

"I mean, dear, that I am going to marry Mr. Grant, and we shall live with him, and he will always take care of us; and you must try to love him, Chris, because I do."

Chris stood upright, a sturdy little figure, with his hands clasped behind him and his eyes glowing with excitement. "But, mother," he cried, in his clear childish voice, "what would *father* say?"

Mrs. Winton started, then leaning forward, she tried to draw the child back to his old resting place. "Father has gone to be in heaven," she said; "but I know that if he could speak to me now, he would say that I was doing right, because when he left us his greatest trouble was to think that there would be no one to take care of me any more."

Chris did not respond to the gentle pressure of her arm. He stood stiffly before her, the gleam in his eyes fading into a look of displeasure. "Father told *me* to take care of you," he said. "I've remembered it lots and lots of times, and you always said I was your little comforter."

"So you are, darling," said Mrs. Winton, "and so you always will be. But you must trust me that I am doing what is right now, though perhaps you cannot quite understand it."

His voice faltered, and big tears stood in his eyes.

"Don't cry, dear, please don't," said his mother, kissing the cheek that felt cold now to her touch. "I shall love you just the same, you know."

Chris gave her a grave little kiss in return. "I know you will," he said. "It is you who don't understand, mother."

Perhaps Mrs. Winton did not understand him altogether, but she knew him well enough to guess what was passing in his mind. Chris was unchildlike, because for a considerable time out of his short life he had had a definite purpose in view. His mother had been his whole world, and he had learnt to look upon himself as her protector, so that now to learn that a new-comer was to fill his treasured place seemed like an earthquake in his life.

He was almost glad when Mrs. Winton got up from her chair at last, and said that they must clear away the dinner-things. "Would you like to go and play with Harry Wilson?" she said, when they had finished.

"No, thank you," said Chris soberly. "I am going to put the wood away in the coal-shed: the man brought it this morning."

He did not take long in finishing his task, but instead of going indoors again, he sat down in the shed, and gave himself up to his thoughts. When four o'clock struck and he went back to the house, he heard voices through the closed door of the sitting-room, and guessed at once who was there.

His heart seemed to get up into his throat and choke him. Somehow, he had not expected this, and it seemed more than he could bear; he could not believe that his mother did not always want him, yet some strange feeling prevented him from going to her now. But Mrs. Winton had caught the

sound of his step outside, and rose at once to open the door. "Come in, dear,'
she said. "Come and speak to Mr. Grant."

Chris straightened himself with an effort, and though his breath came
rather more quickly than usual, he made no other sign of his agitation. He
walked into the room, holding himself very erect.

"Well, Chris, how are you?" said Mr. Grant pleasantly; he was not particularly anxious for the boy's presence at that moment, but he was a good-
natured man, and he felt very kindly towards his future little stepson.

"I am very well, thank you," was the grave answer. "But my *name* is
Christopher."

"Well, my *name* is Richard, but a good many people call me Dick," said
Mr. Grant, with a smile.

Chris did not smile in response. Mr. Grant was leaning in an easy attitude
against the mantel-piece, and the boy stood in front of him, with an expression of earnestness upon his face. Mr. Grant was tall and well-built, and
there was a brightness in his eyes that made his face very attractive. Just now
he was looking his best, for he was feeling happier than he had ever done in
his life before; whereas Christopher's childish brow was clouded with a
heavy weight of thought and care.

CHAPTER III

I T was a brilliant summer afternoon when Mrs. Milman, with Chris by her
side, drove up the long avenue that led to Mr. Grant's house.

The wedding was over, and while Mr. and Mrs. Grant were away the
boy had been staying at the vicarage. He had been looking forward to the
day when he should see his mother again, but now that it had actually come
there was a painful feeling in his mind that he could not express. This strange
big place, with its gardens and stables and its many servants, could not seem
like home to him. *Home* was the dear little four-roomed cottage, with its
familiar shabby furniture, where there had been no one to come between his
mother and himself.

He had never been to Courthope before, and the old butler looked
curiously at him as they drove up to the door. The servants were staid and
elderly people, who had been with Mr. Grant's father before him, and they
dreaded the arrival of a small boy in their midst: "which are all the same,
tiresome little scaramouches!" as the butler remarked to the housekeeper
when she asked for his opinion.

But Chris did not look like a "tiresome little scaramouche" at all as he
alighted quietly from the pony-carriage, and stood waiting till Mrs. Milman
was ready to go indoors.

"Quite the gentleman!" said the butler to himself, as he saw Chris rub his boots upon the door-mat and take off his hat as he entered the hall.

Chris, for his part, looked at the butler in wonder; he had never seen anyone like him before, and he could not think who this elderly gentleman was who seemed to be so much at home in the house.

"Come, Chris," said Mrs. Milman, "we must go out on the steps to welcome them."

She hurried out, and Chris followed more slowly behind till suddenly he stopped aghast. Was that his mother? Ever since he could remember she had been dressed in black, except on the wedding-day, when he had been too confused to notice what she wore. Could it really be his mother in that light-coloured dress, with her hair no longer strained back under a cap, but waving about her forehead? She seemed changed altogether, and with a feeling that the world could never be the same again, Chris slipped away through the surrounding servants, and fled—he knew not where. When he stopped at last, he found himself in a little room that opened out of a long passage. It was prettily furnished, and the windows looked on a garden, gay with summer flowers. He paused for breath, and then, with a sudden cry, threw himself down on the sofa, and broke into a passion of sobs.

It was not long before a sound of approaching footsteps made him start to his feet, and look round hurriedly for some hiding-place. But as he stood uncertainly in the middle of the room, the door opened, and his mother came in.

"Mother!" he cried, and then stopped, for the tears were flowing fast again.

"My little Chris!" said Mrs. Grant, taking him in her arms; and not another word was spoken for some time, for she would not ask any questions.

"How do you like my little room? she said at last.

Chris loosened his arms from about her, and sat up on the sofa. "Is this your sitting-room?" he asked.

"Yes, it has all been newly furnished for me."

She spoke with a fond accent in her voice that showed what a love and confidence had already sprung up between them. Chris looked at her with his great eyes, and read the thoughts that she left unspoken.

"Would you like to come and see your room now?" said his mother after a little silence.

"Yes, please," said Chris, in a low tone.

They had hardly left the room when a step made them turn, and they saw Mr. Grant coming from the library. "There you are, my boy!" he cried. Where were you hiding, eh?"

Chris made no answer, and his mother hastily interposed.

"We are just going up to see his room, Richard," she said. "Will you come too?"

Chris gave her hand a little pull; he had no wish to go and see his new domain if his step-father was coming with him: but his mother took no notice, and went on talking cheerfully as they mounted the staircase.

"This is your room," said Mr. Grant, opening a door as he spoke.

It was a pretty room, simply furnished, but with everything in it that a child could possibly want. Chris said very little, however, and Mr. Grant felt somewhat disappointed. "What a silent little fellow he is!" he said to his wife when they were alone.

"Do you think so?" said Mrs. Grant, rather anxiously. "He generally finds plenty to say."

"Oh! I daresay he is rather shy with me at present," said Mr. Grant; "it will wear off all in good time."

Chris was awake as soon as it was light the next morning, and lay wondering what he should do with himself till breakfast-time. If he had been "at home," as he still called the cottage, he would have gone down-stairs to help his mother, but he had been told that he must not get up till he was called, and the time seemed very long.

The breakfast-room looked bright and pleasant when the bell sounded at last, and his mother was there to greet him, but the meal seemed very formal after their cosy breakfasts together. Mr. Grant read his letters, and turned continually to his wife with questions and bits of news.

As soon as the meal was over, Mr. Grant asked his wife to come into the library. "I will not keep you long," he said; "but there are several things that I must speak to you about."

"I will come back soon, dear," said Mrs. Grant, laying her hand on her son's head as she passed.

Chris had always been used to clear the breakfast-things, and he thought that he might as well do so now. The plates seemed to be heavier and more slippery than those he had been used to, but he managed to make them into a pile, and collected all the knives and forks. He was so busy that he did not hear the door open, nor see the footman's start of surprise as he caught sight of the little figure.

The man stood still for a minute, uncertain what to do, but Benson, who was passing, rushed in with dismay written on every feature.

"Goodness' sake! Master Christopher, what are you doing with them plates?" he cried.

Chris turned round in alarm, and as he did so his foot caught in the table-cloth, and he went down on the floor, drawing plates, cups and dishes after him in one general crash!

There was a shriek from the onlookers, who for a moment were too paralysed with fright to do anything, but in another instant they were down on their knees by the side of the heap of broken crockery.

Chris lay perfectly still under the ruins, and the footman declared that he must be dead, but when they had at last set him free, the child sat up, apparently none the worse. Benson heaved a sigh of relief, but as his anxiety lessened his displeasure increased, and he looked at the little culprit with an air of dignified rebuke.

"What were you touching the table for?" he asked. "Don't you know it's bad manners to go taking things after the company have gone?"

"I wasn't taking things!" exclaimed Chris.

"What were you doing, then?" asked Benson.

"I was only clearing away. I always did it at home."

"That's not a very likely story!" said Benson gravely.

Chris was not accustomed to have his word doubted, and it wounded him to the quick. He was too proud to cry, but his heart swelled within him, and he would have given an indignant answer had not Mr. Grant appeared at that moment.

"Hallo! what's all this?" he asked.

"I don't exactly know," said Benson, "but it's some mischief of Master Christopher's."

Mr. Grant felt more vexed that there should have been a disturbance between the child and the servants than at the loss of his china. "Well, well," he said, "another time don't play so near the breakfast-table, little man."

"I wasn't playing!" burst out Chris; but Mr. Grant had gone, and his exclamation was unheard.

It seemed very hard to him to be so misjudged, but Benson did not see it in the same light. "You shouldn't speak so to the master," he said. "Many gentlemen wouldn't have been so kind, I can tell you!"

Chris saw the justice of this remark. "I'm very sorry," he said penitently. "How long do you think it will take me to save up my pocket-money to buy him some new china?"

The butler smiled contemptuously. "Longer than you can count!" he said. "Besides, it's not the worth of the china; we don't think much about that."

Chris stared at him, hardly believing that he heard aright. The only explanation of such a remark must be that Benson had no experience of life at all, and it would therefore be kind to enlighten him. "Perhaps you don't know how much things cost," he said; "but when you are married and have got a house of your own, you'll know how hard it is to pay bills."

Benson looked at him in utter amazement. "I think you had better go away, sir, while we arrange the room," he said at last.

"He's a rum one!" said the footman as soon as the door was shut; but Benson could only shake his head in mournful silence.

CHAPTER IV

ALTHOUGH Mrs. Grant did all in her power to prevent Chris from feeling the change in his life, it was not possible for her to be with him as much as she had been in the past. Mr. Grant was always willing that the boy should be with them, but still he had a good deal of loneliness to endure.

Chris did not so much mind being alone sometimes, for he had endless ways of passing his time, but what he did feel was that his mother no longer seemed to want his help. He liked to show his love by doing things for her, and now there seemed to be nothing that he could do. Mr. Grant was always taking care of her, and if he ever left anything undone there was a servant at hand to do it.

Several weeks had already passed since Mr. and Mrs. Grant's return home, when some visitors arrived rather unexpectedly. Mr. Lyddon was an uncle of Mr. Grant's—rather a pompous old man, whom Chris took a dislike to at first sight; but his wife was still more trying, for she wanted to know everything, and asked incessant questions.

Their coming seemed to erect another barrier between Chris and his mother, for she was necessarily much taken up with entertaining them.

There was to be a large garden-party one afternoon, and Chris was rather unhappy all day; when the afternoon came he wandered about in his new white suit, feeling very miserable. He was a shy child, and it was agony to him to be talked to by strangers. He stood half-hidden by the shrubs, watching his mother as she received her visitors on the lawn; she looked so utterly different from the mother of old days, that he could hardly bear to look at her. It was all fancy on his part; Mrs. Grant had changed in nothing but the outward circumstances of her life; in heart she was just the same; and if he could only have known it, she was wishing for her little boy at that very moment.

Chris thought that he would go and lock himself into his own room, but as he passed his mother's room he saw that the door stood open, and he paused and looked in. Just inside the door stood a pair of her boots, and flinging himself down on the floor, Chris laid his head upon them, and burst into tears.

"I *do* love her, I *do*!" he said again and again, with a defiant ring in his voice.

After a time he sat up, with the boots jealously clasped in his arms, and looked about him with a new idea in his mind. In days past he had often cleaned his mother's boots for her; he would do it now while there was no one to hinder him.

Soon he was safe in the outhouse where he had often seen the man doing the boots and shoes. There was a variety of blacking-bottles and brushes, and he soon forgot all about his trouble in the interest of his task. He poured on a plentiful supply of blacking, and then applied himself diligently to the brush. He was some time before he was satisfied with his work, but when he stopped at last he was seized with dismay. His white suit was covered with blacking, and when he tried to rub it off, his dirty hands made matters worse at every moment.

What was to be done? If any of the servants should see him, he knew that he should get into dreadful trouble; so he slipped round to a path that led to a side door, hoping to get in unobserved.

Just as he reached it, however, the door opened, and Mrs. Lyddon appeared on the steps, bringing some fresh visitors into the garden. Chris turned to flee, but he was too late; she laid a detaining hand upon his shoulder, and addressed him in her most cutting tones. "Go into the house at once, you disgraceful child!" she said, "and don't dare to appear again."

"Poor little fellow!" said one of the ladies kindly; "he has fallen down and soiled his clean suit.—Have you hurt yourself, dear?" she added, turning to the child.

Chris looked up at her eagerly, but before he could speak Mrs. Lyddon broke in again.

"Please don't encourage him, Lady Fotheringham," she said. "My nephew has trouble enough with him, as it is. In fact, he said the other day that he could not bear it much longer, and I really think——"

The last words were lost as the ladies moved on, and Chris was left standing in the middle of the path, his face crimson with passion.

Mr. Grant had already repented having said anything about the boy to Mrs. Lyddon, whose interference he disliked. He liked children, and Christopher's presence in the house would have been an additional pleasure to him if only he had been more responsive. He did not realise how much Chris felt the sudden change in his life, and he thought that the big house and garden, with all their many interests, must be a continual source of delight to him. Even Mrs. Grant perhaps hardly understood it; she had had so much to occupy her since her marriage, that, though her love for her boy was not in any way diminished, she had not been able to give him so much of her attention.

The little boy had seen so much of the stern realities of life, that Mr. Grant's light-heartedness was a constant enigma to him. Still, he had had a secret liking for him, but Mrs. Lyddon's unkind words had scattered it to the winds. His stepfather had said he could not bear him much longer. Very well, he would take him at his word.

As soon as it was light next morning, Chris stole out of bed and put on his oldest suit; he took the biscuits out of a tin that stood on his table, and put them into his little knapsack. He had quite settled on his plan of action.

The river ran through the grounds, and there was a boat-house on the banks. Chris thought that he would get into a boat, and go down the river till he came to some town, and there he would find work to do, and earn his living, and never let anyone know where he was, and when he was a man he would come back and see his mother again.

It was a true child's plan, full of dangers and impossibilities that he could not foresee, but he was determined to carry it out at all costs, and he soon reached the river, and managed to scramble into one of the boats. It was some time before he could unfasten the rope, but at last he succeeded, and was carried into the middle of the stream. He was a little frightened when he felt how quickly the boat slipped down through the water, but he was too triumphant to feel much fear. He had not been on the water more than a few minutes, however, when he saw something that made his heart beat violently. It was the figure of a man standing on the bank with a fishing-rod in his hand, and to his dismay Chris recognised his stepfather. Hardly knowing what he did, he sprang to his feet; his sudden movement overbalanced the boat, and in another moment he was struggling in the water.

What happened next he never exactly knew, but when he recovered himself again he was lying on the bank, and Mr. Grant was nowhere to be seen. He shrieked aloud in terror, but almost before the cry had left his lips footsteps were heard, and two of the gardeners who had seen the whole thing as they went to their work rushed down to the water's edge. Mr. Grant rose close to the bank. The men clutched him by the coat, and dragged him up on the grass, then, pulling up one of the hurdles, they laid him upon it, and carried him towards the house. He was carried up to his room, and a man sent tearing off on horseback for the doctor. Presently Mrs. Lyddon came out and saw Chris. He had intended never to speak to her again, but he could not restrain himself now. "Where is mother?" he said. "Oh! can I see mother?"

"No," said Mrs. Lyddon coldly. "You have killed Mr. Grant with your mischief, so you had better go to your room, and keep there."

The boy's face turned white, but he made no answer. He had killed his stepfather; no one would ever wish to see him any more.

He dared not go near the river again, it made him feel sick and cold; he ran into the woods that skirted the park, and threw himself down on the ground. It was a bright and sunny morning, and as his shivering little frame became gradually warmed by the sunshine he grew more and more drowsy, and at last dropped off to sleep.

When he woke again the sun was getting low, and he was terribly hungry. The biscuits he carried were very wet, but they were eatable, and getting up slowly, he set off to look for some place where he could spend the night. He had not gone far when he came upon a rough shelter that had been put up by the gamekeepers.

When morning came at last, he found that there was no hope of his walking. The wetting and the fright had taken too much effect upon him, and when he tried to rise he fell back again, sick and dizzy.

Now the thought of his wrong-doing came to add to his troubles. All his stepfather's kind words and deeds came back to him, and for the first time he saw with what jealousy and sullenness he had repaid them. He only wished that he could have a chance of showing his penitence, but Mr. Grant was dead: he had laid down his life for his ungrateful stepson!

The long day wore slowly, and at last Chris became too faint to sit up any longer. He did not hear steps coming rustling through the brushwood, nor see a figure appear at the entrance of the little hut; but when someone knelt down by his side, and touched him, he sprang up with a wild scream.

"Go away! oh, go away! You are dead!" he cried.

"Hush, hush, dear!" said his stepfather tenderly.

Chris lay looking at him with a terrified expression, but he did not try any longer to push him away. "They said I had killed you," he whispered at last.

"Who said so?" exclaimed Mr. Grant.

"Mrs. Lyddon. She said——" But the remembrance was too much for him, and the child began to tremble.

"Never mind," said Mr. Grant gently; "you shall tell me another time. It was only cramp that made me sink, and I was soon all right again. But oh, Chris! you have made us so unhappy by running away."

"Did it make *you* unhappy?" said Chris in amazement. "I thought you would have been glad to get rid of me."

"Never think so again, Chris," he said, in a low tone.

Chris made no answer, but he put both his arms round his stepfather's neck, while the tears trickled down his cheeks.

"Now I am going to carry you home," said Mr. Grant. "I have been looking for you all day, and so have the men; but I am very glad that it was I who found you, because I wanted to give your mother back her little boy myself."

"I thought God was going to make me die to punish me for being so naughty," said Chris, as he laid his head against the strong arm that carried him so tenderly; "but now I'm going to love you all I can to show you how sorry I am."

And though many years have passed since that day, Chris has kept his word.

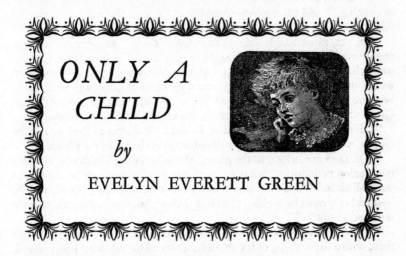

ONLY A CHILD

by
EVELYN EVERETT GREEN

"I т's only a child—shrimping, no doubt, in the shallows."

"What sight you have, Thurloe! I should have taken it for a large bird—a penguin, or something like that."

"You'll see better in a moment. Come on, old man; this shore is none too safe for riding in the dark."

The young men set spurs to their horses and galloped steadily onward over the glimmering sands, which stretched away before them as far as the eye could see. The sky was dull, and out in the west a dusky orange glow lighted up the restless water with a weird and uncanny effect. As the horsemen drew near to the object upon the shore which had attracted their attention from afar, it became plain that young Squire Thurloe had not been mistaken. Alone in the midst of those lonely sands a little boy was sitting, his pale wistful face, full of a strange pathetic fear and misgiving, fixed full upon the glimmering water, creeping slowly, slowly up towards him, whilst the last reflection of the fading sunset seemed to be lingering upon the bright curls which crowned the broad white brow.

Not an ordinary-looking child, by any means; but young men are not wont to pay much heed to the looks of children. Both riders turned a careless glance upon the little fellow as they passed, and met the mute, pleading glance of a pair of dark blue eyes, which appeared to ask for something which the quivering lips would never frame in words; but neither of the pair drew rein. The light was fast fading; their horses were eager for the shelter of a comfortable stable. What was the child to them? His own people would see to him in time. It was no business of theirs.

"What on earth can the little beggar be doing out alone here at this time of evening?" said the squire's companion. "I suppose he is safe from the tide?"

"Oh, yes, safe enough—above high-water mark. I suppose his father is out shrimping somewhere; I thought he looked as if he were taking care of some clothes. This is our way up, old fellow—through this gap, and then we hit the road. Will you come home with me to-night? No? Well, then, here we part company; your way lies to the left, and mine straight on. Good-night; see you again next meet. It's at Sir John's place, I believe."

"I think so. Good-night, Thurloe. I must look sharp or I shall be late for dinner, which, I hear, is an unpardonable sin in the eyes of my hostess."

"If he does not belong to the place," thought Squire Thurloe as his elder companion rode forth, "what on earth can the little beggar be doing out there all alone? I don't see that it's any business of mine. It's only a child—somebody must be looking after him. I don't know why I should trouble my head about it."

But yet he remained motionless in the saddle a full minute longer, and then, with a slight shrug of the shoulders, turned his reluctant horse round, and descended once again the short decline which led to the level waste of sand.

It was no darker than it had been some little time before, for the moon was full, and was now giving a bright light. The squire's far-seeing eyes swept the plain before him with hawk-like glance, and—yes, sure enough, there was the little lonely figure, just where it had been before; only now the golden head was down-bent, and the face hidden between the two hands. He rode quickly forward, and pulled up close to the child.

"I say, my little man, what are you doing out here all alone?"

The big dark eyes, which looked black in the moonlight, fixed themselves wistfully on the speaker's face. In a silvery little voice the child answered—

"I'm waiting for father, please, sir."

"And where is father?"

"Please, sir, he's bathing in the sea. Father is very fond of swimming. I take care of his clothes till he comes back. Sometimes he is a long time in the water, but he never been so long as to-day."

The child continued speaking in short sentences, because the gentleman made no reply. The young squire was, in fact, greatly taken aback. He well knew the perils of this apparently safe-looking shore, and would never have ventured out alone at this state of the tide. He knew perfectly, as he stood there, half afraid to look into the child's face, that his father was no more. But how was this to be broken to the little fellow?

To gain time, he asked a few questions of the boy.

"What is your name, my little man?"

"Jocelyn Carew, please, Sir. Father calls me Jock."

"And what does your father do? And where do you live?"

"We haven't lived anywhere since mother died. Father does a great many things. Sometimes he paints pictures for people to hang on their walls; sometimes he sings, or plays the fiddle in bands; sometimes he conjures, or recites poems. I think father can do almost anything. But we always move about; we haven't any home."

"A better-class vagrant—possibly a decayed gentleman," was the squire's mental comment. And still with the view of gaining time, the young man asked the boy's age.

"Next birthday I shall be six," answered the child, proudly. "Father says I shall be almost a man, then."

It was always "father, father," with the little fellow. He had plainly no thoughts in which the father was not involved. How would he bear the news which must soon be broken to him? The young man had not strength of mind to try and enlighten him yet.

"Look here, my little fellow, it is no good your waiting here any longer. We must send a boat after your father. He has evidently got into some current, and cannot reach the shore again. I will see about all that, and you must come back with me for the present. When they bring your father home you shall know all about it."

The child let himself be lifted up in front of the gentleman on his tall horse, and the squire had the satisfaction of seeing the curly head nodding suspiciously before they had reached the road again.

The little fellow did not hear the words spoken to a pair of stalwart fishermen as the squire rode through the hamlet on his way to his own gates. But the child slept on, soothed by the motion of the horse, and worn out with watching and the vague distress of his own loneliness.

But the squire could by no means share this pleasant oblivion. He was not a little disturbed. It was all very well to know that the housekeeper would look after the child's comfort for the night; but what of that morrow when the truth must be told to him? And what of the future that lay before the little fellow?

"I really don't know why I should bother myself so; he's only a vagrant's child. I mustn't grow sentimental over him. Victoria would not tolerate it for a moment; I know she would send him off straight to the workhouse if she were here, and perhaps she would be right. I know the whole question of the bringing-up of vagrant children is uncommonly difficult, and I have no experience."

When the squire heard that two of the fishermen had come to the house and were inquiring for him, he rose at once to go to them.

It was just as he had expected. The body had been found, washed up at the flow of the tide in a certain bay where only too many other lifeless corpses had been stranded before.

The young man slept restlessly that night, and, waking early, rose and stepped forth into the clear October sunshine, hoping by fresh air and exercise to dispel the mist of unwonted depressions which still hung over him. He had half resolved not to see the child again, to send for the relieving officer and let him be taken straight off by him. In another month he would be the husband of the beautiful Victoria Wellesley, who was soon coming to reign in the old house; and she was the last person in the world to approve of his taking an irrational interest in some unknown waif. No, the whole thing was absurd. He wondered that he had ever dreamed of making a pet of the golden-haired little fellow. Why, before very long he hoped to have children of his own about the old place. What an absurdity to fancy that the little stranger could ever be anything to him!

His meditations had just reached this point, and he had resolved to send off immediately for the relieving officer, when a soft hand was slipped into his, and a sweet little voice said confidingly—

"Please will you take me to my father? They told me you knew where he was."

Here was a pretty situation! Of course he knew where the dead man lay —in a chapel by the sea—and he knew, too, that the kindly fisher-folk would have paid all tender and reverent heed to the last sad offices to the dead. But what was he to say to the child? His mind was quickly made up.

Taking the child's hand in his, he turned towards the sea, saying in a kindly voice, which shook a little in spite of himself—

"Yes, I will take you to your father. Will you try to be a brave, good boy?"

The earnest eyes raised and flashed a strange look upon him. Could it be possible that the little fellow apprehended more than he actually understood? He felt that the tiny fingers clutched his hand more closely; but though there was appeal and pleading in the dark blue eyes, the quivering lips framed no more words, and the young squire, not knowing what to say, remained mute.

The little chapel was not far away, and the door was unlocked. The early morning sun streaming in through the eastern window fell full upon the calm pale face of the dead, stamped with that ineffable peace which is never seen save on the faces of those who have laid down the burden of the flesh.

"Oh," breathed the boy at last, after standing in silence a while, his face irradiated by a wonderful light, his hands clasped behind him in awestruck-wonder, "he has gone to mother; he said he should some day. That is how she looked when she had gone to heaven. He has gone to her now; and, oh, how happy they will be together! Oh, please may I go too?"

"My poor little chap!"

It was all he could think of to say, and the words, accompanied as they were by a look of compassion, seemed to bring home to the child the first sense of his own personal loss. The expression changed for a moment, a wave of some other emotion swept across the upturned face; the child's breath came thick and short. Was he going to break down in wild weeping? For a moment it seemed as if he would; but with a self-control wonderful in one so young, he choked back the tide of emotion, and the squire heard his whisper to himself—

"I will be brave, I will be brave. He said I must not want *her* back. Father, dear father, I will be brave, I will be good. But oh, why did you not take me with you?"

The child sank upon his knees beside the bier upon which his dead father lay, and the young man softly withdrew, feeling that this was a scene upon which no human eye should look.

Rapidly he strode away, his mind in a tumult of conflicting emotion. A baby not yet six years old, and with thoughts and feelings like that! He could not understand it. Let that child, with such a depth of poetry in his nature, be dragged up amongst the outcast population of a great work-house? Never! It might be foolish, wrong, irrational, but the squire's mind was made up. He strode away fast in the direction of one of his own lodges, where his old nurse now lived, pensioned off by his liberality to an old age of peace and leisure, and to her he told his tale in rapid fashion, putting before her a scheme of his own, and asking her if she would help him.

Before he had done, he read assent in her eyes; and she was folding her shawl about her as she spoke at last.

"Take the bairn and give him a home with me? Ay, that I will; and I'd do it for love of the blessed little ones of our Lord's, without the money, squire; though it's like your kind heart to provide for him so liberal like."

"Tush! If you take the care and trouble of him, the least I can do is to provide the funds. Some folks will call us fools, but I think our backs are broad enough to bear their ridicule."

"Ay, ay, let them talk; a few laughs break no bones," answered the old woman with a smile. "But I'll go to the bairn now, and tell him the good Lord has provided a home for him."

"Yes, go to him," said the young man hastily. "You will know how to deal with him: I don't. I'll come down and visit him later, and see how you shake down together."

The young squire was a busy man. He had a large property which he managed himself, and managed well; and he was fond of sport, and gave a considerable slice of his time to shooting and hunting. His approaching marriage gave him extra employment at this time; and yet to-day, as he went about his work, the pathetic face of the little orphaned boy was seldom absent from his mind. It was only a child, a little waif of humanity cast up at his doors: strange that he should take such an interest in him.

Little Jock never pined after, though he never forgot, his father. He loved his granny, as he called the good old woman, with all his heart, and for the young squire he felt an ardent love and admiration. His daily visits were the brightest spots in Jock's life: love was to him the very elixir of life, and the deepest love of a warm heart was now lavished upon the Squire of Thurloe Hall.

But with the advent of a mistress there, things changed considerably. How eagerly did the little fellow await the coming of the carriage that was to bring home the bride! He was dressed in his best clothes, and he was to present to the lady the huge bunch of flowers, the offering from the fisher-folks; and how his heart beat, as the sound of shouting and cheering told him that the carriage was coming, and how eagerly did his eyes scan the handsome, high-bred face, as the carriage pulled up for him to deliver his gift!

The squire's kindly brown face was beaming all over, and he caught hold of little Jock and gave him a kiss that sent the blood rushing to the boy's face. But the beautiful lady only thanked him with careless good-will, and he heard her say to her husband—

"Really, Leonard, there is no need for quite such demonstrative proceedings. Who is the child?"

The answer was lost to Jock, but the squire replied eagerly—

"Oh, Jock is quite a pet of mine. I hope he will be a pet of yours too. Poor little chap, his father was drowned——"

"Surely you have not saddled yourself with the maintenance of a vagrant child?" said young Mrs. Thurloe sharply. "Really, Leonard, you do indeed need a wife to keep you in order."

"He is not a nameless child, Victoria," answered the squire, with more zeal than discretion; "and though I cannot find out about his parentage, I am sure there is good blood in him. You must learn to like him for my sake. He is a dear little fellow. He——"

"I really cannot be enthusiastic over him! If you begin taking him out of his place you will bitterly repent it later. Now let us drop the subject. I am not sentimental, as you know, and there is plenty to think of besides this vagrant boy."

The whole household found a difference now that there was a new hand upon the domestic helm. Mrs. Thurloe was a just and good mistress, but there was something about her which repelled the affections of her dependants, and though they might respect, they did not like her.

Was it the same with her husband? Nobody could say. Outwardly they appeared an attached couple, and their household was governed with clock-work regularity. The squire had his wish, and children were born to him—first a boy, and then two little girls, and the strong affections of his heart wound themselves more and more closely round his little ones with every year. As for little Jock at the lodge, the squire was fond of him and proud of him, though he had now to show these feelings somewhat by stealth.

Mrs. Thurloe disliked Jock with an unreasoning dislike she did not attempt to disguise or explain. "He was only a vagrant's child; it was absurd to make such a fuss over him. He ought to be sent off to the workhouse."

Perhaps one cause of offence was his striking beauty, for her own boy was not beautiful. It was strange, with so good-looking a father and mother, that the child should be so plain. The squire laughed and said that it did not matter in a man, and both the little girls were pretty; but the mother's affections were centred in her son, and she looked upon it as an affront to herself that he should lack personal beauty. He was not an engaging child, either; for the truth of the matter was that he was spoiled to the top of his bent. He was overbearing, tyrannical, and disposed to be a bully; and his father felt keenly that there was something lacking in his training which he knew not how to supply. Perhaps it was with the desire to discover and supplement this lack, of which he was painfully conscious, that the young father at this time cultivated Jock's society more than he had done for many years, actually suggesting to his wife that she should have the boy up to the Hall sometimes to play with little Victor.

"The boy wants a boy companion; the little girls are too young, and no match for him, and he bullies them shamefully. Jock would teach him how to play rationally. It would do him a world of good."

Mrs. Thurloe was at first scornfully indignant at such a proposition; but it had been made in Master Victor's presence, and he was straightway resolved to have Jock as a playfellow. He was by this time five, whilst Jock was nearly twelve. He thought that a white slave to drive about and do his bidding would be fine, and he gave his mother no peace till she had consented.

It was a new and strange life for Jock, but on the whole he did not object. When the squire came himself to join the games, or tell stories to the children, then Jock's cup of happiness seemed full. Jock was soon quite an institution in the nursery; but Mrs. Thurloe's prejudice against the child of a vagrant was never overcome, and she seldom addressed the boy save in sharp speeches, which gave him the sense of having offended her in some unknown way.

"He talks so oddly to the children," she once said impatiently to her husband. "I call him a little sanctimonious humbug. I cannot bear a child to profess that absurd amount of piety. I know he is an arrant little hypocrite at heart. I confess I do not like seeing him so much with the children."

"It is hardly fair to call him a hypocrite or a humbug until one has the chance to see whether or not he lives up to his profession," answered the squire quietly. "Besides, the boy only talks of his feelings, never guessing that they repeat it to us. I agree that I should not like him to talk to us in that strain; but he never does. There is a natural vein of reverence and poetry in a child's nature that must and will find an outlet somewhere. For my own part, I am glad enough for the little ones to make a confidant of Jock."

Mrs. Thurloe tapped her foot impatiently on the turf. She knew that there were subjects upon which she and her husband disagreed, and she resented even the consciousness that he criticised her method of training the children. She knew that he thought their education lacked one essential element, and that he secretly hoped this element was in part supplied to them by Jock. Hence a part of her dislike to the boy.

"Jock, Jock—it is always Jock! I am perfectly sick of the name. I wish you had never taken him up. It is absurd the notice you take of him, and the amount you think of him. He is only a child—and a vagrant's child. I call it a perfect absurdity."

There was no time for a reply. The squire had started to his feet with a quick exclamation, and his wife looked up to see the two little girls racing towards them, their faces blanched with terror. She sprang to her own feet and ran by her husband's side.

"What is it, children?"

"The river—the waterfall—Victor—Jock!" panted the little ones, ready to drop with exhaustion and fear. "Oh, papa, be quick!"

No need to add that injunction; the squire was off like an arrow shot from a bow, whilst mother-love put wings to his wife's feet, and she sped along hardly twenty yards behind him. They knew well the dangerous river-bank, that tempting place just above the fall, where the children loved to play.

When they reached the spot, they saw two boys in the deep water, not twenty yards from the head of the fall. Victor was clinging with the desperate clutch of the drowning to the shoulder of Jock, who had flung one arm round him to hold him out of water, whilst with the other he grasped the branch of the overhanging willow and held on like grim death, though the rigid whiteness of his face, and the unnatural look in his eyes, told the squire at the first glance how terrible was the strain he was putting upon himself.

"Hold on, Jock—one minute—only one minute more!" he cried, as he dashed down to the water, and threw himself along the limb of the same willow-tree within reach of the boys. "Now, Victor, stretch up your hand to me. So—now the other. That is right! Jock! Jock! don't let go, boy! Oh, my boy, what have you done? Take care, Vic! Don't clutch me like that! Let go, child! Ah! it is too late!"

For no sooner did the father release Jock from the clutching clasp of the burden he held, than his own grasp upon the willow-branch relaxed, and before the squire could reach forth a hand to save him, the swirling stream had swept him down out of reach, and the next moment there was a swift flash over the head of the fall, and Jock disappeared from view.

White to the lips with horror and dismay, the squire retraced his way along the branch, and placed the dripping child he carried in his mother's arms. Then, without another word, he dashed along the bank, and plunged down the descent to the lower level, leaving Victor shivering and sobbing, and his wife agitated beyond the power of speech.

The little sisters were now seen hastening to the scene of the calamity, and when they saw Victor safe and sound in the arms of his mother they broke into cries of joy. The little girls clung to their mother, panting out their tale.

"Oh, mamma, it was so dreadful! Victor *would* get on the branch. Papa tells us we mustn't; and when Jock begged him not to, he boxed his ears and called him names. He said *you* would let him, and that you did not let Jock order him about—and then—oh, I can't quite remember how it was, but he was saying naughty things, and making faces at Jock, and he fell off into the water."

"Yes, mamma! and Jock jumped in after him directly, holding by the branch, and got hold of Victor, and called to us to run and fetch somebody, and so we did. But, mamma dear, where is Jock? Didn't he save Victor's life? Oh, he is so brave and good!"

Mrs. Thurloe made no reply, though a strange thrill ran through her. For the moment her whole soul was wrapped up in her son; but when she had seen him safely asleep between hot blankets in bed, she was able to think of that other boy, to whose courage and presence of mind her child owed his life. What had been his fate? Could it be possible that there was the smallest chance for one hurried by the fierce torrent over the rocky waterfall? She shuddered as she pictured the scene. And but for Jock that fate must have been her child's.

"Where is your master?" she asked.

"He has gone to the lodge with the boy."

"Is he——?"

"They say he is dying, but he may perhaps come to himself at the last. The master said he should stay with him to see."

Mrs. Thurloe was throwing a shawl across her shoulders. She stepped out into the dewy freshness of the summer's evening, and walked rapidly towards the lodge, a strange look upon her face.

The cottage door stood open, and the soft light of sunset was streaming in. Jock lay upon the broad oak settle, wrapped in blankets, a strange, sweet smile upon his white face. Bruised, maimed, torn by the cruel pointed rocks was the poor little frame, the lovely face was unscarred, and the child felt no pain from his hurts. He lay holding the squire's hand, perfectly content to know that he was near, and that Master Victor was safe. As the tall form of the lady for a moment blotted out the sunlight, the boy's eyes raised themselves, and fastened upon her face with a pleading, wistful look. For once in her life Mrs. Thurloe was deeply agitated.

"Jock, Jock! what can I say—what can I do for you?"

"Please will you forgive me?" said the child, in very low tones.

"Forgive you for what?"

"I do not quite know," he whispered. "For what I have done to vex you. I could not ask what it was, but I always knew I had done something naughty. You never liked me, and it must have been my fault. But indeed I did not mean it."

The lady's proud head sank beneath the trusting gaze of those blue eyes; a dry, hard sob broke from her.

"Oh, Jock, Jock! it is for you to forgive me!" she answered, in accents too low to reach any ear but her husband's "What can I do to atone?"

Jock's senses were fast failing. He felt himself at peace with all, though he could hear no words spoken by those about him.

"May I send my love to them?" he whispered. "Please tell them it is more beautiful than anything we talked about—all gold and pearl, and the rainbow everywhere. Oh! and the music! I can hear it now so plainly. They are—there they are! Father! Mother—Oh! and——"

The whispering tones ceased. The look of awe and rapture upon the white face deepened to an expression which made the onlookers hold their breath. There was a Presence in that still room which was only seen to one of them, yet all were conscious that it was there.

The Angel of Death had not come alone—there was Another with him. Another—the Angel and Messenger of Life, holding out His hand, and saying to the shadowy attendant with the sword—

"Suffer the little children to come unto Me, and forbid them not, for of such is the Kingdom of heaven."

In the little green churchyard by the sea stands a small marble memorial at the head of one grave—a grave that is always carefully tended, and at most seasons of the year bright with flowers. Children's hands, for the most part, keep that grave trim and flower-decked; and it is there that the children whisper softly together, and tell each other how different "mamma" has been since Jock went away.

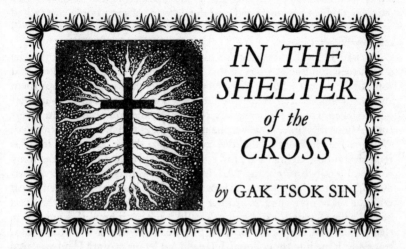

IN THE SHELTER *of the* CROSS

by GAK TSOK SIN

CHAPTER I

'Of all the women in the Flowery Kingdom, few have passed through deeper waters than I have. My father was a squire in a village about a month's journey from here.

I can remember the great Stone-Slab House in which the first ten years of my childhood were spent, especially the view on which I used to gaze from the window of my mother's apartment is impressed upon my memory.

Whenever I shut my eyes, I can see the mountain just as it used to appear when the sun went down and I was awaiting the footsteps of my father, ere he returned from the walk through the plantations of pine-apples and sugar-canes, which he always took in the third watch of the day. Ah, up that mountain we fled, and took refuge amongst its cliffs, shortly after my father brought home a number of books, of which this is one.

So saying, she drew from her sleeve a well-worn, much rubbed book which she passed to me. I had much ado to recognise it as a copy of the Gospel of St. John.

Ah, those books, those books, they eventually led hundreds to forsake their homes and flee to the mountains. I well remember the day when they were brought.

A feast had been given in the village on the preceding day, and a theatre was erected before my father's house, to which all the neighbours crowded; in connection with the feast, which was in honour of Tho-ti-Kong, a tax was levied on the inhabitants of the village; some one, I think, refused to pay his share, which led to a dispute among the parties concerned, and my father was called in to give judgement; the man alleged that he did not pay the amount due because he believed the doctrine of some books that he had bought from a roadside pedlar. It was in some such way that the books fell into my father's hands.

During the next month he did little else but read them. After that he untied their bindings and gave them out leaf by leaf to my brothers and some of the poorer scholars of the village in order that they might copy them and even I was allowed to help bind the new copies. All this time my mother offered incense to the idols regularly, and taught me how to do them reverence. About this time, however, he used to stand and gaze with a puzzled, abstracted air in front of the idol cabinet. One day he called me into his reception room, saying he wished to hear what progress I had made in my studies. I gladly brought my "Advice to the Dwellers in the Inner Apartments," and turning my back to him repeated the last ten pages I had learnt with the aid of my youngest brother. He was greatly pleased, and then said he had a new lesson for me, and he would teach me it himself. I remember that lesson well, for he not only taught me the character sounds but also translated it me into the colloquial. He did not let me go until I had mastered it in both, and could repeat it in either at his command. His old master came in and tarried for him also. He asked me what I was reading, and heard my lesson, but I could tell from his expression something annoyed him. So I timidly inquired if I had said it rightly. He answered "yes," but did not offer to return it me. When my father came, after the usual questions, I heard him say, "Why are you teaching your Golden Flowers (daughter) not to bow down nor worship anything in heaven above or earth below." I did not hear my father's answer, but began to think over the words I had been industriously repeating. The result was that I ran to my mother exclaiming:

"Siong-te si chit e bo nng e;"

"Head above all is one, not two, nor a dozen."

"What does the lesson mean a-ni-a (mother)? If there be but one Siong-te, how is it we have Giok-ong Siong-te, Tho-te-Kong Siong-te, and scores of others?"

My mother made me sit down beside her and then said:

"What else does the lesson teach Chin-Chu (for my name was Pearl of price in those happy days, not Cabbage as it is to-day)?"

"Must not make any graven image of things above, of things below, of things beneath to fall down to worship," I repeated slowly and wonderingly, "But we do mother."

"Did, little one, but run away, and you shall hear all about it when your father tells the others."

I went slowly and thoughtfully towards the common dining-room, in which was placed the cabinet containing the idols and the ancestral tablets. The gods were gone, gone, and in the stead was a scroll bearing the words

I had repeated to my mother. Late that night my father assembled all the household. When they were all gathered together, he talked to them for a long time.

The next day, a number of the literati came to a feast given by my father. I do not know what occasioned it, but many went away looking very angry. That evening, after the household had again assembled, my father broke the idols into fragments, and then taking a bowl of water he dipped his hand in it and laid it all wet on my brother's forehead, saying, "Using the name of the Father, the Son, and the Holy Spirit, I bestow upon you this washing ceremony."

After that day I noticed with sorrow and a pain at my heart, that father's friends among the literati seldom came to call upon him, and when they did come, it was to argue with, and often abuse him.

During the next few months my beloved parent spent much time and labour in teaching us the new doctrines. It was his custom to hear us repeat them to him before the lanterns were lighted. All, save my two eldest brothers, who to my surprise he did not command, but requested them to read and study these strange classics, and encouraged them to tell him their opinions of the doctrines contained therein. My mother, too, took infinite pains to master the simplest of these books, which gave him great pleasure. My father himself had always been a proud man; now he was meek and gentle as a slave. I did not like it.

About this time, at one of the evening assemblies, my brother, father's second son, rose and requested that the washing ceremony might be bestowed on him also. He had scarcely resumed his seat ere man after man rose, and made the same request, owning their allegiance to the Jesus doctrines, and assuming their determination to abide by the teaching of the Jesus classics.

Father fell on his knees, I remember, and in a broken voice confessed his sins and the sins of those assembled with him.

It did not please me. My father was good, and I knew it, so I shouted, "You are a good man, venerable father, you are good," and then began to cry, as I thought of the breach of etiquette I had committed.

A day or two after that occurrence I noticed mother spent much time in weeping, and began to gather articles together from the great cabinets, and pack them into a small dragon box, which my father usually took with him when he went on a journey. Mother stopped my exclamations of surprise with a warning gesture, and I was forced to restrain the tides of astonishment that overwhelmed me. Late one night I was roused by my father, who rolled my *phe** round me, and carried me out beyond the surrounding walls into the unknown world beyond, whither my footsteps had never strayed.

We had been travelling a long time through the blackness, that seemed to

* A thick coverlet or padded quilt.

thicken and deepen around us, when suddenly, borne on the breath of the night, came a shrill faint cry. It appeared to come from far. The silence that followed was broken by the voice of my father. He had been walking close beside us, though I had not known it.

Peeping over a balcony into the great depths below, a number of lights flitting to and fro greeted my astonished sight. At first I thought they were large fireflies, or glow-worms, till I rubbed my eyes, and saw they were crowds of men carrying torches. Then I knew we must be upon the great mountain. Soon the men collected in one vast throng round a large building, evidently attempting to force their way in. At last they broke down the barriers that hinderd them, then crowded in, and hurried out with loads of stuff which they piled in heaps. Jostling, pushing against each other, shrieking, yelling, the mob seemed to have gone mad. They applied torches to the house and to the goods piled up outside, but this brought prompt interference from men dressed in long blue robes, members of the literati. I recognised them at once; but it was not till some wretch in the grip of the demon of destruction managed to elude the vigilance of these leaders of the riot, and set fire to a heap of furniture and household stuff, which, blazing high, threw a lurid light upon the building, and lit up the heavens with a strange red glow, that I realised it was upon the house of my ancestors, the home of my childhood, that the vengeance of the maddened mob was wreaked.

I burst into loud wails, and beat the stone wall with my tiny fists in impotent rage, but father put his face close to mine, and whispered me to be still, or else our enemies might find us. Then we turned away, and that was the last time I ever saw Stone-Slab House'.

CHAPTER II

'WE removed to a small but better house in a small ruined hamlet, which stood on land that had once been awarded to my father for bravery in quelling a rebellion. A large hall was erected in which all the inhabitants of the village assembled early, morning by morning. On every seventh day labour ceased, and the whole day was devoted to the worship of the God of heaven. My father and some of the other men would often go away for weeks at a stretch, taking with them the shoes and embroidery done by the women, and would return oftentimes accompanied by men who like our selves had fled from bitter persecution, brought upon them by their belief in the doctrines of Jesus.

The village increased and prospered, though no one grew rich; and every one seemed happy save myself. I—I hated it all, the place, the people, and above all, the new religion that had brought this change into my life. In the past *I* had been waited on by slaves. Now *I* had to husk rice, prepare the potatoes, wash the clothes. In the past I had been used to long finger nails, jewelled head-dresses, silver anklets, embroidered robes. Now my finger nails were cut in order that I might attend to household matters, and in a plainer garb than any worn by my slaves in olden days was I attired.

One way of escape was open. I was betrothed, had been ever since my seventh year, to the eldest son of a squire in a distant city. Often I wondered with dread whether my parents would find a way to break off the betrothal in spite of its being as binding as the marriage tie, but I never dared speak on the subject or hint that I knew aught about the matter. After I reached the age of fifteen, my mother alluded to the subject, and told me that as my father and she herself dreaded my entering a heathen household, becoming a member of a family that worshipped not the King of heaven, so he had worked and striven in order to gain the wherewithal to pay back the betrothal money, and had determined to try and break off the espousals, but that they thought I should be pleased to be consulted on the subject.

To the utter surprise and dismay of my parents, I was indignant, and professed to be insulted at the proposal to break through the customs of my country. I harped on the fact that I was a true daughter of the Flowery Land and whether the man to whom I was betrothed turned out an idiot or a leper, I would hold myself bound by the contract entered into on my behalf by my elders.

After that, of course, nothing could be done. I heard no more, for it is considered highly improper to let "the youthful dwellers in the inner apartment" know what arrangements are pending relating to their own betrothal.

Negotiations must have taken place between the two families, for in a short time we removed to a house hired by my father in a city distant some thirty *li* from the hamlet in which we had taken refuge. Here we stayed during a period extending over several months. Now my nails were allowed to grow long, and each day my mother with the aid of some hired women and myself cut out, made and embroidered, over two hundred robes. My trousseau I knew—though not a word was said to me on the subject.

We worked desperately, and about ten days before my sixteenth birthday all was done. My trousseau and jewellery were packed into red dragon boxes. Twenty-seven were needed to hold the wardrobe that my mother gave me. In my wedding outfit were included four large washing tubs, a red and gold embroidery frame, thick wadded coverlets embroidered in silks of all the colours of the rainbow, splendid wooden pillows and vases of jade and ebony. It took thirty to forty men to carry my bridal gifts and trousseau. Truly, my father and mother spared no pains to send me to the house of my mother-in-law, surrounded by all the pomp that befitted our old estate.

The evening before the eventful day, on which I was to enter the bridal chair, I was washed in water in which twelve kinds of flowers had been steeped. I remember the feeling of excitement that pervaded the household, and the pained expression on the faces of my father and mother.

After I retired, the sound of their voices reached me till far into the night. I knew they were asking the God of heaven to care for me. I did not want to remember Him, and hoped He would forget me. A voice within my soul told me I had thwarted the wishes of my parents, and this I endeavoured to stifle by persuading myself that I was acting as a daughter of China should act, and following in the footsteps of my favourite heroines.'

CHAPTER III

'THE morning dawned, and I was lifted into the crimson chair and surrounded by a crowd of musicians sent by the bridegroom's people; of all our household, only the go-between accompanied me, but before and behind went a long string of bearers carrying in full view of the admiring bystanders my magnificent outfit. Pale green silk trousers, gold and crimson shoes, orange and purple petticoat, a tunic of turquoise blue, all elaborately embroidered, these with a scarlet robe reaching from head to foot formed my bridal attire.

A golden crown upon my head kept in their place the two veils in which I was enveloped.

At parting my parents gave me that little book, and bade me, if I cared for them at all, show it to no one, throughout my whole life never to part with it, to read it when any opportunity presented itself, and to consult it if trouble or sorrow cast their dark shadows over me.

At last we arrived at the entrance to an extensive mansion, which reminded me forcibly of the Stone-Slab House in which were passed the happy hours of childhood. A theatrical performance was in full swing, delighting an enormous crowd of neighbours. The assembly parted to the right and left as my little cavalcade drew near amid cries of,

"The bridal chair has crossed our threshold,
The bridal chair is in in our midst."

My bearers passed through the various courts till they stayed their footsteps at the door of the great reception hall. Here the chair was put down and the bearers retired, while a crowd of my new relations tried to induce me to step out. Remembering my instructions, I would not move, but wept and moaned in a corner of the sedan. Then a tiny child, tastefully dressed, brought me some sweetmeats on a little silver tray, and in coaxing tones besought me to try the dainties his venerable grandparents had bestowed upon him. I paid no heed to his entreaties, and the child turned away with a grieved air at my unkindness. (The bride is supposed to forget herself in the sorrow of another.) My heart relented at the sight of his distress, and as I was leaning forward to take the proffered dainty to pacify his grief, I was seized and borne struggling and weeping in the arms of two lucky women, across a pan of burning charcoal, into the house, through the brilliantly decorated reception hall, to a tiny room in which I sat motionless, while my robes, sadly disordered by my struggles, were re-arranged. (So far the rules of etiquette had been duly observed.)

Now my mother-in-law and the other females crowded in, longing to lift the thick veils that covered me, but this (to my great joy) the mistress of the ceremonies would by no means permit.

I kept my eyes cast down; even if I had raised them it would have been of little use, for my veils were so closely woven that objects could be seen only very indistinctly through them. Soon I was lifted out and placed beside my husband at the wedding breakfast.

At the end of the feast, of which only my husband had partaken, I was carried back to the inner room. Not long after I adjourned thither I heard, with a heart beating to suffocation, the go-between summon the bridegroom to remove the thick veil that covered me, leaving the one of red fringe. I had not yet seen him, though I had sat beside him at the wedding feast, and did not know how to keep from shuddering as he approached me. He, with quick trembling hands, removed the gauze, and I felt his eyes dwell upon my face before, with a satisfied sigh, he left the room. In vain had I summoned courage to raise my eyes, though I longed to do so while he scanned my face my nerve was not sufficient, and I had not therefore the remotest idea of his personal appearance. He had seen me, but I, I had not yet seen him. Oh, how I wished I had not been so frightened.

I had now to sit at the foot of my bridal couch in the midst of the red boxes containing my trousseau, whilst all my new unknown female relatives and their guests came to examine me, and pass remarks on my personal appearance and dress. This is a critical time for the young bride, for though the relatives and guests have full liberty to remark upon her beauty or ugliness, and say unkind things generally regarding her, yet she is not allowed even by the droop of an eyelid to give expression to her feelings. I sat there while they crowded round, staring straight before me, trying to guess who the various ladies were. Fortunately most of them admired my beauty, one, whom I thought to be a sister-in-law, said I looked proud and haughty; another wondered why my teeth were so white; a third thought I looked bad tempered. An elderly, somewhat stately dame (my mother-in-law I suspected) wondered if my trousseau were at all worthy of the betrothal money they had expended upon me. Some seized my hands and felt them to see if they were soft, and exclaimed at the shortness of my nails. Others lifted up my skirt to examine my feet and see if they were smaller than their own.

So the day wore on, and all the time in the next room I could hear the

merriment of the male guests as they partook of the bridal feast. Evening
was far advanced when the women crowded out. I could hear them setting
the tables, and this was soon followed by the noise of feasting, and I knew
they were regaling themselves on the food left by the men. It was quite dark
ere they finished, and I still sat silent and motionless as I had done all that
long, long day.

Now came the worst hour of the ordeal.

The go-between brought me a tiny cup of tea, and then she on one side
and the mistress of the ceremonies on the other supported me to the great
reception hall, where the man guests were yet carousing. I who had never
seen or been seen by men was now to be exhibited for their entertainment.
Oh, how I hated, dreaded, feared and despised them and myself.

At last I stood in the doorway of the room, and amidst a general shout of
delight the guests came forward, bearing lighted candles in their hands. Their
amusement consisted in urging me to come forward and show my small feet.
I felt their curious gazes resting on my face, taking in every detail of my
appearance, and longed for my protecting veil or that the earth would open
and enfold me in her bosom. In the midst of my misery came a strong impulse to raise my eyes. I knew it would be considered extremely immodest
and unmaidenly, yet I felt a will stronger than my own compelling me. I
struggled with all my might against the feeling, and strove to keep an
unmoved countenance, but my efforts were of no avail, and gradually I
raised my heavy lids to meet the intense gaze of a pair of evil eyes that seemed
to hold mine in thrall while they pried into my inmost soul. A sneering smile
crept over the man's sensual face, and a look of wicked triumph dawned in
his eyes as he slowly lowered them, and then, and not till then could I close
mine. My face was white and drawn. I knew another moment and my feeling would overmaster me. To my intense relief the go-between with the aid
of the mistress of the ceremonies dragged me into a dark corner, and there
they administered a vicious pinch in order to punish me for my bad
behaviour.

Again and yet again I was submitted to the painful ordeal, and had to
suffer the disgusting sallies of the guests. All the time, however, I was conscious of but one: his hateful presence made itself felt. Somehow it obtruded
itself into my inmost consciousness. With a woman's intuition I knew that
the man was my enemy, and I felt instinctively he would work woe in my
new life.

I swooned with relief when I heard the assembled guests throw handfuls
of cash on the table for the honour of having seen my face, which I knew to
be the signal for their departure.

During the next four months the time passed pleasantly enough in reading, talking, and embroidery. I had two hand-maidens, presents from my
father-in-law. I was never blamed, save on account of my forgetfulness to
worship the idols, to place offerings in front of the ancestral tablets, or to

pay the customary reverence to my elders. These were grave faults, and un-
accountable in the eyes of the family of which I was now a member. Pride
forbade me to tell my new relative that my parents thought worship offered
to gods of wood and stone was but a mockery, and displeasing to the one
true God, and that they did not approve of divine honours being paid to the
aged members of the clan.

I was not altogether happy. I felt ashamed whenever I prostrated myself
before the idols. I hated bowing down to the basin of ashes called the "God
of the bedstead," and felt a little frightened whenever I invoked its aid lest
the great Jehovah should visit me in His displeasure and cause me to be
childless.

Somehow, too, the conversation in the women's apartments jarred upon
and left me dissatisfied. Why I hardly knew, unless it was because there was
such a sameness about it. Nothing seemed to interest them but the colours
for their embroidered shoes, and the quality of the paint and powder that
they used. Dress, children, and slaves; slaves, children, and dress—they
rung the changes on these three subjects till I was wearied and longed for
my father's little talks. My two sisters-in-law only yawned if I tried to read
them any of the few books in my possession. Of course I said nothing about
the Jesus doctrines, but oh! how I yearned for some new books. The accomplishments of which I had been so proud were fast slipping away from me
because I had no opportunity for displaying them. For lack of other reading, I would now and again read some of the Jesus classics. They were far
more interesting than the "Doctrine of the Mean," or any Confucian classic
known to me. I never dared to read them if any of my male relatives were
near lest trouble should follow the discovery of such books being in my
possession.

My husband never spoke to me during the first year of our married life.
It is considered improper to do so in public, and at night he was generally
overcome by the fumes of opium. All the male members of the family
indulged in the drug, and even my mother-in-law was a victim to its deadly
influence. The first time I saw her lying corpse-like under the spell of its
noxious fumes I shrank in terror, to the great amusement of my hand-
maidens.

When the four months had elapsed after which it is customary for the
bride to return to her father's home, my mother sent a sedan for me, but I
refused to go, for I dreaded meeting the eyes of my parents and letting them
know that I had deliberately turned to the worship of idols without making
one effort to serve Jehovah, whom I knew well to be the only living and
true God.

All the household praised me for the filial spirit I showed towards my
mother-in-law by electing to stay with her. One thing, as the months sped
by, caused me considerable uneasiness. The man whom I so abhorred and
dreaded was constantly about the house. He never saw me as far as I knew,

E*

but I often caught a glimpse of him through the lattice work that separated our apartments from the reception hall. I could not tell why I so feared and hated him; it appeared to my jaundiced view that he brought with him a shadow, a prediction of evil to come.

I dreaded his presence, and always fingered my charm against the evil eye at his approach. He never indulged in the opium habit, but he gambled from morning till night with the members of our household, and at those games of cards managed to win a great deal, I believe.

I was not aware how dark a cloud had crept over my horizon till the second year after my marriage, when my first child, a boy, was born; then it broke in torrents over our unhappy household.

My husband and his brother were petty mandarins, and held some official position in connection with farming the salt revenue. In their passion for gambling, and in consequence of their devotion to the demon that lurks in the petals of the poppy, they had neglected their duties. Not only so, but to obtain the money that they sorely needed, they had ground the people down into the very dust. At last the populace rose as one man to wreak vengeance upon their oppressors. The tumult was quelled, by the oppressed being vanquished, the down-trodden conquered. But the oppressors were not to escape. Some members of the literati complained of the woeful mismanagement that led to so much unnecessary bloodshed; official inquiries were instituted by the Superior Mandarin, and investigations set on foot. To hush the matter up heavy bribes had to be given to dangerous witnesses, and to obtain the funds necessary for this purpose everything that could be converted into money was disposed of. Much of the wedding outfit of my sister-in-law and myself, with our slaves, were sold for this purpose, and to raise a sum large enough to induce the Superior Mandarin to suspend his investigations, the house itself had to be mortgaged.

The third year after I left my father's roof, the once beautiful gardens and the magnificent courts were overgrown with weeds for lack of workers to keep them in order. The house itself had fallen into disrepair. We all lived in one of the sidewings, the remainder, having been spoiled of all its wealth and beauty, was left unfurnished, and desolation and ruin overhung the place. It seemed as though we dwelt under the spell of some terrible curse.

Hand-maidens, silken robes, delicate jewellery all were gone, and my baby, my boy, was gone too.

One day, while preparing the evening meal, I left my little one, my heaven's gift asleep in an adjoining room. My husband played with him awhile, but the hunger for the opium pipe awoke, and heedless of aught else he was soon lost in magical dreams. Under their spell he did not see that he had left my baby, my precious one, too near the opium-ball. When I entered the room, wondering at the stillness, I found my husband a senseless log, my baby dead, lying beside its father, and still clutching the little brown ball in its tiny fist.

When my husband woke, and saw his son, the hope of his family, dead —the one he looked to as the future mainstay of his falling fortune, snatched from his grasp, an unreasoning hatred towards me took possession of him. I felt he wished to be rid of me—that by fair means or foul he would find opportunity to make me quit my home.

Soon he found the chance he sought.

One evening I saw the man I dreaded enter. In a little while, as usual, he suggested a game of cards, to which my husband eagerly assented. They played two games for some low stake, both of which my husband won. This seemed to annoy my enemy, for he threw down the cards, and said he desired to play for something worth the winning; a hundred dollars would do. My husband haughtily replied he had nothing left worth that; all was lost as his guest knew right well. The man made answer in a significant undertone. The import of his reply I did not catch, but it pleased my husband greatly. He rose, took paper, ink, and pen, wrote a few sentences, and signed them with his seal, then passed it to his guest, who read, and seemed to object strenuously to a clause contained therein; but a glance at my husband's face, which wore a determined and rather irritated air, decided him, and he affixed his signature to the document. All this I could see from where I sat, peering through the lattice. Though I could not hear a word, I *knew* as certainly as though I had read the paper, the stake for which they were playing. My husband lost, my enemy won, and the stake for which they had played was—myself.

I tottered towards the bed, and threw myself thereon in an agony of dread. How I lived through that night, I know not.

The next day my husband informed me that he owed the sum of a hundred dollars. I was a childless wife, he had legal right to divorce me, so had sold me to a near neighbour.

One thing he had insisted on, for which I thanked him, and that was the insertion of a clause in the deed of sale to the effect that I was to be recognised as the legal wife of the man who had bought me. I did not need to be told who had purchased me.

The next day a go-between conducted me to my new dwelling. There I became the wife of the man whom my soul abhorred. The life I endured at his hands drove me to seek refuge at the feet of the Crucified'.

Here a fit of stormy sobs shook Chhai So's frame, and her voice ceased, and through the silence, in the darkness of that night, I heard the dropping of her tears.

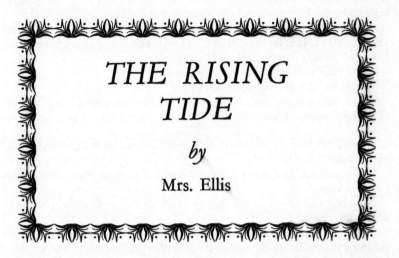

THE RISING TIDE

by

Mrs. Ellis

T HE stranger who visited the residence of Mrs. Falkland, on the western coast of England, could not fail to be struck with the picture of peace and comfort which her home presented. She was a widow; but her solitude was cheered by the society of a son and daughter, whose characters were now sufficiently matured to render them in all respects companions to their mother.

It was on a September evening, that Mrs. Falkland and her daughter in company with an elderly gentleman, sat upon a balcony commanding the view of a wide expanse of ocean and of sky, where the sun was just sinking below the horizon.

The village lay in a narrow dell, through which a little river forced its way along a bed of rocks into the sea; and though the sands on either side the stream looked as safe and solid, they were said to be dangerous to cross in the vicinity of this stream. Still it was a thing of such frequent occurrence for horses and travellers on foot to pass that way, that no one thought much about the danger; and especially as the road along the beach was so much nearer than any other from the village to the neighbouring market town. The chief difficulty arose from some of the rocks jutting so far out into the sea, that all passengers were obliged to pay attention to the state of the tide, or the probability was, that even while plenty of space remained within the bay, they might find themselves hemmed in at these points by the waves having reached the rocks.

The country people, however, knew these dangers well, and strangers were under less temptation to seek the nearest way to the town; so that all the record of accidents on this spot, were a few stories of by-gone days, kept up by the fishermen and old women of the village.

"We who live in the midst of the noise and the tumult of cities," said the visitor, "may almost be allowed to envy you the repose of a life like this—so free from anxiety, so tranquil, and so calm."

"And yet," said Miss Falkland, "we have our cares."

"Impossible! Julia. What can they be?"

"As a friend of my father's, I need scarcely scruple to speak to you of anything connected with the happiness of our family. You know my brother?"

"Yes; and a finer youth I never saw, than George Falkland, when he was last in town."

"He is, indeed, the kindest of sons, the best of brothers. But even he may have his faults."

"The faults of youth—mere thoughtless follies. He will grow wiser with advancing years."

"I wish it may be so. But at present he seems so much fonder of gay company than of his quiet home, that my mother seldom knows a happy day. Not that he is addicted to any particular vice, at least that we know of; but wherever he goes, he has a habit of staying out late at night, which throws my mother into such a state of nervous anxiety, that her health is seriously injured; while he, on the other hand, is so annoyed by what he calls her unreasonable solicitude, that he will not deny himself a single hour of convivial enjoyment for the sake of her peace of mind."

"Youth and age," replied the visitor, "are apt to differ on such points; and perhaps both are incapable of making sufficient allowance for the feelings which operate with the other. Yet, so long as your brother visits only in respectable families, and does not attach himself to any companion of bad principles, I should feel great hope of his ultimate recovery from these errors."

"But there is the root of our anxiety," said Miss Falkland, with increased earnestness. "My brother attaches himself, by a very close intimacy, to a young man of the worst principles—a Ralph Kennedy, the only son of a worthy old man in this village, whose grey hairs may truly be said to be brought down with sorrow to the grave, by this ungrateful son. It is reported that he sits up night after night, working at his desk, in order to keep a situation for his son, which his own infirmities have long since rendered him unequal to. And yet this young man—this Ralph Kennedy, is so idle and unsteady, as to be wholly unfit to succeed his poor father in a place of trust."

Miss Falkland prepared to lead her visitor into the house; when, rising from his seat, he observed, for the first time, that a quiet-looking young girl apparently about eighteen, and dressed in white, had been their companion on the balcony; and with a sort of instinctive curiosity, he directed an inquiring look to Miss Falkland, which seemed to say, "Whom have we here?"

"It is only my cousin, Grace Dalton," said Miss Falkland, understanding him perfectly.

Seeing the girl did not attempt to rise, the old gentleman still lingered. "Won't you catch cold, my dear?" said he, with that familiar, but well-meant kindness with which old gentlemen are apt to address those who are between girls and women.

Grace Dalton rose, and thanked him respectfully, but immediately resumed her seat; and the door was closed upon the lighted room, and she was left to her evening meditations, and forgotten. Indeed it was very easy to forget Grace Dalton. She was an orphan, too, and very poor; but surely it is not possible, in such a kind world as ours professes to be, that these two facts should constitute any reason why persons are more easily forgotten. Oh no! It was because Grace Dalton was diminutive in her person, simple in her dress, timid, gentle, unobtrusive, and not remarkably pretty, that she was so often, and so easily forgotten; and though she was a poor relation, and always came last into the room, and looked so humble, that she might have almost claimed pity from a stranger, it frequently fell to her lot to find no room left for her at table.

Yet for all this, the humble orphan had her own little world of interest, in which she lived, perhaps, a life of deeper feeling, because it was so seldom shared with others. What was the reason why she sat out so late this evening, no one asked, nor would they, perhaps, have felt more curious, had they seen the tears that were fast falling from her eyes, as she bent over the balcony, with her forehead resting on her arm. Perhaps it was something in the conversation which had pained her, for she was strongly attached to her cousin George, and often ventured to take his part, even when he was most in fault. She could not be made to see the desperate nature of Ralph Kennedy's principles; and thus she fell a little into disgrace, both with the mother, and the daughter.

Meanwhile, seated around a social board, a little company of choice spirits, with George Falkland at their head, laughed away the last hours of daylight, and hailed the lamps that seemed to dance before them as bright harbingers of a happier and more joyous night.

George Falkland had that day left his mother's house, in company with his friend, Ralph Kennedy, who was in great request at all the convivial meetings in the neighbourhood since his unrivalled good spirits made him a welcome guest wherever he went. It is true, he seldom went away from these meetings in a state very creditable to himself—it is true, he made his own gratification the sole object for which he lived—it is true, he left an aged father to toil for his support, because he had too much of what is called spirit to devote himself to any kind of regular pursuit. Yet, notwithstanding all this, he managed to keep what is considered good society; and to maintain for himself the character of being a "good fellow"—"his own enemy," it was granted; but still he was accounted the enemy of no one else and the best companion in the world.

On the night described, they had stayed late, and the moon had risen high before either of them thought of returning home. At last, when Kennedy had sung his best song, Falkland rose from the table; for no one cared after that to hear an inferior voice.

"Come, come," said Falkland, laying his hand upon the shoulder of his friend, "it will take us a full hour to ride home, and we had better have the benefit of the moon over the sands; for I fancy neither you nor I see so steadily as we did this morning."

"Sands!" exclaimed half-a-dozen voices at once. "You won't go by the sands to-night."

"Won't I, though?" said Kennedy, rising, and immediately joining his friend; while both supported the dispute, until it ended in a bet, which appeared to render the enterprise of going by the sands, altogether much more attractive.

The two friends then mounted their horses, and set off merrily, taking the road which led immediately down to the beach. It was a beautiful night. A breeze had sprung up from the sea, and a few distant dark clouds came floating along with it towards the moon; but still she rode high in the heavens, and her light was almost like that of day.

Many were the lively jests with which the travellers amused themselves by the way; for Kennedy, though scarcely able to keep his balance on his horse, had often, when in that situation, a spirit of drollery about him, more amusing than in his sober moments, to those who cared not from what source it came. All his odd movements, all the strange accidents which happened to him under such circumstances, he could turn to jest; and the laughter and merriment with which they now pursued their way towards the sands startled from behind the shadow of a rock an old fisherman, who was watching his nets.

They had passed him by with a slight good-night, when Falkland wheeled round his horse, and asked him how long it would be before the tide would be up, and if they had time enough to reach the second headland which jutted out into the sands.

"Time enough," said the old man, "if your horses are good. The tide won't be up to the crags yonder, for half an hour yet." And he pointed to a heap of black rock, at some distance out to sea.

The travellers now set spurs to their horses, not so much from any fear of the tide, as from the mere hilarity of their own spirits, which could not be satisfied with any sober pace. Capable, however, as Kennedy had been of keeping his seat under more favourable circumstances, he fell from his horse the moment it struck into a gallop; and whether from the violence of the fall, or the novel position in which he found himself, he became so bewildered and confused, as to be long before he could regain his seat. Even then he rode with his head sometimes bent over the neck of the horse, and sometimes thrown back, while the loss of his hat, and other accidents, occasioned both laughter and delay.

Then—was it the moonlight that lay so white before them on the sand? No: it was the tide running up in long sheets of hissing foam, each one stealing farther than the last.

"Set spurs to your horse," cried Falkland, "and ride, Kennedy, ride, for your life!"

He did so, and down he fell again upon the sand; and the foam curled up and around him, and then retreated, while he mounted again to make another fruitless attempt at greater speed.

"We shall escape yet," said Falkland. "We are just upon the crags, and when these are passed, we have but the river, and all will be over."

It was in vain, however, that Falkland rode close beside his friend, and stretched out his arm to keep him steady. He appeared to have become more and more confused with each repeated fall, while the unequal nature of the ground rendered it impossible for their horses to find safe footing, or to keep pace with each other. Falkland himself was but just able to think, and to wish that they had taken the route above the cliffs. He even stopped, and looked for a moment towards the land, to see if there was no place where it was possible to ascend, but in vain; and the next moment they plunged into the stony bed of the stream, and found themselves in deep water.

Kennedy had now fallen forward on his horse. The animal grew terrified, and, rushing desperately amongst the rocks and the foaming current, it shook itself loose from its rider, and then plunged forward, and left him to struggle for his life.

Falkland had now but one object—to place the wretched man behind him, and trust to his own animal for sustaining both. For this purpose he stretched out his arm, and caught the hand of his friend, at the moment when he was rolling down the stream. He even succeeded so far as to lift him upon his horse, but his strength was unequal to keep him there. He had become utterly helpless, and it now seemed as if, in attempting to save him, both must perish. Still, however, Falkland resumed the attempt. He even succeeded again, and was only defeated by Kennedy falling this time with his hand clenching the coat of his friend, with a wild and desperate hold, which it was impossible to shake off.

"My mother!" cried Falkland, as if the fierce waves could hear him. "My poor mother! She will never survive this night, if I am lost. It is yet in my power to save her from a broken heart."

With that he tore off the fragment of his dress, which that doomed and drowning man still held by, and with one plunge of his horse, escaped out of the bed of the swollen torrent.

The window of Mrs. Falkland's chamber looked upon the garden, that of Grace Dalton towards the yard, where it was impossible that a horse should enter, without her hearing it. What, then, was her surprise to hear the well-known signal of her cousin, without any previous notice of his coming! With a stealthy step, she trod as usual past the door of her aunt's chamber, and descended to the hall, where, drawing aside the bolt of the outer door, she stood expecting that her cousin would enter.

"I want to speak with you, Grace," said he in a voice so little like his own, that she started back. "Come away from the door, and be very, very quiet, while I tell you a sad story."

"Go on," said Grace, trembling all over. "I am quiet. Has anything happened?"

"Come out farther still," said her cousin; "and now be sure you do not make the least noise." He then whispered close to her ear, "Kennedy is lost!"

A shriek so loud that it seemed to ring through the vault of heaven, was the answer of poor Grace.

"There, now!" said he, grasping her arm, and speaking more angrily to her than he had ever done before. "You have done the very thing against which I warned you. I would rather have given you a thousand pounds than you should have uttered that scream."

Lights were now glancing in all the windows of the cottage, and before many minutes had passed, Falkland was compelled to describe to the whole assembled household, every particular of the sad catastrophe. It was not difficult to read in his haggard countenance the terrible conflict he had sustained; and while one brought him cordials, and another chafed his cold hands, Grace Dalton, who had wont to be the first to render all these offices of kindness, was the only one to stand aloof, as if altogether stupefied by what had passed.

"Why do you stand there, child?" said Mrs. Falkland in her anxiety for her son. "Go up stairs and bring dry clothes for your cousin."

The poor girl went up stairs as she had been told, but what it was to fetch, she could not by any possibility remember. Her delay was the cause of much chiding, which seemed to produce no effect upon her senses. As regarded all present things, they were quite gone, until Falkland called her to him, and whispered to her with a shudder on his lips, "Take that coat, Grace, and hide it, so that I may never see it more. The part that is torn away is where he held me with his dying grasp."

Grace Dalton took the coat as she had been requested, and no one knew how she disposed of it, for it was never seen again.

"And now," said Falkland, when his strength had been in some measure restored. "I have a hard duty to perform. I must go to old Kennedy, and tell him what has happened."

With this intention, he rose up, and even went as far as the door, when turning back again, he sank down into a chair, exclaiming, "I cannot meet that old man! My heart fails me when I think that Ralph was the only relation he had in the world—the only being he ever seemed to love. Will none of you go with me?"

"I will go with you," said Grace.

"You, child!" was the general exclamation. But, finding that, although little could be hoped from her assistance, she was in reality more willing than any of the party, it was at last agreed that she should accompany her cousin.

"Come then," said Falkland. "For once I will lean on your arm, instead of you on mine; and, if you like, Grace, I will tell you as we go, all the particulars of this melancholy story. Would you like to hear it?"

"Yes; only I am afraid I shall not be able to repeat it."

"Nonsense! You should nerve yourself to these duties. If it is difficult to you, think what it must be to me, who have still his death-grasp on my person; his last moan in my ear; his——What ails you, Grace? You are cold, child. The morning air is too sharp for you. Here, take this shawl, for they have given me more than I can bear; and you have no bonnet. What a foolish girl you are!"

Grace made no reply: but her teeth absolutely chattered; while the ghastliness of her countenance gave her cousin fresh cause to think that the grey dawn of morning, now spreading over earth and sea, was too cold in its autumnal chill for the delicate frame of his companion, and he drew her closer to his side, and held her hand in his, with a brotherly tenderness for her bodily comfort, which he had been less ready to feel for that of her mind.

"There," said Falkland, for he had already commenced his story, "it was in the direction of that stunted tree, half-way between the first point and the river, that Kennedy first fell from his horse. Look, Grace."

"I am looking," said Grace. "At least, I will look if I can, but the wind blows so fiercely." And she shaded her eyes with her hand, while her cousin went on with his story.

Long before he had concluded the melancholy detail, they found themselves before the humble home of Kennedy's father.

It was a second-rate sort of house; and the one domestic who waited upon the old man, was yet too soundly asleep to hear their summons, for they knocked in a trembling and hesitating manner. At last one bolt was drawn away, and then another, and then the door was opened by the old man himself, who stood before them with an inquiring gaze, while he held in one hand a lighted candle, which had burned down into the socket.

Grace Dalton looked at her cousin. His lips moved—his voice faltered—he could not utter an articulate sound.

"Perhaps you will allow us to come in," said Grace; "we have come to speak with you on very important business."

"Business?" repeated the old man, as well he might, at that hour of the morning, and with such guests. They were both silent; while the quivering fingers of Grace Dalton played amongst her hair, and her open lips were pale as ashes. At last she spoke.

"I think, Sir, you are aware where your son spent last evening."

"I know little of where he spends his evenings," replied the father, "and it has become a matter of small importance to me."

His apparent coldness, while it shocked the feelings of Grace Dalton, gave her nerve to proceed, and she related the whole account of the fatal catastrophe, exactly as it had been told to her, only pausing occasionally to ascertain whether she ought or ought not to proceed.

"Go on," said old Kennedy, every time she stopped, in a deep-toned and sepulchral voice; but he never once looked up, nor changed his attitude, nor unclasped his hands, that were closely folded together, with his lips pressed upon them, and his elbows supported by the arms of his chair.

"Go on," he repeated, until the whole had been told; when he simply asked—"And the body?"

"I have stationed six fishermen from the village," said Falkland, "along the bay, and three beyond the crags; but they say it is impossible it should be found before the tide goes down. I shall then|be on the beach myself, and see that nothing is neglected. In the meantime, if you would like Grace Dalton to remain with you, she will be most happy to render you any assistance in her power."

"Who is Grace Dalton?"

"The young person who has accompanied me."

"I would much rather be alone; and, perhaps, the sooner you both leave me, the better."

There was no forcing their presence upon him after this remark; and the two cousins arose, and left the room. They had not left the outer door, however, before their progress was arrested by the sound of deep groans from within. They paused; for it was not easy to leave an aged man, under such circumstances, alone. They paused; for pity, as well as horror, seemed to chain them to the spot; and now they discovered that those strange and awful sounds were the strong prayer of mortal agony—that prayer which is wrung out from the human soul by its necessity, not by its inclination or its hope.

"He did love him, then!" exclaimed Grace Dalton; clasping her hands together; "He did love him as a father ought to love a son! May blessings fall upon the head of that old man!"

"Why, Grace," said Falkland, as he led his cousin away from the house of mourning, lest by again yielding to her own emotion, she should be the cause of interruption or alarm to others—"How is this? You are over-whelmed with gratitude, because a stern old man is melted into common feeling by the death of his son. For my part, I should have felt more pity for him had he received the first intelligence more like a father, and a christian man."

"We cannot all feel alike," said Grace, "nor make the same display of sorrow when we do feel it. I confess, like you, I was shocked at the seeming apathy with which our intelligence was at first received. But those fearful groans, George, they surely tell of more than common grief."

All the distance from the village to the beach, was now scattered with groups of people, who, some of them from mere curiosity, and some from feelings of deeper interest, had left their homes, to hear if there were any tidings of the body, or to learn if anything more remained to be told than the melancholy story which had already circulated from house to house with the usual number of variations and additions.

Falkland and his cousin approached the scene of interest from one point; his mother and sister, with their household attendants, from another. Way was respectfully made for all, and they stood together for some time without uttering a word, except to ask and tell in what manner old Kennedy had borne the intelligence of his loss. All looked towards the sea; and Grace Dalton, though she trembled violently, dashed away her hair from her eyes, and looked more intently than any of the watchers there.

The next moment she was shooting like an arrow across the sands, straight on to a crag of black rock, which was just beginning to stand out above the shallow waves, and beside which some of the fishermen were now seen to be gathering themselves into a group.

"What can be the matter with Grace?" said Mrs. Falkland, observing the strange movements of her niece. "She seems to have quite lost her sense with this melancholy affair. You were wrong in taking her with you, George. She has no spirits for such scenes as these."

"You are mistaken in Grace, I assure you," said Falkland. "She was of the greatest possible use to me this morning, and behaved like a heroine. But see! They have found him at last. I am sure that is the body."

It was true. The wretched man had not been washed by the waves to any great distance from the spot where he perished, probably owing to his dress having become entangled amongst the rocks. There he lay, stretched out upon the sand, one of his cold hands still clenching, with an iron grasp, the shred of Falkland's coat, which he had torn off when they separated for the last time.

Nothing now remained to be done; and, while all stood around, uttering their different exclamations of regret, Grace Dalton remained on her knees beside him, stooping down with her head so low, that she could have heard the faintest breath had it passed his lips; though her hair fell down and shaded her face, so that none could see in what manner she was holding her strange communion with the dead.

Bitterly would Mrs. Falkland have reproached her niece, had she known why, amongst that crowd of strangers, she had stood the first—why she had approached the nearest to that awful spectacle—why she had been the only one to endeavour to unclench that cold hand—why she alone had hoped against hope, that there might still be life. Happily for poor Grace, the strangeness of her conduct met with no farther censure than its absence of decorum deserved, and this was even pardoned in consideration of the childish weakness with which she was so often charged; for, like most persons in her situation, she had often to bear the blame of a fault, and its direct opposite, at the same time.

No extenuation, however, ought to be offered for the chief fault of which Grace Dalton was guilty—that of loving a dissipated and unprincipled man. She felt that she deserved no pity, and therefore she asked for none. She had her punishment within herself; and the perpetual sense of condemnation which she bore about with her, made her still more meek, and humble, and submissive under reproof, than she would otherwise have been. Nor did she regard the errors of Ralph Kennedy with more toleration, in her own mind, than the rest of the world evinced towards them. In proportion to the high estimate of what she believed to be his virtues, was her fear, her sorrow, her hatred of his vices. These, however, she never spoke of, except to himself. There were others to do that, she thought; and when so many voices were against him, there was the less need of her's.

Thus she was often thought to look with too lenient an eye, both upon his conduct, and that of her cousin George. The fact was, she loved her cousin because she believed that he loved Kennedy; and, had those who charged her with indifference to their vices, only followed her to the little chamber which she occupied alone—had they watched her there, when every other member of the household was wrapped in sleep, they might have seen such tears, and heard such prayers, as would have convinced them that vice in any form, but particularly in those she loved, was no matter of indifference to her.

But to return to our story. The father of Ralph Kennedy saw, from the point of land on which he stood, that three or four fishermen were gathered together on one particular part of the sand, and he knew from the number of persons who hastened towards the spot, that they had found the body of his lost son. It was not in his nature to connect himself with a crowd, especially on such an occasion. He therefore returned, silently and alone, to his own dwelling, where he gave the necessary directions to his only domestic, and then shut the door of his chamber, and listened for the footsteps of those who should bring home the dead. They were long in coming; and the servant had time to make ready a little parlour, considered more particularly as her master's own apartment, for it was here he used to keep his books, here he used to sit through the midnight hours, waiting and watching for his son's return, it having been his custom never to allow any other person to be disturbed by his late hours.

Notwithstanding the dreadful calamity which had so recently taken place, it did not so nearly touch the family of Mrs. Falkland, but that all was peace that day within her dwelling. Falkland, wearied out with excitement, had returned to rest; and by the time their evening meal was prepared, he was able to join his mother and sister once more around the social board. He and his mother sat again on the rose-covered balcony, their hands clasped together in that expressive silence, which conveys more meaning to the heart than the most eloquent words. His sister, too, was there, and Grace Dalton; and all looked towards the sea except Grace, who seemed to be teaching the clematis where it ought to climb, though her small hands trembled so that she could scarcely guide its fragile twigs.

The subject of their separate thoughts was the same—the awful night that was past; when, another wave of that angry flood, another cloud over that clear moon, a moment less of time, and that vigorous form, so rich in all the gifts of nature, so animate with life, and adorned with youthful beauty, might have been stretched upon the silent bier in a house of mourning and desolation.

"I cannot tell," said Falkland, as if thinking aloud, "how it was that that poor fellow so entirely lost his presence of mind. He had no more power to help himself, than a child would have had under such circumstances. And yet to see the mirth of his merry face not half an hour before, when we rode down to the beach, and the cliffs echoed with our laughter. When I think of this, and the last look of agony I caught as he fell back in the water, his clenched hand still holding that shred of my dress—Oh, mother! it makes me wish to hide myself in the earth, or in some place where this horrible vision never could pursue me."

"He was so unprepared, too," said Mrs. Falkland, "and such a character!"

"There are many persons," said Grace, "who die in their own chambers, and with all the warning of long illness, as unprepared as he was."

"Ah, Grace," said Julia Falkland, "will you never see these things as you ought to see them?"

"When young women like you," observed the mother, "who have been virtuously brought up—when such make excuses for the vices of men, what can we expect?"

"Shall I bring your shawl, dear aunt?" asked Grace. "The evening air grows cold."

"Perhaps we had better all retire," said Mrs. Falkland.

"No, no," said George, detaining both his mother and his sister. "And you, too, my poor little Grace. You shall no longer stand shivering there. Come sit down near to Julia; for I want you all to witness this night, that I discharge my conscience of a load, so far as it can be discharged by an act which refers merely to the future. Would to heaven it could expiate the past.

"I now want you all to hear me, and to bear witness to my vow, while I look to yon dark sea with the same clear moon—the same blue skies above me—I want you all to bear witness to my vow, when I promise, that, as God will give me strength, from this time henceforward, I never more will grieve my poor mother's heart as I have done—I never will stain my own character, nor suffer the moral degradation which man must suffer under the mastery of wine, and in the fellowship of those whose only enjoyment is the excitement for the moment, purchased by the sacrifice of domestic peace. Now, this is my vow. My mother, my Julia, my poor Grace, you must all help me to keep it."

A solemn silence followed. The mother's hands were for a moment clasped together in the attitude of thanks giving, until her feelings burst all bounds, and she actually sobbed aloud. Julia leaned her head upon her brother's shoulder, while her tears fell thick and fast upon his bosom. Grace alone was silent, and wept not like the rest.

They were a happy little party who sat beside Mrs. Falkland's cheerful fire that evening, for they were happy in that peaceful solemn feeling, which, beyond all others, deserves the name of happiness. They were happy in knowing that evil was renounced, and good, at least, intended—happy in confidence restored, in affection valued, in trust held sacred, and in peace regained. If Grace Dalton looked less cheerful than the rest, it was only that she had a different way of showing her satisfaction; for none were more thankful than she was for the resolution her cousin had made. Nor was he unconscious of her meaning, when she held his hand at parting for the night, and looked up into his face, and bid him such a kind good-night, as spoke the true language of affectionate regard.

The following morning Grace Dalton was able to put in practice a plan she had formed for visiting the father of the deceased, without appearing designedly to obtrude herself upon his notice; and in this she obtained the full approbation of her aunt, who was extremely anxious to adopt some mode of expressing her sympathy with the bereaved parent. He was, however, so little known to any one, so reserved and inaccessible in his own character, that this was an object of no easy attainment; and had not Grace been a more than commonly willing messenger, and so meek, besides, as not to shrink from the probability of meeting with a repulse, Mrs. Falkland's intended kindness would never have been carried into effect.

There were many considerations now to be entered into with regard to the funeral, in which female aid was not altogether out of place; and Grace began, by consulting with the servant, and occasionally sending messages to the master, which he answered promptly, and without evincing anything like displeasure, but rather as if relieved from a burden, by others having taken this affair upon themselves. Grace had imagined it would be so, for she possessed that kind of intuitive insight into character, which a naturally strong power of sympathy affords, and which is, perhaps, more serviceable, in the common events of life, than talents of a higher and more distinguished order.

Thus, before the day of the funeral arrived, Grace Dalton had become a sort of authorized assistant in the melancholy preparations; and retiring and modest as was her general bearing, her aunt and cousins were surprised to find the tact and skill with which she contrived to manage these affairs, without appearing to manage them at all. Mrs. Falkland and her daughter had both made the same experiment, and had both failed. They were too much of fine ladies to suit the taste of such a man as Kennedy; and, besides, they were now too happy to sympathize with him in reality, though they spoke fluently and well in the language of condolence. Grace, on the contrary, seldom uttered an expression which could lead the reserved and solitary to think that he himself was the subject of her observations. He only noticed that she took a part in the preparations for the funeral; and he thought it was quite right for those who had a taste for such things, to take them into their own hands.

And now the morning of that day had come, and all things were in readiness; and Grace Dalton felt that her melancholy task was done; for what right had she to take part in the mourning? what right had she even to be seen to weep? for what were the Kennedy's to her?

While she was occupied, while she trod with gentle step about the house, and felt that she had an errand or duty there, she was comparatively happy. She could even pass the door of that silent room, though she had done this as seldom as possible; but now that all was ready, that the grave claimed its own, and the sacred charge must be resigned, she felt a strange sinking of the soul, a sense of forlornness in her unpitied grief, under which her spirit failed; and having occasion to follow the servant into the room where the father sat alone beside the closed coffin, she lingered there a moment, to see if she might not be permitted, though silently, to mingle her sorrow with his.

"Is all ready, child?" said the old man, in a voice at once so gentle and subdued, that Grace was encouraged to approach nearer; and after answering his questions, she bent her head upon the coffin, and gave way to her tears.

It was the hour of final separation. Both felt it to be so; and the old man sat at the head of the coffin, his hands clasped together, as if their firmly knit grasp gave him strength to bear his affliction; while the gentler form of the orphan girl was bowed as if with mortal anguish. And there she wept as if her heart was breaking; and the father was too deeply wrapped in thought to ask what right she had to grieve. Sad and solemn were the moments which the two mourners thus spent together. They were too soon interrupted; and old Kennedy rose from his chair to meet the strangers who came to perform their appointed office. He rose from his chair, and motioned for them to proceed with their duty; but his knees shook beneath him, and he dashed his hand across his brow as if to clear his vision, or to sweep away some image that still lingered before his sight. He soon recovered himself, however, and with no arm to lean upon, no near relative to wear so much as the outward garb of woe, he walked after the coffin to the place of burial, and stood with his head uncovered during the solemn service beside the last home of his only child.

The next day, however, Grace Dalton found, or made, an excuse for calling at the house; and not having been able to accomplish this before the evening, she was agreeably surprised to find that her appearance had not only been expected, but wished for.

"I thought you long in coming," said old Kennedy.

Simple as were these few words, they had a powerful effect upon the orphan girl, who felt that a way was now opened for the kindness she had found it so difficult to express.

The next morning she was the bearer of a present from her aunt; and so she went on, stealing upon the heart of the solitary, until he began to converse with her perhaps more freely than he had done with any one for many years of life. Grace had observed, that for some time he had been busily arranging his books and papers; she had observed also, that he was always at home; and she was not surprised to learn that he had resigned the situation, which, but for the sake of his son, he would never have held so long.

"My wants will now be so few," said he, "that it would ill repay me to be spending the little time that is left me on this side the grave, in toiling for myself."

Yet how to pass the time when no longer stimulated to exertion, was to him a far greater difficulty than he had apprehended; and, like many others similarly circumstanced, the lengthened hours of his aimless existence were filled with murmuring and discontent. Even common kindness, from whatever hand it came, with the exception of that of Grace Dalton, was scarcely received with gratitude.

"I cannot tell," said he to Grace one day, "why Mrs. Falkland thinks I have more relish for dainties since the death of my son, than I had before. She never sent me these delicacies when he was living, and might have shared them with me."

"It is the only means she has of showing you her kind feeling," observed Grace.

"And why does she wish to show it? Is it not enough to feel kindly, without telling others that you do so?"

"But you know, dear sir, that sympathy is nothing, if locked within one's own bosom."

"Don't talk to me of sympathy. I am weary of the word."

It was not always, however, that Kennedy spoke thus to Grace. He was sometimes harsh even to her, for it was his nature to be so; and those who speak of great afflictions, or even of great events of any kind, wholly changing the tone and bias of natural feeling, know little of that nature of which they speak. There is but one change from which we have a right to anticipate any radical or lasting result, and even that leaves the same tone and bias to be striven against so long as life remains.

Still it was soothing and pleasant to that solitary and friendless man to have the orphan girl so near him, though, why she came so often, and lingered so long about him, he was wholly at a loss to imagine. She herself scarcely knew the nature of her own feelings. That she loved him for his own sake, was scarcely to be supposed; and yet she did love him with a strange kind of tenderness, which made her long to call him father; and one day, when they sat together in the sunshine at his door, and his manner was more than usually cordial, she looked up into his face, and ventured to ask him if she might call him father. But a cloud immediately settled upon his features, and he answered in words which poor Grace was never able to forget.

"No, no, child. You are going too far now. That I like you to come here, I will not deny; and that you sometimes while away the long hours, and make my life less weary, I can say with truth; but that any other voice than *his* should call me father, is a thing that cannot be. No, no. When you have known what I have known, you will understand how nature has her broken cords, which it would be a poor mockery to pretend to tie again. No, no. I have been a parent, and I have heard the cherub-voice of infancy lisping the name of father. As time rolled on, I have listened to the same sound, until it swelled into more meaning, and sunk into my soul, filling all its vacant chambers with the melody of love. Yes, morning after morning, I have been aroused from slumber, when the early birds had scarce begun their song, by the fond and playful touch of my own, my only child. And now these things come back to me in my desolate old age, and I cannot— no, I must not let you call me father."

"Forgive me," said Grace, with a voice that could scarcely articulate, "forgive me. I am an orphan. I never knew what it was to use the name of father, or of mother."

"Poor child!" said Kennedy; and he took her hand, and drew her so near him, that she ventured for the first time to lean her head upon his shoulder, and weep.

In the mean-time, all was peace and joy in the habitation of Mrs. Falkland. It was frequently observed of the good lady herself, that her youth had returned with all its freshness and vigour; for her cheek now bloomed with health, and her step was light and active, as in by-gone days. It was impossible for her son not to notice this change, or to deem it otherwise than cheaply purchased by the sacrifice he had made. Not that he ever estimated very highly the mere personal gratifications he had now given up; the sacrifice was, in the position he had held amongst a certain class of society, who now looked upon him as a sort of traitor to the pledge of good-fellowship which his previous conduct had implied. Nothing was said to him on the subject, for there was a dignity and determination about George Falkland, which effectually repelled familiarity, whenever it was his wish to do so; but his presence became evidently an intrusion amongst his former friends, diffusing over every countenance a silent gloom, like that which would naturally be produced by the entrance of a suspected person into a secret council. He was, in short, considered as a sort of spy upon their action, and such being the general feeling towards him, it became less difficult to withdraw himself entirely from their society.

Still there were some who entertained for George Falkland more than the common regard of mere acquaintanceship, and who felt a sincere regret to lose from their social circle a companion whose position in society, whose talents, and gentlemanly manners, alike combined to render him a valuable acquisition to whatever class he might attach himself.

With these friends it was a real difficulty to Falkland to maintain the ground he had so recently, and, in their opinion, so unreasonably taken.

"Why should you think so much," they used to say, "of that luckless Kennedy? He was a low fellow, after all, and if he was drowned by the rising of the tide, it has only made us all the wiser, by teaching us not to ride home by the beach when we have been out to dine."

To these remarks George Falkland would sometimes reply with a visible shudder; for, as he told his cousin Grace, he never afterwards could rise from the dinner-table without realizing again the grasp of that clenched hand, when the last hold of the drowning man was upon him.

There was one family in particular, with whom George Falkland always found it difficult to adhere strictly to the resolution he had formed; and on one memorable day, he had just begun to think, that as more than a year had passed since the death of poor Kennedy, he might surely satisfy his friends by remaining with them at least an hour beyond his usual time. He had even filled his glass again, on the strength of this determination, when his better feelings gained the mastery, and he rose suddenly from the table, and wished the party good-night.

It was a fine moonlight evening in October, when he rode slowly along his lonely way, too happy to accelerate his speed, in the thought that he had escaped, though narrowly, from breaking his solemn vow. Wrapped in these reflections, and the many thoughts to which they gave rise, he was suddenly startled by the sound of a carriage advancing with unusual rapidity towards him; and, drawing up his horse to listen, he heard the clatter of horses' hoofs at full gallop. His next impulse was to alight, and it was well that he did so, for in a few seconds the carriage was before him, and it was only by the steadiness of his eye and hand, that he was enabled to lay hold of the rein of the affrighted animal, and arrest its furious course.

"My father!" cried a feeble voice at that instant, and Falkland then saw for the first time the figure of a female in the carriage, who implored him with all the strength she retained, to assist her to go back in search of her father. With difficulty, however, could she make herself understood; and such was the agitation under which she laboured, that her simple story was long in being told. It was no other than this, that her father having got out of the carriage to adjust the rein, while thus engaged, the horse had suddenly started off, and, as she believed, had dragged the carriage over him;

and with astonishing presence of mind, she had remained perfectly quiet, while the horse was going at its utmost speed. Had Falkland been a few minutes later, a sudden turn in the road, with a steep descent on one side, would probably have terminated her existence; while, had his eye been less steady, or his hand less firm he might never have been able to stop the terrified animal, and thus to rescue from an awful death, the gentle being who now leaned upon his arm, and urged him to go faster, and faster still, though her own strength was scarcely able to support her to the spot where she believed her father to be laid.

What, then, was her astonishment, to see his well-known figure hastening towards her, evidently in the possession of his accustomed health and strength. The consequence was a very natural one. Her reason, which had withstood the shock of terror and distress, gave way under that of unexpected joy, and the daughter sank senseless into the arms of her parent.

The following morning found both the strangers welcome visitors beneath the roof of Mrs. Falkland. Miss Cameron, for that was the young lady's name, was sufficiently recovered to know that her father was safe, and by degrees the whole came back to her recollection, and she talked and smiled with the rest of the family, at the providential meeting between her and George Falkland, who did not fail to recall, in his own mind, the temptation he had been under to remain an hour longer with his friends, by which means he would not only have broken a promise now kept inviolate for more than twelve months, but would have lost the opportunity of saving the precious life of a being, who struck his youthful fancy as the loveliest he had ever beheld.

Mr. and Miss Cameron were well known in the neighbourhood, but it so happened that they never had been introduced to the Falklands before. Their meeting now was of a kind to make their acquaintance more intimate than years of common visiting could have rendered it; and the first awakening of kind interest to which an awful and alarming event had given rise, was followed by a frequency of intercourse, in which George Falkland considered himself richly rewarded for the few instances of self-denial in which his natural inclination had been crossed; but most of all, for that particular instance which had been the means of introducing him to the society of Miss Cameron.

But why prolong a story of love, which all understand, though few know how to speak of? Suffice it, that not twelve months after this event, the bells of the village church were ringing merrily one fine evening in July, and Mrs. Falkland and her family were all in readiness to welcome home the heir of her house and name, with his beautiful bride, once Miss Cameron, after their marriage tour. And not the inmates of his mother's establishment only, were expected to rejoice, for there were tables spread upon the lawn, and rustic seats made ready, and Grace Dalton was passing from one to another, placing the crowning dish of plenty on the board, and arranging the accommodation of all, even the poorest and the meanest of her neighbours from the village.

At last the sound of carriages was heard. The gates were thrown open, and the happy travellers looked out, and saw what a welcome awaited them. Nor were they too fastidious to despise the rural minstrelsy of that humble place. A band of village musicians struck up a lively air. A troop of children then came hand in hand, after them their parents, followed by the young men and maidens of the village, and took their places at the tables under the spreading trees, with the green turf for their carpet, and the cloudless skies for their canopy.

Those who argue that there is no social enjoyment without strong stimulus, might have been defeated in their theory that night. Whether it was the want of taste in the inhabitants of that obscure village, or their folly in being so easily contented, we will not pretend to say; but, certainly, there was no lack of harmless mirth, of happy faces, of laughter and good fellowship, that night.

There was no longer any need for Grace to exercise her ingenuity in entertaining the company, or setting them at ease. She was now liberated from all duties of that description, and, turning into a shady walk, she indulged herself with the luxury of believing she was alone. What then was her surprise, to see the figure of old Kennedy leaning upon his staff!

With the privilege of a child, to which he appeared to consider her entitled, she went and stood still beside him; for she knew his temperament too well to break upon his silent moods by addressing him abruptly.

"They seem very happy," said the old man. "I told you that I would not come, for I thought I could not bear it. But as I sat alone in the twilight, it rushed into my mind that I would just come and see how it might have been with *him*—if—if—" and he dashed a tear from his eye, while his words seemed to choke him in the utterance.

"Ay, there they are," said he, after a long pause. "There is the bridal party come out. See how graciously they go from one table to another; and, hark! what is that which George Falkland is telling them?"

They both listened; and as the gay and happy party approached nearer, they could distinctly hear George Falkland bid them all welcome, and receive their good wishes in return.

"I have treated you with the usual kind of hospitality," said he. "I have given you nothing to excite your mirth, but I hope you have not been the less happy. I cannot for my own part forget, and I am sure you would not wish me to forget to-night, that had I, on one occasion, staid one hour later at table, or even taken one glass more, I should not only never have known the happiness of calling this lady my wife, but in all human probability she would never have seen the light of another day."

"Yes, child," said Kennedy again, as if the train of his thoughts had scarcely been interrupted, "such might have been *his* situation. And you,

Grace Dalton, might have been leaning on his arm like yon happy bride. But what have I said, my child? and why do you weep as you did on the day of the funeral?"

"Because I loved your son."

"You loved him!"

"Yes. And he loved me—at least, he told me so."

"Then come to my bosom," said the old man, opening his arms, "and you shall be my child indeed, and I will be your father. Now, now I understand you. Yes, lean on this withered bosom; there is warmth in it yet. Sweet as an angel's visits have been thine to me; but from this hour let us never part again."

And it was so, that Grace became an inmate in the humble abode of the old man, and dwelt with him until his dying day; and sweet and salutary was the influence her mild and chastened spirit exerted over him. The arguments of a more powerful reason, his morbid mind would, in all probability, have repelled; but the persevering solicitude of a meek and quiet spirit, few can resist.

The little property which Kennedy had possessed, he bequeathed to Grace Dalton at his death. When that event took place, she put on mourning as if she had been his child; and perhaps few parents are followed to the grave with sorrow more sincere, than was her's for her adopted father.

*He knelt down and placed his
hand upon the child's heart.*

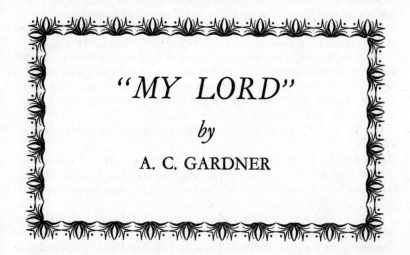

"MY LORD"

by

A. C. GARDNER

CHAPTER I

"Y lord, come here this minute. Oh, Mr. Parker, do you call
him; he won't mind me a bit;" then in a rapid descent from
threatening to coaxing. "Now, there's a dear little gentleman,
come out of that nasty, dirty water, getting your lovely new clothes in such
a mess too—do, there's a dear."

"Shan't," was the offender's sole response.

"Did you *ever* see such a boy?" Jane exclaimed despairingly. "It's one
person's work to see as he doesn't kill himself, let alone keep him clean. My
lord, if you don't be good, I'll run straight in and tell your——" But here
the girl stopped suddenly. There was now no "papa" to be told of his boy's
naughtiness, no "papa" to be held up as a threat or a warning; of not more
than three hours ago all that was mortal of the late Lord Donne had been
deposited with great pomp and ceremony in the family vault.

Something in the nurse's unfinished sentence attracted the child's attention, for suddenly desisting from his new amusement, he sat down on the
grass, and, crossing his legs in a little old-fashioned manner, he began eating his apple, his eyes fixed on the clear sky overhead.

How could people see into the workings of that little boy's heart; how
could they understand how the father could be to his only child a father in
name alone, a person to be feared, to be dreaded, not loved, whose only
recognition of his son had been a few formal words morning and evening
or a cold handclasp—never a kiss, never a caress to the motherless little one,

in whom the father saw not the helpless babe, but the cause of his wife's death, that wife the only being in the world he had ever cared for.

The doctor's words, "The baby will live, but Lady Donne must die," had in that one moment closed for ever the father's heart against his son.

"Reggie, Reggie, where are you?" came in clear accents through the still air. The child ran forward to meet a slender black-robed figure, who was coming swiftly forward, and who knelt on the grass and took him in her arms.

"Oh, Reggie dear!" she began; then changing her tone, "but I won't wait to scold now. Come in with me; someone wants to see you."

On the terrace a gentleman was standing watching the pair as they advanced.

The boy darted forward and clasped him impetuously round the knees.

"It's cousin Rex," he cried delightedly, "my own cousin Rex! Oh, Rex, won't we have fun together now you are come, you and Mona and me! It will be just like old times."

Just one year ago the three had met for the first time, which was when Mrs. Meredith and her daughter had come to stay at the Park. Now, Lord Donne had never cared particularly for his half-sister Marcia. She had been one of the foremost to object to his marriage. He was a man who resented interference, and he never forgave her the part she played then, so, when she wrote suggesting a short visit to him, although he could not put her off, he hit upon a plan for making her stay a short one. Knowing her views with regard to her daughter's making a good match, he wrote to his dead brother's only son, a clerk in the Foreign office, cordially inviting him to spend a few weeks at Donne Park.

He knew the young man had not a farthing beyond his pay, and promised himself some amusement out of the once dreaded visit.

All turned out as he had wished. Mona and Reginald, or, as he was called, Rex Donne, fell in love with each other. Lord Donne took care that they should have every opportunity for doing so, whilst he smiled grimly over Mrs. Meredith's ill-concealed wrath and chagrin. That visit was the one bright spot in Reggie's life; for in the rides, drives and picnics the happy lovers did not forget the little lonely boy; but it came to an end all too soon; matters at last reached such a climax that one morning boxes were hurriedly packed, and Mona, all tears, was whisked off by her indignant mother, who loudly declared that she had been the victim of a plot, and that she would never set foot in Donne Park again. The next day the dog-cart took Rex to the station, and with him every vestige of Reggie's pleasant time disappeared. From that day to this, the lovers had not met.

After Rex had affectionately greeted little Reggie, he turned to Mona, and took both her hands in his.

"And now tell me," he said, in a tone as if they parted but a few hours ago, "how and where you have managed to spend the last year."

"In so many different places," she answered, tossing back her bright hair:

"France, Switzerland, Germany—mamma was determined to let me see the world and society."

"And after all, did Mrs. Meredith succeed in making you forget me?" Rex asked, ignoring the latter part of her speech. Mona's eyes fell, and a vivid blush overspread her face.

Rex clasped her fingers still more tightly, but said nothing further *then*.

Little Reggie stood by a patient listener, looking with pleased eyes from one to the other.

"Mona looks very pretty to day, Rex, doesn't she?" he remarked presently, critically surveying his blushing cousin. "She has such nice red cheeks." Whereupon Mona bent down to kiss him and to hide those same cheeks from Rex's gaze.

"And now, sir, give an account of yourself," she said after a pause, during which she was busily arranging little Lord Donne's necktie; "pray what brought you here; and what do you think mamma will say to you?"

Rex drew a comical face.

"Poor Mrs. Meredith! I really do think she would like me well enough if I were not such a terrible detrimental*—that is an unpardonable sin in her eyes. And what do you think now, Mona?—by way of a climax, she and I are made joint guardians of this young gentleman! I had a letter from Brown and Jepson yesterday, summoning me here, but I could not get away in time to hear the will read; not that it made much difference, for my name was not mentioned as a legatee."

"Then that explains it," said Mona thoughtfully. "I could not make out what was the matter with mamma; she locked the door of her room so that I should not see her, and she looked so angry when she came out of the library after seeing the lawyers—she pushed me away when I went up to her."

Mona had tears in her eyes as she said this. Her mother might be harsh, unsympathetic, often unjust, but with it all she loved her very dearly.

Rex looked at her compassionately.

"Perhaps she is afraid that I shall make too much of my rights as guardian," he went on, knowing that Mrs. Meredith must have guessed the drift of his uncle's will, and that her daughter had not. "If so, she need not be afraid. You and she together will look after Reggie better than I could; my duties will not begin before his school days, at any rate, and by that time who knows what may happen? someone may take it into his head to leave me a large fortune."

He was laughing, but Reggie was gazing into his face with very serious eyes.

"Are you very poor, then, cousin Rex?"

"Well, I *could* do with more money than I have, laddie."

"What would you do if you were rich, Rex?" the child continued.

* In society slang, an ineligible suitor.

"Well, let me see," Rex answered gaily, falling into the little fellow's humour. "In the first place, I would have a beautiful house; then I should have plenty of servants, plenty of horses, plenty of carriages, then, best of all—stoop down, Reggie (he had caught the boy in his arms)—"I must whisper this—best of all, our dear Mona should be the queen of it all; now, isn't that fine?"

"And where should I be, Rex?"

"Oh, by that time you would be a big boy, in school, perhaps, making a lot of friends and learning to play cricket and football, and of course, you would come over and spend all your holidays with us. We would always keep one room that we would call Reggie's room, and you should have your own pony that no one else, not even Mona, should ride on——"

"Yes, Mona could," said Reggie, looking at her lovingly. "But go on, Rex—what next?"

"Tea next, laddie, if I mistake not," as a servant appeared from the house to summon his little lordship to the nursery; "no, don't ask Mona to go in with you. You have had her to yourself for the whole of three days; you must spare her to me now."

Lord Donne seemed at first a little inclined to rebel. It had been Mona's custom to have a cup of tea at the same time that he took his; but after a short struggle with himself, he went off obediently, chattering volubly as usual. He looked back once to shout out—

"Make haste and get rich, Rex!"

The others watched him disappear within doors. There was a smile on both faces, for they were very fond of their small cousin, who all unconsciously barred the way for Rex to rank and fortune. Perhaps that thought had more than once crossed his mind. When this thought did come—for it would be useless to deny that it came sometimes—it is but fair to add that Rex did fierce battle with it, and never allowed it to gain mastery.

"I have many things to say, dear. Will you come with me to the old place?"

Together they walked in silence, following a path well known to both, which presently widened into moss-carpeted glade. Here Rex stopped and faced his companion.

"Darling!" he said, "here, we were interrupted a year ago, when I would have told you of my love. I believed then that though no words were spoken, you knew that I should never love anyone but you; now, after one look into your dear true eyes, I know that you too are unchanged. Are you *my* Mona still?"

"Can you doubt it, dear Rex?" she answered; and she let him press kiss after kiss upon her lips.

"A year ago!" he began presently. "Is it possible that twelve months have actually gone by since we last stood here and your mother appeared upon the scene? How severe she was! Darling, what would you do now if the branches of that tree yonder were suddenly parted and you saw her face? Tell me, would you shrink and tremble as you did then, and creep closer to me until I could hear your heart beat against my arm?"

"I should be braver now, Rex," she answered, with a swift upward glance into his handsome face. "I should say now that I loved you with all my heart, and that neither life nor death should separate us."

"My own sweetheart," said Rex, softly laying his cheek against hers. "You know, my darling, that I cannot claim you yet, that we may have to wait for years even?"

"Yes, Rex, but I can be patient."

"You will have a hard time of it, dearest," he said, rather ruefully. "Your mother will do all in her power to banish me from your memory; and can I blame her? Then there are sure to be lots of fellows ready to come forward; fellows with heaps of money too; confound them!"

Mona laughed.

"What a silly boy you are! Can you not trust me, dear?"

"I am wrong, dear one, very wrong,—I *do* trust you! I won't torment myself any more. Now, I want you to tell me what you thought of my letting you be taken away from me a year ago, with seemingly so little opposition on my part. Did you think meanly of me?"

"I don't know what I should have thought," said Mona very demurely, "if I had not happened to see your letter to mamma."

"No! did she show it to you?" cried Rex in surprise. "I never hoped for that."

"Yes; she said it was right I should see it, and so I read how my dear boy promised that he would not say a word of love to me nor try to see me even, for a whole year. He said he owed it to the mother of his darling that he should not take advantage of her daughter's youth, and that perhaps, after all, her love for him was only a passing fancy. Foolish boy! as if I did not know my own mind! and then the letter left off by saying at the end of that year—" her voice faltered.

"At the end of that," cried Rex triumphantly, "not all the mothers in the world should keep my darling from me if she still cared for me. Mona, the year is up to-day; I knew your whereabouts all the time, thanks to poor uncle Donne, though perhaps his motives were none of the best, and if I had not heard that I should meet you here, I should have followed you to Rome, there to learn my fate. Now, sweetheart, let us delay no longer, let us tell your mother all. She may be more generous than we think."

So they slowly moved away from the place which had witnessed so many happy meetings, and wended their way back to the house.

Reggie had been eagerly watching for their return from the nursery window, and directly he caught sight of them rushed down-stairs to meet them.

"What an age you have been!" he called out. "Nurse wouldn't let me look for you, because she said I ought to be punished for getting my clothes in a mess—and so I timed you by the big clock over the stables, and you have been away a whole hour and a half!"

He looked so aggrieved that the others felt bound to apologise.

"Well, old fellow, we have had a lot of talk about," said Rex; and, "Dear Reggie, I am so sorry," came from Mona.

"A lot to talk about," he said contemptuously: "I should think you had. Wasn't it rather mean of you, cousin Rex, to keep Mona so long?"

Rex replied only by hoisting the little fellow on to his broad shoulder.

"What did you talk about?" his lordship next inquired curiously.

"Tell him, Mona," said Rex, looking at her roguishly.

She stammered and hesitated, but could apparently find no words.

Reggie regarded her patronisingly from his height, and steadied himself by putting one small hand on her head as she walked beside him.

"Never mind, Mona.—Rex, *you* say."

"Well, I'll tell you one thing I said. I asked Mona to be my wife some day."

"Oh—and then?"

"Why, then I believe I kissed her."

"What did she say?"

"The darling girl said yes, she would marry me some day."

Lord Donne was very thoughtful for a moment.

"Some day," he repeated presently; "does that mean when you are rich, Rex?"

"Yes, dear boy."

He was so quiet after this that Mona looked at him anxiously.

"You are not sorry, Reggie, are you?"

"Sorry, Mona? Oh no! glad; I was only thinking."

"Well, out with it, laddie," said Rex kindly.

He hesitated a little.

"I wanted to know if what Jane told me just now is true."

"And what did she say?"

"Why, she said that I had lots and lots of money, and that this house is mine, and the gardens, and everything, and that even the shops and the post-office in the village are all mine. It isn't true, Rex, is it?"

The child's voice was trembling, and Rex could see there were tears in his eyes.

"Should you not like it to be true, Reggie?" he asked very quietly.

"Oh no, I think it is *horrid*," he said, bursting out crying, "that just a boy like me should have so much, and you be poor. Rex, dear Rex, can't I give it all to you and Mona?"

Rex sat down on the stone balustrade that ran round the terrace, and waited until Mona had somewhat soothed the excited boy; then, seating him on his knee, he spoke—

"Now listen to me, old fellow," he began, "and I will try and make things clear to you. It is true that you will one day be very rich indeed; but only think, Reggie, of all the good you will be able to do with your money. You will be able——"

Reggie interrupted him impatiently.

"But you can do all that, Rex. Oh do, *do* take my money."

"My dear little boy, it is quite impossible," his cousin said, trying to suppress a smile. "Why, people wouldn't let you give away your money! No, no, my boy, we must be patient. I shall work like a horse, and perhaps by the time you are a man I shall be rich, too."

"Is it only because I am little that I can't give you the money?"

"That's about it, Reggie."

"And when I am a man, I can do what I like?"

"With a great deal of it, yes."

"But what if I don't ever grow up to be a man?" Reggie said.

Rex jumped up quickly.

"I'll tell you what, laddie, I am going to have one race up and down the terrace. Now, see who'll get to the last vase of geraniums first. Reggie, start fair; your foot is at least an inch before Mona's!"

In a moment everything but the excitement of the race was forgotten, and when little Lord Donne, all flushed and breathless, his curls streaming behind him, triumphantly came in first, every vestige of the previous conversation had vanished from his mind.

But those last words of his were never forgotten by the other two. "What if I don't ever grow up to be a man!"

CHAPTER II

POOR Rex was sitting gloomily enough on a garden-chair which he had dragged into the full blaze of the summer's sun; his father's regiment had been stationed in India, where he was born, and his early years were spent there, which may account for his predilection for great heat. He had been reviewing his prospects, not for the first time by any means, and the result had not been satisfactory. Furthermore, Mrs. Meredith was clearly keeping out of his way.

No amount of calculation would double his income or increase his savings; the last year he had managed to put by a little, certainly, but such a very little, after all was said and done, and he became very melancholy as the chances of his marriage seemed so remote.

"I don't know what else I can cut off," he said to himself ruefully. Here he stooped and picked up the cigar, and looked at it affectionately. He paused, and gave a huge sigh. "Yes, I will do it. I'll do it for her— she's worth any amount of sacrifice. Come, my old friend, I will smoke you to the very end; you are the last cigar I shall have for many a long day!"

He was comforted that he had hit upon a plan for saving a few more pounds, and began to feel more cheerful. He then, for the first time, became aware that Reggie was no longer with him. He rose up with a slight feeling of compunction.

One of the under-gardeners happening to pass by, Rex hailed him.

"Have you seen Lord Donne anywhere?"

"Yes, sir; not a minute ago he was running as hard as he could go towards the shrubbery."

There the young man hurried, but for some time he looked in vain for the child. He was turning away when the sound of sobbing attracted his attention, and, pushing aside some overhanging bushes, he at last discovered him.

Flung face downwards on the grass at the foot of an arbutus, there Reggie lay, crying as if his heart would break, his whole frame convulsed with grief.

Rex stood still in utter astonishment. Was that the merry, mischief-loving little light-hearted boy, with whom tears at all were a rare occurrence, who was weeping in such a strange, unchildlike manner?

He went up to him, and kneeling by his side, put one hand gently on the bowed shoulder.

The boy started as if he had been shot.

"Oh, Rex, is it you? Please, please go away," and he tried to hide his tear-stained face with both his small palms.

Rex put his arms round him and drew him to a sitting posture.

"Tell me what it is all about, laddie. Hush, dear boy! don't sob like that—you frightened me."

"Oh, I can't tell you, Rex; I can't tell anybody."

He was getting so agitated that his cousin refrained from pressing him; he only said quietly—

"Do you know, Reggie, that if you cry any more you will be quite ill? and you wouldn't like that, would you?"

He was not prepared for the answer.

"I *would*, I *would*," the child said energetically. "Oh, I *would* like to be very, *very* ill."

Rex was really shocked.

"Reggie," he began, very gravely, "you must tell me what has happened. I don't like to see my dear little boy so distressed. If you don't tell me yourself, I must take means to find out."

If he thought that would rouse him he was mistaken, for Lord Donne never moved.

"No, Rex, I can't tell you—I wish I could—but it's no use." The disjointed sentences came in gasps: "I—oh, I *do* wish I were dead."

Rex saw it would be only cruelty to torment him further. The first burst of grief having subsided, he seemed worn out; so, taking him up, he carried him into the house, and delivered him into Jane's charge with strict injunctions not to leave him. Then he walked rapidly towards the inn where he had taken quarters, for he suddenly remembered that he had several business letters to write which must be sent off by that day's mail.

The letters took up more of his time than he had anticipated. Truth to tell, thoughts of Reggie and his grief would come continually between him and the paper; and he had scarcely finished them when his landlady came in.

"What, dinner already, Mrs. Jennison! I thought I should have had time to run up to the Park."

"Yes, sir; it has gone six, but the post don't go out till half-past, and my Sam won't take five minutes going to the office."

"I have positively been three hours over them," said Rex to himself. "I do hope that dear little boy is all right; he quite worries me. Hark! Mrs. Jennison, what's that?" he cried suddenly; "it sounds very much like a runaway horse!"

"Yes, sir, it do," said the woman, going over to the window and peering out; "Lor', sir, whatever can be the matter? It's one of the grooms from the Park, and he's coming here, I do believe."

In another moment Rex had flown down-stairs, and was outside just as the man drew rein by the inn door.

"Accident up at the house, sir," he gasped out; "Lord Donne, sir; I'm just on my way to the doctor's," and was off again at full speed.

Rex ran through the village and up the lane which led to Donne, almost before the words were out of the man's mouth. The park was traversed in a very few seconds, and with one bound he was up the stone steps and into the hall.

Mona came swiftly forwards to meet him, her face as white as death.

"They have not moved him," she began, speaking hurriedly. "He is there, just where he fell."

"How did it happen?" Rex asked briefly.

"He was sliding down the banisters, and must have turned giddy, we think; but all we know is that there was a scream, and then a crash, oh, such an awful crash!"—Mona shuddered—"the sound rings in my ears now."

Rex went quickly to where the little fellow lay. Someone had placed a pillow under his head. He looked very much as if he had just fallen asleep, save that his cheeks were too pale, and he was so quiet, so very quiet.

He looked questioningly into Mona's face.

"He moaned when we tried to raise him," she said in a low voice, the tears falling down her cheeks. "Oh, he lives—he must live; he can't be very badly hurt!"

As if in answer to her words, Reggie at that moment unclosed his eyes.

"Do you know me, laddie?" said Rex, bending over him. "Old fellow, it's Rex—you know Rex?"

F*

"Yes, I know Rex," the child repeated, as if he were saying a lesson.

Just then the doctor appeared, a good-tempered-looking, red-faced little gentleman, who had known Lord Donne from babyhood.

The first thing he did before making his examination was to administer a restorative which brought the colour a little back to the white cheeks.

"Well, young sir, and pray what new mischief have you been up to? Sliding down the banisters, eh? Ah, that's it!" He went on talking as he rapidly passed his hands over the child's limbs.

"Well, how do you feel? As if you could run upstairs and come sliding down again, eh? Where are you hurt? Come, tell me."

"My foot hurts," said Reggie; "nothing else."

In a moment the shoe and sock were off, and a large bruise was discernible on the delicate flesh.

"Pooh! that's nothing," said the doctor, "not even the skin broken! Now, see if you can move."

The boy tried to obey, but could do no more than raise his head. He sank back with a sigh.

The brisk little man was watching him intently.

"Ah—hum!" he ejaculated, as he saw the failure; "does your back feel bad?"

"No; only I feel so heavy and funny altogether, and my head is just like it was that time when I drank all the wine out of the decanters."

There was a tiny gleam of fun in his eyes.

"Ah, I remember; a nice job I had to make you take the emetic."

"You won't give me medicine now, doctor, will you?"

"No, no; don't be afraid: I shan't give you medicine," said the doctor cheerily.

But Rex, who stood the nearest to him, was almost certain that he saw tears in the little man's eyes.

As he rose after his examination, Mona went up to him.

"It's nothing very serious, is it, Dr. Farmer?"—she was feeling reassured by his manner—"Reggie will soon be about again, I hope?"

"Nothing very serious, my dear young lady!" he exclaimed, as he drew her a little aside; "but, indeed, it is VERY serious—*very* serious!" he repeated.

"Is he going to be very ill, then?"

"He will not be *long* ill," said the doctor, laying a stress upon the word.

"Doctor, you don't mean—you *can't* mean—;" Mona gasped out as she seized his arm.

"Hush! he must not be agitated," he said, warningly, guessing the right way of calming her, "you will only hasten the end!"

The poor girl gave a faint groan, and staggered back. Rex's arms were open to receive her, and they tightened round her protectingly.

Presently she raised her head.

"I will be calm now, Dr. Farmer; I won't give way again. I must learn all there is to be done."

"That's brave," said the little man, approvingly. "Now all you have got to do is to keep him and yourself as quiet and composed as possible; he will suffer no pain—he will go off as peacefully as if he were falling to sleep."

"And when will it be?" Rex asked, knowing that Mona could not put the question.

"I do not know exactly: you see, the back is broken, and there are internal injuries besides; I cannot tell how far these may extend. He may die early in the night—more possibly before morning approaches. He will certainly not see another day."

"Die in the night—*this* night?" Mona asked, in a tone of such utter horror, and with such white lips, that the doctor turned sharply to Rex.

"Better take her out and give her some fresh air; she will break down in a minute; then let her have a good cry—that will relieve her. I will see if I can move him up-stairs, where he will be more comfortable, and then I must be off. Sad business, very—nice little boy, too."

Under his supervision Reggie was carefully placed on a mattress, which was then carried up-stairs and placed on the bedstead in his own little room, a snug little chamber facing the west.

Then the doctor approached to take leave.

Reggie's little hand seemed quite lost in the doctor's large palm.

"Well, sir, I've got to say good-bye. Lots of other sick folks waiting to see me."

"What were you all talking about in the hall?" the child asked, without answering his remark. "Was it about me?"

"Heyday, what's all this! Can't we talk about anyone else, pray?"

He tried to speak carelessly, but he could not meet the little fellow's penetrating gaze.

"You *were* talking about me," Reggie said confidently, "and I believe I am going to be very ill, Dr. Farmer. Am I going to die?"

The doctor blew his nose vigorously.

"Dying, indeed! and what do you know about dying?"

"I don't know much about it," the child said, looking with great solemn eyes full in the doctor's face, "but I know I should like to die."

For once in his life, Dr. Farmer was at a loss for words; his eyes wavered and fell.

"It would be better for everybody if I died," the little fellow went on; "and Mona says that Heaven is, oh, *lots* better than here; and then, mamma is in heaven you know."

"Ah—hum! yes, of course."

"I heard you tell Mona, 'before morning,'" Reggie went on persistently; "was that about me too? was I to die before morning?"

"There, there, there, I can't stop talking any longer. Good-bye, my little man: God bless you."

Yes, actually the cynical old doctor, who was more than suspected of holding very peculiar, if not positively atheistic views, said "God bless you," to the little boy who lay there dying.

It was as well none of his supporters were there to hear him.

Then he stooped down and touched the child's lips with his grizzled moustache, a thing he had never done before, and hurried from the room.

On the threshold he met Mona, outwardly at least composed.

"Don't weary him with much undressing," he said, as he stood aside to let her pass; "and one thing more. You are spared a great deal; the child knows he is dying."

*   *   *   *   *   *

The evening was very still and warm. The windows were thrown wide open, but not a breath of air stirred the lace curtains or fanned little Reggie's brow.

The sun was sinking in all its splendour behind the distant hills, and the sky was flecked with tiny cloudlets of purple and crimson.

The child had not spoken for a long time, but lay quietly with one hand fondly clasped in Mona's.

Rex stood a little in the shadow of the bed, and all three were silently watching the glorious sunset.

Suddenly the great clock over the stables struck eight.

"That's my bedtime," said Reggie excitedly, "and, Mona, I haven't said my prayers."

"Say them now, dear."

"But I can't kneel," he said, with a little sob in his voice; "it won't seem like prayers."

"Never mind, my darling—the dear Lord knows you can't help it. See, I will kneel for you."

"Yes, that will do," he said, contentedly; then, folding his hands together, he closed his eyes. Rex hid his face, too, and for a short time there was perfect silence in the room.

Presently Reggie stirred, and gave a sigh of satisfaction.

"Rex," he said by-and-bye, looking up into his cousin's face, "you will marry Mona very soon, won't you?"

"Yes, dear boy, if you wish it."

"Oh, I do, I do, so much—and you will be *very* happy, won't you?"

"Don't you know how we shall miss you, darling?" Mona answered, with a little break in her voice. "We can't be very happy just at first."

"Then as soon as you can," he said, rubbing his cheek on her hand. "Promise you won't miss me for very long, or I shall be sorry I am going to die, not glad."

"Glad!—oh, Reggie!"

"Yes, dear; you know what I mean; for then Rex will have my money."

Mona looked up frightened into Rex's face.

He came forward and bent over the bed.

"Reggie, my boy, how did you know—who told you I should have the money—afterwards?"

The boy answered rather dreamily—

"I heard Jane talking about it to-day—was it to-day? it seems so long ago—she was talking to Morgan, the gardener, who squints. I was on the other side of the hedge."

"And what did they say?"

"Jane said you were in love with Mona, and then Morgan said it was a pity you were not 'my lord,' for then you would have plenty of money and could marry her; but now you were as poor as a church mouse, and must just about hate me—a little brat of a boy—for standing in your way."

So long a speech tired the little fellow, and he lay back panting on the pillows; but he evidently had something else which must be said, he looked so earnestly in Rex's face.

"When you found me to-day—you know when—I had just heard them. I couldn't tell you then, but I can now."

"And do you think I hate you, laddie?" He tried in vain to steady his voice.

"No Rex—oh, no, dear Rex!" was the eager reply; "I never thought it; but I couldn't help being glad when Dr. Farmer said I should die. It wasn't wrong, was it? but I *was* glad!"

The young man drew a long deep breath, and his troubled gaze for one moment met Mona's. There was an expression in her eyes of almost terror-stricken horror as with parted lips and clasped hands she leant forward. Had the suspicion momentarily occurred to her that what had happened was not purely accidental?

Perhaps he read something of her half-framed thought, for he bent quickly over the child once more.

"Reggie, my boy, you never told me how this came about—this tumble of yours, you know. How did it all happen?"

The little white lips quivered, and large tears welled up into the big dark eyes.

"Oh, Rex, I was so naughty. I am so sorry now—but I was running away from Jane. She was wanting to brush my hair, and she does pull it so; and I knew the quickest way was to slide down the banisters. I'd done it hundreds of times before, and never got hurt. Rex, don't be angry with me; I'll never do it again."

The old unconscious childish promise! How strange it sounded now!

Rex laid his lips tenderly on the little fellow's brow.

"I'm not angry with you, laddie—never think that. There, don't speak any more for a bit. Forgive you, dear boy? yes, with all my heart and soul!"

Then he went over to Mona, who was trying to suppress her sobs.

"Oh, Rex, how cruel of them—how cruel!" she said, piteously. "If he had only not heard those servants talking so heedlessly, so wickedly! Oh, what can we do?"

"Nothing, my darling," he replied gently. "Do you not see that he is happy in the very knowledge that we shall owe all to him—that he has given me my wife? Don't let him see your tears love; it will sadden him, and he is dying so peacefully."

So they returned to Reggie's side, and for a long long time no one spoke.

Mona now and then whispered in the child's ear, and he answered in the same tone; but Rex could not catch a word of what they said, only after each sentence he saw the little face grow more calm and tranquil.

And so, one by one, the last beams of the sun faded away, and all became grey and chill.

Mona rose and gently closed the windows, but no one suggested lights; it seemed as if they wished to make the day as *long* as possible. Was it not his last?

"Rex?" said Reggie once more, after a long silence.

"Yes, laddie."

"Isn't that Thomas outside?"

"Yes, my boy, I think so."

"Please, I want to see him."

So the old servant was summoned and stood respectfully near the door, looking with pity and awe at the dimly defined figure of his little master.

"Thomas, do you know I am going to die?"

The man felt a choking in his throat, and could not answer until another more peremptory "Thomas!" made him say reluctantly—

"Yes, my lord."

"Then by to-morrow morning Mr. Donne will be 'my lord' instead of me."

"Yes, my lord," repeated the man, in wonder this time.

"So I want you *now*, before me, to call him 'my lord,' just once, so that I may hear, or else I shan't ever, and I *do* want to."

There was an awkward pause; Thomas fidgeted about uneasily from one foot to the other. At last, willing to humour the little boy's wish, Rex gave some trifling order, to which the man responded—

"Yes, sir——my lord, I mean!" and fairly bolted from the room.

Reggie closed his eyes with a sigh of relief.

"That's right!" he said, in a tone of great satisfaction; "now I don't think I want anything more."

As the night advanced, his mind began to wander, and then the cousins learnt how much the idea had taken hold of him that he was better dead, better out of the way; that he was only a little useless boy, and that he was "in Rex's way—in Rex's way," as he pathetically reiterated again and again.

Poor Mona's tears fell thick and fast as she listened to the feeble voice; even Rex's caresses and entreaties were for once powerless to assuage her grief; it was in vain he tried to soothe her.

At about three o'clock the dying boy's delirium vanished, but the look in his eyes made Mona send for Aunt Marcia, who came in feebly crying and wringing her hands. She had begged that she should not be summoned unless it was absolutely necessary, as she could not look upon pain, and her nerves were so highly strung that she felt she should be useless in a sick-room.

As soon as she saw the little white face lying back on the pillows, she wailed out—

"Mona, how can you stay there and watch him die?" and forthwith went off into a fit of hysterics.

Mona bent over Reggie anxiously as Mrs. Meredith was taken from the room; she so feared that the noise had disturbed him; but he had evidently seen and heard nothing of what had happened; he lay there quite quietly, with his eyes closed.

Once he spoke, but so softly that she had to place her ear very close to his mouth to catch the words.

"Before morning," he said, "before morning!" and then she knew he was referring to the doctor's words.

Suddenly he opened his large eyes to their fullest extent and looked with a rapt expression into the beautiful face leaning over him.

"It is almost morning, Mona!"

"Yes, darling, almost."

Rex went to the window and drew aside the blind.

"Not *almost*, dear boy, but *quite*. See! the morning has come!"

And, indeed, the short summer's night had ended, the first streaks of dawn already appeared in the sky—but for Reggie there was no daybreak on this earth. For him.

> "   .   .   .   .   the morning
> Broke on the golden shore."

She felt, rather than saw, that Arthur Grey was standing a couple of yards away.

MYRTLE'S HERO

by

JENNIE CHAPPELL

CHAPTER I

"WELL, dear, it certainly will be interesting to meet him again after so many years. Quite like the first chapter of a story."

"Anna, I *am* surprised at *you*!"

"Why? I'm not aware that I have said anything very shocking."

"I *did* think *you* were above all that—that vulgarity! I imagined it was enough for Mrs. Greene to sidle and smirk, and Myra to titter and suppose that 'something' will be likely to come of it, and to feel that all the feminine spy-glasses in Burfield are centred upon me, without my wise, calm, common-sensible Anna joining in the persecution. It is mean and cruel of you!"

"O Myrtle!"

They were as great a contrast to one another, these two friends, as might well be conceived. Anna Rushton, more than ten years the elder, with her quiet matronly grace, served, folks said, as an excellent foil to the nineteen-year-old maiden whom it was her office so often to chaperon. And never was the contrast more striking than at the present moment, when the pale refined face of the one, crowned by its dainty widow's cap, shone out, marvellously softened, from the twilight shadows, and the vivid, untoned beauty of the other—carmine cheeks, and black-fringed eyes, and the glory of bronze-brown waving hair—was intensified by the amber firelight, in the glow of which, low on the rug, she sat.

"Don't say, 'O Myrtle!' in that martyr-like tone!" expostulated the young girl, flashing upon her friend a pair of darkly blazing, indignant eyes. "It is I who am the martyr, I think."

"I'm very sorry."

"No, you're not! or you wouldn't join the multitude in tormenting me to death about that wretched man. It's *not* interesting—not in the very least. It is a horrible nuisance. I heartily wish his mother and mine had not been such dear friends: and more, that he and I had never entertained one another with milk-and-water and bread-and-jam, and fought over Noah's wife——"

"Oh! you quarrelled sometimes, did you?"

"Yes; and I slapped his face, I remember, and made him cry. I'm glad of it! I feel as if I should like to do it again."

"I should like to ask you if you think it fair towards this unoffending young man to entertain such feelings as those."

"He isn't unoffending," protested Myrtle wilfully. "He has offended me deeply."

"By coming back to his home, and seeking out his childhood's friends?"

"By publishing abroad how very fond we were of one another in those remote days, and setting all Burfield on the *qui vive*. So perfectly idiotic of him! You see, we were in our teens when last we met—at least, he was—and all the sentimental old maids, and all the simpering young ones in the place, will be on the watch for symptoms of the tender passion. Fond of him, indeed! I couldn't bear the little sop! He was a miserable little cry-baby at the age I best remember him! Pale, thin, and yellow-haired, with weak red eyes. Frightened of everything, from a black-beetle to a brass band, and generally suffering from mumps."

"Poor little fellow!" exclaimed Mrs. Rushton, though laughing in spite of herself. "But was he not clever?"

"He had a very big forehead, and was kept away from school because of a supposed tendency to St. Vitus' dance. They were the only signs of genius I ever heard of," said Myrtle, with a wicked relish.

"Not the conventional type, certainly," admitted Mrs. Rushton, with some reserve.

"But if he were endowed with every charm of mind and person (as the old fairy tales say), he should receive no grain of encouragement from *me*!" protested Myrtle. "The knowing folks who have made up their minds that Arthur Grey is coming to Burfield on purpose to marry Myrtle Vayne, and that she is ready and waiting to say, 'Yes, please!' shall find themselves, for once, mistaken. I mean it," she added, nodding her pretty, proudly poised head with an air of great determination. "I shall snub him from the first."

"I can well sympathise with your annoyance at meddlesome tattle," she began. "But, dear, if I were you, I would not be too positive——"

An impatient reiteration of her resolve was already forming itself on the girl's rebellious lips, when a servant tapped at the door with a letter for Miss

Vayne. One glance at the superscription changed the whole current of Myrtle's thoughts.

"It's from *Pen and Ink*!" she eagerly cried. "I know you will excuse my tearing it open."

" 'Excuse,' my dear! I am as anxious to learn the contents as yourself. (The gas, Esther, please.) Of course it is about your poem?"

But Myrtle was lost to all else. Anna saw a great radiance break over her expressive face.

"Rejoice with me!" she cried, springing to her feet and waving the letter aloft. "I've won the five-guinea prize!"

"Is it possible? Oh, my dear, I do indeed congratulate you. How splendid, Myrtie—oh, how splendid!"

"And the examiner, they say, speaks highly of it," continued Myrtle, her eyes and cheeks ablaze with exultation. "Fancy, to be spoken highly of by *him*! That is honour, if you like, Anna! Just think of it!"

"Who was the examiner?"

"*Who*? Why, Cleveland Kestin—the future laureate; the greatest poet (next to Shakespeare) who ever lived. And my poem has been 'spoken highly of' by *him*! Anna, shall I ever be able to sleep again?"

"You excitable child! Will you think me a great dunce, Myrtle, if I confess that Cleveland Kestin's works are all but unknown to me?"

"Then they must not be so another hour! I will fetch you 'A Wayside Garland.' I made sure you had read it long ago. I thought *everybody* had. Such gems, Anna! no love-nonsense! To have won the prize is very nice, but—to have been 'spoken highly of' by *Cleveland Kestin*!—that is the reward, Anna, that is the crown. Why I should feel honoured beyond expression to be allowed to clean that man's boots!"

She danced out of the room in a whirlwind of ecstasy, and "Oh, Myrtie!" half sadly, was all that her friend could say.

CHAPTER II

A RTHUR GREY'S conduct had not been quite so "idiotic" as Miss Vayne imagined. He had only, with touching ignorance of the weaknesses of womankind, confided to his particular friend, Mrs. Wright, the fact of his having still in his possession a tiny doll which Myrtle had once given him in exchange for a gilt whistle. Mrs. Wright, thinking the incident "so *very* pretty!" had repeated it to Mrs. Greene, who had in her turn retailed it to Mrs. Thompson and the younger Miss Trotley. Before the week was out, indeed, all Burfield had heard of it; but that was not Arthur's fault.

It was beneath Mrs. Greene's roof that the ex-playfellows first met after their seven years' estrangement, and their hostess contrived, with short-sighted self-gratulation, that Mr. Grey should take Myrtle in to dinner. Had she possessed one particle of really sympathetic insight into either character she would carefully have avoided such an arrangement. But, like most conceited folks, she frequently blundered.

Arthur Grey, the shy, quiet student, always at his worst in company, was little prepared for the honour thus conferred upon him. The rosy, red-haired hoyden whose dash and daring had led him captive a decade earlier, had developed a stateliness positively regal. He scarcely dared to look at her, and his tongue, the more he longed to utter some graceful and agreeable speech, the more seemed tied.

The girl herself, as we are aware, was already the centre of observation, and her conjectured feelings were the subject of much idle gossip. For Burfield was a small place, whose small happenings were few and far between, and Myrtle Vayne was its chief heiress and belle. Her annoyance therefore was only natural; nor was it likely to be soothed by Mrs. Greene's ordering of affairs, and the consequent glances of would-be sympathetic interest which Miss Trotley ever and anon cast at her across the table. But this was no excuse for the unkind frigidity of her demeanour towards her companion.

"Just the same top-heavy head!" she was saying to herself, with a sidelong glance at his massive brow. "I wonder what sort of a mouth he hides behind that imposing beard? Weak enough, I daresay; but I forget. His eyes are still like a ferret's, evidently, which is the *raison d'être* of those blue spectacles. How disfiguring they are! He is certainly broader and better grown than I should ever have expected; but a good tailor can manage all that.—Thank you; a little water, please."

"Fire? a smell of fire?" someone was saying. "Yes, surely there is. It is the odour of wood smoke."

"I smell it, too!" said someone else.

"Jecks!" cried Mrs. Greene to the servant, "find out where it comes from, will you?"

"It's only the gardener burning up branches, ma'am; and the wind brings it all this way."

Thus answered Jecks, promptly allaying all fear.

But Mr. Grey was ashen pale, and trembling so violently that Myrtle took the water-jug from his hand only just in time to save its contents from being spilt.

"Thank you," he said gently, adding, after a few moment's pause, as he wiped his face, "I am ashamed of myself for being so much affected, but a peculiar faintness comes over me invariably at the bare mention of *fire*. You remember my weakness of old, I daresay."

His tone was appealing, and the shame he confessed only too visible on his crimsoned brow. Myrtle was boiling over with contempt.

"It is one of the few things that I do remember," she cruelly replied.—

"Miss Trotley, would you be so kind as to lend Mr. Grey your vinaigrette?"

The instant the words had left her lips, Myrtle felt as mean as she deserved; and beneath the focussed gaze of the whole table experienced a deeper, because more justly merited, share of confusion than her victim.

Not another word was interchanged between them during the remainder of the meal.

It was useless for Myrtle to argue with herself that Arthur Grey's pusillanimity was despicable—that no being worthy the name of man could permit himself to give way to such weakness. She felt as though some hunted creature had fled to her for sanctuary, and she had basely betrayed it.

She passed the next hour like one in a dream, all the surrounding brightness quenched by an overwhelming sense of her own barbarity. Her every emotion was intense and all-absorbing, and, outwardly calm and stately, she passed into the drawing-room with her whole soul bowed in remorse.

Mrs. Greene at her side was asking if she did not think Arthur vastly improved; and who would ever have expected that delicate boy to grow into such a fine young man? At any other time this talk, from its obvious intention, would have exasperated Myrtle into pungent retort; but just now all her exasperation was expended upon herself, and she replied "Yes," "No," and "Really!" with such docile acquiescence that Mrs. Greene was puzzled. What did the lovely Myrtle really feel?

CHAPTER III

"THERE! Shall I do? Do I look fit to present myself?"

Myrtle, as she spoke, swept into the drawing-room, where Mrs. Rushton was already waiting for her.

"Yes, dear, you will do very nicely, I think," replied Anna quietly, though her eyes and smile were full of admiration for the slim but statuesque figure that stood before her, robed in velvet of the richest pansy shade, and with a single scintillating diamond clasping the foamy lace at her throat.

"I hope I don't look like a common fashionable miss," Myrtle continued. "I want to give the impression of a person of at least *some* mind. I'm sure *he* would despise a girl who was frivolous and silly. Oh, Anna! I wonder whether he will have anything to say to me beyond just 'How d'you do?'"

Anna knew perfectly well that the unnamed "he" was the adored poet whom Myrtle worshipped from afar.

"I daresay that, as the writer of that prize poem, you may receive rather more than ordinary attention from him," she replied.

"How I wish I were pale!" cried Myrtle, catching sight of herself in a glass as she drew on her gloves. "Who ever heard of a woman with an ounce of brains having such milkmaid cheeks as mine? Ugh! What *could* I do to give myself an intellectual aspect just for to-night?"

"Borrow Mr. Grey's blue glasses!" suggested Anna, laughing. "You know Mrs. Greene's opinion of them."

"Ah!" said Myrtle, becoming suddenly grave; and she did not speak again until the two ladies were nearly half-way to their destination.

Rather more than an hour's drive brought them to the outskirts of Sydenham, and five minutes more to the residence of the genial editor of *Pen and Ink*. Here were assembling most of the contributors to that pleasant little weekly literary prize.

Eagerly her eye scanned the various groups of talkers for a face and form which should at once proclaim the bright particular star of all that galaxy. She felt sure that she should recognise the author of "A Wayside Garland" the moment her gaze rested upon him. "Something" seemed to tell her that he was tall and dark, with an eagle countenance, thoughtful and pale, deep-set eyes, keen yet meltingly tender in their glance, and with loose waves of coal-black hair flung nobly back from his high and gifted brow.

"He is not here," she whispered.

"Who?" asked Mrs. Rushton, rather densely.

"Cleveland Kestin. I'm sure he is not. There is no one here, I am certain, who would be capable of producing such thoughts as his. The editor particularly said that he would be present, too."

"He may come later on," said Anna consolingly. "What a prevalence of spectacles and eyeglasses, Myrtle! And how fond the ladies seem of short-cropped hair!"

"Yes," Myrtle assented dreamily. Suddenly she gave a sort of gasp. "Anna!" (under her breath). "*Who* is that?   Look! Don't you see him? Next that lady in black silk. How *in* the world did *he* get here!"

Mrs. Rushton followed Myrtle's gaze, and her own was arrested by the pink-flushing face and blue spectacles of Arthur Grey!

"Really!" she exclaimed, as much surprised as her companion. "How very odd! But possibly he may be a private friend of the editor's or have been introduced by someone else."

"How astonished he will be to meet us here!" said Myrtle. "I suppose we must speak."

Half an hour later, Myrtle was chatting with the lady winner of the latest essay prize, her eye furtively watching the door and her ear only half attentive to the subject in hand, when the editor's fussy little wife came bustling up to her, followed with obvious reluctance by Mr. Arthur Grey.

"Miss Vayne, my dear," she said, "my husband tells me that you have so often expressed an interest in the author of 'A Wayside Garland'; and Mr. Kestin, I'm sure, would like to know the young lady whose poem on 'Winter' was so fortunate as to meet with his special approval in our late competition.—Mr. Cleveland Kestin, Miss Myrtle Vayne!"

"Most happy!" murmured the poet, with crimsoning ears and the air of one who would have been thankful to take refuge beneath any article of furniture that seemed handy.

"But—but—*Arthur Grey*! I don't understand!" faltered Myrtle.

"The other is my pen-name," explained Arthur awkwardly. "You—you didn't know I wrote?"

"I had not the faintest idea of it! And the 'Garland,' too! It seems impossible!"

"Oh—ah—yes," rejoined Mr. Grey, fidgeting with his cravat as though it were choking him. "I did that ever so long ago."

Silence. Miss Vayne appeared absorbed in twisting the tassel of her fan, and the poet in the contemplation of the toes of his boots.

"I admire your book very much," said Myrtle next. "I am never tired of reading it."

She flashed one glance up at him from those wonderful eyes of hers, then their dusky fringes drooped lower than before; but that brief glimpse of glory was sufficient to retard the recovery of Mr. Grey's self-possession.

"Oh—er—did you? I mean, are you? That is to say, most happy!" he mumbled.

It was a wretched interview. Myrtle did not know whether to laugh or cry.

"So fortunate, my dear," said the editor's wife, "to have been able to have Mr. Kestin with us this evening—we always call him by the name we were first familiar with. He has been telling my husband that he has just accepted an appointment in New South Wales, and must sail the end of next week. Such a loss he will be, both personally and as a contributor to our magazine. A dear, nice fellow he is! and *so* kind and truly good!"

CHAPTER IV

A YOUNG silvery moon was peeping between the still leafless branches of the aspen-tree as Myrtle paced the garden alone in the spring gloaming. A strange restlessness had possessed her for hours past, and she was now drawn out of doors by a futile, irresistible desire to hear the approach and departure of the train which was to convey Arthur Grey on the first stage of his journey to the Antipodes.

For a while, following that startling revelation anent the writer of "A Wayside Garland," it had been doubtful whether Arthur Grey would rise to the honours of Cleveland Kestin, or the poet descend to the level of poor Arthur Grey. Disenchantment is a painful process to enthusiastic youth, and the substitution of the real for the ideal often involves a fearful mental wrench. But it is the real, after all, that throbs with feelings like our own, that may be strengthened by encouragement or crushed by neglect. The struggle in Myrtle's breast was not for long: her ideal poet of the raven locks and eagle eye melted into thin air, and she accepted the blushing, timid playfellow of her childhood as the human channel of those sublime thoughts which had so often lifted her above herself, and filled her with love and yearning for the Divine.

She drew her fleecy wrap around her, and leaned upon a railing, lost in pensive reverie. She would not own, even in the depths of her own inner-most consciousness, that Burfield would seem colder and life greyer when Arthur was gone out of it; but she would have liked to tell him, humbly and gently, how sorry she was for her unkind, her insulting behaviour to him at their first meeting, and to have received from his own lips an assurance of pardon. Never yet had an opportunity of doing so presented itself, for the young man's shy shrinking from her, by no means diminished by their singular *rencontre* at Sydenham, hindered the securing of even one minute's *tête-à-tête* with him.

A trembling glow shot upwards into the blue-grey sky, and as suddenly died. It came again—a strange red light, waxing and waning intermittently for a few seconds, then burning brighter still. A subdued hum was growing in the air, becoming articulate at last in the dread cry of "Fire!"

It was not in the direction of the village that the warning glow arose, but from a group of cottages lying half a mile further up the London road, and so much nearer to Myrtle's home.

Full of sympathetic excitement, the girl rushed back to the house.

"A fire! a fire, Anna!" she cried. "Carter's End is alight! Put on your hat and come!"

"Carter's End! Poor Snookes's place? Are you sure?"

"Quite sure. You can see the glow from the end of the garden. I am afraid more than one cottage is caught. Come, Anna! Be quick!"

"We cannot do any good by going," said Mrs. Rushton reluctantly. "Women at such a time are always in the way."

"More shame for them, then!" rejoined Myrtle warmly. "*I* shall go whether you do or not. We might be able to help by passing water-buckets, or something."

In less than five minutes both ladies were at the scene of action, albeit the elder vainly sought to keep at some considerable distance from the crowd.

It was the end cottage of the block that was alight—not Snookes's, but the next, inhabited by a labourer, with his wife and children. It had been no difficult matter to get them all safely out, but now strenuous efforts were being made to save their poor little home. The wooden beams and thatched roof of the place blazed like a pile of faggots, and there was not a moment to lose.

"They have saved most of the things," said a familiar voice at Myrtle's side. "They will have to give over now."

Startled beyond expression, she turned, and saw the slight figure of Arthur Grey—slight and small indeed in comparison with the stalwart sons of labour among whom he stood.

"I thought you had started ere this," she said.

"I found that the next train would serve me quite as well," he replied, reddening even in the fiery light to find that she had noted the hour fixed upon for his departure. "And," he added, in an almost inaudible tone, and with averted face, "I thought I would make one more effort to conquer my weakness. So I am here."

"I am *so* glad," murmured Myrtle. "I have been so sorry ever since—"

But her long-delayed apology was even now arrested on her lips by the heart-broken wail of a little child at their feet—one of those that had been brought out from the burning house.

"My kitties! Oh, my kitties! Oh, my dear, dear little kitties!"

"What is the matter, dear?" asked Myrtle, stooping to take the child's hand.

"My kitties! They're all burnin'! They'll be all burnt up! Oh—oh—oh!"

"Be thankful for your own life, and don't yell like that for a cat's!" said a woman roughly. "You might ha' been burnt up yourself."

But the little girl was inconsolable. Evidently the recollection of her pets had just crossed her mind. "My kitties—in the basket! Oh, my dear kitties!" she sobbed.

"I'm afraid it is too late to save them now," said Myrtle. "Poor things! How cruel that they should have been forgotten! The roof looks every moment as if it would fall in."

She turned to speak to Arthur again, but found instead, Mrs. Rushton at her side.

"Myrtle! Myrtle! What *is* he going to do?" the latter was excitedly asking. "It is madness! Surely they will never let him?"

"Has he gone to get my kitties?" asked the child.

Myrtle stood white and rigid, her eyes wide and fixed with terror, her breath all but stayed.

"It is sheer insanity!" Mrs. Rushton cried. "He will never come out alive. Yes—here he is! No—yes! and he has got them!"

"Hurrah! Hip—hip——"

But the ringing cheer died away in a groan of horror. The upper windows, with part of the wall, fell forward, and Arthur Grey was buried in the ruins.

* * * * * *

White and weak, he leaned among the pillows of his invalid chair, and his right arm lay for ever helpless at his side; but the unconquerable rosy red surged warmly as ever over his worn temples as Myrtle came in, radiant as the May sunshine, and laid a bunch of gold-crowned narcissus in his hand. She smiled down at him with wistful tenderness; he smiled up at her admiringly. A tabby kitten—one of the rescued three—uncurled itself upon his knees and began to purr.

Myrtle stroked the little silky ball with gentle touch, but the kitten was not in her thoughts.

"Do you know," she said, after what seemed a long silence, as she watched her own white fingers smoothing the striped fur, "that they are going to hold a thanksgiving service in the church-room for your recovery?"

"I had not heard," he replied. "It is too much—altogether too much."

"You are the hero of Burfield!" said Myrtle.

"I was afraid—horribly afraid!" he owned. "That was why I went to the fire. I determined, with God's help, to conquer my despicable cowardice. And they were all His creatures—I mean the sobbing child and her poor little pets—and I could not bear the thought of it. But I was sick with fear all the time."

Myrtle was silent, but her heart was swelling with thoughts too deep and —shall we own it?—too tender for words.

"I've lost that appointment," Arthur resumed. Then added, as by a sudden impulse, "Do you know why I accepted it so hurriedly?"

"No. How should I?"

"It was to get myself out of the way. Out of your way!"

Myrtle's tears welled over, and dropped upon the flowers in his hand.

"And I despised you, and thought you weak!" she murmured. "Oh, forgive, forgive!"

"Should I have done right, Myrtle?" he whispered.

"No, no, *no*! Oh, how I misjudged you! You—braver than the brave!"

He drew her scarce resisting head downward to the pillow beside his own, and leaned his brow, unchidden, against her wet cheek. Her lips were quivering with sobs; she could not speak, but her soul was deeply glad. What mattered his weakness, his shrinking, his shyness, now? What cared she that the fleshly garb of her poet wore blue spectacles and—had now but one arm! Beneath it all throbbed the mighty heart of a hero, and that heart was hers.

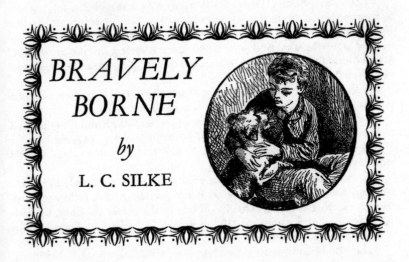

BRAVELY BORNE

by

L. C. SILKE

CHAPTER I

ANGER

'There, Rough, old fellow, that's all I've got to give you;' and the speaker, a boy of about eleven, flung the crust which had been given him for his own supper to the dog who stood looking at him with wistful eyes.

The bread was soon devoured, the scotch terrier wagging his tail, and afterwards licking the face of the boy, who was half lying, half sitting upon the brick floor.

'Dear Rough! I think he gets fonder of me every day; don't you, mother?' he said, turning to the only other occupant of the room, a woman who was busy preparing something hot for her husband's supper.

'Maybe he do; but I'm sure he always was as fond of you as he could be,' she returned. 'He's a good faithful creature, though he ain't what one would call a beauty.'

'He is in my eyes; and I wouldn't give him in exchange for the handsomest dog in all the city. Rough's worth the lot of 'em. He knows we're talking about him; he knows everything. And he knows how I love him, too,—better than anything in the world, 'cept you, mother;' and the boy drew the animal towards him, and laid his face down against the rough, shaggy back which had earned for him the name Archie had given him.

'Well, it's time to be going for father's beer,' returned Mrs. Wood, taking no notice of the latter part of her little son's speech.

'Come along, Rough; we'll look sharp won't we, doggie?'

Rough was on the alert in a moment; but his young master rose in a less nimble manner, as if it were an effort to him, and he would gladly have remained where he was. And as he stood up he revealed, not the usual light, active form of a boy of his age, but a poor deformed figure and thin, almost shrunken limbs.

His slow movements expressed such weariness, that the mother turned to him gently, saying, 'Does your back ache to-night, dear?'

'It ain't so bad, mother, only I'm tired; and so Rough and I'll go to bed as soon as we come back, unless father wants to send me out again.'

'I'll go myself if he does,' rejoined Mrs. Wood. 'It's time a lad like you was a-bed already.'

The two inseparable companions accomplished their errand; and in returning, Rough came bounding on before, whilst Archie followed more slowly, carrying the beer carefully. When he drew near the door, he hesitated, for he heard sounds of talking within, and therefore knew that his father was already there.

As he stood leaning against the lamp-post which was opposite their door, the young face, which had appeared so gentle whilst the boy was fondling his dog before the fire, hardened into a look expressive of fear. He reluctantly entered the cottage.

He was immediately greeted by, 'Now then, boy, I'd like to know what you've been about all this time! Don't stand gaping. Look sharp, and come across and set the jug down here,' thundered Wood, with a motion of the hand which showed that he was prepared to let the lad feel its weight.

Archie saw the scowl on his father's face, and still hesitating to come closer, remained standing in the doorway. At that moment Rough, excited by his run, suddenly bounded with one of his joyous springs upon his young master; and whether the boy was off his guard, or his father's threatening words and manner made him nervous and rendered his grasp less firm, certain it was that he started violently, and let the jug which he held fall to the ground, where it lay broken into several fragments, its contents spilled on the floor.

With a oath Wood seized a thick stick, and, rendered more powerful than usual by his passion, in an instant felled the dog to the ground. Uttering piercing cries of pain, the animal turned his wistful eyes on his young master, and tried to drag himself towards him; but his hind limbs hung powerless, and all he could do was to look up piteously.

Archie sprang to him and took him up in his arms, almost unconscious of a stinging box on the ear dealt him at the same time by his father.

Burning with indignation at sight of the injury done to his faithful Rough, he turned and confronted the angry man with flashing eyes, his face working with emotion, as he exclaimed, in an outburst of passion,—

'Just see what you've done to my dog, father! How dared you? You might have beaten *me*—you've done it often enough—but you'd no right to lay a finger on Rough, for he didn't belong to you, and if he dies I shall hate you; I know I shall always hate you!'

The boy seemed beside himself as he stood there pouring out his passionate words, his cheeks flushed crimson, his whole form trembling from the force of the feelings surging within him.

Wood remained for a moment as if petrified by the boldness of the lad. But it was only for an instant that surprise stayed his arm. The next it would have descended with all its weight upon the boy's shoulders, had not Archie, with a smothered cry, darted through the door into the darkness. Then he hurried on, his dog tightly clasped in his arms, and his whole frame still quivering with the convulsive sobs which shook him; whilst he pressed Rough tenderly to his breast as he heard the poor creature's low moan of pain.

Thus he hastened on and on, knowing not whither, and caring not, so that he put a safe distance between himself and his father. At length he found himself by the river, among the docks and wharfs, where, coming to a shed, he crept into it, and flung himself down on the ground, pillowing Rough's head on his arms, whilst he stroked the poor, disabled limbs of the faithful creature, who looked up at him with his grateful eyes, and licked his hand to thank him.

Archie's tears were dropping fast upon him by this time; and seeing him crying the dog began, as was his wont his low plaintive whine, not on account of his own hurts, but in sympathy with his master's distress.

CHAPTER II

WILL HE DIE?

IF ever deep, unselfish affection existed between human being and dumb animal, it did between Archie and Rough, who had been the solace of many a solitary hour; in fact, since the day when the forlorn creature had strayed into the court where the deformed boy lived, and with his piteous eyes had seemed to beg for a crust the boy was munching, which was generously given him, the two had been scarcely an hour apart.

Archie had spoken nothing but the truth when he said that next to his mother the dog held the first place in his affections; and how warm those were none but his mother knew—except, Rough. And now, could it be that Rough was going to die—killed, by his father's hand?

As the thought came into the boy's mind his face darkened, and he set his teeth and clenched his little hand; but the next instant he felt Rough's tongue licking his cheek, and as he turned and bent over him, his expression melted into a look of tenderness and love.

'Oh, Rough! my poor doggie! if I could only do something for you! If I'd known what father was going to do, he should have beaten *me* instead of you—beaten me as much as he'd a mind to, but never you, Rough. Oh, 'twas cruel of him! for you never done him no harm; you never done no harm to nobody; you've been the best dog as ever lived!'

Rough seemed to understand all the boy was saying, for he lifted his eyes to his young master's face as if to thank him for his love.

'Oh, Rough, you mustn't die!' exclaimed Archie, seeing something in the dog's look which he had never observed there before, and guessing what it meant. 'Whatever should I do without you?'

But Archie's love could not prolong his favourite's life, nor restore the paralysed limbs; though he sat with him in his arms, caressing and talking to him all through the night, indifferent to discomfort, alive only to one fact—that soon the faithful animal would no longer be able to respond to his caresses; the loving heart would have ceased to beat; the eyes have closed for ever.

And when morning broke it found Rough stretched out stiff and motionless, and Archie sobbing out his distress over the body of his dumb friend.

His grief was real and heartfelt; for Archie was but a child, though with feelings deeper and more sensitive than those of childhood usually are; whilst his lonely life, which had given him so few objects to love, had intensified the affection with which he clung to those one or two. Therefore he felt as if his heart would break as he looked upon Rough stretched upon the cold ground, and thought of all he had been to him, and all he should miss in him.

Then, after a while, noticing that it was beginning to get light, he sprang to his feet, and taking up the dog, walked on till he came to the drawbridge near. Picking up some stones, he fastened them to him, his tears falling meantime, as he murmured to himself,—

'Nobody shan't do no more harm to you, poor old Rough. I'll put you out of their way, so safe that nobody'll ever be able again to give you so much as a cuff or a kick. I won't forget you, Rough; don't you fear that. I *couldn't* forget you, if I was to try; for I shall miss you every minute of the day.'

With a fresh burst of tears he went on,—'Oh, Rough, Rough, you were the nicest playfellow I ever had. You never laughed at me because I'd got a hump on my back; you never stared at me or turned away from me 'cause I wasn't straight like other chaps; but you loved me just the same; and when I was tired, you'd come and lie quiet, and when I wanted a game you was always up to that too; and we used to keep each other so warm at nights, and whenever I woke up then I'd you to talk to! And now I must put you away out of sight! Oh, Rough, Rough!' and the little fellow sobbed in a passion of grief.

But once more he roused himself, fearful that people would soon be coming about; and making a desperate effort, he dropped the dog from the bridge into the middle of the river.

He could not restrain a cry as he heard the splash in the water; and covering his face with his hands, he leant sobbing against the railing.

At length the little woe-begone face was lifted, just at the moment when a girl of about fifteen, with a basket on her arm, set her foot on the bridge. Their eyes met; and something in Archie's look seemed to appeal to the girl's compassion, for she glanced at him again, and appeared to slacken her pace as she drew near.

There was something in her too which attracted Archie, and made him look at her a second time.

'Haven't I seen you before?' she exclaimed, looking down upon the boy as he sat huddled together, shivering; for winter had not yet taken his departure.

'Maybe you have,' replied Archie. 'It ain't difficult to remember me when you've once seen me,' he added, with bitterness in his tones.

'Oh, I didn't mean that,' returned the girl earnestly; 'but I'm sure I used to know you. Oh, I remember, 'twas when we were living in Angel Court; you used to live there too, didn't you?'

'Yes; we live there now.'

'We didn't stop there long, because father didn't like it much, and he wanted to be nearer his work. He works at the docks, and I'm taking his breakfast now. I must go on, too, or he'll think I'm late.'

'And will he beat you for it?'

'*Beat* me! father beat me!' exclaimed the girl in surprise.

'Yes; my father would; and I thought most all fathers were the same: that they didn't do much else.'

Bessie Martin—for so the girl was named—might have felt inclined to smile at Archie's word, but for the earnest manner which accompanied them, seeming to tell that the child spoke from sad experience.

'I can't remember father ever beating me. He's too kind and good.'

'D'you love him?' asked Archie.

'Yes, of course I do.'

'I don't love *my* father,' said the boy, in an undertone, from between his set teeth. 'I don't love him, I almost hate him!'

'Oh, how dreadful!' exclaimed Bessie, shocked at such expressions, and noticing the darkened look which passed over poor Archie's face as he said the words. 'I wouldn't talk like that if I were you; it sounds so wicked like.'

'Ah, you don't know what he's been and done, or perhaps, if you was me, you'd feel the same.'

Archie burst out again into such bitter crying and sobbing, that Bessie could only stand by, feeling compassion for such genuine sorrow though she knew not yet the cause of it. She uttered a few words of sympathy, and Archie, when he glanced up, saw such a kind look resting on the frank, open face, that he felt suddenly prompted to unfold his grief to her, and told of poor Rough's untimely end.

Bessie could not quite understand so much feeling being expended upon a dog; but she saw that Archie's sorrow was real; and her own heart being a large, warm one, ready to enter into everybody's troubles, and to love every one in need of her love, she set herself to try and console the poor boy under his loss. But Archie was not to be consoled; at least not yet. Time might soften his trouble, but at present it was too fresh upon him, too real a thing to be put aside, even though it was only a dog he was mourning.

At length Bessie declared 'she must make haste to father, for it would not do to keep him waiting for his breakfast; but she should have to come back that same way, and then they could have another talk.' When she returned, Archie was still in the same position.

'Father said I might bring you this,' she began, addressing him, and holding out a thick slice of bread.

Archie received the bread with thanks; but when he tried to swallow a morsel, a choking feeling came in his throat which made him lay it down again.

'Well, keep it,' said Bessie; 'if you can't eat it now, I dare say you'll be hungry by-and-by.'

After a little more conversation, and having told where she lived—which was almost within sight of the bridge—Bessie said she must go home, as she had plenty of work to do, and so departed.

CHAPTER III

STILL IN TROUBLE

ARCHIE knew his mother would be out to work that day, as she frequently was, her husband spending so much of his earnings upon drink that the portion he gave her was insufficient to maintain herself and her boy; and therefore she was glad to 'turn a penny,' as she expressed it, in any way that presented itself.

So she often took a day's charing or washing; and thus it was that Archie had often depended for society upon Rough.

The remembrance of the words he had spoken to his father the previous evening in his passion came back to his mind, and made his heavy little heart yet heavier, as he found himself anxiously wondering how it would be with him when next they met. Would he thrash him? or how would he punish him?

He wished he could keep out of his way for ever. He had never had much from him but blows, and cuffs, and angry words; and now he had killed his Rough, and that he never could forget nor forgive.

His attention was attracted by some fine large vessels which were being towed into the basin. The sight of them seemed to inspire him with a sudden thought.

'Why shouldn't I go to sea, like Bob? What a first-rate idea that would be!'

For a moment the child's eyes brightened, as if they had caught a ray of hope; but soon his look fell again as he turned away, saying to himself,—

'I couldn't leave mother; for she's got nobody but me, now that Bob has gone away from her; and if I went too, she'd have no boy at all. I ain't much good, I know; there ain't much as I can do for her; still, maybe, I'm better than nobody. Poor mother! I daresay she's a-fretting about me, wondering what I did last night. I'll go and try to meet her as she leaves her work. Let's see; this is the day she always goes to Mrs. Black, and she don't keep her late; and if I go and hang about there, I'll be sure to see her as she comes away.'

Archie accordingly did so. Mrs. Wood folded her arms round her boy, gave him a kiss, whilst a tear came into her eye as she felt the half-convulsive way in which he clung to her for a moment.

'Oh, Archie, how I've been fretting about you! Whatever became of you last night?'

'Oh, I managed fine, mother. I crept into a sort of shed place I found down by the docks, and I watched poor Rough all night. But he's dead mother,' said the boy, looking up.

'Dear, dear! Poor dog! How sorry I am!'

Archie's tears were again rolling down his cheeks.

'Father didn't mean it, dear,' she went on. 'He only gave the dog a blow, and he couldn't tell as 'twould hurt him so.'

The boy's eyes gleamed with an indignant light, but he said nothing more; only inquired, 'Is father still angry with me, mother?'

'Ay, he's angry; there ain't no doubt about that.'

'Dreadful angry?'

'Ay, I'm afraid so. You shouldn't have spoke to him like that, Archie.'

'I know, mother; but I was in a passion. Oh, 'twas cruel of him to strike at Rough like that!' and Archie's face again grew dark and hardened-looking.

'Father had been drinking last night, and you know when he's like that it don't do to provoke him.'

'And perhaps he'll have been drinking again to-night, and then he'll give me ever such a beating. Oh, mother!' exclaimed the little fellow pitifully, wincing at the bare idea of what he would have to endure.

G

As the mother looked down upon the poor, deformed little figure before her, her heart cried out that 'it was indeed cruel to strike at such a lad as that;' and a sense of indignation stirred within her. But Mrs. Wood was of a passive nature, and had not much energy of character. She was strong to endure, but not strong to resist; and what little spirit she once possessed had been long broken by her violent-tempered husband. Violent-tempered he was when under the influence of drink; and though sometimes he would go on pretty well for a while, at other he would come home night after night the worse for liquor. At those seasons it was useless to reason with him or oppose him; and the poor wife knew to her cost that, it only made matters far worse if she interfered. She felt she could do nothing now to help her little son, though she saw him standing with drooping head, and knew that his poor heart was bleeding for the loss of Rough, and shrinking from what he might have to suffer at his father's hands.

'I haven't yet told you all as father said, Archie,' she began hesitatingly.

'What is it, mother?'

'Well, he declares—though I don't scarce know how to tell it you, my poor boy—as he won't have you come nigh the place again. After daring of him as you did, he says you shall just go your own ways; and if he catches you about he'll thrash you as he never did afore. Oh, Archie, whatever shall we do? It'll break my heart to go on like this much longer!'

It was Archie's turn now, on seeing his mother's distress, to try and act the part of comforter.

Swallowing down his own dismay, and endeavouring to put on one side the feelings of despair which were creeping into his heart, he answered, 'Don't you take on so, mother. Oh, I'll find a place somewhere.'

'Look here. They've paid me a shilling for what I done to-day, and here 'tis; you shall have it, Archie. But I don't know where to tell you to go, nor what to do.'

'I know what I'll do. I met a girl this morning down at the docks—a real, nice, kind girl, and she give me a piece of bread. She lives hard by there; and I'll go to her; maybe she can tell me of somewhere to sleep. It's a good way off there, safe out of father's reach.'

Then the boy related what had occurred since he had darted out of the house on the previous evening. But soon a clock striking, told Mrs. Wood it was time to hasten home to prepare her husband's supper. The two must part.

'We must be patient, Archie, and maybe happier times 'll come. Many things seem hard; but I've heard the parsons say as that's 'cause we don't see plain, nor know what it's all to lead to. So let's try and not feel angry, but put our trust in the good Lord; for He *is* good, though He do send us troubles sometimes; for He comes and helps us bear 'em, or we shouldn't be able to hold on nohow.'

When Archie left his mother he sauntered towards his old post on the drawbridge, meaning to try and find Bessie Martin; for there was something in her face that attracted him, and made him feel sure that she would befriend him if she could.

He took a long time to reach the docks, not only because it was a good distance, but also because he felt so weary, his heavy heart seeming to make his footsteps drag heavily too. He had a sense of being an outcast, and felt utterly wretched and forlorn; for the exhaustion of his body reacting upon his mind, made him take even a more gloomy view of things than he might have done at another time. But the long night of sleeplessness, the long sorrowful day which had succeeded it, during which he had almost fasted, were all telling upon his delicate frame, which was little fitted to stand much exposure.

At length with painful steps he reached the bridge and standing where he stood that morning, he leant his arms upon the railing, and soon his head sank upon it, such strange sensations creeping over him that he felt as if he were slipping out of life, down, down into the waters below, to rejoin Rough there. That was his last thought as he quietly sank down fainting on the ground.

CHAPTER IV

NEW FRIENDS

A RCHIE was conscious of nothing more, until he saw a face full of kindness bending over him. He could not understand; but he was too tired to think, and again closed his eyes.

Then he heard a voice saying, 'Come, come, my little man, this will never do. Try to swallow some of this. It will make you feel alive again in no time.'

The speaker held a flask to the boy's lips, and induced him to take a sip. Then Archie looked up again and gazed inquiringly upon his new friend.

He was a middle-aged gentleman, rather stout, and with a countenance upon which it was impossible to look without feeling the better for it, so full was it of kindness and benevolence, so overflowing with cheerfulness and good-temper. But it was chiefly when, as was now the case, his sympathies were called out, that the gentleness and tenderness which dwelt in that large heart were expressed upon the features, and made the fine countenance so singularly sweet and attractive a one that no heart could resist its influence.

It was now gazing down pityingly upon the poor boy, whose looks and condition appealed strongly to Dr. Oldroyd's easily-awakened feelings of compassion.

'Is your home far off, my boy?'

'I an't got no home, sir. I mean I durstn't go back to it.'

'How is that? Tell me all about it, my lad.'

Archie did so. Led on and drawn out by his companion, he related the whole of his tale, even to the passionate words he had in his anger spoken to his father.

'But where were you thinking of going for the night?' he asked at length.

Archie told him of his thoughts respecting Bessie Martin.

'A very good idea,' rejoined Dr. Oldroyd. 'I know something of them, for I attended a little boy of theirs in an illness; I daresay you can manage to walk that distance. Do you think you could get along now if you were to try?'

Archie was quite sure he could; but in spite of his efforts his steps were so feeble and lagging, and he felt so dizzy at times, that he was very glad of a little support from Dr. Oldroyd.

At length they arrived and Bessie opened the door, with a mingled look of pleasure and surprise upon her face—pleasure at seeing Dr. Oldroyd, who with both rich and poor was a welcome visitor wherever he went, surprise at finding him accompanied by Archie.

'Will you walk in, sir?'

'Yes; we are come to have a few words with you. Is father at home?'

'Yes, Sir.' And Bessie led them in, and placed seats for them, whilst John Martin rose and came forward, expressing heartfelt pleasure at sight of the good doctor. He seemed something like her, with the same frank, kindly look upon his face; he had a quiet way of speaking, very different from the loud, harsh tones he was accustomed to hear from his own father.

When the doctor had told the lad's tale, he turned kindly towards him, saying, 'We'll try and find some sort of a shake-down for him here ourselves. He don't look fit to go much further. I daresay you'll be able to manage something for him, eh, Bessie?'

'Oh yes, father; we can easily make him up some sort of a bed.'

'Ah, that will be better than I had hoped for,' said Dr. Oldroyd. 'I shall feel I am leaving him in good hands. And now, my boy, good night. You'll be all right after a long sleep, but I should like to see you again to-morrow. I shall be busy and out all day, but do you think you could find your way to my house in the evening? Bessie here can tell you where it is.'

Archie's face showed how delighted he should be to have a chance of seeing the kind gentleman once more; and then, after a few words in a low tone with Martin at the door, Dr. Oldroyd departed.

After he had left, Archie sat for a moment, feeling very shy; but the feeling was soon dispelled by Martin, who crossed over to the lad, and, looking down upon him, said kindly,—

'Poor little chap! You'll be glad to get to bed, I expect, for you are look-ing as white and tired as if you was almost done up. Come, Bessie girl, give us a bit of supper, and then see what you can manage for the lad's bed.'

'I thought perhaps he could turn into Jim's bed for to-night, father, if you didn't mind,' returned Bessie, in a low voice, looking doubtfully at Martin, as if not quite sure how he might take the suggestion.

'Ay, ay, so he shall. The thought of little Jim ought to make us kind to every lad for his sake,' he murmured in a low tone; 'and, if he was here, he'd be glad enough to give his bed to this poor boy. Go and get it ready, will you, Bess?'

The latter hastened to obey, and returned to the kitchen whilst her father and Archie were still sitting at their supper. The former was trying to persuade the latter to eat more, but the boy had not much appetite; and when in an unguarded moment Martin made some allusion to Rough, whose story Bessie had been relating to him before Dr. Oldroyd knocked at the door, the sorrow, which he had partly forgotten for the time being, swept back upon him with such force that, unable to control himself, he buried his face in his hands and sobbed afresh. It was not loud grief, but so deep and evidently beyond the boy's power to restrain, that Martin hastened to do his best to soothe him.

'There, there, don't cry like that, my lad. I didn't know you'd take on so, or I'd have thought twice afore I said anything about the poor dog. But you're tired out—come with me, and I'll show you where you can sleep for to-night.'

The man led him up a steep staircase into a little room above, where in a corner stood a small bed, which he said was to be his, the larger one being Martin's. Then he helped the lad to pull off his things and tumble into his bed.

A softened, saddened look rested on Martin's face the while, for his thoughts had gone back to another young lad of about the same age, who had lain down upon that little bed, and had never risen from it again, but had turned his tired face to the wall, and fallen into that last long sleep, from which there is no awakening on earth. It seemed to open his honest heart towards other lads, especially this poor deformed boy, who appeared to feel his troubles to be such great ones, and to suffer accordingly.

'Make haste and go to sleep, my little lad; and after a good night's rest maybe things'll look up a bit, and not seem so dark like.'

And then, with the remembrance that on the morrow he was to see again the gentleman who had been so good to him, and whom he already loved with all his warm little heart, he lost all consciousness of everything, and slept soundly.

CHAPTER V

DR. OLDROYD

ARCHIE slept long the next morning, for Martin in getting up was careful not to disturb him; and when he at last awoke, and hastening to dress went downstairs, he found Bessie had already taken her breakfast.

But she had kept some for him, and as he sat eating it, whilst she was busy cleaning and dusting the neat little room, they had a long talk together. Bessie told him how she had kept father's house for him ever since mother died some years ago, and how kind father was, and how she looked forward to his coming home in the evenings.

And then she spoke a few words about little Jim, whilst Archie listened eagerly. She told how kind Dr. Oldroyd had been to him; but the tears came into her eyes as she said how she missed the little brother, 'for it isn't very long since he went; and he was ill a good while, so I got accustomed to having him about, and to be always thinking what I could do for him; that made me miss him all the more.' And as she went on to tell of his patient ways, Archie found himself remembering many times when *he* had been very impatient, and had murmured bitterly in his mind because he was not like other boys.

When Archie arrived at Dr. Oldroyd's that evening he was shown at once into his study, the doctor having given orders to that effect. Now, as Archie entered the room, and remained timidly standing near the door, he turned round towards him, with one of his pleasant beaming smiles on his face.

'So you have found your way here, my little lad. That is right. Come nearer and let me have a look at you, and see whether your night's rest has done you all the good it ought.'

Archie came nearer, and Dr. Oldroyd put his hand upon his shoulder, his keen, quick eye scanned the thin, delicate features of the boy. Last night the little face had not looked over-clean, stained as it was by traces of tears which had been brushed away by dirty, unwashed fingers, that had left their mark behind; but now Archie had given it an extra cleansing in preparation for this visit; and it shone and glistened from the effect of the polishing it had received.

After a little talk, Dr. Oldroyd said, 'Now, my boy, I want to ask you a few questions about that poor back of yours. You mustn't mind them,' he added, as he saw the lad's face flush crimson, and noticed his sensitive shrink-

ing from the allusion, 'because they are for your own good. It is not out of
curiosity, but because I'm a doctor, you know, and so I should like to see
whether anything could be done.'

'Oh, sir, could it ever be made straight again?' exclaimed Archie, with
breathless eagerness, his whole face suddenly kindling into an expression of
such intense, ardent longing, and wild hope, that Dr. Oldroyd was half
alarmed at the effect of his words.

He replied hastily, 'No, no; at least I can't tell unless you let me examine
it. But don't raise your hopes so, my boy, in case of disappointment. I'm
very much afraid nothing can be done; still I should like to see whether there
is any chance of it.'

The light died out of Archie's face. The ray of hope which had passed like
a lightning flash through his mind, awakening thoughts that had made his
heart beat high for the moment, was gone, leaving darkness and hopeless-
ness behind.

'My poor boy! Is it such a great trouble to you?'

Dr. Oldroyd's question received no answer; save, indeed, that given by
the lad's gesture as he turned his face away, apparently afraid lest the starting tears should be seen. For though Archie had sobbed in uncontrollable
grief over poor Rough, he was in general reserved about showing his feelings; and none, not even his mother, guessed how heavily his trial weighed
upon him.

Besides his being hump-backed, Archie was so short as well, and didn't
seem to grow like other boys; and sometimes the fear had forced itself upon
him whether he ever would get any bigger, but would be through life, not
only deformed, but a dwarf—something to make everyone who passed him
turn round and look after him, and perhaps point the finger at him. Oh, how
he envied the tall, straight, active boys he met in all directions; who could
run, and jump, and climb, and even fight one another; whilst he, after only
walking a short distance, was often glad to lie down and rest his weary,
aching back.

So Dr. Oldroyd's question received no spoken answer, for Archie could
not have put all those, his feelings, into words; in fact, no words could
have expressed them. But, when the doctor had made his examination, it
was with piteous eyes that Archie looked up into his face, as if entreating
him to say there was hope, and yet feeling sure there was none.

'I'm afraid it must be a life-long trouble, Archie,' he said gently.

The lips quivered, and the little downcast face was very sad; but Dr.
Oldroyd held one of his hands in his own warm grasp, and that seemed to
help him to control himself.

'But perhaps if we were to have a talk together about it we should find it
need not be such a great trouble after all, or at least learn how to bear it
better. Sit down here, Archie, and warm yourself, whilst we talk the matter
over.'

And then Dr. Oldroyd tried to show the lad why it was that troubles came; that they were all meant as blessings, and would prove such if used aright.

'You have a heavy cross to bear, my little fellow; heavier than most of us; and you are so young too!' said the kind doctor compassionately; 'but if you take it up bravely and bear it patiently it will be exchanged for a great reward some day. It has been sent you in kindness; for you know Who it is lays it upon you, don't you, Archie?'

No reply coming, Dr. Oldroyd continued, 'It is your Heavenly Father; and therefore, you know, it must all be in love, because He *is* your Father.'

But the word 'Father' kindled no answering look in the boy's face. Dr. Oldroyd noticed it, and guessed the cause. With a pitying glance towards the boy, and a feeling of indignation stirring within him that any parent should so abuse the sacred name of father, he tried another strain.

'You have a mother, I think you told me, Archie?'

'Yes, sir.'

'And is she kind to you?'

'Kind! Oh, ain't she just! Why, she's my *mother*, sir.'

'And therefore you think *must* love you! And if you are in trouble, does she try and comfort you?'

A softened light came into Archie's face now, as he recalled all the tenderness she had always shown him, and how she had always shared in all his troubles. Especially he thought upon their meeting yesterday, when she had pressed him to her so closely; and child though he was, he knew well enough that she would gladly bear every one of his little sorrows for him and instead of him, if she could.

'Ay, she just do try to comfort me—always—as much as ever she can.'

'Then listen, Archie. God says, "As one whom his mother comforteth, so will I comfort you."'

Archie looked up musingly. This was a new view to him.

'It is God who has given you this cross to bear; but He feels for you, and knows exactly how heavy it is, and longs to comfort you, just as your mother does. For He is so tender, Archie! more tender than your own mother even.'

The boy was listening attentively, with his eyes fixed upon his kind friend's face; but when the latter paused, he said in a low tone,—

'Then why did He make me hump-backed? or why don't He make me straight now?'

'Ah, that is one of the things we cannot understand, Archie; at least, not here, though you will when you get to heaven. Then you will see that it was all in kindness that He didn't make you straight like other lads. Perhaps it was that your troubles might teach you to go to Him, who loves you not the less, but rather the more, because you are different from most boys.'

'But now, Archie,' said Dr. Oldroyd, after a time, 'we must think what is to be done about father. For your mother's sake, you must try and get him to forgive you and let you come home again, for she must want her little boy back with her.'

'But he won't forgive me; he's too angry with me.'

'Well, we must see if we can't persuade him. Do you think if I went and had a talk with him it would do any good?'

'He'd hearken to you, sir, if he would to anybody,' said Archie confidently.

'You think so, do you? Very well, then, I'll try to-morrow; and you come here again in the evening to hear if I have been successful. No, stay, that would be too far out of your way if, as I hope will be the case, I am able to tell you to go home afterwards; I will call round for you at Martin's, if you will keep in the way. At least, I will come and tell you what father says.'

At this moment the door was suddenly flung open, and a boy of about Archie's age burst into the room in an eager manner, exclaiming, 'I've finished my lesson, papa, so now I can come and sit with you.' Then, as he perceived Archie, he added, 'I didn't know you had any one with you.'

'That doesn't matter, my boy; we have finished our talk, so you needn't go away.'

The new-comer upon this advanced nearer his father's chair, and stood with one arm resting on the back of it. He was a bright, handsome lad, with regular features and curly brown hair. A very winning face it was, full of fun and good temper, and perhaps telling that its owner possessed a larger share of heart than of brains.

Dr. Oldroyd caught Archie's eye fixed upon him with a wistful, admiring gaze; and as he glanced at the two lads, so differently gifted and circumstanced—the one full of health and vigour and boyish beauty, the other sickly, stunted in growth, and deformed—his compassionate heart felt more than ever for the poor lad whose lot seemed one of such privation. Ah well! he would try if he could not brighten the little fellow's path.

'How are the rabbits to-day, Georgie?'

'Oh, they're all right, father. Should you like to have a look at them?' added the boy, with a smile.

'Well, you may bring them here for a few minutes if you like, for I fancy Archie there is fond of animals, so I daresay he would like to see them.'

George hastened away, and soon returned with two snow-white rabbits in his arms. Putting one down on his father's knee, he allowed Archie to take the other. The poor lad, who possessed that innate love for dumb animals which so often accompanies a large, tender heart, was delighted with the soft, warm creature, and pressed it to him caressingly, gently stroking it and laying his cheek down against its white back.

'Aren't they beauties?' said George.

'Ay, that they be, and no mistake,' returned Archie warmly. And soon the two boys were deep in discussion about their particular merits, Dr.

G*

Oldroyd trying to keep the conversation strictly to the rabbits, and avoid all allusion to dogs.

Archie was loth to put his new favourite down, but it was time now for him to be going, and Dr. Oldroyd said he should come again some day to see how they were getting on.

'Mr Martin will let you sleep there again to-night, I suppose?' he asked.

Archie thought he would, and departed, Dr. Oldroyd having first renewed his promise of coming round to see him on the following evening.

Martin was perfectly willing again to give the boy a shelter under his roof; and upon Archie's producing his shilling, and begging him to take it, saying he was afraid it wasn't near enough, but it was all he had, the other replied,—

'Keep it, my little lad, keep it. You'll be certain to want it fast enough, so you needn't be in such a hurry to part with it; and as long as ever I have got a bit of sup to spare, I hope as I'll always be glad to share it with a poor, friendless little chap. Put your money back in your pocket. If I wouldn't take Dr. Oldroyd's last night when he wanted to pay me for taking of you in, I ain't likely to take everything as you've got from you yourself. No, no; you sit down instead, and make a good, hearty supper. Our crust won't taste none the worse, will it, Bess, because we've give a part of it to the little lad?'

CHAPTER VI

LEARNING PATIENCE

THE next evening Archie was anxiously awaiting Dr. Oldroyd, to learn the result of his promised visit to his father. At length the footsteps which so often brought hope and comfort to many an oppressed heart in that great city were heard approaching; and when they reached Martin's door, Archie was standing there, ready to receive his kind friend with a bright smile of welcome.

'It's all right, my boy. Father has promised to agree to your coming home again. But you must try for the future not to vex him; and you must bear it patiently if he gets angry with you sometimes. It isn't right for a boy to answer back, or speak to his father as you did, Archie; though I know it was hard upon you to see your dog injured before your eyes,' added Dr. Oldroyd, wishing to soften his reproof.

After a few words of leave-taking, and thanks to the Martins for all their kindness, Archie prepared to set off, Dr. Oldroyd having said he would walk part of the way with him, as he had something more to say to him.

'You can come and see us sometimes, can't you?' said Bessie. 'We should like to hear how you are getting on.'

'Ay, I'll come sure enough,' returned Archie. 'You've been so kind to me here that I ain't like to forget it;' and then he ran off after the doctor.

'You must tell your father, Archie, that you are sorry for your behaviour the other evening,' he said, as they walked along.

Archie did not reply.

'Aren't you prepared to do that?' asked Dr. Oldroyd.

'I don't know as 'twould be true, sir,' answered Archie, in a low voice; ''cause I should be pretty sure to do the same again if poor Rough was here and he struck at him. 'Twas a cruel shame! Don't you think it was, sir?'

'You mustn't look at that, Archie, but at your own part in the matter. You must think whether you are doing what is pleasing or displeasing to your Heavenly Father. Eh, my boy?'

'I never thought on it like that afore,' was Archie's brief reply.

'Then think of it now, my lad.'

When Archie reached home his father was sitting beside the fire smoking. He did not turn round, nor take any notice when the child stole in, and was received by Mrs. Wood with a smile, and warm though silent embrace. Nor when Archie, trying to screw up his courage—as he felt the promise he had given Dr. Oldroyd before they parted must be kept—timidly advanced nearer, saying, 'Father, I didn't ought to have spoke to you like I did t'other night; I was a bad boy to get into such a passion,' did he make the slightest sign of being conscious of his presence.

Archie, thinking he had not heard, repeated his speech; but his father's eye still remained fixed upon the fire; so he retreated to the little table at which his mother was sitting working, and drew up a chair beside her.

A few minutes afterwards Wood rose and went out, to Archie's great relief, and then he and his mother had a happy half-hour talking over his new friends, and his good fortune in falling in with them. Then he went off to his little bed; and though when he found himself there for the first time without his faithful Rough, he shed a few silent tears over his memory, his last thoughts were of Dr. Oldroyd and the words he had spoken to him that evening when they were sitting by his study fire.

After this things went on for a time much as usual, Wood taking little notice of the child, who, however, shrank from him more than formerly.

Some times when his mother was out working he would go to Bessie, who taught him hymns; or to the good Dr. Oldroyd, when noticing his intelligence, he offered to teach him. He progressed well in his lessons.

Thus the days for a time went on smoothly and more happily than formerly with Archie, who was learning many things, but chiefly that highest and sweetest of all lessons, to know more and more of the love of his Saviour, and in gratitude for that love to strive to please Him in every word and deed.

But after this pleasant life had lasted thus for a time, it was suddenly interrupted by an accident which occurred to Wood, who, while engaged in his work, fell from a scaffold, and was taken up much injured. He insisted upon being carried to his house, rather than to the hospital, and was accordingly conveyed thither. Fortunately for him, Dr. Oldroyd happened at that very hour to be paying a visit to a sick person in the same court, and with his usual kindness came across at once and attended to his hurts.

Archie and his mother had enough now upon their hands in nursing and waiting upon the invalid, whose sufferings made his temper more irritable than ever, so that it was next to impossible to please him or to do anything right in his eyes; whilst many hard, bitter speeches—which perhaps in Archie's case would have been accompanied by cuffs and blows, had not weakness rendered the hand powerless—were poured upon them.

After a time, Wood being better, and thus requiring less watching, though still unable to leave his bed, Mrs. Wood, whose earnings were more than ever needed now, again went out by day to work, leaving Archie to wait upon his father. The boy shrank very much at first from being thus left alone with him; but there was no help for it, and so he tried to face his task bravely.

And when, often for an hour at a time, his father would appear to be dozing, he would softly sing to himself, in his low, sweet voice, the hymns he had learnt to love so much.

One day Wood had been in a good deal of pain, and had, in consequence, been more than usually exacting and impatient, and hard to please. Archie had tried to do his best, in spite of his weariness both of mind and body; but he was learning to seek for strength from above, and by its help he was enabled to take in silence, and without replying, the irritable fault-finding, which was all the return he received for his patient efforts to give satisfaction.

Sitting down on a little stool near the fire, though expecting to be called again in an instant to bring or do something, as had been the case almost every minute throughout the morning, he buried his face in his hands, wondering how much longer he should have to go on thus. Then all Dr. Oldroyd had said to him about being patient came into his mind, and he began to fear he had been very much the contrary, in wishing that his weary task might soon be ended. To soothe himself he softly chanted some of his favourite verses, the sadness which was filling his little heart giving a plaintive ring to his voice which made it more than usually sweet.

After a time, wondering at his father's silence, he looked across to see if he were asleep, and found him lying with open eyes looking at him.

'Why do you stop?' asked Wood, abruptly, as the boy paused. 'Go on singing.'

'What shall I sing, father?' inquired Archie, astonished at the command.

'Anything. Them things you're always a-singing.'

Then this was not the first time his father had been listening to him; and, moreover, he liked to hear him. Archie was pleased, and sang out clearly and firmly one hymn after another, until he had run through them all. Then he paused.

'Haven't you ere another?'

'No, I don't know any more; but I could sing'em all over again, if you'd like.'

'Sing away, then,' was the abrupt reply; but when next Archie had occasion to perform some little service for his father, the latter received it with a 'Thank you, boy,' which was something quite unusual; whilst all the rest of the day his manner was kinder and gentler.

After this the boy sang day by day, whilst the sick man lay and listened to the simple words telling of a dying Saviour's love, and of a full, free pardon for all erring ones who come and cast themselves with all their sins before the Redeemer's feet, entreating Him to wash them in the blood He shed for them. All this fell upon the ears of the man who had long been deaf to such things, and sinking deeper yet, reached his heart, and took firm root there.

The hard heart was becoming softened and melted, surely if slowly; and at the same time, gradually and almost imperceptibly, Archie was making his way in, and winning for himself a place there such as he little dreamt or imagined. And Dr. Oldroyd, who always seemed to know the moment when to speak or when to be silent, watched for his opportunity, and tried indirectly to help on and deepen the impression already made.

'What was it the doctor was saying to you t'other day about a cross, Archie? What did he mean?'

' 'Twas only a few words about something as he'd talked of afore one day.'

'Well, what was it? What did he mean by your taking up your cross?'

'He meant bearing troubles patient-like—without grumbling at 'em.'

'And what troubles have you got to bear?'

Archie was silent, reluctant to give an answer. But the question was repeated in a way which gave him no choice but to reply.

'Well, for one thing, being hump-backed, and so different from other fellows,' he said in a low tone.

'Is that a trouble? Do you make that a trouble, boy?' asked Wood, almost sharply, with a sudden change of voice and look.

'I can't help it,' murmured poor Archie. 'I do try not to mind, but—'

'But what? Go on, boy.'

'It seems so hard sometimes. Though p'raps some day I shall get not to care; for Dr. Oldroyd says as God wouldn't have made me crooked if He hadn't knowed somehow as 'twould be the best thing for me.'

'God didn't make you crooked. He made you straight enough,' said Wood, abruptly.

'Then who did make me crooked?'

Ay, who did? Archie's question remained unanswered. His father gave one long, searching look into the boy's countenance, many expressions flitting across his own meanwhile, and then he turned his back upon his little son, and his face to the wall, and thus remained without speaking for more than an hour.

But all that evening his eyes followed Archie's movements with a new look in them; and the latter several times found them fixed upon him musingly.

CHAPTER VII

SUFFERING

As soon as the invalid began to be able to sit up and move about a little, Archie was allowed to resume his visits to Dr. Oldroyd's; and it soon came to be an understood thing that on his return he should relate to his father all that had passed, and all that the doctor had taught him, Wood appearing glad of anything that might relieve the dreariness of his long confinement to the house.

And these visits were a source of the greatest pleasure to Archie, not only because he loved the short lesson from Dr. Oldroyd, and the brief conversation which generally followed it, but because, now that the evenings were light, George Oldroyd would often, before he left, take him out into the courtyard at the back, where the rabbits and other pets were kept; and there the two boys, so unlike in most other respects, found they were on common ground.

Many an hour they spent together, devising improvements in rabbit hutches, in which Archie showed himself the more skilful of the two, or in planning better arrangements for the other pets, among which George numbered a guinea pig, and a little mouse, which was a most clever, knowing little fellow, and always showed off his accomplishments best when Archie was present, the boy seeming to have a knack of speedily winning the love of all dumb creatures.

But as the long days came on, and the heat grew greater and greater, Archie's feeble strength seemed to feel it, and he began to flag more and more. For a time it passed unnoticed, as he never even complained, and his spirit helped him to bear up; but the walk to Dr. Oldroyd's took him longer and longer to accomplish each time.

It was so gradual a change that for a while it escaped Dr. Oldroyd's observation; but at length he began to perceive that the lad was drooping, and one evening, when the heat was more than usually oppressive, and Archie could not conceal his weariness, his pallid cheeks startled the kind doctor.

'We won't do any more lessons to-night,' he said, shutting up the book. 'You don't look fit for it. Anything particular the matter, eh?'

'No, sir, thank you.'

'Is it only that you are tired, or does your back hurt you?'

'It aches, sir; but it almost always does that.'

'Then you must rest it more, Archie. The long walk here is too much for you, I expect.'

'Oh no, indeed, sir, it ain't,' rejoined Archie, earnestly. 'I'd a deal rather my back did ache than miss coming here.'

Dr. Oldroyd smiled.

'But I can't allow you to come if it does you harm,' he said kindly.

Archie's face lengthened; and he looked up wistfully, as if to beg the doctor not to carry out such a sentence; but he had no time to say more, as at that moment Georgie burst into the room in his usual fashion.

He wanted Archie's help in the yard in some fresh arrangements he was making there.

'Archie is tired this evening. I don't think you must ask him to come now,' said Dr. Oldroyd.

'Oh, but I can't manage without him!' exclaimed Georgie.

'Mayn't I go, sir? Indeed, sir, I ain't too tired,' said Archie, rising.

'Well, then, don't let him keep you too long. Mind, Georgie, Archie has a long walk home before him; so don't keep him working at your affairs until he is altogether done up. Learn to be considerate and thoughtful for others, my boy.'

'Come along then, Archie;' and the two lads went out together.

They found their occupation one of engrossing interest, and for a time all went well, until it came to the hanging of the magpie's cage in a different place, more out of reach of the numerous cats which prowled about.

'I want it hung just up there,' said Georgie, pointing to a particular spot, whilst Archie stood by waiting to execute orders.

'But I can't reach, Master George, without something to stand on.'

'What can we find? Here, this will do, won't it?' said Georgie, dragging out of a corner a disused wooden flower-stand, composed of two or three little shelves, rising like steps one above another.

'Will it bear me, do you think, sir?'

'Oh, yes; it'll bear you fast enough.'

Archie ascended one or two of the steps, and with the hammer raised in one hand, and in the other a nail which he was preparing to drive into the wall, was suddenly startled by a shout from Georgie.

'Not there, Archie, that won't do; it'll come just in the way of the rabbit-hutch. It must be ever so much higher.'

Archie, standing on tip-toe, tried to stretch his arms up the required height, but he could not reach the precise spot pointed out by Georgie, who, with an impatient exclamation—'How stupid you are! Here, let me come

and do it; I'm taller than you'—made a sudden movement which gave a
push to the light stand, and destroying Archie's balance, made him fall to
the ground.

'You haven't hurt yourself, have you?' said Georgie, somewhat carelessly,
too intent upon his occupation to think much of a tumble which to himself
would have been a mere nothing.

Without waiting for an answer, he sprang upon the steps, and soon
accomplished the driving of the nail at the desired height. But when that
was done, and he looked round, he found his companion was only just
beginning, slowly and with difficulty, to rise from the ground.

'Why, what's the matter?' he asked hurriedly, alarmed at Archie's white
face. 'Are you really hurt? I'm sure I'm very sorry I made you fall. I didn't
mean to push the steps like that.'

'Oh, it ain't much, sir; leastways, I daresay it'll soon go off,' said Archie,
though the look of pain on his face belied his words.

'Can't you get up? Shall I help you?'

'No, thank you, sir; I'll manage it by myself;' and Archie, catching hold
of some support near, pulled himself up, though with lips so tightly pressed
together that it showed it was all he could do to keep from uttering a
groan.

Georgie stood by, looking on with concern whilst Archie leant against the
wall, wiping from his face the drops of moisture which the suffering he was
trying so bravely to conceal had brought there.

'Don't mind me, Master George,' he said, as he noticed the latter's look.
'I shall be all right in a minute, I daresay; and you haven't hung the cage up
yet. Let us see if it'll do now.'

Georgie put the cage in its place, and was highly satisfied with the arrangement; and then, as there was nothing more to do, Archie prepared to
to take leave, concealing to the last the pain every movement cost him, lest
Georgie should be distressed at it; whilst the latter, to whom falls and
tumbles meant only a few bruises, of which he would not dream of com-
plaining, and little thinking of any more serious results, went indoors, and
finding his father had gone out for a short time, took up a book, and soon
forgot everything in the thrilling interest of the story he was reading, which
was full of wonderful adventures in foreign lands.

Poor patient Archie meantime took his painful way homewards. Very
slow and weary were his steps; whilst he had to sit down and rest so often
that he began to wonder how he should ever manage to reach home at all.
The pain in his back was such as he had never felt before; so great that it
was almost past endurance; but still he plodded on as best he could.

Both mother and father were in; but Archie no longer dreaded meeting
the latter, for he seemed to be growing kinder almost every day, and had not
once since his recovery from his accident gone back to the drink, which had
formerly made him so irritable and violent.

Mrs. Wood was alarmed at her little son's looks, as he stole in and sank down upon a chair.

'Why, whatever is the matter with you, Archie? Whatever have you been about? You are looking nigh as white as a ghost!'

Wood looked up from the paper he was reading as he ate his supper, and glanced across inquiringly at the boy.

'What is it, dear?' went on Mrs. Wood, as she put her arm round the lad, who laid his head wearily against her.

'It's my back, mother. It's so bad I don't scarce know how to bear it!'

Wood's face seemed to grow red at these words, and there was an odd twitching about his mouth; but without speaking he rose, and turning his back upon them both, stood looking out of the window.

'Poor child!' said the mother. 'Then you'd best go to bed at once, dear; maybe you'll feel better there.'

'I'd rather bide still a bit first, mother; it hurts so to move. I'd bear it better,' he added, with a patient smile on the little thin face, 'only I'm so tired to-night;' and the boy's voice had a weary sound in it.

Wood turned round with a strangely softened look on his face.

'If it hurts you to move, my lad, I'll carry you upstairs, and so save your walking. You needn't be afraid to trust me,' he added, seeing Archie's look of surprise, 'for I won't be rough with you; I won't hurt you.'

His manner was almost as if he were entreating a favour; whilst as he stooped to lift the boy, and the latter put his arms round his neck, and he felt how light was the child's weight, and how thin the arms which had never before clung to him like this, a sudden gush of tenderness seemed to spring up within him, making him lay his burden down on the bed so carefully, that one would scarcely have thought it possible such gentleness could come from a great, strong man, whilst Archie fancied he heard him murmur, 'My poor little lad! my poor little lad!'

'Thank you, father; 'twas so kind of you to bring me up,' he said, with a grateful look.

Wood gave one glance at the poor little suffering face, and then, as if he could not trust himself to speak, he hurried downstairs, leaving Mrs. Wood, who had followed them, to look after Archie's wants.

'What is it has made you so bad, Archie? What have you been about? Have you given yourself a hurt anyhow?'

The boy hesitated for a moment, and then replied, 'I had a fall this evening, mother; that was all.'

'Ah, maybe that gave your poor back a twist. Dear, dear! how sorry I am! But let me see if I can't make you more comfortable; and maybe, after a good night's rest, you'll be better.'

When Mrs. Wood, some time later, again went downstairs, her husband turned round to ask how the boy was.

'He seems in a deal of pain, poor fellow,' she answered, meeting her husband's look with one full of reproachful sadness.

'Mary don't; I can't bear it!' exclaimed Wood, with a sudden outburst of feeling. 'It cuts me to the heart to hear him say that, when I know how different I've always been. And it do seem as if the punishment of my sin was to last for ever, and grow heavier just when I'm beginning to wish to do better! Oh, if I'd never given away to that fit of passion! for now I can't undo it, though I'd give a deal to be able to.' And the strong man's voice was broken and husky.

The wife was much moved by this unexpected display of feeling. Drawing nearer, she laid her hand on her husband's shoulder, saying,—

'He don't know nothing about it, for I've never told him. And he'll learn to love you if you'll only be kind to him, for he's got as loving and tender a heart as any lad living. 'Twould make him so happy, poor fellow, if you'd always be like you were to-night.'

' I mean to try. I hope as I'll be a better father to him for the future; for the little lad has taught me many things all that time whilst I was laid up abed, and he used to sing to me. And it all seems to take such hold on me; I can't shake it off, nor get it out of my thoughts nohow. I see now what a brute of a father—ay, and husband too—I've been! You've been very patient with me, Mary, and forgiving; and as to the boy—there, I can't say nohow all as I feels about him; only I think I could a'most lay down my life for him tomorrow if 'twould do him any good!'

A thankful light shone in Mrs. Wood's eyes, making them very soft and bright, whilst her heart overflowed with happiness at finding that the hopes which she had been secretly cherishing of late were not without a good foundation.

CHAPTER VIII

A CONFESSION

ARCHIE passed a sleepless night of pain, and the next day was no better. He could not rise from his bed, but lay there in constant suffering, though trying all the time to bear it patiently, and not utter a murmur.

But this uncomplaining endurance appeared to touch his father to the quick; and when, after he came home from work in the evening, he agreed to look after the lad whilst Mrs. Wood went out to do some errands, he sat beside him with so sorrowful an expression on his countenance that Archie noticed it and wondered what brought it there.

'Is the pain as bad still?' asked Wood at length. 'Don't it get no better?'

'No, father, not yet; but maybe it will soon.'

'You couldn't sing to-night, I s'pose? You're too bad for that?'

'I could try, if you like, father;' but the faint tones of the voice showed the impossibility of the thing, and made the father hasten to say,—

'No, no, my boy. Make haste and get better, and then you shall sing again.'

However, Archie did not get better, but rather worse; and when the evening for him to go to Dr. Oldroyd's came round he was still confined to his bed, suffering the same pain.

When the doctor found that the lad did not present himself, he feared something must be amiss, remembering how fragile he had looked the last time he had been there. Always prompt in action, and never sparing himself when a kind deed was waiting to be done, Dr. Oldroyd resolved at once to go and look after the boy; for he knew no slight obstacle would have prevented him from coming.

Mrs. Wood opened the door to him; and from her he learnt the state in which Archie had reached home that last evening he had been out, and how much he had suffered since.

'I am the more sorry to hear it,' remarked the doctor, 'because he had been previously so pulled down by the hot weather that he can have very little strength left to help him to bear up.'

But he found the boy even worse than he had expected; and as he took his feverish hand in his, and felt his feeble pulse, he looked very grave.

'Why did you not send for me before?' he said, turning to Mrs. Wood. 'I would have come directly, and I might have been able to do something for him.'

'Well, we hoped, sir, as he'd get better, and there'd be no call to trouble you; but we were just thinking if we mightn't make so bold as to send to-morrow if he wasn't better.'

'I don't want to bother you with many questions, my boy,' said Dr. Oldroyd, sitting down beside him, 'but I want to know how this happened. Your mother tells me you had a fall.'

'Yes, sir.'

'But where did you fall, and how was it?'

Archie hesitated. 'I fell off some steps, sir.'

'But how was that? How came you to fall?'

Archie did not reply; only looked distressed, and seemed to beg not to be questioned further.

'Well, well,' said Dr. Oldroyd, 'if you can't tell me now, perhaps you will another time. But I must hear how you are feeling, and all about it, that I may know what to do for you.'

And then Dr. Oldroyd promised to send him a soothing draught, which would help him to get some sleep; and also some little dainties from his own table to tempt his failing appetite.

'Your mother tells me you have been a good patient boy, Archie,' he said, rising. 'How is it you have been able to bear it all so bravely?'

'You said, sir, Jesus would help me, if I asked Him; and I have asked Him,' answered the boy, almost in a whisper. 'And when I mind, sir, all as you've told me about what He's done and borne for me, why I feel as if I could bear the pain, and a deal more too, without a word, if 'twould only show how I love Him.'

And as Archie's face kindled with the feelings which carried him out of his shyness, and made the features which were sharpened by suffering light up with a smile, which showed that, child though he was, he had learnt to take up his little cross cheerfully and lovingly, Dr. Oldroyd felt his eyes becoming dim with a moisture that rose into them. He had to clear his throat and blow his nose vehemently, as though suffering from a violent cold, before he could speak, and then it was only to say,—

'I'll come and see you again to-morrow morning, and I hope I shall find you a great deal better then.'

When Dr. Oldroyd reached his home, Georgie came forward to meet him, saying, 'Where have you been, papa? I came to look for you as soon as I had done my lessons, but I could not find you anywhere, nor Archie, either; and this is his evening.'

'I have just been to him. He is ill, Georgie.'

'Is he. Poor Archie! What is the matter with him, papa?'

'There seems to be some fresh injury to the spine. He seems to have hurt himself in some way, and his stock of strength is so very small at the best of times, that I'm almost afraid it may go hardly with him. I was quite startled at the change in him.'

'Oh, papa, how sorry I am for him! But it seems so sudden; it isn't long since he was here!'

'No; it was that same evening that he crawled home so ill and went to bed, and he hasn't been able to get up since. He says he had a fall; but I can't get him to tell me anything more. I suppose you don't know anything about it, Georgie?' Dr. Oldroyd suddenly asked, as he remembered the two lads going out into the yard together that evening.

'No, papa. Oh, stay'—and Georgie's face flushed crimson, whilst a look of distress came into it, as the circumstances of that evening, which he had since quite forgotten, darted into his mind.

'What is it, Georgie? Speak out.'

'Oh, papa, he fell here; it was my doing. I gave a push to some steps he was standing on, and he fell right down. But he didn't say he had hurt himself so much.'

'Because, as you know well enough, Archie isn't a lad to complain; but how could you be so cruel and thoughtless,' said Dr. Oldroyd sternly, 'towards a poor deformed boy, who ought to be treated gently by everybody? How came you to do it?' And an indignant light flashed in the doctor's eye.

'Oh, papa, I didn't mean to do it; I didn't know he would fall.'

'It wasn't in anger, then? I know how hasty you often are, Georgie.'

'No, indeed, papa, I wasn't angry; I was only a little bit impatient because he couldn't do what I wanted in a minute. But I shouldn't have cared for such a tumble a bit. I'll tell you exactly how it was, papa;' and Georgie related all the circumstances truthfully and honestly.

'Still, it was very thoughtless of you, Georgie,' said his father, 'and it is a punishment to you for yielding to impatience, for you have brought great suffering upon the poor boy.'

The tears came into Georgie's eyes.

'But he did not tell me it was you who had caused his fall,' went on his father. 'I could get nothing from him when I questioned him. I little thought it was my own boy who had done it.'

'I'm *so* sorry, papa,' said Georgie, sobbing.

'I'm sure you must be; and so am I,' returned Dr. Oldroyd gravely.

'But he will get better, won't he?' asked Georgie.

'I don't know, my boy; I can't say; for he isn't like a lad who has a good strong constitution to work upon. But we must do all we can for him.'

'Let me go and tell him how sorry I am, papa. I'm sure I didn't mean to hurt him; for I do like Archie; he's worth all the boys I know put together almost.'

'But I hope you wouldn't willingly have hurt him, even if you hadn't liked him.'

'I mightn't have been so sorry for it,' was Georgie's candid answer. 'But what can I do to make up to him for it? May I go and see him?'

'Not now; it is too late, and I couldn't have him disturbed again to-night. But you shall come with me when I go to-morrow, and see him for a few minutes. He is too weak to bear much; but you can just tell him in a few words how sorry you are.'

Georgie did not recover his spirits that evening, but went off to bed early; and the next day, when according to his father's promise he was allowed to see Archie, he was so shocked at his altered looks that his grief broke out afresh.

'Oh, Archie, do forgive me; I know I oughtn't to have been impatient, but I never thought you would fall; I never meant to hurt you.'

'Oh, I know that, Master George; please don't take on so about it. 'Twas all my being so clumsy and stupid; it wasn't your fault at all.'

'Oh, but I know it was; I ought to have been more careful with you, because you can't stand knocking about like I can. I wish I could bear some of the pain for you, Archie.'

The latter smiled one of his sweet, grateful smiles; but he had no time to say more, as at that moment Dr. Oldroyd returned to the room, and seeing his little patient could not bear more excitement just then, sent Georgie downstairs.

'Please tell him not to fret over it, sir,' said Archie, as the doctor came to his side; 'for it wasn't his fault, sir. He did nothing more than anybody would have done; 'twas just an accident.'

'Very well, my boy, I'll tell him what you say. And should you like him to come and see you again?'

'Oh, d'you think as he would, sir? That would be good of him!' exclaimed Archie, as earnestly as his feeble voice allowed. ' 'Twould quite make up for being ill to have you and him come in sometimes.'

'My poor boy!' murmured Dr. Oldroyd, marvelling at the depth and warmth of the affection that dwelt in the heart of the little untutored lad.

'But yet you are a happy fellow, Archie, aren't you? for you've always one Friend close at hand, whom you love; and you know how to go to Him and tell Him all your troubles. He'll take away this pain, and make you well again if He sees right; and if not—well, when you get to heaven there'll be no pain there.'

And the good doctor, who could never witness suffering, especially in a child, without feeling his compassion moved, found himself sending up a secret petition that God would bless his skill, and make it avail for the little fellow's relief.

That evening, when Wood came in from his work and went upstairs to sit with his little son, as had become his custom since Archie had been ill, he found him, as he fancied, even worse than usual. A strange softness and tenderness always came over Wood now in the presence of his boy, when the formerly harsh voice became low and gentle, and the frequently angry looks of past days were exchanged for sorrowful, pitying ones.

The heat had been great that day, and still was so, which naturally made Archie more languid than ever; and as Wood sat looking at him in silence, a sudden fear darted into his mind that it might be the boy was not long for earth, that perhaps his weary little course was almost run, and the burden laid upon him, which he had tried to take up so uncomplainingly, was soon to be laid down and exchanged for a bright reward. Wood's thoughts might not, perhaps, have been clothed by himself in these words, but they were something to the same effect.

Archie, noticing his silence, said, 'Didn't you find it terrible hot at work to-day, father?'

'Ay, it was hot, and no mistake. But is it that as makes you seem so much weaker to-night, Archie? or is it that the pain ain't no better?'

'Maybe, it's a bit of both, father. But,' he added, seeing the sad expression on the face turned towards him, and wishing to chase it away, 'Dr. Oldroyd says up in heaven there won't be no pain, so it's only just to bear it for a little while.'

'A little while!' cried Wood, with sudden alarm in his tones. 'Oh, Archie, you don't mean—you don't feel as if——'

He could not finish his sentence, but Archie understood it.

'I don't know, father; but sometimes as I lie here I think how nice 'twould be to go there and be made quite well and straight, which I never can be here.'

A sort of shiver ran through Wood's frame, as if he had received some sudden thrust or stab.

'Oh, Archie, forgive me!' burst from the strong man in accents of agony, as he sank down beside the little bed, and buried his face from sight. 'Archie, can you ever forgive me? Oh, tell me that you do before you go!'

'Forgive you, father? What for?'

'For making you deformed, Archie!'

A moment's pause followed those last words, when the silence in the room was so profound that it could be almost felt. Wood seemed as if he could not trust himself to look towards his boy but went on,—

'It was my doing, Archie. God made you straight enough, but I, in a fit of passion, when I was half drunk, did you such an injury as you've never got over. Your poor back has got worse and worse, and now it's come to this! But, oh, Archie, I don't think as the pain you have to bear can be much worse than what I feel at seeing it!'

'Dear father!' murmured Archie softly.

'I didn't used to care,' went on Wood, as if he felt forced to tell everything; 'at least, I used to try not, and I know I've often been sharp and cross with you, just because the very sight of you minded me how bad I'd been, and made me angry with myself. But I see it different now, and I'd give anything to be able to make it up to you. Don't hate me, Archie, now you know it was all my fault you're hump-backed.'

'Hate you! oh, father, please don't say such things! I was a bad boy once, and talked like that, but 'twas wicked of me, and I wouldn't say such words now; for it wouldn't be true—how could it, when you're so kind to me!'

'But you can't love me?' And Wood lifted up his face with a wistful, yearning look upon it.

' I can, father. Indeed I can, and I do. You're so kind now,' he repeated; and the boy took one of the large, rough hands between his smaller ones caressingly.

That touch seemed to unlock the pent-up feelings in the strong man's breast. He bent his head, and hot tears fell upon his boy's hand. His heart was melted within him. Always a man of strong feeling, and little used to disguise of any sort, the tide of remorse and sorrow, of longing to undo the past, and of passionate love for the lad beside him—his own child, to whom he had done a life-long injury, and who, just as he was learning to love him, was perhaps about to pass away from him—swept over him with such force that his soul was, as it were, bowed to the ground; and in broken accents he testified to the genuineness of his penitence by doing that most difficult thing for a parent, humbling himself to ask forgiveness of his own son.

Archie was almost awed at sight of his father's emotion.

'Indeed, father, you needn't mind so much for me. I don't care for it now like I used to once; for Dr. Oldroyd has told me what a heavy cross Jesus bore for me, and he says if I bear this little one patient-like, 'twill show as I'm trying to please Him. And I would like Jesus to know how I loves Him! So I don't want it different, father; indeed I don't. There's no call for you to fret so over it.'

'Bless you, my boy! bless you for them words. But when I think of your being like that all your life through——'

'Maybe it won't be so very long,' said Archie, as his father broke off without finishing his sentence.

'Oh, don't say that, my boy,' cried Wood, almost entreatingly. 'I know that then you'd be set free from all your pain; but oh, Archie, we want you here; we couldn't do without you nohow!'

'Dear father!' said Archie, with a new sense of gladness in his heart at finding such love bestowed upon him. 'But I s'pose it'll be just as God chooses, won't it, father? 'Twould be nice to go to heaven and live with Jesus; but Dr. Oldroyd says, if I ask Him, Jesus will come and be always with me here, and then I could still stay with you and mother. It'll be nice any way. But I'm *so* tired now, father;' and the boy's voice died away to a whisper, whilst he lay looking white and exhausted upon his pillow.

'My poor little lad! I've been letting you talk too much,' exclaimed Wood, in tones of self-reproach. 'Let me see if I can't make you more comfortable; and then you try and go to sleep.'

Wood carefully and tenderly tried to lift and put him into an easier position; but his heart ached as he saw the marks of pain and suffering on the young face, and the exhaustion which could not be concealed. Was he, indeed, passing away? Would they only have him with them for a little while longer? At these thoughts tears again filled his eyes, as he gazed mournfully upon the little form on the bed.

Archie, glancing up, saw the sorrowful look, and tried to smile; and then, with one hand in his father's, his eyes closed, and he seemed about to sleep. The other did not move or stir, for fear of disturbing him; and thus Mrs. Wood found them when she next came into the room.

He made her a sign to be cautious not to disturb the boy, and then whispered, 'You go to bed when you like, Mary; I'll stay by him to-night.'

'You don't think he's worse, do you?' she asked anxiously, still in a whisper.

'I don't know; he's very bad, that's certain. But I should like to sit beside him; and I'll call you if you're wanted. You see I couldn't move, 'twould wake him.'

Mrs. Wood, looking down, saw that the child's fingers had closed upon those of the father, and in spite of her anxiety on Archie's account, a sense of gladness filled her heart to see the two united to one another. She would leave them thus together. There was a work going on in which she would not desire to meddle, only rejoice over it, and give thanks for it.

Archie's sleep did not last long, and pain and restlessness succeeded to it; but all through that night, whenever he opened his eyes, he found his father's fixed upon him sorrowfully and sympathisingly; whilst the hard, rough hand, the weight of which Archie had so often felt in former days, smoothed his pillow and ministered to all his little wants with a gentleness of touch such as only the deep love now stirring within his heart could have taught.

For the parental feelings which had been lying dormant, or apparently dead, for so long, now seemed to have sprung into life with all the greater force from having been so long repressed. He seemed as if he never could do enough for the lad; and all through the weary hours of restlessness and sleeplessness tried by every means in his power to soothe the sufferings of the boy, to whom each movement brought such pain.

Archie looked up gratefully into his face, and once when he was bending over him, whispered, 'Kiss me, father.'

Wood stooped down and touched the thin cheek with his lips, evidently trying to control his feelings the while, lest he should disturb his boy; but he could not forbear saying in a low tone,—

'You love me, Archie, in spite of all?'

Archie's smile and look of affection were answer enough.

'Then I'll believe as Jesus loves me too, and is ready to forgive me for all as ever I've done!' murmured Wood, in an undertone.

And notwithstanding his sorrow and anxiety, a look of peace and gladness stole into his face.

CHAPTER IX

WOOD VISITS DR. OLDROYD

THOUGH Archie for a time had seemed to improve, he gained ground so slowly that he almost appeared to be at a stand-still. It caused him still great pain to move, and he was unable to sit up, whilst his strength did not return. But Dr. Oldroyd kept a cheerful face in the little fellow's presence, and never let him see that he felt any anxiety.

It was one evening, just at this time, that Dr. Oldroyd was sitting in his study when a servant came to inform him that a man of the name of Wood was asking if he could speak to him for a few minutes.

'Certainly; let him come in here,' was the reply; and Wood was accordingly shown in.

'What is it, Wood? Archie is not worse, I hope.'

'No, doctor, I don't say as he's worse; but then I can't say as he seems any better. And that's why I've made bold to come to you to-night, sir, to ask of you what you thinks about him, 'cause I'm most always out of the way when you come to see the lad. What's your 'pinion, doctor?

'Well, he doesn't get on very fast—not as I should like to see him.'

'But what I want to know, sir, is, do you think as he ever will get on?'

'I hope so. This hot weather is against his gaining strength for the present.'

'Ay, that's true. But, to come to the point, doctor, do you think as he'll ever get up again, or will always have to be a-lying down, like he is now?'

Wood's voice trembled as he asked the question, and then he bent forward in breathless eagerness to await the answer. There was a moment's pause before it came.

'I see no reason why he should not get better, and be able to do as much as he could before; but it may be a tedious affair.'

'Thank you, sir, for them words,' said Wood, with a look of infinite relief. 'They've took a load off my mind.'

'What did you fear?' asked Dr. Oldroyd.

'Why, that the poor little lad might be all his days as helpless as he is now —perhaps live on, but never be no better. And I thought perhaps you know'd it, only didn't like to tell us. And oh, sir, if it had been so, I don't know how I could have borne it.'

'You are very fond of your boy, and I don't wonder at it.'

'Oh, it ain't that only, but—but because of its being all my doing.'

'Your doing? How so? The boy, I am sorry to say, met with his fall at my house.'

'But it wasn't that as did it, was it, Sir?'

'Not altogether, of course, for such a trifling fall would have been nothing to another lad, whose spine was not already weak and delicate. If there had been no mischief there previously, it is not probable all this would have resulted from it. And, moreover, he had not been looking well or strong for some time before; he had flagged very much, and that was against him, and made him less able to bear up against the pain.'

'My poor little chap! Everything has always been against him, but his father's hand most of all!' exclaimed Wood, in a low tone of pain and self-reproach.

'Nay, he tells me how very kind you are to him,' said Dr. Oldroyd.

'Does he?' said Wood, drawing his hand across his eyes. 'He's the gratefullest little chap as ever I knew, that's certain. But ain't he told you nothing more, sir?'

'No.'

'Never told you how I've served him days gone by?'

'Only about the affair of the dog. And that was a good while ago, just when it had happened.'

'Then you never knew, sir, how he came to be deformed like he is?'

'Not exactly. Your wife, when I asked her one day, said it was the result

of an accident when he was quite a little fellow; but I thought from her manner that it pained her to refer to those times, and so I let the matter drop.'

'Well then, sir, I'd liefer you knew how 'twas. I shall feel more honest-
like when you knows the worst. 'Twas *I* as did it, sir, as caused the accident;
'twas all along of me and my passion, for I've mostly been a violent sort of
a man, leastways whenever I was in drink.'

A look of shame rested on Wood's face, showing that it cost him an effort
to make the confession. As Dr. Oldroyd did not speak for the moment, he
continued,—

'You're shocked, sir, I see, and well you may be; but I've been punished
for the sin.'

'And a heavy punishment it must indeed be, my poor fellow! And yet
God has been very merciful to you in putting such a forgiving spirit into
your boy, that he loves you instead of bearing you a grudge.'

'Ah, it's that as cuts the sharpest of all! If he was to be sullen and sulky
over it, I shouldn't feel it half as much as now, when I see his patient ways,
and how he's always trying to make the best of it, that I mayn't be too much
cut up about it. He's the tenderest-hearted little chap as ever breathed.'

'He certainly has a wonderful warm, grateful little heart. We must try to
get him about again, with God's blessing; and then I am sure he will not
regret the illness which has drawn you both so much more closely together.'

'Oh, if I could but think as he'd get well!' exclaimed Wood earnestly. 'If
I could make him so by giving everything as I can call my own, I'd do it
cheerful! But there ain't nothing as I can do.'

'We must leave him in God's hands. He is the great Physician. But still
there is something you can do.'

'Me, sir? What, sir?'

'You can pray for the child; you can take him to Jesus for healing. You've
learn't to go to Him?'

'Ay, I have,' returned Wood in a low tone. 'I've been to Him to ask of
Him to forgive me, for I felt as I couldn't hold on nohow like I was. Something seemed a-crushing of me to the earth, and I couldn't get no comfort
nowhere; for when I thought on all as I'd done and been, I felt as if I was
too black to lift up my head for shame. But then I thought on them lines as
I heard the boy singing so often,—
            "Foul, I to the fountain fly,
              Wash me, Saviour, or I die;"
and said I to myself, "You go and try Him, William; for there's no one else
as can do anything for you," and so I went to Him, and I haven't felt like the
same man since. And every time I see how forgiving the boy is, I think as
sure the Saviour's more forgiving still.'

Wood, carried away by his feelings, had spoken out with the unreserve of
an honest working man; and as he paused, Dr. Oldroyd, with a sudden impulse, held out his hand to him.

'My good fellow, I see you have caught at the one truth which all, rich or poor, need to learn. You've found the only true happiness!'

'And 'twas through the boy as it come to me. So you can fancy, sir, how I loves him!'

CHAPTER X

A DELIGHTFUL CHANGE

AFTER Wood had left, Dr. Oldroyd set himself, as he had already done so many times, to ponder Archie's case, and think whether anything more could be done than was being done already.

He sat for some time with a grave, thoughtful face, revolving many schemes in his mind; and at length he seemed to have hit upon something satisfactory, for, exclaiming to himself, 'I have it,' he drew pen and paper towards him, and hastily wrote a letter, which he at once dispatched to the post. The result of it was the arrival, a day or two afterwards, of Mrs. Bennett, Georgie's old nurse, who had been almost a mother to him since Mrs. Oldroyd's death, until her own marriage, a year of two ago, had forced her to leave her boy for the first time since his birth.

But as her new home lay only ten miles off, there was a frequent interchange of visits, for Dr. Oldroyd had a sincere regard for his faithful servant, and was always glad when she could come to stay with them for a few days; whilst Georgie welcomed her with real pleasure, having by no means lost his warm affection for his kind nurse and foster-mother. Moreover, Mrs. Bennett, being comfortably married to a farmer, living in the pleasant seaside village of Stoneycombe, Georgie was sent to pay her a visit whenever his father thought he was needing a little change; and thoroughly the boy enjoyed those visits. But this time Mrs. Bennett's coming had no reference to Georgie.

'How should you like to go for a bit to the seaside, Archie?' Dr. Oldroyd asked the next day, when paying his little patient a visit.

'Go to the seaside, sir?' exclaimed Archie in astonishment.

'Yes. Do you know what it's like? Have you ever seen the sea?'

'No, sir. I've never been out of this place.'

'Ah, then you can have no idea how delightful it is to stand beside it and watch the waves coming in, and feel the cool breeze blowing on your cheeks. Why, I shouldn't wonder if it would put a colour into even your pale face, and make you well and strong in no time.'

'Oh, how nice 'twould be to go there!' said Archie, as if speaking of a thing quite impossible and out of his reach.

'And the place I am speaking of is quite in the country, in the midst of beautiful green fields and orchards full of fruit-trees, where there are no streets like there are here, with endless rows of houses, but beautiful flowers and shady trees, making it seem cool even on such a hot day as this.'

'Oh, what a jolly place! Shouldn't I just like to be there!'

'Well, that was what I was asking you. Should you like to go there?'

'*Me*, sir?' asked Archie, looking as if he almost thought his kind friend must be making fun of him.

'Yes, you; I mean what I say; I am in earnest, I assure you. And if you would really like to go, and father and mother will let you—and I'm pretty sure they will—I can arrange all about it. My little boy's old nurse, who lives there, says she is quite ready to take you back with her, and look after you until you are well again. She is kind to everybody, and would be especially so to you, for I have told her all about you, and she says she'd be very glad to do all she can to help make you well again.'

'Oh, sir!' was all Archie could exclaim, surprise and pleasure at the prospect opening before him depriving him of words.

'She lives at a nice farm-house,' continued Dr. Oldroyd, 'where there are no end of animals about, from horses and cows down to kittens and chickens. And then when you are stronger you'll be able to go down on the shore and pick up shells and seaweed, and all sorts of things you never saw before.'

Archie's eyes were glistening at the bare mention of so many delights. But all at once his face clouded over.

'What is the matter?' asked Dr. Oldroyd, noticing the change.

'If I can't get no better, sir, how shall I ever be able to go there?'

'But you will get better, I hope. and I don't mean you to wait until you are well. I mean you to go first, and then see how quickly you will get better afterwards.'

'What, go just as I am, sir?'

'Yes; at least, as soon as ever you can bear to be moved. It isn't a very long way off; and we'll make the journey as easy as possible for you. And when once that is over, and you've been there a few days, with the fresh, cool sea-breezes blowing in at your window, I expect you'll feel a different fellow, and will soon be asking to be allowed to sit up.'

The new hope with which this conversation had inspired Archie had so good an effect upon him that, after two or three days had gone by, Dr. Oldroyd thought the short journey might safely be attempted. To make it as easy as possible he proposed sending the lad in his own carriage, in which they could arrange for him to lie down almost as if in his own bed; and Mrs. Bennett, who had become warmly interested in his case, was quite ready to bestow her utmost care and attention upon the little fellow. She would have done so for his own sake; how much more when he was a little patient of her old master's entrusted to her care!

Wood carried the boy tenderly in his arms downstairs, and laid him beside Mrs. Bennett in the carriage; and the pain the movement cost him was bravely borne by the patient little fellow; though by the time they reached Stoneycombe Farm he was too exhausted to be able to take much notice of things around. He only knew that Mrs. Bennett's husband had come and lifted him out of the carriage, and taken him upstairs into a pleasant, cool room, where everything looked so bright and smelt so fresh that it seemed to revive him at once. But Mrs. Bennett advised him not to talk, but to keep quiet for awhile and try to sleep; 'For after that you'll feel ever so much better,' she said; and Archie, immediately trying to obey, had soon dropped off into a sleep, sounder and sweeter than any he had enjoyed for a long time.

When he awoke Mrs. Bennett was sitting beside him with her work in her hand, and through the open window came in the songs of the birds outside, and the scent of the honeysuckle which peeped in at the casement, whilst a gentle breeze floated the curtains and even fanned his cheeks. How different from the close, hot room in Angel Court, where the atmosphere was so stifling, and the sounds heard outside were generally those of quarelling, or disputing, or scolding!

'How nice it is here!' he exclaimed, with an air of thorough enjoyment. 'I've never heard the birds singing so close to my window afore; for there weren't no birds in Angel Court. But I s'pose they live in that big tree there. I can see the top of it as I lie here, and the beautiful blue sky.'

'Oh, yes; we've plenty of blue sky and fresh air here. It's very different from the town, where there's always smoke, and dust, or dirt. You'll soon get well here.'

'And then I shall be able to go out and have a look at the sea. I've never seen it yet; and I'm longing so to see the waves Dr. Oldroyd has told me about, and all the other things!'

'And if you wait patiently I hope you'll be able to in time. You can't expect it all in a day, you know.'

'I'll try and be patient,' said Archie, with a little smothered sigh, having rarely felt such a longing to be up and out of doors as at that moment, when the bright sunshine seemed so tempting, and so many novel sights were awaiting him.

But he turned from those thoughts to make the most of what he had, and listened with a keen delight to all the farm-sounds which came in through the open window—the lowing of the cows, or the trampling of the horses' feet as they were led into the yard; the quacking of the ducks, or the cackling of the geese; no matter what it was, it all seemed to have the charm of novelty for him. And when Mrs. Bennett brought him in a bunch of flowers from the garden, and laid it down beside him, it was long before he had ceased admiring their beauty or enjoying their scent.

Sunday morning came; and the sounds and signs of busy life about the farm, which had been borne in to him through the open window on other

mornings, were hushed; a great calm seemed to brood over the little
village.

But later on another sound fell upon the air; the clear note of the church
bell calling the people to come up to God's house, and there mingle their
praises and thanksgiving for all His mercies towards them. After the bell
had ceased all was very quiet for a while, both in the house and out of doors,
until suddenly Archie heard the echo of a man's footstep on the stairs. There
was something in it which seemed familiar to him; and yet it was not like
the tread of Mr. Bennett, who sometimes came up to see him. Then whose
could it be?

The next moment the door opened, and his father stood before him.

'Oh, father, however did you come here?' cried Archie in astonishment,
whilst he held out his arms with a bright smile of welcome.

'Well, I wanted to see how my little lad was a-getting on, and so I walked
over. Are you glad to see me, Archie?' he asked, with a pleased smile, as he
saw the look of happiness on his boy's face.

'Oh, ain't I just! How good it was of you to come!'

'And how are you, my boy? Getting on a bit?'

'Oh, yes; fine!'

'And you like being here?'

'Ay, I should think so! It's so cool here, and Mrs. Bennett's so kind, and
there's such lots of sounds to listen to as come in at the window, so that I
knows pretty nigh all that's going on, though I can't get out to see it all.
But maybe I shall soon; for Mrs. Bennett says as soon as I'm able to be carried out of doors the sea-breezes 'll blow on me, and she expects make me
strong and able to walk in no time.'

'God grant it may be so!' murmured Wood in an undertone.

Then Archie asked after his mother, and the two had a long talk about
home affairs, and spent a very pleasant day together, Mr. and Mrs. Bennett
insisting upon Wood's remaining until the evening.

The next week showed a visible improvement in Archie's condition; so
much so that when, towards the end of it, Dr. Oldroyd drove over to see
how his little patient was going on, he was much pleased with the measure
of success that had already attended this new scheme.

'We shall soon have you about again, my boy, I hope,' he said; and his
words called up one of Archie's very brightest smiles in return.

It was a great event to the boy, and seemed indeed like getting on when
he was pronounced well enough to be carried downstairs, and laid on a litle
sofa in the pleasant farm kitchen where Mrs. Bennett sat, and where, through
the open door, he could look out and see a great deal that went on without.
Especially was he delighted with the chickens, which came pecking up the
food Mrs. Bennett scattered for them almost up to the very door, and the
pretty pigeons, which often fluttered down, and were so tame. Moreover,
people constantly came and went, making it lively; whilst the little patient

boy soon won the hearts of all around; and first one, then another, would bring him anything they thought might amuse him.

So he was very happy, but there were better things yet to come, for, as soon as he was able to bear it, Dr. Oldroyd sent down a sort of invalid chair, in which Archie might lie or sit, whichever he liked, and be drawn down to the beach, where he was longing to go, for, though so near the sea, there was no view of it from the farm-house itself.

Archie's delight was great on its arrival, and that evening a consultation was held as to who should be found to draw it. The boy was lying on his little sofa, whilst Mrs. Bennett was sitting near with her work. This was the time of day Archie liked, for then he could have a quiet talk with his kind friend without the many interruptions which occurred during the busy hours; and he had learnt to love a talk with her as much as George Oldroyd did.

'I think Bill Green could be spared the best of any of the lads to draw you,' she was saying; 'and though he's a rough-looking sort of a boy, I know he has a kind heart, and would be careful. But we must see what Mr. Bennett says about it.'

'I haven't seen Bill yet, have I?'

'No; I don't think he has happened to come in since you've been downstairs, but he works on the farm; and, poor boy, he hasn't a very happy home. They say he's stupid, and doesn't seem to have much brains; but I think it's more because he doesn't seem to have any one to love him, and call out what is in him. He always seems to me like a lad who has been cowed by harsh treatment.'

'Hasn't he a father and mother?'

'Yes, he has a father, but he'd almost be better without him, for he's been a confirmed drunkard for years; and his mother is only a stepmother, and she hasn't a good temper, and doesn't seem to like the boy. I'm always sorry for him. But there's a baby now; and I saw Bill one day when I passed their cottage sitting at the door nursing it as carefully as any woman could do. So I'm sure he has a good heart, only he's always so shy and silent one can't get at him.'

The next morning being beautifully fine and bright, Archie, who was all eagerness to go out for the first time to explore the country round, was carried down and placed in the chair.

Bill Green was standing by, waiting to draw it, and Archie looked a little inquisitively at his new companion. He was a big, awkward fellow, with a heavy face, which seemed to express nothing save stupidity and sullenness. But he gave one stealthy glance at Archie, looking at the fragile delicate features as curiously as if they had belonged to some being of a different race. Certainly the intelligent, expressive little face of the town boy presented a great contrast to that of the other.

Then the little procession started; Mrs. Bennett walking by Archie's chair, and cautioning Bill to go gently and very carefully. The caution was not needed twice, but neither Mrs. Bennett nor Archie were able to get a word from Bill in reply to their remarks, the utmost he would give them being a nod of the head when 'Yes' was required for an answer.

Archie enjoyed his ride with the keen sense of pleasure sure to be felt by one who had so long been confined to a bed of sickness and suffering. And then all the country sights were so new to him and so delightful—the lanes and hedges, the fields and meadows, the larks singing overhead, or the sparrows hopping and pecking on the ground—all were something to admire, and awaken fresh interest. But when they came within sight of the sea, lying sparkling and shining in the sun, with its waves breaking on the shore in foam of dazzling whiteness, which they tossed aloft in wreaths of graceful spray, his delight and admiration were almost too great to express in words. He gazed in silence, with a look and smile of intense pleasure resting on his face, seeming as if he never could withdraw his eyes from the grand spectacle stretched out before him. And then the sea-gulls, flashing in the sun, came in for their share of notice, as well as the cliffs, which stood out in all their glistening whiteness, contrasted with the blue sky above and sea beneath.

CHAPTER XI

A NEW HOME

THE heat of summer was over, and autumn had now come, with its bright, pleasant days, and chilly mornings and evenings, which made a good fire very acceptable. The trees among which the long, low, dark-red brick buildings of Stoneycombe Farm nested were already beginning to strew the gravel path leading up to the house, and the lawn in front of it, with bright, many-coloured leaves, which they flung in a shower upon the ground every time a gust of wind came swaying their branches, and forcing them to part with their leafy treasures.

All this time Archie had been steadily gaining health and strength, until now the chair was no longer needed, as he was able to walk quite as far as he had ever done. A very happy life he had been leading all these weeks at the farm, learning to love Mrs. Bennett more and more, whilst Mr. Bennett was always kind to him; and he and Bill had grown greater friends than ever. Many a talk had the boys held together, all Bill's reserve having melted away, until he had learnt to confide everything to Archie.

'He don't want no book-larning, then?' said Bill, one day, with a sigh of relief. ' 'Cause I couldn't never manage anything that way!'

H

'No; Jesus only wants us to love Him back again,' said Archie; and poor Bill, with his dull understanding but warm heart, felt that he could do that —nay, that he already did, for there were thoughts and feelings stirring within him, new and strangely sweet, which made him long by every word and deed to please that unseen, gracious Friend.

Archie now was out of doors almost all day long, drinking in fresh strength with every salt breeze, and finding endless objects of interest both on the seashore and in the well-stocked farmyard, where he had made acquaintance and friends with every living creature, great or small, and had gained by his own observation such a stock of information with regard to their ways and habits, that Dr. Oldroyd, who drove over now and then to see his little patient, was astonished and much pleased at his intelligence.

George Oldroyd, too, had been over several times to spend the day, and greatly had the two boys enjoyed those times; for to both of them the farm possessed endless attractions, only equalled by those of the seashore, which were indeed great and never-failing.

Wood had also walked over sometimes on a Sunday, and very much had enjoyed a stroll on the sands with his boy; whilst even Mrs. Wood had managed to get out once or twice to have a peep at Archie.

But now he was pronounced well enough to return home, and though sorry to leave Stoneycombe where he had been so happy, it yet was pleasant to look forward to going home to his father and mother, who were longing to have him back. Besides, Dr. Oldroyd had said they would resume the evening lessons together as soon as he returned, and Archie looked upon the hour spent with the doctor as one of his happiest times.

But Bill was almost inconsolable at Archie's depature, and could only be cheered at all by the prospect which Mrs. Bennett held out, that she hoped Archie would come again some day to pay a visit to the farm, for Dr. Oldroyd had said that whenever he got to look ill again he should send him down there at once.

Mr. Bennett, who was going into the town on business, drove Archie in his gig to the place of meeting, where it had been arranged Wood, as it was his dinner hour, should be waiting for them. He was there, his eyes beaming with pleasure at Archie's bright looks and smile of delight at seeing him again. Then, after a few words of honest, hearty thanks to Mr. Bennett, he took his boy's hand in his, and turned to go homewards.

'But which way are you going, father? This won't lead to Angel Court, will it?'

'No; but we ain't a-going there now. We've moved from there.'

'Have you?' exclaimed Archie. 'Oh, I'm so glad! I never liked Angel Court. But you never told me!'

'No; we kept it as a surprise for you. And where do you think we've gone? Where should you like best to go and live?'

'Well, I've often thought how I wished we could have one of them pretty little cottages down near the docks where Bessie Martin lives; where it ain't shut up and built in so close, like Angel Court, but all open and cheerful-like. But of course that would be too grand for us; so it can't be there!'

'Yes it is, Archie; only two or three doors off Bessie Martin's.'

'Oh, father!' and Archie stopped short in his astonishment, and turned to look up in his father's face to see if he could really mean what he was saying.

'Ay, I mean it; it's true. I thought as you'd be pleased!'

'Oh, ain't I just! I never dreamt of anything half so jolly! But however can you afford it, father? It must cost a great lot more than t'other place.'

'I can afford it just as I might have afforded it long ago, if I'd been a better man; just by bringing home all my earnings, instead of spending of 'em at the public-house; that's how |I'm able to manage it. But see—here we are, and there's your mother a-looking out for you at the door.'

Mrs. Wood seemed to have grown years younger lately, so happy an expression had replaced the anxious one of former days; and very bright she looked as she clasped her boy in her arms, and murmured words of thankfulness at having him back again well and strong.

Then Archie was all eagerness to see over the new house, and take a look upstairs as well as downstairs; so his mother accompanied him, well pleased to listen to his expressions of delight at everything.

When they returned to the kitchen, Wood came forward with something in his arms.

'What have you got there, father?'

'You shall see. It's a present for you.' And he displayed to view a pretty little black-and-tan terrier dog.

'For me!' cried Archie in surprise. 'For my very own?'

'Ay; I've been a-training of him for you, and he can sit up, and beg, and do lots of tricks. He's very affectionate, too; and so, perhaps, some day— when you've got to be fond of him—he'll make up partly for the other dog'.

It was the first time Wood had ever alluded to poor Rough, nor had Archie mentioned him for a very long time, though he had been far from forgetting his old, faithful friend.

'Oh, how kind of you, father!' said the boy, looking up, pleased and grateful. 'How good of you! And when I don't deserve it nohow either; for I was a bad boy, I know I was, to get into such a passion, and be so angry. But you've forgiven me, father?' and Archie took one of Wood's hands between his own.

'Ay, ay, no need to ask that,' said the other, looking down upon him fondly. 'The little dog there can tell you that. Look, he's jumping up on you; he's wanting to make friends with you.'

'And what's his name, father?'

'Well, he's been called Tiny, but you can call him anything as you choose, for he's your dog; he don't belong to anybody else; so you can give him whatever name you like.'

'I think Tiny is a very good name 'cause he is such a little bit of a thing. He's the prettiest little doggie I ever saw.'

'We've a many mercies to count up; so many we couldn't ever have done telling of 'em,' said Wood, in a softened tone; whilst his eye rested tenderly, and yet mournfully, upon his deformed boy's happy, smiling face, as if he felt and was ready to own that some of his choicest blessings had come through the little fellow whom formerly, to his lasting sorrow, he had treated so harshly and injured so deeply.

But all that seemed to have been mercifully forgiven him; and the grave expression on his face was chased away the next moment by Archie himself, who, catching up Tiny in his arms, and glancing from one to the other, exclaimed joyously, 'Oh, father, oh, mother, how jolly it is to be at home again! But I can scarce believe yet as we've really come to live here! It seems too good to be true! But now I shall be able to go in and see Bessie Martin every day! And Dr. Oldroyd said I could go to him this evening, and then I shall see Master George too! I'm sure as there ain't a happier fellow in all the town than I am! Is there Tiny?'

And the boy turned to have a romp with his dog, filling the cottage with his merry laughter, which the creature's lively tricks and ways called forth.

GOTT SENT HER

by

LILLIAN STREET

"SHTAND op, my little frent, and let me look at you. How many years haff you? Ach! haff you no tong, then!"

The little creature so interrogated was seated on the old German's doorstep in the sun. She had been there for hours, Julia, the maid-of-all-work, told him, and nothing would move her.

"Where is your muzzer, my dear?" That word was magic.

"Rosy's mammy has gone to London—she will come back for her soon."

The old German left her and called to Julia, a buxom country girl, good-nature dimpling all over her fat red face.

"Wat can we do with this little childer? Do you zink the muzzer will com' back?"

"Lor', sir, it's to be hoped so!"

"Bott I haff heard that sometime in England the muzer do not return, and you haff to drain op the little one yourself. We will see what Heinrich will say."

Twelve o'clock struck, and the click of the garden gate announced the return of Heinrich from school. He was a tall, handsome lad of fourteen; like his father in the dreamy sweetness of his expression, but of a stronger, more masterful build; and there was a token of intellectual promise on his broad brow, and a world of thought in his dark eyes.

"You lovely little being! Where did you drop from?"

Heinrich held out his hand, and Rosy wriggled, then got up slowly and put her plump little fist in his kindly grasp.

"Who is she, father?"

The old German was watching the meeting with a pleased smile.

"Her muzzer left her here this morning, and no-poddy knows anyzing more."

Heinrich whistled.

"But I suppose she'll come back before the night."

He lifted the child in his arms, and carried her into the house.

"Rosy hungry!" she cried, when she saw the smoking dishes. "Boy feed her."

He unfastened the bonnet-strings and the little cape, and kissed the soft little arms that locked themselves a moment round his neck, and then proceeded to feed her from his plate.

The German sat opposite, gazing at the picture they made with an artist's delight, and sighed that his hand could no longer work. And Julia made up her mind Heaven had sent the child, and immediately commenced preparations to fit her into the tiny house. When tea was over, she ran to the village to spend her savings in a few necessaries for the child's comfort, and came back to take possession of her.

But Rosy was fast asleep in Heinrich's arms, and he would not have her disturbed. The lad had pushed his books away from him, and was gazing across the sea, entirely absorbed in his new treasure.

It was the old story. Rosy's "muzzer did not com' back," and Rosy was thrown on the mercy of the kindest beings that ever breathed, and into the danger of being entirely spoilt.

She was a wild little creature, that loved to roam by herself on the seashore, sockless and shoeless, when the tide was low, and to chase the butterflies across the rippling sands. Only Heinrich had the slightest control over her; from the first she had shown her preference, and his word was always law.

So the years flew, and Julia taught her to make the blue serge gowns that had at last to cover the pretty legs; and with the long dresses came long musings and awakening thought. In what relationship did she stand to these people? By a freak of memory she had no recollection of life apart from them; and when she questioned the old German he would answer—

"Ach! you mustn't zink about such zings, my lofe; Gott sent you to us, and it is goot for us to be togezzer."

But at last she made up her mind to question Heinrich.

He had developed into a strong man, and was earning his living as usher in the grammar-school at X——, three miles away. How his soul loathed the drudgery only himself knew. But the sacrifice of his dream of a student's life at Leipzig he gladly made for the sake of the two who were dearer to him than any distinction the cultivation of his intellectual powers might have brought him. Nevertheless, the picture of "the might-have-been" could not be entirely effaced, and it was before him in all its rosiest colours the evening Rosy sought him to solve her questionings.

Her quick glance at his wistful look across the sea set her wondering in a new direction, and when he looked up with a smile and asked her what she wanted of him, she threw herself on her knees beside him and cried out—

"Tell me what you see, Heinrich."

He started, and put up his hand to pull off the net Julia made her wear, and to let the rich gold hair fall in its beautiful masses round her shoulders.

"Shall I tell you? I see a great throbbing city where men and women are struggling and straining for what is greatest and best; and the more they strive the more they find to gain—the greater the great becomes, the better the best."

"I know," she interrupted; "I have read about it. And there is a huge, big school there where you can learn everything you want to know, and become great and splendid yourself. Heinrich! you must go there! And you shall be greater than them all!"

"Hush!" he whispered. "We were talking about dreams."

He wound the gold locks round her throat and tilted back her head to gaze into her face. And then he realised for the first time her succeeding beauty—how Nature was moulding her with every grace and charm of womanhood. And he bent and kissed her. And her woman's heart leapt in her bosom at the touch, and all her being moved to his.

"Heinrich!"

She gazed into his eyes, half-fearful, half-wondering, and caught up her hair in the net again, and waited for him to speak.

"Rosy," he said at last, "it is you who must go away from here. You must go out into the world and see other men and women. You will be a very beautiful woman, and there is a great future before you."

"I can do nothing," she answered, "and I only want to be beautiful for —for your sake. But I will go, Heinrich. I *will* go!" she went on passionately.

"Why should I be a burden, a stumbling-block, because I am a woman? I am strong, and I can work."

Then it was that she discovered she possessed the gift of a rich voice. And a piece of fortune decided her destiny.

One Sunday evening a great singer from London was coming to stay with the squire, and the best must be done for the honour of the village. A look from Heinrich told her to consent to lead the choir. And when the day came she took her place behind the rustic lads, glad to put her power to use.

And the result was, the London singer gave his host no rest till he had taken him to the cottage on the cliff and brought him face to face with the beautiful singer.

In a moment Heinrich knew her fate was sealed—that the man before him was already his rival. Young, handsome, and gifted, how could she resist what would of necessity be the outcome of the lavish admiration he poured unrestrainedly upon her? He made his request then and there. If they could find her a home in London, he would give her lessons and fit her for a great career.

There was a flush of joy on her face.

"Oh! shall I make a lot of money?"

"If you are a success you will doubtless be rich."

"I will work hard; I want to be very rich," she cried, throwing her arms round the old German's neck. "Let me go!"

"Wat do you zink, Heinrich? Can we let her go?"

"Yes, she must go," he said quietly.

And so it was arranged. A home in a family was found for her, and Heinrich took her there.

"Will you promise, darling, to come back to us if you are the least unhappy?" he said anxiously, at the parting.

"How brave that would be!" she laughed. "No, Heinrich, I shall wait to be happy till I am with you again."

And he sighed, almost wishing he could believe that.

Eventually came the date for her *début*. Oh! if they could come! But the old German was ill, and Heinrich could not leave. But he walked to the nearest town the next day to get the London papers, and read the accounts of "the singularly beautiful and superb new contralto" with burning heart and flushed cheeks.

Three years passed by, and the singer came to the village again. He brought them vivid accounts of her success, and the great impression her beauty was making.

"One day," he said condescendingly, "I shall make her my wife. But not till her name is ringing through the world and can rank with mine."

Heinrich clenched his hands and looked him keenly in the face.

"You shall only marry her for love of her," he said.

And the old German looked up with a wan smile.

"She will not marry wizout lofe, our little Rosy. Gott sent her to us, and I zink she would rather com' back to us and be poor again."

"Well, well," the singer laughed, "she has a decent sense of gratitude, I suppose, and every penny she earns is practically mine."

Heinrich sprang to his feet.

"You shall be paid back every farthing, if I have to work the flesh off my bones to get it. She shall never marry you—never!"

"That must be her decision," the singer sneered; "and I have heard little whispers of growing rich in order to send somebody to Leipzig."

"That! Is that her idea?"

"What a cleffer childer it is!" the old German cried, laying his hand on Heinrich's shoulder to suppress his vehemence. "Bott tell her we do not want for money. Heinrich here will be ver' rich when I die—he has not heard, bott I haff saved—I haff been selfish not to let 'im go before—bott I was lonely!"

Heinrich's arm was round his father's neck.

"I would never have left you, and I never will."

The singer went back to London, and he did not tell Rosy these things; but he brought her gradually to understand the debt he expected her to pay and then her position flashed upon her. If she married him, the sacrifice would be supreme. If not, all the money she was making must be given to him, and her darling project thrown to the winds.

She decided; and he did not wait till she should become famous—Heinrich's wrath had been ominous, and he did not mean to lose her.

"When we are married I will take you to them," he said caressingly. "You must not tell them a word about it till the day, my queen. Your friend Heinrich was a little bit in love with you himself once, you know, and we won't let him anticipate the pain he may feel, poor fellow!"

That was generous. And she let him caress her cheek, but she shuddered away when he attempted to kiss her lips. Heinrich had been a "little bit in love" with her *once*, and no one should wipe out the memory of the kiss he had given her the night he had awaked in her her woman's soul.

On the day fixed for her marriage there was a storm raging over the little village by the sea, and the old German watched for his son's return from X—— in nervous apprehension. The news from Rosy had not reached them till the ceremony must have been over, and Heinrich had gone to his work without making a single sign.

Julia watched her old master anxiously all day, and had failed in her efforts to make him eat or rest. Towards the evening he grew more feeble, and his restlessness increased. Heinrich was later than usual, and suspense became intolerable. He opened the door and looked out, and a gust of wind blew the lamp from his hand and shattered it to pieces.

Julia rushed forward at the noise, but too late to stop him flying from her in a fit of frenzy. She shrieked after him and tore into the darkness; but madness was upon him, and lent him lightning speed, and she was obliged to give up the chase and return; and it was not until midnight that Heinrich and the villagers with their lanterns came upon him at the foot of the cliff. He was lying dead in the arms of a woman. They carried him back, and the woman followed. No one noticed her, and it was not till they had undressed him and washed the poor bruised corpse—he must have fallen from the cliff, they thought—that Heinrich remembered how they had found him, and went to look for the woman.

She had thrown off her bonnet and cloak, and was pacing the little sitting-room in an agony of sorrow. Her golden hair had fallen round her, and her face was wet with tears.

"Rosy!"

She was on his breast, and not till he had held her in a long, agonised embrace did he remember—

"Where is your husband?"

H*

The voice was hollow, and he pushed her from him, but his grip was on her wrist.

"Heinrich! Heinrich! pity me! I ran away. Oh! Heinrich! I could not marry him. I left him all my money—and I only meant to have one last look at you—through the window—one last peep at the sea. And then the dear father—I found him lying there—oh! Heinrich, he was alive! He kissed me—and I told him——"

Her sobs choked her, and Heinrich stretched out his arms.

"My darling! *Mine, mine,* at last! We are alone in the world, you and I, but we will never part again. My love!—Oh! my father, if you could know of my joy!"

NOBODY LOVES ME

by

Mrs. O. F. WALTON

CHAPTER I

OLD GRUMPY'S HOME

THE great church clock, in the most crowded part of that crowded city, was striking eight.

It was a solemn old clock, and it spoke very slowly and distinctly, as if it thought that the people who lived round the church were not able to count quickly, and as if it were afraid they would make a mistake, and would lay the blame on the clock.

The children heard it, and they left their mud pies in the gutter, and ran to their homes. The bricklayers, who were mending the church porch, heard it; and they threw down their trowels, and hurried away to their breakfast. All the wives and sisters and mothers, in all the streets and alleys and courts near the old church, heard it; and they filled the tea-pots, and buttered the toast, for the husbands and fathers and sons who were coming in for breakfast.

Old Grumpy heard it, as she was raking the ashes out of her little grate.

'One—two—three—four—five—six—seven—eight!' counted Old Grumpy, and then she went on with what she was doing, without taking any further notice; for it made no difference to her. No one was coming in to breakfast; she had no husband, no brother, no son, to care for. Old Grumpy live alone, and she liked to live alone; she was quite proud of saying that she loved nobody, and nobody loved her.

She was a thin, bony old woman, with a hard and cross face. Even the children ran away from her for she never smiled or spoke to them, but stalked on, with her lips tightly pressed together, as if she had made up her mind to be the Ishmael of the court—her hand against every man, every man's hand against her.

Ivy Court was certainly not like the ivy in anything—for there was nothing green, or pretty, or bright about it. The first part of the court had a double row of houses, but at the end of this there was a narrow passage, which wound round two sides of the graveyard of the old city church, and here the houses were only on one side, and looked upon the high grimy wall of the churchyard. Old Grumpy's house was the last one; she only rented the upper room, and it was neither a very large nor a very cheerful place to live in. Still she stuck to it, year after year, and it would have broken her to leave it for another. The walls were black; her old four-post bed was hung with faded chintz more filthy than the walls; and if you had been able to see through the dust and cobwebs that covered the window-panes, you would have seen nothing but the bare wall opposite, and the tops of two or three sooty gravestones which were taller than the rest, and which seemed to be peering over the wall at the inhabitants of Ivy Court. It was a dismal prospect, and perhaps Old Grumpy thought so, for she never tried to clean the windows, but allowed the dust to thicken there unchecked.

No one in the court knew anything about the strange and disagreeable old woman. They did not even know her name. The children who lived near her had given her the name of 'Old Grumpy,' because she always spoke in a surly, unpleasant voice. But the children who had given her the name were children no longer. They had all left Ivy Court; some of them were married, and some of them were dead. Yet, although they had left, Old Grumpy's name had been passed on to the next generation, and the children who lived in the court at the time this story begins still ran away, calling out, 'Old Grumpy! Old Grumpy!' whenever the old woman came out.

Poor Old Grumpy's life had been a very cheerless one. She was born in a workhouse, and her mother had died when she was only two days old. She remembered very little about her childhood, except this one thing, that nobody cared for her. And when she was a child, this often troubled her. Other children had mothers, other children had homes, but she had not a relative in the world, and her only home was the workhouse.

There was one evening, when she was about nine years old, which Old Grumpy had never forgotten. She had been sent on an errand for the matron, and was coming home through a narrow street, full of working people's houses. It was seven o'clock, and she could see the cheerful firelight in many a happy home as she passed by. It was Christmas Eve, and there was a merry family party gathered round the fire in nearly every house. The child felt a strange, hungry feeling in her heart as she looked at them. Oh, if one of those bright little houses had been her home!

But it was the last house in the street which she remembered best of all.

There was a bedroom on the ground floor, and on the table was a candle. The child peeped in, and saw four little beds, and in the beds four little fair-haired children. And there was a fair-haired mother, going about amongst the cots, shaking up the little pillows, tucking up the blankets, and kissing the little rosy cheeks. Then she took up the candle and was going away, but the children called her back again and again, for more and more kisses.

The poor child outside, who had no one to love her, turned away with tears in her eyes. She could not remember that any one had ever kissed her; she wondered if her mother had kissed her before she died. Her mother had had fair hair, so the old workhouse nurse had told her, and was very pretty. The child wondered whether, if she had lived, she would have tucked her up, and made her cosy when she went to bed.

Poor Old Grumpy had never forgotten that night; but as the years went by, and she grew older, she grew at the same time harder. Nobody had ever loved her, and so she resolved she would never love anybody. She could do quite well without their love, she said to herself. Nobody had ever been kind to her, so she made up her mind not to be kind to anybody. All the world was against her, and she was against all the world.

Yet, ever and again, that old, hungry feeling, which had come into her heart on that Christmas Eve so long ago, came back to her, in spite of herself.

Unloved and loveless, she still at times yearned both to be loved and to love.

CHAPTER II

THE FIRST LINK

OLD GRUMPY was raking her grate that cold morning, when the solemn old church clock was striking eight. She had just raked out the ashes, and was hunting in a dark dirty closet by the fireside for some pieces of stick, which she could use to light the fire, when she heard a step on the staircase.

It was not a heavy step, and it was not a loud step, and it was not a quick step. On the contrary, it was very light, and very quiet, and very slow. And yet it was such an unusual thing for Old Grumpy to hear any step at all on her staircase, that she paused in what she was doing, and listened.

It could not be a child, she thought; could it be a dog, or a rat, or a bird?

Curiosity led her to open her door and look out. There, on the landing close by her, and looking up piteously into her face, was a visitor waiting to be let in. It was a little black half-starved kitten.

Now Old Grumpy had the greatest contempt for cats. A neighbour of hers, the old man who lived in the downstairs room, had a cat, a great tom-

cat, with a long bushy tail, which used to sit on his back when he was at
work, and follow him like a dog. Old Grumpy had the greatest contempt
for this cat, and for old Joel's affection for it. It was a wild, ferocious creature. No one dared to touch it. The children never ventured to pull its tail,
or to drive it about the court, as they did all the other poor miserable cats
which had the misfortune to live there; and there was not one of the neighbours, men or women, who would have dared even to stroke it.

Yet with Joel the cat was always gentle and obedient. He was very fond of
this cat; it had been his companion for many years, and its tricks were the
pride of the old man's heart. But whilst they amused old Joel, they disgusted
Old Grumpy. 'Silly old fellow!' she would mutter to herself, as she heard
the cat leaping in the room below. 'Silly old chap, to be wasting his time
over an ugly creature like that!'

These being her sentiments, it was not to be expected that Old Grumpy
would receive her visitor with open arms. Her great idea was to get rid of it,
and that as quickly as possible. She accordingly gave it a kick, and shook her
shawl at it; but the kitten only crawled a few steps from the door, and lay
down again. It seemed quite weak and exhausted, as if it had spent all its
strength in climbing up the staircase.

Old Grumpy closed her door, and went back to her fire, hoping that the
kitten would soon go away; but whenever she paused in her work she heard
the same doleful sound outside.

'Mew, mew, mew, mew,' said the kitten again and again.

And it went on, long after the fire was lighted, and the kettle had boiled,
and the old woman had made herself a cup of tea.

'Mew, mew, mew, mew;' but the sounds grew fainter and fainter, and at
last they ceased altogether.

'That tiresome little thing is either gone or dead,' said Old Grumpy to
herself.

But which was it? Had it gone? Or was it lying stiff and dead at her door?

Old Grumpy tried to forget the kitten entirely, yet in spite of herself she
kept wondering what had become of it. At last she thought she would just
look out for a moment, to see if it were there or not; she could shut the
door again if it were still alive, and if it tried to get into her room.

So she looked out, and the kitten was still there, and it was not dead. It
was evidently very ill, so ill and weak that it did not even try to crawl to the
door; but it looked in at the fire in Old Grumpy's grate, which was burning
brightly, and it looked up in the old woman's face, as if it were asking her
to let it in.

It was a very strange thing, but at that moment, as Old Grumpy saw the
kitten looking in at the fire, her thoughts went back to that cold Christmas
Eve, nearly sixty years ago, when she had looked in at the bright firesides of
that little back street. It may have been the thought of that night, so long ago,
yet so well remembered, or it may have been the plaintive cries of the kitten,

which began again as soon as she opened the door, or it may have been the recollection and the cries together, which touched the soft part in Old Grumpy's hard heart. Anyhow, the old woman suddenly changed her mind, lifted it in her arms, and carried it into her room.

The kitten had been shamefully ill-treated; a wicked boy had pelted it with stones, which had broken its leg, and given it a terrible wound on its head. Old Grumpy bound up its leg, bathed its wound, gave it milk out of her own saucer, and let it lie on her knee.

The kitten purred its thanks. And as the day went on, strange to say, the old woman, who had never loved any one before, began to love the kitten; and, *not* strange to say, for it was the natural consequence, the kitten began to love her.

It seemed very strange and very sad that the wealth of love God had given her, that power to love which He gives to all alike, should be squandered on a kitten! It surely was very sad, that the love which might have made so many around her happy, the love which might have helped the poor tired mothers in the court, nursed the sick children, and cheered those more helpless than herself, should have been hoarded up, only to be given to a poor little kitten, which would have been more than content with so much less.

But still it was the beginning of better days for Old Grumpy. She was learning to love, that was something; she was learning the pleasure of being loved, that was more.

And is it not, sometimes, a very little thing, a thing more insignificant and useless than a kitten, which is the first link in a chain which leads on to very important things?

CHAPTER III

MISSING

IT was a new feeling for Old Grumpy to have any one to care for but herself. She had been so long accustomed to get up in the morning, with no thought except 'What shall *I* eat?' or, 'What shall *I* drink?' or, 'How shall *I* be clothed?' that it was a curious and pleasant change for her to have even a kitten to care for.

The first day it followed her into the court, it made quite a sensation among the neighbours. A boy, not knowing that it belonged to the old woman, and thinking that it was a strange cat which had come over the churchyard wall, was seizing it by the tail, when Old Grumpy suddenly turned round on him, and gave him a blow which made him fly out of the court, screaming. Then all the neighbours came out to see what was the matter, and stood still in astonishment, as they watched Old Grumpy petting and fondling the kitten, and looking wrathfully after the boy as he ran into the street.

'What's come to the old woman?' said one to another. 'Who ever would have thought it?'

But old Joel was very scornful, quite as scornful as ever she had been of him. 'Such a creature!' he said. 'A poor miserable, bony, half-starved kitten! If it had been a cat like mine'—and he glanced up at Tiger, who was sitting on his shoulder—'no one would have said anything about it. But a black-and-white kitten! Ugh!'

But Old Grumpy heeded them not. It was enough for her that she had found some one to love her. She made a soft bed for her kitten to lie on; she gave it the best she had in the house to eat; she bought a piece of blue ribbon, and tied it round its neck; and she talked to it, and stroked it, and petted it from morning till night.

By degrees the kitten grew into a cat, and became soft, and sleek, and well fed, and a great contrast in every way to what it was when it had begged to be let into her room that winter's morning, as the great church clock was striking eight. And as the kitten was growing into a cat, Old Grumpy's love for it was growing at the same time. The cat became the one thought of her life; and from living so much alone, and from speaking so little to those around her, she spent all her time in talking to her cat; and, after a time, the cat began to talk to her, at least the old woman thought it did. And when she went to the shop at the top of the court to buy her tea and sugar, she would repeat in her strange, muttering way, half as if she were talking to herself, half as if she were talking to her neighbours, what her cat had said to her as it lay on her knee. It would tell her how comfortable it was, and how it loved her, and how glad it was she had taken it in. So the old woman said, and so she firmly believed. The neighbours laughed at her very often, and made great fun of the idea of a cat talking; and old Joel said it clearly proved that *she* was mad, and ought to be taken to the ' 'sylum;' yet Old Grumpy held to her tale, in spite of everything that was said to her.

But one morning, when the old woman had been to the workhouse, to fetch her weekly allowance of half-a-crown and two loaves of bread, she came home to find a trouble awaiting her.

The cat had disappeared. She had left it asleep in the chair by the fire, and she had locked her door. The door was still locked when she came back, but the cat was gone. She called it by all the many names she had given it; she hunted for it under her bed, and in the dark closet by the fireside, and in every nook and corner of her room but the cat was not to be seen.

Then she remembered the window. Yes, it was open! The cat must have jumped on the churchyard wall, and then down into the court. In great haste and with trembling steps the old woman went out, calling the cat again and again.

Old Joel came out of his door and laughed; the neighbours stood at their doors and laughed; no one had seen it, no one had heard it, no one knew anything about it.

Having searched the court from end to end, Old Grumpy opened the iron gate of the churchyard, and hunted amongst the graves. Sometimes stumbling over an old stone, sometimes sitting to rest on a crumbling monument, sometimes calling, sometimes searching, but never finding; so the old woman spent the greater part of the day. Then she wandered down the street, asking of every passer-by, walking down every court, calling for the cat at every turning. Still she did not find it; there came no answer to her calls.

Night came on, and still Old Grumpy wandered. She could not bear to lock her favourite out; she could not bear to think of the empty desolate room without it. So she walked on the greater part of the night, and her neighbours, as they woke from their dreams, still heard her cries for the cat, as she paced up and down the court.

The next day she still searched; and the next, and the next; indeed, her whole life at that time became one long search, and when she came to her room, to eat or to sleep, it was only to make fresh plans for finding her cat.

But all these plans were fruitless; the cat never returned to its old friend. Whether it had strayed away, or had been stolen, whether the cat had deserted her, or whether the neighbours had been treacherous, and had made away with the cat, Old Grumpy never could determine. But, whatever had been the cause of her loss, the loss remained the same. The cat was gone, and it never came back again.

But the old woman was changed; she was no longer satisfied with the lonely selfish life she was leading. She had known what it was to love, though she had only loved a cat; she had known what it was to be loved, although only by a cat.

As weeks went by, and she began to despair of finding her cat, she began to look around, almost ravenously, for something or some one to love. She tried to make friends with the children of the court, but they had lived all their lives in such fear of her, that they ran away when she called them, and hid themselves when they saw her come out.

Then she would wander up and down the street, looking for other children, that she might kiss them as they went by. Sometimes she would kiss the forehead of a little girl on her way to school, who would look curiously at her, wondering who she was, and where she came from. Sometimes she would stop a group of little children, walking out with an aunt or mother, who would ask Old Grumpy where she lived, and who would receive no answer.

As the days went by, this craving to be loved grew stronger and stronger; the old woman's brain, which had never been strong, began to be quite bewildered and troubled by it; and it was a sad sight to see her wandering up and down the court, muttering to herself over and over again, 'Nobody loves me, nobody does! nobody loves me, nobody does!'

CHAPTER IV

THE SECOND LINK

OVER and over again, till the neighbours were tired of hearing her; over and over again, till her head ached at the sound of her own voice; over and over again, as the church clock struck one hour after another, Old Grumpy repeated the same words, 'Nobody loves me, nobody does! nobody loves me, nobody does!'

But at last, one day, there came a change. She was leaning against the churchyard wall, watching the neighbours filling their pails at the pump in the middle of the court. Suddenly she found herself listening to their talk.

'There's nothing to be done,' said one woman; 'she must go to the house at once. Mrs. Perkins has sent for the officer to come and see about it.'

'Poor bairn; it's a pity!' said another. 'She's such a pretty little thing. I'd have kept her, I'm sure I would, but my Bob wasn't willing, he wouldn't hear of it. He says we've got plenty already!'

'And so you have, Mrs. Wilkins,' said an old woman, who was waiting with a jug. 'Why, you've six, haven't you? No good ever comes of doing for other folks' children; nobody thanks you for it!'

'What's that?' said another woman.

'Why, it's a woman that has just died, at Mrs. Perkins' lodging-house, over the way there; she went there last night—very bad she was when she arrived. They got her to bed at once, and fetched a doctor, but she died in the night; and there's a little girl left. Mrs. Perkins has just sent to the work-house for them to send on and see about it.'

'Is it a baby?' asked the new-comer.

'No, it's a little girl about as big as our Kate, going on five, I think; and so clean she is, and nice little clothes too!'

'Who are they?' asked the woman.

'Mrs. Perkins doesn't know; they don't belong to this part at all. By what I understand, she was travelling through to her own parish, so I expect they'll send the child on there.'

'Poor bairn!' said the woman. 'I must go and have a look at her;' and she hastened out of the court and went across to the other side of the street, where Mrs. Perkins' lodging-house stood.

Old Grumpy got up, and came nearer the pump.

'Would they give her to me?' said the old woman, suddenly clutching one of them by the arm.

'Who's that?' said the woman, starting and turning round, for she had not seen her coming. 'What does she say?'

'Would they give the bairn to me?' repeated the old woman.

'No, I shouldn't think so,' said the women in a chorus. 'You wouldn't know how to look after her!'

'She looked after her cat well enough, anyhow,' said a man, who was standing at a door, smoking his pipe.

'Well, to be sure, so she did!' said one of the women. 'But what would she keep her on? She couldn't keep a child out of her parish pay.'

'I would work for her,' said the old woman, lifting up her thin bony hands. 'I would work for her as long as I could crawl about. Oh let me have her, let me have her! I'll be ever so good to the bairn. Nobody loves me; nobody does!'

'Well, I'll go and see Mrs. Perkins about it,' said the woman who had been the chief speaker.

Old Grumpy stood at the entrance of the court, watching Mrs. Perkins' house anxiously. It was a high house, with many rooms in it, and it looked if possible, more forlorn and dirty than the row of forlorn and dirty houses in which it stood. The dirty ragged blind was drawn down in one of the upper rooms, and Old Grumpy fancied the mother of the child must be lying there; and she wondered what she was like, and if she was at all like her own mother was, when she had been laid, dead, in a ward of the work-house hospital. The poor child, she thought, was left motherless, just as she had been; but if only they would let her have it, then it should never have to say, as she had said, oh, so many times, 'Nobody loves me, nobody does.' She would love it as much as if it were her own child, that she would! Ah, *how* she would love it!

It was a long time before her neighbour appeared again, and when she did it was to beckon Old Grumpy to come in.

'*Her!*' said the landlady contemptuously, when she saw her.

'Let her try, poor old thing!' said the woman of Ivy Court. 'We can send the bairn to the house if she doesn't look after her; and we will all keep an eye on the child, and see no harm comes to her.'

'Well, have your own way,' said Mrs. Perkins; 'it doesn't matter to me. But you'd better take her and be off, before the officer comes down. It's not very likely he'll let that crazed old body take her. I needn't tell him there is a child, if you're off at once.'

'Where is she?' asked the woman.

'She's in the kitchen, playing with my Sally Jane and Anna Maria; she doesn't know her mammy's dead. I told her she was poorly, and wanted to be quiet, and sent her downstairs.'

'I'll go and fetch her then,' said the woman; and she soon returned, lead-ing by the hand a tiny child, with soft dark brown hair, and large dark brown eyes, very pretty, as the neighbours had said, but very thin and pale, so thin and pale that there were tears in the woman's eyes as she brought her in; and she whispered to Mrs. Perkins that 'It was clear it wouldn't be for long; the bairn would soon be with her mother again.'

'I'll be ever so good to her,' said Old Grumpy, as she took her hand. 'Don't you be afraid of me; I'll be ever so good to her.'

Ivy Court turned out, as they walked through, to see Old Grumpy's child. Some said it was a shame to let the child go to such a place as that; the workhouse would have been far better for her. Others, and the man with the pipe was among their number, said it would settle the old woman's mind, and keep her from having to go to the asylum. Old Joel, who was standing with Tiger on his shoulder, thought it a good joke, and laughed so loud as Old Grumpy passed by, that the man with the pipe came across the court, to bid him to be quiet, and to mind his own business.

The old woman walked on, heeding neither the remarks of the neighbours nor the laughter of old Joel. She felt as if she were in a dream. Now, at last, she had found something to love; now, at last, she would be happy. None should rob her of this darling; nothing should ever part them. The child would love her, and would grow up to be a comfort and a joy to her, and they would be so happy together. Old Grumpy saw all the future spread out before her, in a very bright and beautiful picture, as she opened the door for the child to go in.

And the One who was still standing outside her door, the living, loving Lord, of whom the old woman still knew but little, and cared less, was another link to the chain which was to lead her to Himself.

When would the chain be finished? There were more links yet to follow, sorrowful links for Old Grumpy, before the last link came, which led her to the Lord Himself.

CHAPTER V

THE WHITE LILY

OLD GRUMPY put the little girl on a stool by the fire, and stood looking at her, with such a loving, kind, motherly smile, that the neighbours would not have known the old woman if they had seen her.

'What do they call you, my pretty darling?' said Old Grumpy, gently.

'Lily! Mother calls me Lily. Where is mother? I want to go to mother.'

'That *is* a pretty name!' said the old woman. 'I never heard a prettier name than that.'

'Mother brought me a posy of lilies one day,' said the child, 'and she said their faces were as white as mine.'

'They couldn't be much whiter, poor lamb,' said the old woman; and she was going to take the child on her knee, when suddenly it struck her how dirty she was beside the child. The child's fair skin had not a speck of dirt on it, and her print frock, though it was faded and patched, was clean and tidy; her pinafore was as white as washing could make it, and her soft brown hair had evidently been brushed and cared for. Such a clean pretty little thing she looked, as she sat on the stool by the fire. Old Grumpy had never known before how dirty and forlorn she was; she did not like to touch the child with those dirty hands, or to take her to sit on her knee, while she had that dirty ragged apron on.

"Where is my mother?" said the child, crying. 'I want to go back to her.'

'Mother's gone away,' said Old Grumpy; 'you're coming to live with me, my little darling. I'm your mother now.'

'Oh, no, no, no,' sobbed the child, 'no, no, no! I don't want to stop here. Take me to my own mother. I want my own mother.'

The old woman tried to comfort her, but in vain; the more she talked to her, so much more the child cried and sobbed, and asked to be taken to her own, own mother.

'What's the matter with the bairn?' said old Joel's voice, at the bottom of the staircase. 'Are you a beating of her already?'

Grumpy did not deign to answer him, but tried once more to quiet the child. She took her on her knee, in spite of her dirty apron, she kissed her, she offered her a piece of sugar, she called her all kinds of loving and endearing names, and she made her numberless promises of what she would do for her and get for her if she would be a good girl, and not cry any more.

But it was all of no use. Little Lily still sobbed on, and still cried, 'Take me to my mother, do; I want my own mother.'

At last, in despair, the old woman took her up in her arms, and carried her down the court to the house where the man with the pipe had stood at the door. The man was not there now, but his wife, a little rosy-cheeked woman, was hanging some clothes out to dry, on a line which went across the court.

'Well, I never!' said the woman. 'Why, here's Old Grumpy and her bairn. What's the matter with the little 'un?'

'She doesn't like me,' said the old woman, bursting into tears. 'She does nothing but cry for her mother. Whatever shall I do with her, Mrs. McKay?'

'Poor wee lamb!' said the rosy-cheeked woman. 'Let her bide here to-day; she'll maybe get settled a bit. Our Georgiana Maria will mind her.'

It was a distinguishing feature of Ivy Court, that nearly all the children in it had two Christian names, by which two names they were always called. The fashion had been started by Mrs. Perkins, who was a much-respected person, because she lived in a front house, and because she took in lodgers. It was agreed by all the neighbours that Mrs. McKay had chosen the finest names of all; and as for Georgiana Maria, her name was considered to be unrivalled in beauty. She was a little girl of eight years, as round and rosy as her mother, and with as bright and pleasant a face. She took the sobbing child in hand at once, dried her tears on her pinafore, took her in the kitchen put her on a stool by the fire, and brought a picture-book for her to look at.

After a time the sobbing ceased, and the child seemed happier. 'She'll be all right now,' said Mrs. McKay. 'Let her stop here till to-morrow, and she'll settle down a bit.'

'Very well,' said the old woman; 'but you'll be sure and let me have her then. You won't take her away from me, will you?'

'Oh, never dear,' said rosy Mrs. McKay, laughing. 'We've got plenty of 'em here; we don't want any more, *I* can tell you.'

The first thing the old woman did, when she got to her room, was to lock her door, to draw down the old ragged blind before her window, and to stop up the keyhole. Then she drew from under her bed a small square box. The box was locked, but Old Grumpy cautiously unfastened her dress, took out a key which was tied round her neck, and opened it. Inside there was another box, smaller still, made of cardboard, and tied up with a piece of faded blue ribbon. The old woman untied the string and looked in. There was not much inside the box, only a wedding-ring, a lock of fair hair, and a small book. The ring had been her mother's, and the lock of hair had been cut off by the workhouse nurse, after her mother was dead.

Old Grumpy wrapped these things carefully up again, and took out the only other thing in the box, a small leather purse. In this purse she had put all her savings. Not that she had ever had much to save. She had been in many situations, but she had been the drudge in them all, and had done a great deal of work for very little money. Still, though she had received little, she had spent less; and, by degrees, and careful stinting and scraping and hoarding, she had got quite a little fortune in the old leather purse; at least, so it seemed to her that morning as she counted it.

Why she had saved it, she could not have told. It had never been of any use to her. Most of it had been locked up in that box for many years; and yet, though she had often been very poor, and though sometimes she had not known where the next meal was to come from, she had never touched this little hoard; she had even felt as if she would rather starve than make it less. But for the sake of the child some of it must be spent. It was a great wrench to part with it; but it must be done.

'Anything for that pretty bairn!' she said to herself; 'anything for her!'

CHAPTER VI

THE MYSTERIOUS LETTER

O LD GRUMPY took some shillings out of the purse, and hurried away to the shop. The woman of the shop was astonished when the old woman asked her for soap and soda, a sweeping-brush, and a scrubbing-brush.

'Well, I never!' she could not help saying to her husband. 'Whatever can she be going to do?'

Old Grumpy hurried back to her house, and began her cleaning in good earnest.

Joel, in the room below, could not imagine what was going on. Such a knocking and thumping and scraping, such a brushing and rubbing and scrubbing overhead; he thought that the old woman had at last gone quite mad, and that he ought to leave word at the asylum at once.

But Old Grumpy worked on, all through the day; and the evening sun-beams, which came streaming in through her window, must have been as-tonished to see the change in her little room. The window was bright and clean, so that they had no difficulty in getting in; the dead flies, spiders, and cobwebs had disappeared; the ceiling was whitewashed, the walls were swept, the floor was clean, the grate was brushed with black-lead; even the handle of the little closet by the fire had been polished till it shone like gold.

But the sunbeams were to see more changes still, when they looked into Old Grumpy's room the next day; for that night a paperhanger and painter, who lived in Ivy Court, came after working-hours, and hung the walls with a bright, cheerful paper. The old woman thought this paper would help to amuse the child, for it was covered with pictures of carriages and horses, and of grand ladies and gentlemen, in bright blue dresses and scarlet coats. Then the man gave a coating of paint to the door and chimney-piece and closet, and the little room looked as clean and pretty as it could possibly be made to look.

Meanwhile Old Grumpy had been very busy on the landing. She had washed the chintz on the bed, and her own clothes, and everything in the house that could be washed.

When Lily was brought home the next day by kind little Mrs. McKay, the old woman's joy was complete; for the child did not cry, but amused herself by running round the room, counting the horses on the walls, and choosing which of them she would like to ride, if she were a lady.

Only at night, when she had had her bread-and-milk, and was sitting by the fire in a little nightgown Mrs. McKay had given her, did the child begin to be sorrowful.

'My mammy's never coming back no more, Grum,' said the child. 'Mrs. McKay said so.'

'Poor darling!' said the old woman, kissing her gently. 'Poor little lamb!'

'Where's heaven, Grum?' said the child, presently, as she put her toes on the fender to warm them.

'Well,' said the old woman, 'I don't know. Some folks say it's in the stars; but I don't know, they're such little things, is the stars. Maybe it's behind the blue sky, if only we could see there.'

'What's my mammy doing there, Grum?' asked the child.

'Singing,' said the old woman, decidedly.

Lily sat looking into the fire, watching the flames darting up the chimney, her large brown eyes wide open, and her thoughts far away with her lost mother.

'What's she doing *now*, Grum?' she said, after they had been silent some minutes.

'Singing, my bairn, singing,' repeated the old woman, for she thought she could not have heard her before.

'When will she stop singing?' asked the child.

'Never no more,' said the old woman; 'they do nothing but sing in heaven.'

'How tired she will get!' said the child, wearily. 'How very tired! Doesn't God never let them rest?'

'I don't know,' said the old woman. 'I don't think so.'

'Will she sing all the time we're in bed?' asked the child.

'Yes; they say it's never night there,' said Old Grumpy. 'I've heard folks say so, lots of times; but I don't know if it's true!'

'Oh dear, she *will* be tired!' said the child.

She let the old woman lay her in bed, and wondered what heaven was like, and whether her mother was happy there, till she fell asleep.

Grumpy sat for some time beside her, watching her pretty little face as lovingly and tenderly as her dead mother could have done.

Then came a rap at the door, and Old Grumpy opened it cautiously. To her surprise there was Mrs. Perkins waiting to be let in.

'Hush!' said Mrs. Perkins, motioning with her hand for her to be quiet. 'Don't say a word, and I'll tell you what I've come for.'

Whereupon Mrs. Perkins unbuttoned her ulster, and took out from under it a small carpet-bag.

'There,' she said, mysteriously, 'you keep that bag. It has got a few of her clothes in it, and it's yours by right now you've got her,' pointing, as she spoke, to the sleeping child. 'How are you getting on? Dear me, what a nice clean-looking place you've got!' she said, looking admiringly round the room.

'We're getting on all right,' said the old woman; 'I'm as fond of her as if she was my own.'

'You couldn't be much fonder,' said Mrs. Perkins. 'Now then, just you remember about that bag. Nobody knows about it, you understand. If they was to get sight of it at the house, they would be wanting to take the child, and I might get into trouble, so I never told them. You understand? Well, good-bye;' and in a moment Mrs. Perkins was gone.

Old Grumpy stooped down by the fire, and in the dim light, for the fire was dying out, she unpacked the bag. It was nearly filled with little Lily's clothes, pinafores, and night-gowns, a Sunday frock, a tidy little jacket and hood, several pairs of knitted socks, and a little pair of shoes.

But there was one other thing in the bag which troubled Old Grumpy not a little. She had taken out all the little clothes, and was feeling with her hand at the bottom of the bag, that she might be sure that she had found everything, when she discovered a pocket inside the lining at the side of the bag.

She put her hand into this pocket, and brought out from thence a letter. It was fastened up, directed, and stamped, ready for the post. How much the old woman wished that she could read, that she might know what name was written on the envelope! To whom was the letter addressed? Mrs. Perkins had evidently not found the pocket, nor seen the letter, or she would have mentioned it to her. And now, what ought she to do about it?

CHAPTER VII

ANYTHING FOR THE CHILD

THE more Old Grumpy looked at the letter she had found, the more troubled and perplexed she became. No doubt the letter was addressed to some relative of the dead woman, and no doubt if the officer had it, he would be able to find out who she was, which Mrs. Perkins had said he had been quite unable to do. Ought she not to take it to him to-morrow, when she went to the house for her bread?

But every day that passed, her little Lily grew more dear to Old Grumpy's heart. Every day that passed, made her less inclined to post the letter that might be the cause of taking the child from her.

Although Lily never forgot her own dear mother, and although she still talked much about the heaven where she was gone, and wondered many times in the day what she was doing, still she was as happy as a little bird in the old woman's room. It was no longer a dark and cheerless place; the sunbeams, as they looked in, saw a happy little girl there, who was more of a sunbeam in the once dismal place than they, the sunbeams, were themselves.

Old Grumpy's life was now a very happy one. The letter seemed to be the only cloud in her sky. When her little girl was talking to her, and she was listening to her pretty voice; when she was walking hand-in-hand with her in the fields outside the city; when she was making a chain of the daisies she had gathered in her walk, and when she was hanging them round the old woman's neck; when she was hugging her, and stroking her face, and calling her 'her own dear, darling Grum;' then the old woman's happiness was complete.

The neighbours were very kind; many a little present for the child found its way to Old Grumpy's room. Sometimes it was an old frock, carefully patched and mended; sometimes a pinafore which had been outgrown; sometimes it was a new little garment, bought with pence which had been carefully saved for the orphan child; sometimes it was only a pudding, or a cake, or a biscuit; but, whatever it was, it was given cheerfully and gladly, and was thankfully received by the old woman, as adding to her darling's comfort. As for her own small hoard in the box under the bed, it grew less and less; but each time Old Grumpy took from it, she did so with greater pleasure and with less pain. 'Anything for my pretty child,' she would say each time to herself, as she unlocked the box.

Every one in the court was fond of 'Old Grumpy's bairn,' as they called her. Her quaint, quiet, old-fashioned ways won all their hearts. Even old Joel would call her into his room, and would make his wonderful cat go through its performances for her amusement; and when she clapped her hands with delight, he would pat her on the head and tell her to come again, for she was 'as welcome as never was!' The children followed her about as if she were a newly-arrived curiosity, and were always kind and gentle to her in their play.

But Mrs. McKay's Albert Joseph was her great ally. He was a quiet, grave-looking child, very unlike his noisy brothers and sisters. When they were scampering about the house, or playing at marbles in the court, he would sit on his stool before the fire, gazing at the flames and thinking.

What Albert Joseph's thoughts were, no one had ever been able to discover, until 'Old Grumpy's bairn' arrived on the scene. Between Lily and Albert Joseph there sprang up a great and firm friendship. They were never tired of being together; they would sit side by side for hours in the sunshine on one of the doorsteps of the court, or would wander hand-in-hand down the street, looking in at the shop windows, or would stand gazing in at the churchyard gate, watching the sparrows hopping from tree to tree, and sitting on the old smoky gravestones, near the churchyard wall.

'Grum,' said Lily one day, 'Albert Joseph thinks.'

'What does he think?' said the old woman, stopping in the midst of her washing. 'His mother says he thinks a many things; what is it now?'

'He thinks,' said the child, 'that my mother isn't always singing in heaven.'

'Why, what does he think she does, then?' said Old Grumpy.

'He thinks she works for God,' said the child, reverently; 'and he thinks, maybe, she goes to see the stars, and all the beautiful places God made; that's what Albert Joseph thinks! He says his Sunday-school teacher told them all about heaven last Sunday. However does she know about it, Grum? Has she been there?'

'No, my lamb,' said the old woman. 'She couldn't go there till she died; maybe she's read about it.'

'But how did the books know about it?' said the child, still more puzzled. 'Somebody must have been to see.'

'Well, bairn, I don't know; I only know folks learns a lot in books, and they seem to think it's true.'

Lily lay still, watching Old Grumpy, who was very busy with her washing again, scrubbing and rubbing her little darling's clothes, that she might make them as white as snow.

CHAPTER VIII

THE BEAUTIFUL GARDEN

THE very next Sunday afternoon, Albert Joseph and Lily started together, hand-in-hand, to go to the Sunday-school. Old Grumpy felt very lonely when they were gone; she could not read, and Sunday had always been a long day to her before Lily came to her. But on Sunday afternoon she and Lily had gone for a walk together in the fields outside the town, and it had been a happy time for Old Grumpy. Now she sat watching the clock, and counting the minutes till Lily's return.

The old woman felt quite rewarded for sparing the child, when she saw her bright, happy little face as she ran into the room, eager to tell of her adventures.

'Oh, Grum, Grum,' she said, 'dear old Grum, I wish you were a little girl, and could come with me.'

'Was it so nice, my bairn?' said the old woman.

'Yes, Grum; I'm going to tell you all about it,' said the child, seating herself on a stool at the old woman's feet. And taking both her thin wrinkled old hands, she kissed them, and then she put them on her little pale cheeks, and made them stroke her face, again and again.

'It was about a garden, Grum, such a pretty garden, prettier than the garden of that big house near the cemetery, where you and me peeped through the gate, 'cause I asked teacher, and she said it was.'

'Did she?' said the old woman, smiling at the child's bright face.

'Grum,' said Lily, suddenly, as she was eating her bread and butter, 'what's a *skellington*?'

'I don't know, I'm sure,' said the old woman, laughing. 'I never heard of such a thing.'

' 'Cause Joel was talking about a *skellington* to-day,' said the child.

'Joel talks a lot of nonsense,' said Old Grumpy, scornfully. 'He's always talking some sort of rubbish to that ugly old cat of his.'

'It wasn't the cat he was talking to,' said the child, 'it was Mrs. McKay. When me and Albert Joseph was coming home they was talking together, and Joel, he pointed at me, Grum, and he said I was as thin as a skellington.'

'Joel had better mind his own business,' said the old woman, sharply; 'don't you go and listen to what Joel says; *he* doesn't know, a silly old fellow like him! A skeleton indeed! What nonsense!'

Nevertheless she looked at the child very anxiously, more anxiously and carefully than she had ever done before. Yes, she was thin, very, very thin; the old woman was forced to acknowledge this, in spite of herself.

'But you always *were* thin, you know,' she said, as she took the child on her knee; 'always a little thing, you were! And it's a deal prettier too to be thin. So Joel may say what he likes; you and me don't care about him; do we, my beauty?'

Thus the old woman tried to lull her fears to rest. But when Lily was in bed, and the candle was put out, she sat beside her, watching her very anxiously by the flickering light of the fire.

And this Sunday evening the clock on the mantelshelf seemed to speak. As the pendulum swung backwards and forwards, it seemed to be repeating over and over again the child's words:

'A skel—ling—ton, a skel—ling—ton. He said—I was—a skel—ling—ton!'

And so it went on, the same words repeated so often, that Old Grumpy's head ached with the sound.

She felt angry and impatient. Why was not her little girl as strong and healthy-looking as the McKays or Perkinses? Why did not God Almighty make her so? They had plenty of children; she had only this one.

Old Grumpy felt angry with God. She knew very little about Him, but she knew that health and strength are His gifts. Why then did He not give them to her darling? She felt angry, too, with herself, that she had not noticed before how thin and delicate her child was, that she had not watched her more carefully, and that she had not kept her indoors when the wind was cold, and fed her with more strengthening things. But, most of all, she felt angry with old Joel. He had never liked her, never been friendly to her; she and Joel had always 'had words' together, and no doubt he was glad her child was like a skeleton. He was an ill-natured, cross, disagreeable old man, was old Joel.

Such were Old Grumpy's thoughts, when they were disturbed by the sound of a man's step on the staircase. Who could it be? She opened her door cautiously, and she saw, standing before it, the very last person she expected to see. It was old Joel himself.

It was the very first time he had come to Old Grumpy's room, and she was not at all prepared to give him a welcome. She felt very much inclined to shut the door in his face, without waiting to hear what he had to say. But perhaps it would be a good opportunity to tell him to mind his own business, and not to chatter and gossip about her child again.

CHAPTER IX

GRUM DOES NOT CARE

'WELL,' said Old Grumpy, gruffly, 'what do you want?'

'Is she asleep?' said Joel, peering into the room, and taking no notice of the cold reception he met with.

'What business is that of yours?' said the old woman, angrily.

'Now, then,' said Joel, 'don't be so stingy, ole woman. You and me never *has* hit it, I *know* that; but we'll let bygones be bygones, as folks say. Now look ye here; I like that little lass *uncommon*—I do, indeed.'

'You're not the only one that does that,' said Grumpy, still unmoved.

'Never said I was,' answered Joel; 'but look ye here what I've brought her! Just you put it by her pillow, that she may find it when she wakes up in the morning. It's the New Year, to-morrow is; and it's a New Year's present from me to the little lass.'

So saying, Joel thrust a parcel into Old Grumpy's hands, wished her good-night, and went quickly down the stairs.

The parcel was tied up in a very much crumpled and soiled piece of newspaper, and a piece of thick string was knotted tightly round it. On it was written, 'For Lily, with old Joel's love.' She laid the parcel by the child's pillow, and waited as patiently as she could for New Year's day.

That was a very long night; at least, it seemed so to Old Grumpy. The church clock seemed slower in his movements than ever, and when he solemnly proclaimed twelve o'clock, and announced to Ivy Court, and to all the neighbourhood, that a New Year had begun, his voice sounded very terrible to Old Grumpy. For the clock on the mantelshelf was still ticking the same words.

'He said—I was—a skel—ling—ton.'

What would the New Year bring to herself, and to her child? Could it be that it would see her once more left with nobody to love her? Old Grumpy slept very little that night, and was truly glad when the morning came, and the child awoke. Of course she caught sight of her parcel at once, and of course she wanted to know what was in it, and of course the old woman at once jumped out of bed, and brought the biggest knife in the house to cut the string.

Inside the parcel was a little frock, made of soft warm plaid, which Joel had bought for the little girl, and which Mrs. McKay had made for her. It was so warm, and so pretty, and fitted her so well, that Old Grumpy's eyes filled with tears as she dressed her in it; for it was Joel's present, the present of 'the ill-natured, cross, disagreeable old man' as she had called him only the night before. She took hold of Lily's hand, and went downstairs.

'Joel,' she said, 'I'm right 'shamed of myself; it's a real beauty, that's what it is!'

'She's as welcome as never was,' said the old man. 'Bless her! She *does* look a little lady now! Will she give old Joel a kiss for it?'

The child ran forward, and jumped on his knee, and throwing her arms round the old man's neck, she kissed him again and again; and he felt well repaid for the self-denial it had cost him to save the money for his New Year's present.

The little frock was warmly lined, and was made high in the neck, and with long sleeves. Joel had particularly requested Mrs. McKay to make it thus.

'No cold winds will get to you now, little lass,' he said, as he wished her a happy New Year. 'You'll get as fat as never was!'

But, though Joel's frock kept Lily so warm and snug, and though Grumpy watched her child more carefully than ever before, and though she went again and again to her little hoard for money to buy all kinds of tempting things for her to eat, still, somehow or other, the child did not grow either fat or rosy. And when the winter passed away, and the warm spring days came, she grew very tired.

'She was not ill, not at all ill,' Old Grumpy often said to herself, as she answered her own fears; 'only a little white and thin, and not very strong; but spring weather was very tiring to every one, and she would be all right again in a few weeks.'

One Sunday afternoon Lily came in with so much colour in her pale face that the old woman thought she had never seen her looking so well; but it was only a flush of pleasure, and did not last long.

'Grum,' she said, 'dear Grum, they've been singing about me at school!'

'About you, my pretty bird,' said the old woman; 'what does she mean, Albert Joseph?'

' She means the hymn,' said the little boy; 'it was about a lily.'

'Yes, and we learnt the first verses,' said the child. 'Would you like to hear it, Grum?' And the two children sang the hymn to her.

'Isn't it beautiful, Grum?' said Lily, with a sigh, when she had finished; 'and the teacher said—— Tell Grum what teacher said, Albert Joseph.'

'Teacher said that was the way to get to heaven. Did you ever tell Grum about Adam and Eve, Lily?'

'Yes, she told me,' said the old woman; 'that was her first Sunday.'

'They were bad, you know,' Albert Joseph went on, 'and all their children were bad, and we're bad too.'

'Grum doesn't think we are,' said Lily.

'Teacher said so,' said Albert Joseph; 'but she told us such a beautiful story. Tell her, Lily.'

'It wasn't about a garden this time, Grum,' she said; 'it was about a hill, like the hills outside the town.'

'And on the hill there was a cross,' said Albert Joseph, 'and the Lord Jesus hung on it.'

'Ay, I've seen a picture of that in a shop window,' said Grumpy.

'He loved us so much,' said Lily, 'that He died instead of us,—*instead* of *us*. Think of *that*, Grum!'

'Did He, my dear?' said the old woman, smoothing out her darling's dress, and evidently not thinking of what she was saying.

'Isn't it wonderful, Grum?' asked the child.

'Isn't *what* wonderful, my bairn? You've got a wonderful bright colour in your cheeks; I'd like Joel to see you now! I'll give him a call; maybe he'll come up and have a look at you, and see if you ain't getting a rosy girl. We'll have to call you Rosie, instead of Lily.'

'Grum doesn't care about it,' said Albert Joseph, when she left the room.

'Yes, she does,' said Lily; 'she didn't hear, I think.'

CHAPTER X

OLD JOEL'S LETTER

'You *do* care; don't you, Grum dear?' said Lily, when Joel had gone downstairs again.

'Care, what for?' asked the old woman; 'for *you*, my darling?'

'No; for that beautiful story,' said the child. 'Don't you see, Grum, we *can* go to heaven, though we *are* so bad; because Jesus has been punished instead of us.'

'Teacher told us about a man,' said Albert Joseph.

'Yes, a bad man,' said Lily, 'who was going to be put in prison. He had to pay ever so much money, or else go to prison.'

'And he hadn't any money,' said Albert Joseph; 'not a farthing!'

'And then a gentleman went and paid instead of him,' said Lily; 'such a kind gentleman. And teacher asked us if the man would have to pay too!'

'And we all said "No," ' said Albert Joseph; 'and then teacher told us it was like Jesus and us. Jesus had been punished, and paid for us, and we could go free.'

'Isn't it wonderful, Grum?' said Lily again.

'Yes, I s'pose it is,' said the old woman; but she asked no more questions, and began to be very busy, getting out the tea things and preparing for tea.

Lily watched her for some time, and then she asked suddenly, 'Grum, what else do you think teacher said? She said, if the man would have nothing to do with the gentleman or his money, why then he'd have to pay himself!'

'Yes,' said Albert Joseph, 'he'd have to go to prison, because he couldn't pay; he hadn't any money. And that's why she taught us that verse, and wanted us to say it to God.'

'And teacher said, if we ask Him, He will make our souls white like the lily,' said the little girl.

'Yes, and take all the bad in us away,' said Albert Joseph; 'so me and Lily are going to ask Him, Grum.'

'Come and say it too, Grum,' said Lily, pulling her by the apron.

The old woman could not refuse the child. It was the first time she had knelt to pray for many, many years; but though she repeated the words after her darling, she was not praying; she was thinking of her, and not of the loving Lord, who was standing, waiting to bless her. The third link must be added to the chain before Old Grumpy would care for His love.

And the third link was coming very quickly. For her Lily, her lovely cherished flower, was fading fast.

Every one knew it except the old woman, who loved her so much, and who watched her so tenderly.

Mrs. McKay knew it; and she wiped her blue eyes many times in the day, as she thought how soon her Albert Joseph's little companion would be gone. Mr. McKay knew it, and he took his pipe out of his mouth, and looked after her each time she passed down the court. Mrs. Perkins knew it, and she would tell her lodgers, over and over again, how *she* had said when the mother was dying, that she and the child would not be parted long. All the neighbours in Ivy Court knew it, and the little presents that found their way to Old Grumpy's room were more numerous than ever. Old Joel knew it, and he would carry the child up the stairs in his arms, when she came in, that she might not be tired, and a tear often fell on her little arm as he did so. Even the children in the court knew it, and would stroke her face, or kiss her cheek, or bring her flowers as she passed by. But Old Grumpy would not believe it; she shut her eyes to it, and refused to allow it was true. Yet day by day the child grew thinner and more languid; day by day the cough, which had at first come so seldom, increased and grew worse; day by day Lily grew weaker and more weary.

One by one, all her little ways were changed. She no longer sat on the doorstep or played in the court. She no longer looked in at the shop-windows with Albert Joseph, or stood at the churchyard gate watching the sparrows. And at last the day came when Joel carried her upstairs for the last time.

But Old Grumpy did not know it. She would be better in a few weeks, she said. But the weeks on earth were getting very few for little Lily; she was going to the land which is very far off, the land where her mother had gone before.

'It's a pity this is such a cold place,' said old Joel, one day; 'such cold east winds we get here; and it's so damp too. If she could only go for a bit to a warmer country, maybe she'd get over it. I *have* heard of folks getting better when they went away.'

All at once there flashed into the old woman's mind the remembrance of the letter in the box. Perhaps there was some one belonging to the child who lived in a warmer country, and who would take her for a time, and then bring her home again, well and strong. Would she ever come back? That was the question. Was it not more likely, that once having found her, they would keep her altogether? There was a fierce struggle in the old woman's mind. But true love for the child won the victory over selfish love for her.

'Anything for her,' she said, 'anything for the pretty bairn! If the letter is to any one in a warmer country, it shall go; if it breaks Old Grumpy's heart to send it.'

She took it from her box, and hiding it under her apron, she took it to Joel.

'Joel, man, you can read,' she said; 'have a look at this!' and she told him where she had found it, and why she had hidden it so long.

Joel put on his spectacles, and read the address—

'Mrs. Havercroft, Elm Cottage, Near Bideford, Devonshire.'

'It's a fine warm country that is,' said old Joel; 'one of my mates came from there; I know all about it.'

Grumpy was almost sorry to hear this; now she must find out more.

'Open it, Joel, and see who it's to,' she said; 'we shall need to know that.'

So Joel opened the letter and read:

'My dearest Mother,—Lily and I are on our way to you, and hope to be with you in two days' time. I am very ill indeed, and am coming home to die. Since John was taken, I've had a hard time; I took in washing, and went out to work. That is why I never wrote all these months. I couldn't bear to tell you; I was afraid you would fret. Mother, I have learnt to love Jesus, and He has forgiven my sins, and I shall soon go to be with Him. I know you will look after my darling when I am gone. Hoping soon to see you,

'Your loving daughter,
'Emily Turner.

'P.S.—We left our old home and went to Northampton, so I never got any letters from home for a long time.'

I

'It's to Lily's grandmother,' said Old Grumpy. 'Now, Joel, you must write me a letter to go with it.'

So Joel, with much trouble, and with many mistakes in spelling, wrote as follows:—

'DEAR MADAM,—I hope this finds you well, as it leaves me at present. Your dawter died in this citty, near two yeers ago; and an old lady took the child, and a blessed child she is, and as welcum, when she comes to see me, as never was! And Old Grumpy (meaning the old lady) makes a hidol of her, and loves her like her own. But she (meaning the child) is ill, and thin. And she (meaning the old lady) is willing to spare her to you, if you can fetch her to Devonshire, which folks say is a warm country.

'But if you will let her come back again, as soon as restored to health—for reason of *this*, that we can't get on without her—you will for ever oblige all parties concerned.

'From you sincere friend and well-wisher,

'JOEL SMITH.

'Address—"Mr. J. Smith, Ivy Court, Cathcart Street, Ledminster." '

This curious letter gave great satisfaction to Old Grumpy, to old Joel himself, and to Mrs. McKay, who alone was admitted into their secret. The old woman posted it herself. She felt as if her heart would break as she saw the letter fall into the box, for surely soon some one would be coming for the child.

She little thought who was coming, nor how soon!

CHAPTER XI

THE THIRD LINK

SEVERAL days went by, and no answer had come to old Joel's letter. And each day Lily grew weaker. The doctor whom Joel had fetched to see the child said that he could do nothing for her; they were to give her anything that she could take, and keep her as quiet as possible.

Lily was very happy; every one was so good to her, she said.

Albert Joseph came the moment that school was over, and spent all his playtime with her. Mrs. McKay came in and out all day long, and helped Old Grumpy to make the child's bed, and to get her all she wanted. The neighbours were constantly asking after their little favourite, and sending her tempting dishes, which they thought she might fancy; and poor old Joel deserted his cat, and sat beside her for hours together.

The child did not talk much now; it tired her so much, she said. Only she would often raise herself, to put her arms round the old woman's neck, and to kiss her, and sometimes she would say:

'Grum, dear Grum, you *do* care, don't you?'

And the old woman would answer, struggling to keep back her tears, 'Yes, my bairn, I do care for *you*, very, very much.'

'But you must care for Jesus too, Grum,' the child would say, 'that's what I mean; for Jesus dying instead of us; don't you remember, dear Grum?'

And then she would be tired, and lie down again. They often thought she was asleep, and would move about quietly, and speak in whispers, and then she would open her eyes and smile at them, and would say, 'I'm not asleep, Grum; I was thinking about my hymn. Every one in heaven is white like the lily!' said the child, 'teacher said so; but she said we must be made white *here* first.'

'I'm sure you're white enough, my pretty little lass!' said the old man.

'Only my face is white; not my soul. Not till Jesus washed me. But I've asked Him. And teacher said He would.'

Then she was tired, and fell fast asleep. She slept so long, and so soundly, that they grew quite hopeful. Surely it was a good sign, and she would awake refreshed and better.

Then a step came on the stair; but a step so noiseless, that the old woman and Joel did not hear it.

Only the child heard it, and she looked up and smiled, and then went at once, and gladly, with the One who had come for her.

And stronger, more loving arms than old Joel's carried the tired child up to the home of rest.

The old woman did not know that she was gone, and when Joel told her, for a long time she would not believe it. 'She was only sleeping; she would be waking soon,' she said. But when Mrs. McKay came, and convinced her that Joel was right, the old woman sat down on a stool by the fire, and rocked herself backwards and forwards in the agony of her grief. She did not speak, or take any notice of those around her. She only rocked herself and moaned.

So she sat the whole of those three sorrowful days in the darkened room, with the child beside her. She ate what they gave her; but she did not seem to know what she was doing, and looked strangely at them all the time.

Then they took all that was left of her darling away; and still Old Grumpy did not move, nor cease rocking herself backwards and forwards. It was not until all this was over, and the neighbours had gone home, and the little room was empty and desolate again, that old Grumpy spoke, and then it was only to break out with her old terrible wail, in a voice so heartrending that Joel in the room below stopped his ears, that he might not hear it. 'Nobody loves me; nobody does! Nobody loves me; nobody does!'

'She's gone quite mad again,' said the neighbours; 'poor old soul! can nobody do anything to bring her to herself again?'

But, though they stood talking of it by the pump for hours together, no one could think of any plan for comforting the old woman.

'Nobody loves me; nobody does!' the old woman moaned on, all through the night. 'My cat loved me, and I lost her; my darling loved me, and I've lost her too. Nobody loves me; nobody does!'

The last links were being added very quickly to the chain now. The living, loving Lord, who had stood so long outside her closed door, had His hand on the latch now. He was leading her on, by this dark and sorrowful way, to Himself and to His love.

There was great excitement in Ivy Court about two days after the child's funeral. It was caused by the arrival of a respectably-dressed middle-aged woman, who was a stranger in the town, she said, and who wanted Mr. Joel Smith. It was the child's grandmother. She had come at last; but she was too late to see her little grandchild. Mrs. McKay took her into the house, and with many tears, the little blue-eyed woman told her the sorrowful story. She told her of her daughter's death—of the way in which the old woman came to have charge of the child—of her great love for her—of the way in which she had toiled for her, and denied herself that she might keep her—of her terrible grief now that the child was dead.

'She's almost crazed,' said Mrs. McKay; 'she does nothing but rock herself, and say over and over, "Nobody loves me; nobody does!" You'll maybe wonder we let her have the poor bairn; but she wasn't crazed while she was here, not a bit, I *do* assure *you*!'

'God knows I'm only too grateful to her for being so good to my Emily's child,' said the poor grandmother, wiping her eyes. 'But why did I not get this letter before?' she asked, taking her daughter's letter from her pocket, and pointing to the date. 'I thought Emily had forgotten me; I wrote to her again and again, and got no answer.'

'Well, mum,' said Joel, who had come in while they were speaking, 'I'll tell you how it was you didn't get it. That old body, they're speaking of— she that has had care of that blessed child—*she* found this letter. But she didn't find it afore she had got to love the child. And she felt it would break her heart to lose her; and not being a scholar, you see she couldn't read it, and she didn't know who it was for. So, you see, she hid it away, and kept it as close as never was; and none of us never got a sight of it! So that's just about where it is,' said old Joel; 'and I'm not going to say it was right of Old Grumpy, quite the contrairy! But the love for the child was what drove her to it; and I'll take it as a great favour, and as kind as never was, if you won't go for to mention it to her under present circumstances.'

'No, indeed, I won't say a word,' said the poor grandmother. 'I'll only thank her for being so good to her. I should have come before; but the bad news about my Emily knocked me up so, and it's a long journey. But I'll go and see Mrs. —— *What* is her name?. I never heard her proper name, I think.'

'What *is* her name, Mrs. McKay?' said Joel, turning to her.

' 'Deed, and I don't know,' said Mrs. McKay.

'I *do* assure *you* I don't know! You see it's this way, the children in the court, long whiles ago, gave her the name of "Old Grumpy," and we've all stuck to it—not that she's grumpy a bit now, poor old body, not at all! But if you be so kind as to call her "Grum," ma'am, she'll be best pleased; that's what the child called her! It was always "Grum, dear Grum." Can't you hear her sweet voice, Joel?'

'Ay,' said Joel, with a sob, and wiping his eyes with his coat-sleeve, as he left the house to show Mrs. Havercroft the way to Old Grumpy's room; 'she was a blessed child yon was, and as welcome as never was!'

CHAPTER XII

THE CHAIN COMPLETED

OLD GRUMPY was sitting in her desolate room, rocking herself backwards and forwards, and uttering the same pitiful moan.

'Nobody loves me; nobody does! Nobody loves me; nobody does!'

She heard footsteps coming up the stairs; but she took no notice of them. It was, she thought, only Mrs. McKay coming to bring her a cup of tea.

She heard a knock at the door, but still she did not move, she only rocked herself again with the same sad wail:

'Nobody loves me; nobody does! Nobody loves me; nobody does!'

Then she felt a hand laid on her shoulder, and she heard a voice close to her ear.

'Thee mustn't say that,' said the voice; 'thee must never say that again; it isn't true!'

What was it in the voice that reminded her of her little girl? Old Grumpy started and turned round. It was not a child's face that she saw, but the face of a middle-aged woman, whose hair was streaked with grey, and whose eyes were full of tears. And yet there was something in the face, too, which reminded her of her darling.

'Are you her grandmother?' she said.

'Yes,' said her visitor, 'I am Lily's grandmother, and I have come to thank thee for all thee hast done for her. I want to tell thee how grateful I am to thee, and how I pray God to bless thee for it.'

Old Grumpy gave up rocking herself, and let Mrs. Havercroft take her hand, and hold it lovingly between her own.

'We have both had trouble,' Lily's grandmother began, as her tears fell on the old woman's hand.

'Trouble—trouble—trouble,' Old Grumpy interrupted her, drawing away her hand, and beginning to rock herself again—'trouble—trouble trouble—the world is full of trouble; I've never had nothing but trouble! I've lost them all—all I ever cared for. Nobody loves me; nobody does! Nobody loves me; nobody does!'

'Thee mustn't say that,' said Mrs. Havercroft, in a very firm and decided voice; 'stop, dear Grum, stop! It isn't true, and thee must never tell a lie.'

'It *is* true,' said the old woman, almost fiercely; 'nobody loves me; nobody does!'

'Hush, dear!' said Lily's grandmother, in a soothing voice, as if she were talking to a child,—'Hush, dear!—quiet! Will thee listen for a minute, Grum? Lily would like thee to listen; wouldn't she? Lily would say, "Grum, dear Grum, stop a minute—*please* stop a minute, and listen to my grannie!" '

The voice reminded her so much of the child's that it quieted her at once —she did not speak or move again, but clasping Mrs. Havercroft's hands tightly within her own, she waited to hear what she had to say.

'I want thee *never* to say again, "Nobody loves me," Grum. Because, dear Grum, it's a lie; it isn't true. I know somebody who loves thee far better than our darling did. He does indeed, Grum, and she would tell thee so if she were here. The dear Lord loves thee, Grum. He came all the way from heaven because He loved thee, and He died for thee on the cross. Think of that, Grum!'

Then the old woman spoke—'Ay,' she said, 'that's just what she said when she lay a-dying, "Grum, dear Grum, you *do* care, don't you?" she said, "for Jesus dying instead of us?" '

'Does He really love me?' repeated the old woman slowly.

'Yes, He really does,' said Lily's grandmother, 'and He wants thee to love Him. Ever since thee wast a little child He has been waiting for thee to love Him, and He is waiting still.'

'How do know He loves me?' said the old woman. 'Who told you?'

'He told me Himself, Grum,' said Mrs. Havercroft.

'Told you Himself—how?'

'In the Bible, Grum—it's a letter from Him thee knows.'

'And it's really true?' said the old woman, looking her well in the face.

'Oh! Grum, if I could only make thee know *how* true it is!' said Lily's grandmother, with fresh tears in her eyes.

'And He died instead of me,' repeated the old woman; 'my darling said so.'

'Yes, instead of thee, Grum. Thee couldest never have gone to heaven, never have gone to the lovely land where our little girl is now, not with thy sins, Grum.'

'Ay, that's what she said again,' said the old woman. ' "Adam and Eve was bad, and all their children was bad, and you and me is bad too, Grum," she said; "and God won't have us in heaven, like we are now, Grum." '

'Lily used to say a bonny little prayer,' said the old woman, 'and she made me say it too. She said it scores of times, over and over again:

' "Oh! wash me, Lord, I pray Thee,
    That so my soul may grow
As pure as is the lily,
    And whiter than the snow,
Pour down upon me, daily,
    Thy Holy Spirit's dew,
To cleanse me, and to strengthen,
    And give me life anew."

It was almost the last words she said.'

'Let us say it now, dear Grum, thee and me,' said Lily's grandmother. 'The dear loving Lord is in the room now, Grum; think of that!'

'Here, in *my* room?' repeated the old woman, doubtfully.

'Ay! that He is, waiting for thee to come to Him, Grum. He sees thee, though thee don't see Him. Let us go and tell Him thee wants to love Him.'

So the two knelt down together, in the once dark and desolate room. But it was not dark now, for the Sun of Righteousness Himself was there, shining into Old Grumpy's soul; and it was not desolate, for His unchanging, unfailing, unending love was filling her poor, sorrowful old heart.

'Dear Lord,' said Lily's grandmother, 'Grum thanks Thee very much for dying instead of her. She thanks Thee for Thy love, and for waiting so patiently for her. Dear Lord, save her now; shine in her heart now; make her happy in Thy love now; and don't let her ever say again that nobody loves her. Lord, we know Thou loves her; help her to love Thee back again, for Thy Holy Name's sake. Amen.'

CHAPTER XIII

EVERYBODY LOVES ME

THE great church clock was striking eight, in the same solemn and deliberate way in which it had struck that morning, now so long ago, when Old Grumpy was lighting her fire, and the lost kitten was mewing at her door.

The great church clock was striking eight, and Old Grumpy counted the strokes as she sat in her chair by the fire, just as she had done that other morning, so many months before.

'One—two—three—four—five—six—seven—eight!' counted the old woman. And the voice of the clock set her thinking.

She would not hear its voice many times more; for this was the last day she would spend in her old room, that room in which she had spent so many years, and which she had thought it would break her heart to leave.

How much had happened in that little room! Old Grumpy could not leave it without a pang. There was the smart paper on the wall, with the ladies and gentlemen going to the hunt, which had amused her little girl so much and so often. There was the stool on which she had sat, and the window seat into which she had climbed, and the shelf on which she had kept her pretty little cup and saucer, Mrs. McKay's present to her at the fair. Then there was the clock on the mantelshelf, still ticking away, as it had done on the last night in the year, and saying over the same words in Old Grumpy's ears:

'He said—I was—a skel—ling—ton.'

She was going to leave all these well-known things behind, and Mrs. McKay was to get them sold for her, at some auction, after she was gone. She could not leave them without tears, and she would take the remembrance of them with her wherever she went. She would often picture to herself that little room, with the sunbeams shining in at the window, lighting up the pictures on the wall, the faded chintz, and her little girl's pretty hair, as she sat on the stool at her feet.

This was her last day in her old home, and she wanted to think it all over before she went away. All the old cheerless days she had spent there came back to her mind, when she had been even proud of saying that she loved nobody, and nobody loved her. How wretched she had been then, and how foolish! She saw it all now.

And then she remembered the day when she had first begun to love; the day on which that poor kitten had come to her door. She remembered how strange it had seemed to her to have anything to care for, and how still stranger it had seemed to have anything to care for her. And then the cat had been lost, and she was left unloved again.

But after that her darling had come. Old Grumpy covered her face with her hands as she thought of this, and of the happy time that followed. And then God had taken her, and once more she was left alone, and, as she thought, unloved.

But now the Lord Himself had come, the living, loving Lord, and had lighted up her dark heart with the sunshine of His love. How wonderful it was! It seemed to the old woman too good to be true!

And now what could she do to show her love to Him? That was the question. That was the one great thought in the old woman's heart. He had done so much to prove His love for her; how could she prove hers in return?

Thank God, He was going to give her a good opportunity for doing so. She was going back with her little girl's grandmother to her home in Devonshire, that warm country where she had so longed to send her fading Lily; and Mrs. Havercroft had told her that there would be plenty for her to do there for the Lord, and for the Lord's people.

Lily's grandmother was a Bible-woman, and worked hard amongst the poor mothers in the parish in which she lived, trying in every way she could to lead them to the Saviour, and to help them to keep straight on the way to heaven. She lived alone, for her husband had been dead many years, and all her children were married; and she had asked the old woman to go back with her, and to spend the rest of her days in her little home.

'Thee wilt go from Ivy Court to Ivy Cottage,' she had said, 'so it won't seem strange to thee. Only we've got some real ivy there, covering us up to the chimney, and sweet fresh air blowing all round us; it will do thee good, dear Grum. And thee wilt keep my house, and have all cosy and snug for me when I come in tired from my work, and thee wilt help me to look after the sick folks, and the poor tired mothers; and the dear little children who've got no mother to look after them, thee wilt love them, and help them, Grum, for our little girl's sake, and for the Lord's sake; won't thee, Grum?'

And the old woman had answered, with her eyes full of tears—'God and you are both too good to me, Mrs. Havercroft!'

No one in Ivy Court had taken any notice of Old Grumpy the day she had first come to live there. No one had asked who she was, or where she came from, or why she came there. But it was very different on the day that she went away.

Although it was very early in the morning when the old woman started, everyone was up to see her off, and to give her a kind word at parting. Everyone in the court knew her now, and they knew where she was going, and why she was going, and they all wished her a happy journey, and a comfortable home at the end of it.

Even the children wanted a kiss of Old Grum before she went away. Indeed, they had all so much to say, and so many wanted to shake hands with her, that it is more than likely that she would have missed her train, had not Mrs. Havercroft, who had been lodging for the last few days with Mrs. Perkins, come into the court, and hurried her away to the cab, which was waiting outside.

But even that was not the last which Old Grumpy saw of the inhabitants of Ivy Court, for old Joel, Mrs. McKay, and Albert Joseph ran to the station, and were on the platform to say good-bye again, and to wave their pocket-handkerchiefs to her till she was out of sight.

'Why *everybody* seems to love me now!' Old Grumpy said, with tears in her eyes, as the train moved away.

I*

Old Grumpy wishes she could read

THE TWO BENS

by

AN UNKNOWN AUTHOR

B IG BEN had just struck seven; little Ben, sitting on a seat on the Embankment, looked across and counted the deep strokes. Ben was hump-backed, pigeon-chested, and altogether rather a miserable little object, yet his face had a bright intelligence and alertness that made him almost attractive.

He was short, and the parapet of the Embankment is high, but by placing his toes on the little projection, and hooking his outstretched arms over the the broad top, he was able to look over. It was a very fair scene on which he gazed; the sun was setting, its level rays turned the muddy Thames water into a golden stream. His toes slipped, and he came down, grazing his cheek in so doing; he did not climb up again, but sauntered on, taking very little notice of the other ragged children who played about noisily. Across the water was St. Thomas's Hospital, and Ben was fond of watching the sick people, who spent a good deal of time in the fine weather on the verandah outside the wards.

The sun had gone down now, all the lights had faded out of the sky, and a little chilly breeze came from the water. Ben had crossed the bridge and passed the hospital, and was walking by the archbishop's palace and St. Mary's Lambeth. He knew he liked the place, but could have given no reason for so doing; he liked, too, to look at the curious half-pagan monuments in the churchyard, which was so still and peaceful amidst the stir and turmoil of the sordid life around.

Ben turned to go back the way he had come. Most of the seats on the Embankment were occupied, but on one there was only an elderly gentleman at one end, and Ben took his place at the other, glancing now and then at his companion, as though to intimate that he was quite ready for conversation. Evening had quite settled down, and the great bell stuck eight.

"Same name as me," said Ben, after counting the strokes.

"Indeed?" said his companion, looking a little amused.

"Yes," said Ben; then, as if he must do the honours of the place, "Often come here?"

The gentleman bent his head.

"Wonder I ain't seen you. What, going already, guv'nor? I'll look out for you to-morrer."

Mr. Grange went on his way, feeling curiously interested in the little waif. He had been bitterly disappointed in one he deeply loved, and from that time had shut his heart against love and friendship. For many years he had led a solitary life in his old-fashioned house in South Lambeth. Of late, he had taken to walking on the Embankment at night, sometimes not returning home till the small hours. His selfish, bitter life had left its impress on his face, which was by no means attractive now.

Yet somehow little Ben had been attracted by it; and next night, when Mr. Grange took to pacing the Embankment, he found the little arab following him.

Perhaps he was tired of his loneliness; and the boy seemed safe to speak to, and there was no one to notice; so, almost to his own surprise, the solitary man took to talking to his small admirer.

"You ought to be in bed," he said once, when it was late; but Ben's patient little shadow still followed his.

Ben grinned. "Ain't got no bed; sleep under arches if the coppers don't move me," he said.

"But haven't you anyone belonging to you?"

"Only him," answered Ben, with a sweep of his arm.

Mr. Grange was puzzled; there was no one very near him, but the great clock was chiming the quarter.

"Him," explained Ben; "he's just like a brother, and we've got the same name; and he don't never go on at a fellow, but just speaks kind and cheerful; even when it's too foggy to see him, he speaks up to say he ain't a-going to leave me."

Mr. Grange looked at the eager face rather pityingly, "So that's why you like to be here?" he said.

"Yes; seems as if he looks kind of sorrowful when I've been away long."

"Can you read, Ben?" asked Mr. Grange suddenly.

"No," said Ben. "When I lived with Aunt Bet, before she was took, someone said I had oughter go to school, but Aunt Bet ups and says, 'Bless yer soul! don't bother the boy; he'll never be a growed-up man: and better for him, such a poor little 'natomy,'" he concluded, as calmly as if talking of someone else.

"Do you know what she meant?" asked Mr. Grange.

"Meant I shall die," Ben said indifferently.

"Have you ever heard of God, Ben?" said Mr. Grange.

"Him as people speak to, though they can't see Him?" said Ben, in an awestruck whisper.

"Yes, Ben; may He take you to Himself when you pass from this world!"

Ben would have liked to ask some questions, but Mr. Grange had turned away, and was striding hastily homewards. The man was strangely stirred and shaken by the child; the voice of conscience which he had stilled for so long was making itself heard again. For long he had kept apart from his fellowmen, holding out no helping hand to those who were perishing around; now he was making up his mind to help the poor little deformed waif who had come into his path.

Next evening Mr. Grange went to the Embankment rather earlier than usual; Ben was there, but was not looking out for him, and he watched him from a distance. He felt shy and nervous over the task he had set himself, and wondered which would be the best way to put it to the boy.

Ben had hooked himself on to the wall in his usual fashion. When "Chi-ike!" suddenly yelled a voice in his ear; it was only a boy coming up from behind, who intended no harm. Ben was startled; his hands and feet slipped, he struggled for a moment, then fell backwards in a heap.

Mr. Grange looked to see him get up as if nothing had happened; but, instead, when he tried to rise he sank back again with an agonised groan.

"Why, you aren't hurt?"

"I dunno," Ben gasped; but some of the terror left his face as Mr. Grange bent over him. "No, don't touch me; let me be here," he cried out.

"But I must. There, my dear lad, the worst part is over," Mr. Grange said quite tenderly, as he held him in his arms; but he was quite at a loss what to do next. However, the other boy had a suggestion ready. "Take him to the hospital, Mister," he said, nodding towards St. Thomas's; "they'll do him good."

"Thank you," said Mr. Grange, moving off quickly. The doctors at the hospital looked very grave over little Ben; there was an internal injury, they said, and they might have to perform an operation; at any rate, they must keep him; and Mr. Grange went away, knowing that the little fellow was in good hands.

When he went to the hospital next day, he was told that Ben was in a serious condition, and must have been before his fall. Lying in his white bed in a nest of pillows, he greeted his friend with a smile that had something of entreaty in it.

"He wants something, sir," said the nurse who was standing there; "it's someone he wants to see, I think. 'The other Ben,' he calls him."

"The clock; isn't that it?" asked Mr. Grange; and Ben brightened and looked more satisfied. The ward he was in did not face the river; but when the authorities were told of the boy's great desire, he was moved into another; and whenever the weather permitted, his bed was wheeled outside.

"It's very comfortable here," he said one day to his friend; "and the big 'un, he's easy in his mind now I'm so well off."

Mr. Grange had bitterly regretted that his resolve to help the little waif had come so late; very falteringly, feeling how far behind he was in practice, he tried to teach the child of better things. It was quite wonderful to see how much Ben could grasp and understand, and it seemed as if the evil amidst which he had lived had not been allowed to harm him. The Good Shepherd had watched and guarded His lamb, and now was leading him into the fold of Paradise.

"He just has been kind!" said Ben one day, as he looked at a picture of the Good Shepherd, "and I can't do nuffin for Him; and the thorns hurt Him so."

"You are doing something for Him now, Ben, as you try to be patient in your pain and weakness," said Mr. Grange gently.

Ben shook his head. " 'Tain't nuffin!" he said. "He's done such a lot for me."

Such a lot! Aye, He had indeed; but Mr. Grange's heart smote him as he thought of the boy's deformed, neglected, unloved life, and of what his own had been. How was he treating the Heavenly Father who had done so much for him? At that moment he made a prayerful resolve to do better in future.

"Stop with me, guv'nor," pleaded Ben one day, in a strangely weak voice; the thin little fingers grasped his own, the great dark eyes looked at him imploringly, and Mr. Grange stayed.

Ben's was the only bed out on the verandah, and it was sheltered as much as possible; the boy had begged so hard to be where he could see his namesake, that he had his way. Mr. Grange sat at his side; nurses and doctors came to look at him every now and then, and went away again softly.

Ben lay very still; when Big Ben chimed the quarters or struck the hours he responded with a smile or weak motion of his hands. His fingers plucked at the counterpane; once Mr. Grange laid his own on them, but they would not be stilled.

"Guv'nor, where are you?" he cried presently.

"Here I am, my dear; I have not left you."

"I can't see you; it's getting very dark. Oh, guv'nor, hold me!"

The boy's eyes were dim and frightened, and he moved his head from side to side.

"Lighten our darkness, we beseech Thee, O Lord," prayed Mr. Grange, in words with which he had once been familiar.

Morning light was very near for Ben, though over the city the sun had set and twilight was fast turning into darkness. " 'Tain't dark now," he said, as if surprised, as he turned his head restfully. Then he lay still.

And Big Ben, as it solemnly struck seven, almost seemed to tell of a triumph.

*   *   *   *   *   *

Ben's is a very short, perhaps unsatisfactory, life-story; but there is one at least who is ceaselessly thankful for it. Mr. Grange no longer lives a selfish, solitary life; and in helping others he is himself blessed: in making them happy he finds true happiness.

"Alva Chisholm! Is it you?
Where are you going?"

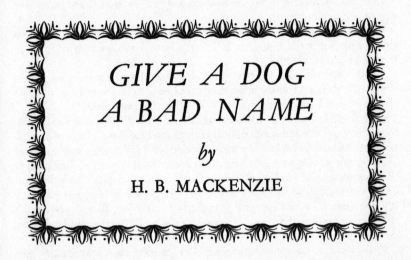

GIVE A DOG A BAD NAME

by

H. B. MACKENZIE

CHAPTER I

"GIVE a dog a bad name, and he may as well earn it. The old divines believed that the devil of old time appeared to men, saying, 'Ye are gods; therefore know yourselves gods'; but he appears to me now with this temptation, 'Thou art a sinner; know thyself, show thyself, a sinner.' "

Alva Chisholm threw himself back in his chair and stared defiantly into the fire. He did not look exactly like a social pariah, yet in effect he had declared himself one, and, strangely enough, he was so in truth. A young fellow of nineteen, undoubtedly clever, well connected, not unhandsome, and with good prospects of success later on in life—he was at present in the University studying medicine—young Chisholm was about the last person one would have supposed likely to attain to such a position. Chisholm had come from some remote eastern district a year or two ago, entered the University, and got so far on in his career with honours. He had but lately come to the highly select suburb in which he now abode, and taken up his residence with a clergyman's widow struggling to keep up an appearance of "refinement" on a small pension and two or three boarders. It was by this suburban society that Alva was ousted and ejected, declared to be an improper companion for innocent youths, and a still more undesirable acquaintance for innocent maidens. How all this came about no one seemed exactly to know. It was vaguely hinted that Alva was "fast," that he kept late hours, that he "took more than was good for him," that he flirted with "servant-girls," that he seldom attended church; but no one seemed in a position exactly to prove any of these statements.

Of Alva's few friends, Bertie Ferrier was, perhaps, the only one who thoroughly believed in him. He it was to whom Alva now poured forth all the bitterness of his soul.

"I am quite reckless, Ferrier—upon my word I am! I have reached that stage of soul-deterioration in which a man ceases to be ashamed of his own wrong-doing. I am expected to do evil. Why, then, not do it?"

"Alva, old boy, don't!" pleaded the other lad. He did not well know what to say, seeing he was not pharisaical enough, to read Alva a lecture on self-control and humility. He was a fair-haired, boyish fellow, not half so clever as Alva, but with a warm, generous heart that swelled with indignation at Alva's wrongs. "It's a shame! It's too bad!" he blurted out. "Alva, I've got an idea into my head. If I can carry it out, things will be changed for you a bit, old man. Be sure they will! I won't tell you it yet, though; but don't speak of going to the bad yet, until you know what I've in my mind, will you, Alva?"

"Oh, I can't promise anything. I feel in the mood to-night for any mischief, any evil, Bertie."

"Alva, I wish you wouldn't!" said the lad, seriously. "I know you are often tried sorely, but what do you need to care for people that you would not choose as your friends anyhow? In a year or two, when you are making a great name for yourself, these very people will wish for your friendship and you can give them the cold shoulder then. Well, I must be off, old fellow. Keep yourself cool, and remember there's a stiff exam. to-morrow."

"Good-bye, Bert. No. 'Earthly Paradise' or music-hall for me to-night, I fear. Be sure you tell the Rev. Osgood and his female supporters that I was sober when you left me," said Alva, as he dismissed his visitor. Bertie was organist in the parish church, and had an engagement there that night.

*   *   *   *   *   *

"I give you my solemn word, mother, I've never seen Alva Chisholm intoxicated once. As for that cock-and-bull story of his going into the servants' premises at Dalcluthan, it arose from the simple fact that the housemaid was the daughter of an old nurse of his own, but for some reason he didn't want to tell that. . . Come, mother, be your own sweet, reasonable self; don't listen to all these tattling scandal-mongers say."

Pretty Mrs. Ferrier hesitated, smiling into her boy's eager face, and looking hesitatingly at the tall, slim figure of a girl in the window-recess. Before she could answer Bertie, the figure moved towards the comfortable, homelike fireside—in which the little group of mother, son, and a fat tabby made a pleasant picture—and Anne Ferrier's clear, strong voice spoke out.

"I think Bertie is right, mother. We must ask that poor lad to see us. If he *is* going wrong, there is the more need why we should help to bring him right. If he is falsely maligned, then *we* are doing a great wrong by heeding what is said about him. I have always felt inclined to speak to him, but some foolish prejudice has kept me from doing so. But I shall now. I am afraid we have been helping to drive the poor lad into the wickedness of which he may never have been guilty, as Bertie says."

And her decision carried the day. Alva Chisholm would no longer be an outcast from society.

CHAPTER II

ANNE FERRIER was six-and-twenty, a tall, handsomely moulded young woman, with that air of strength and independence which a liberal education, good health of body and mind, and the sense of being respected and relied on, give to a woman. She had not been beautiful as a young girl, but many considered her so now in her young womanhood. Anne was clever; she had passed with honours in local examinations, and had taken her degree at twenty-three. Yet no one condemned her for that; no male creature passed coarse jests on a woman's aspirations after knowledge; Anne was never stigmatised as being "mannish" or "strongminded." The age for that is passed.

Everyone in Pentland heard of Alva's being "taken up" by the Ferriers, and the news created quite a little sensation in the circle to which the Ferriers belonged. No one dreamt of remonstrating with Anne on the subject; but her conduct was criticised unfavourably by many. "Anne Ferrier likes to do things that no one else would dream of doing," was the least hostile animadversion passed. And mothers still told their daughters. "You are not to recognise *that* Alva Chisholm in the street, even if you *do* meet him at the Ferriers'."

One evening, Anne Ferrier, hastening to catch a suburban train homewards, passed the door of the "Earthly Paradise." Anne, being an intelligent woman, knew enough of this modern Eden to understand how many ruined Adams it periodically cast out from its bosom. She merely glanced at its tempting entrance, glowing with rosy lights which showed long vistas beyond, like the entrance of an enchanted fairy palace; but just as she did so, a young man, coming along the pavement, was entering it. Anne looked sharply at him, with a sudden start. He evidently did not notice her.

She went up, and laid a very quiet hand on his arm.

"Alva Chisholm! Is it you? Where are you going?"

He looked at her without answering. Her steadfast eyes seemed to hold his. He could not look away from her, but the expression in his own dark face was something like that of a criminal caught in the act. He had gone very pale, and his lips twitched nervously.

"I am very glad I met you," said Anne calmly. "Will you come home with me, Alva? or are you going anywhere?"

Without a word, he turned and walked by her side towards the station. Anne kept talking of indifferent subjects, her companion hardly answering her. Anne had never seen him look as he did now; for the first time, she began to realise that there had been some truth in all the stories of evil told about him. The train she had meant to catch was gone, so there was nothing for them to do but to await the next one.

"We can sit in the waiting-room: it is not cold," Anne said, in her decided way. They went in together, and Anne, taking a seat, pointed Alva to one.

Then suddenly he burst out.

"Why do you ask me to sit near you?" he said hoarsely. "You know what I am now, Miss Ferrier—unworthy your friendship, unworthy your recognition! You can't think I am worth redeeming any longer. I am bad, though not so bad as others would make me; but I shall be some day. It runs in my blood. My father—you would not speak to me if you knew what he was."

"Hush, Alva! Not speak to you! Why, I would do that even if you were as bad as you make yourself out; and what have you to do with your father's shortcomings? Don't begin to believe in heredity, and all that nonsense. Wickedness is not a consumption or mania of the moral nature, it is an individual choice. What's wrong, Alva? Don't look like that! Do you think I am going to condemn you?"

'If you do, then I am lost for ever," said the lad hoarsely. "Miss Ferrier"— he laid his hand impulsively, yet reverently, on her arm—"I don't know what possessed me to go to that place to-night; it was the devil's own tempting. I have never gone near it since—since I knew you. Before then, I used to go. Bertle never did. He had not the temptations, you see. . . . When a fellow is alone, and has no friends, and has never known what a happy home is, life looks pretty black sometimes. No one seems much to care whether he goes to the bad or not."

Anne's eyes were wonderfully soft as they looked at him now. "If you would like to tell me your story, Alva, I should like to hear it. Think I am your elder sister to whom you are telling it."

So, drawn out by her questions, he told it. It was not a long one, and not uncommon, though Anne would fain have thought it so. The story of a man's evil, sensual life, ruinous to his own body and soul, ruinous to the gentle woman whom he had done the injury of marrying, was but the story of many another. Alva's father had died, but only after his wife had sunk into a heart-broken grave; then, but years after, the elder brother had gone too, paying the debt of his own and his father's sins by an early death.

When he ended, and looked into Anne's face with eyes dark with the intensity of his feeling, he saw that hers were full of tears.

"Alva," she said, not turning from him, and speaking in the low, emphatic way that always marked earnestness with her, "it is very good of you to tell me all this. You have been—brave and—strong. You will gain the victory soon. When you do, Alva, you will come to me, won't you, and I shall crown you victor?"

He looked at her with an expression she could not quite make out, but which troubled her vaguely. She went on—

"Will you promise me two things, Alva, now? The first is this: that you will always come to us whenever you feel the—the temptation to go to a place like the 'Earthly Paradise.' The second is, that you will always remember I am like your elder sister, and tell me what you would have told her if you had one."

His dark face crimsoned all over. For a moment he seemed to hesitate; then, stooping down, he raised her two gloved hands to his lips.

"I promise," he said solemnly. "With God's help, I shall come to you a victor some day."

CHAPTER III

SEVEN years later, Alva Chisholm, now a specialist in one of the London hospitals, returned to Pentland for a short visit. Why he came he hardly knew. A strange, dull longing, which nothing seemed to conquer, to see once more the woman to whom he owed so much, had come upon him. He knew the meeting would give him almost intolerable pain; for he had never seen her since he had received from her that letter, of which he could not think even now without an after-pang of the crushing pain it had caused—the letter in which she had said—

"And now, dear Alva, my dear friend, my almost brother, whom I love as if he were in truth my brother, I am going to tell you the secret none know yet but mother and Bert. I am going to be married very soon—in two months; and, Alva, I am very, very happy. . . . "

The first person he met at Pentland was Bertie Ferrier. Bertie had blossomed into a full-blown medical practitioner, and had started his practice in his native Edina. As Chisholm was getting off his train, Bertie emerged from another carriage. The two old friends met face to face.

"Why, Chisholm!"

"Why, Bertie!"

That was all; but hand clasped hand in a grasp that told of a friendship which never should sink into a thing of the past. Each saw great changes in the other; but perhaps that in Chisholm was the more marked.

"How are they all?" he asked, when he had answered Bertie's eager questions. "Your mother and—and sister?"

"Mother is all right, but poor Anne is having a hard time of it. You haven't heard from her lately, I suppose? I know you have been corresponding pretty regularly, but—it is her husband—poor Ralph Stenhouse; he's terribly ill—going fast, I fear. You will come along and dine with us to-night?"

"Thank you, I will. What is the matter with him, Bertie?"

"Diphtheria of a slow kind. He has been ill a week, and it has developed with alarming rapidity within the last few days. I have sent for Professor Wynton for a consultation this afternoon. Will you come along too, Chisholm? I know the throat is your speciality."

"I will," said Chisholm, after a moment's pause.

Within four hours he found himself in Anne's house.

Mr. Stenhouse, who was younger partner in a large manufacturing firm, had his house some miles out from Edinburgh. Bertie and Chisholm went out together, and met there the great specialist, Professor Wynton. A brief introduction and explanation were all that passed between the three men, who were then conducted in silence by the servant to the sick-room. As they entered it, a figure rose from a distant part of the darkened room, and came forward with a swift, noiseless footstep to meet them. At the first glance, Alva Chisholm knew it, changed though the face turned towards him was.

She recognised him at once, and, after bowing to the Professor, turned and hid her hand in his with one of the rarely beautiful smiles which were all her own.

"Alva! Forgive me for calling you that; but it seems so short a time, after all, since we first met. You are well—and prosperous? I am so glad."

She quietly left the room, and the three doctors were alone.

*   *   *   *   *   *

"There is only one resource left which we can have any hope of success in," said the great Professor sententiously.

The two younger men assented; they knew well enough what that resource was.

Alva Chisholm gave a glance backward at the bed. The patient was unconscious now, and would probably remain so until the end—if the end it was to be. He had been a stalwart man, of iron constitution; the sinews of his hands, the muscles of his arms, which had not been wasted by the disease, so rapid had its progress been, showed that. The face lying upwards on the pillow had been a fine, even a noble one; not a patrician face, with haughty curves and delicate features, but the strong, purposeful one of a man of energy and will, with the grand lines of resolution and power, of work planned and work accomplished, in it; the face of such a man, as Anne Ferrier would surely have loved. Looking at it, Alva Chisholm no longer hated the man; no longer felt the awful, devilish temptation to desire the death of Anne's husband; no longer had any more in himself to conquer.

He turned to the Professor very quietly.

"Of course, we know what you mean. Tracheotomy would mean instant death here. There is little rallying power left, and what there is must be carefully husbanded. . . . If you wish to try another operation, I am ready to aid you."

"Consider well what it is you offer, Dr. Chisholm," said the Professor, with his usual dignity a little quickened, after a pause. "In an operation of this kind there is always a certain amount of risk. You *might*—there is the possibility—you might succumb; and in such a case you know how narrow is the chance of recovery."

"A professional man does not usually consider such risks," said Chisholm quickly. "Besides, it is no greater than other risks. . . ."

Without flinching, heedless of the terrible risk he was taking, Alva opened his mouth and bent over the unconscious man.

Two hours after, and all was over. The patient, with closed eyes and moist skin, breathed freely and softly. Anne, kneeling by his bedside, thanked God with streaming eyes; and Alva Chisholm, victor at last, walked quietly toward his lodgings.

CHAPTER IV

"I WOULD not have told you, Anne. Heaven knows, you have had anxiety enough lately, but we thought—it was better that you—that you might like to see him," stammered poor Bertie, with a choke, that he vainly tried to cover.

Anne rose up slowly. She was very pale, but she gave no other sign of feeling.

"I will go now, Bertie. Ralph is quite easy now."

In a few minutes brother and sister were walking to the station.

"You thought he was so well—that there was no fear?" Anne said. "Oh, Bertie! is it not too sad? He has literally given his life for one who was not even his friend!"

"It came very suddenly—in the middle of the night," said Bertie slowly. "Anne, isn't it an heroic ending, after all, for his life—his useful, brave, unselfish life? Do you remember how the Pentland folk used to black-ball him, and ostracise him from society?—and how you took him up, and braved their jeers at your latest fad? He is repaying you now, Anne, fourfold! But I verily believe you made a man of him."

The door was opened by Alva's landlady, who shook her head in reply to Bertie's question, then in silence led the way up to that silent room in which, alone, friendless, single-handed, Pentland's social pariah was fighting his last grim battle.

Anne went forward to the bedside. A moment's long, earnest gaze into the darkened eyes, whose weirdly wistful look told her, as nothing else could, how near the end was, and Anne had fallen on her knees, and taken in her own the damp, chill hand. She bent her head, and caught the whisper—

"Anne—I have come to you—to be crowned victor."

A burst of scalding tears came to her eyes.

"My brave Alva—my boy once more as in old days! Alva, say but one word more; you have been victor over self?"

A faint smile touched the feeble, chilling lips.

"Yes—now. . . Anne, kiss me."

She obeyed, her warm lips touching his cold brow in a long, pure kiss. When Anne lifted her head, his eyes were closed. She sat quietly, holding his hand still, till Bertie touched her on the shoulder.

"Come, dear," he said, in a choked voice. "You can do no more. It is all over."

Then she saw it was so indeed. He had entered "the tragical portal of Death."

An hour after, Anne came for her last look.

She bent and reverently kissed the cold face once again. In death the face seemed smiling and calm; it was as if it had been very welcome at the last, and that the touch of the chilly fingers had been "soothing and serene."

Anne smiled also as she turned to Bertie.

"I shall not weep—I, who have crowned him victor, Bertie," she said, though her lips were tremulous.

Bertie did not know what she meant. None but Anne knew how fair were the laurels with which she had crowned her boy-lover. None on earth but Anne should ever know how great a victor he had been.

LITTLE MEG'S CHILDREN

by

HESBA STRETTON

CHAPTER I

MOTHERLESS

IN the East End of London, lying near to the Docks, there is a tangled
knot of narrow streets and lanes, crossing and running into one another,
with blind alleys and courts leading out of them, and low arched passages, and dark gulleys, and unsuspected slums, hiding away at the back of
the narrowest streets; forming altogether such a labyrinth of roads and dwellings, that one needs a guide to thread a way among them, as upon pathless
solitudes or deserts of shifting sands. It was called Angel Court.

There was certainly an advantage in living in the attics of the end house
in Angel Court, for the air was a trifle purer there, and the light clearer than
in the stories below. From the small windows might be seen the prospect,
not only of the narrow court, but of a vast extent of roofs, with a church
spire here and there, and the glow of the sky behind them, when the sun was
setting in a thick, purplish cloud of smoke and fog. There was greater quiet
also, and more privacy up in the attics than beneath, where all day long
people were tramping up and down the stairs, and past the doors of their
neighbours' rooms. The steep staircase ended in a steeper ladder leading up
to the attics, and very few cared to climb up and down it. It was perhaps for
these reasons that the wife of a sailor, who had gone to sea eight months
before, had chosen to leave a room lower down, in order to mount into
higher and quieter quarters with her three children.

Whatever may have been her reason, it is certain that the sailor's wife, who had been ailing before her husband's departure, had, for some weeks past, been unable to descend the steep ladder into the maze of busy streets, to buy the articles necessary for her little household. The only nurse she had, and the only person to whom she would entrust her errands, was her eldest child, a small, spare, stunted girl of London growth, whose age could not be more than ten years, though she wore the shrewd, anxious air of a woman upon her face, with deep lines wrinkling her forehead, and puckering about her keen eyes. Her small bony hands were hard with work; and when she trod to and fro about the crowded room, from the bedside to the fire-place, or from the crazy window to the creaking door, which let the cold draughts blow in upon the ailing mother, her step was slow and silent, less like that of a child than of a woman, who was already weary with much labour. The room itself was not large enough to cause a great deal of work; but little Meg had had many nights of watching lately, and her eyes were heavy for want of sleep.

The evening had drawn in, but Meg's mother, her head propped up with anything that could be made into a pillow, had watched the last glow of the light behind the chimneys and the church spires, and then she turned herself feebly towards the glimmer of a handful of coals burning in the grate, beside which her little daughter was undressing a baby twelve months old, and hushing it to sleep in her arms. Another child had been put to bed all ready, upon a rude mattress in a corner of the room, where she could not see him; but she watched Meg intently, with a strange light in her dim eyes. When the baby was asleep at last, and laid down on the mattress upon the floor, the girl went softly back to the fire, and stood for a minute or two looking thoughtfully at the red embers.

"Little Meg!" said her mother, in a low, yet shrill voice.

Meg stole across with a quiet step to the bedside.

"Do you know I'm going to die soon?" asked the mother.

"Yes," said Meg, and said no more.

"Father 'll be home soon," continued her mother, "and I want you to take care of the children till he comes. I've settled with Mr. Grigg downstairs as nobody shall meddle with you till father comes back. But, Meg, you've got to take care of that your own self. You've nothing to do with nobody, and let nobody have nothing to do with you. They're a bad crew down-stairs, a very bad crew. Don't you ever let any one of 'em come across the door-step. Meg, could you keep a secret?"

"Yes, I could," said Meg.

"I think you could," answered her mother, "and I'll tell you why you mustn't have nothing to do with the crew down-stairs. Meg, pull the big box from under the bed."

The box lay far back, where it was well hidden by the bed; but by dint of hard pulling Meg dragged it out, and the sailor's wife gave her the key from under her pillow. When the lid was open, the eyes of the dying woman rested with interest and longing upon the faded finery it contained—the bright-coloured shawl, and showy dress, and velvet bonnet, which she used to put on when she went to meet her husband on his return from sea. Meg lifted them out carefully one by one, and laid them on the bed, smoothing out the creases fondly. There were her own best clothes, too, and the children's; the baby's nankeen coat, and Robin's blue cap, which never saw the light except when father was at home. She had nearly emptied the box, when she came upon a small but heavy packet.

"That's the secret, Meg," said her mother, in a cautious whisper. "That's forty gold sovereigns, as doesn't belong to me, nor father neither, but to one of his mates as left it with him for safety. I couldn't die easy if I thought it wouldn't be safe. Meg, you must never, never, never let anybody come into the room till father's at home."

"I never will, mother," said little Meg.

"That's partly why I moved up here," she continued. "Why, they'd murder you all, if they couldn't get the money without. Always keep the door locked, whether you're in or out; and Meg, dear, I've made you a little bag to wear round your neck, to keep the key of the box in, and all the money I've got left; it'll be enough till father comes. And if anybody meddles, and asks you when he's coming, be sure say you expect him home to-day or to-morrow. He'll be here in four weeks, on Robin's birthday, may be. Do you know all you've got to do, little Meg?"

"Yes," she answered. "I'm to take care of the children, and the money as belongs to one of father's mates; and I must wear the little bag round my neck, and always keep the door locked, and tell folks I expect father home to-day or to-morrow, and never let nobody come into our room."

"That's right," murmured the dying woman. "Meg. I've settled all about my burial with the undertaker and Mr. Grigg down-stairs; and you'll have nothing to do but stay here till they take me away. If you like, you and Robin and baby may walk after me; but be sure see everybody out, and lock the door safe afore you start."

She lay silent for some minutes, touching one after another the clothes spread upon the bed, as Meg replaced them in the box, and then locking it, put the key into the bag, and hung it round her neck.

Her mother turned her face round to the wall with a deep sigh, and closed her eyelids, but her lips kept moving silently from time to time. Meg cried softly to herself in her chair before the fire, but presently she dozed a little for heaviness of heart, and dreamed that her father's ship was come into dock, and she, and her mother, and the children, were going down the dingy streets to meet him. She woke with a start; and creeping gently to her mother's side, laid her warm little hand upon hers. It was deadly cold, with a chill such as little Meg had never before felt; and when her mother neither moved nor spoke in answer to her repeated cries, she knew that she was dead.

CHAPTER II

LITTLE MEG AS A MOURNER

FOR the next day, and the night following, the corpse of the mother lay silent and motionless in the room where her three children were living. Meg cried bitterly at first; but there was Robin to be comforted, and the baby to be played with when it laughed and crowed in her face. Robin was nearly six years old, and had gained a vague, dim knowledge of death, by having followed, with a troop of other curious children, many a funeral that had gone out from the dense and dirty dwellings to the distant cemetery, where he had crept forward to the edge of the grave, and peeped down into what seemed to him a very dark and dreadful depth.

"You've got no mam but me now, baby," cried little Meg. She sat still for a while, with Robin lying on the ground beside her, his face hidden in her ragged frock; but the baby set up a pitiful little wail, and she put aside her own grief to soothe it.

"Hush! hush!" sang Meg, getting up, and walking with baby about the room. "Hush, hush, my baby dear! By-by, my baby, by-by!"

Meg's sorrowful voice sank into a low, soft, sleepy tone, and presently the baby fell fast asleep, when she laid it upon Robin's little mattresses, and covered it up gently with an old shawl. Robin was standing at the foot of the bed, gazing at his mother with wide-open, tearless eyes; and little Meg softly drew the sheet again over the pale and rigid face.

"Mother is going to live with the angels," said Meg.

"What are angels?" asked Robin, his glittering black eyes glancing at the bed where she lay in her deep sleep.

"Oh, I'm not quite sure," answered Meg. "Only they're beautiful people, who are always white, and clean, and shining, like that big white cloud up in the sky. They live somewhere up in the sky, where it's always sunny, and bright, and blue."

"How'll mother get up there?" inquired Robin.

"Well, I suppose," replied Meg, after some reflection, "after they've put her in the ground, the angels 'll come and take her away. I read once of a poor beggar, oh, such a poor beggar! full of sores, and he died, and the angels carried him away somewhere. I thought, may be, they'd come for mother in the night; but I suppose they let people be buried first now, and fetch 'em away after."

"I should like to see some angels," said Robin.

They were silent again after that, looking down upon the quarrelling children, and the drunken men and women staggering about the yard below. Now and then a sharper scream rang through the court, as some angry mother darted out to cuff one or another of the brawling groups, or to yell some shrill reproach at the drunken men.

"Meg," said Robin, "why do they call this Angel Court? Did the angels use to live here?"

"I don't think they ever could," she answered, sadly, "or it must have been a long, long time ago. Perhaps they can't come here now, so they're waiting for mother to be taken out to the burying-ground, afore they can carry her up to the sky. May be that's it."

"Meg," whispered Robin, pressing closer to her side, "what's the devil?"

"Oh! I don't know," cried Meg; "only he's dreadfully, dreadfully wicked."

"As wicked as father is when he's drunk?" asked Robin.

"Oh! a hundred million times wickeder," answered Meg, eagerly. "Father doesn't get drunk often; and you mustn't be a naughty boy, and talk about it."

"Meg," he said, at last, "does the devil ever come here?"

"I don't think he does," answered Meg, with a shrewd shake of her small head; "I never see him, never. Folks are bad enough without him, I guess. No, no. You needn't be frightened of seeing him, Robbie."

"I wish there wasn't any devil," said Robin.

"I wish everybody in London was good," said Meg.

It was dark already in the court below; and here and there a candle had been lit, and placed in a window, casting a faint twinkle of light upon the gloom. The baby stirred, and cried a little; and Meg lifted Robin down from his dangerous seat, and put two or three small bits of coal upon the fire, to boil up the kettle for their tea. She had done it often before, at the bidding of her mother; but it seemed different now. Mother's voice was silent, and Meg had to think of everything herself. Soon after tea was over she undressed Robin and the baby, who soon fell asleep again; and when all her work was over, and the fire put out, little Meg crept in beside them on the scanty mattress, with her face turned towards the bed, that she might see the angels if they came to carry her mother away. But before long her eyelids drooped over her drowsy eyes, and, with her arm stretched lightly across both her children, she slept soundly till daybreak.

No angels had come in the night; but early in the morning a neighbouring undertaker, with two other men, and Mr. Grigg, the landlord, who lived on the ground floor, carried away the light burden of the coffin which contained Meg's mother. She waited until all were gone, and then she locked the door carefully, and with baby in her arms, and Robin holding by her frock, she followed the funeral at a distance, and with difficulty, through the busy streets. The brief burial service was ended before they reached the cemetery, but Meg was in time to show Robin the plate upon the coffin, before the gravedigger shovelled down great spades-ful of earth upon it. They stood watching, with sad but childish curiosity, till all was finished; and then Meg, with a heavy and troubled heart, took them home again to their lonely attic in Angel Court.

CHAPTER III

LITTLE MEG'S CLEANING DAY

AFTER a week was past, Meg and her children made a daily expedition down to the docks, lingering about in any out-of-the-way corner till they could catch sight of some good-natured face, which threatened no unkind rebuff, and then Meg asked when her father's ship would come in. Very often she could get no satisfactory answer, but whenever she came across any one who knew the Ocean King, she heard that it would most likely be in dock by the end of October. Robin's birthday was the last day in October so her mother's reckoning had been correct. Father would be home on Robbie's birthday; yet none the less was Meg's anxious face to be seen day after day about the docks, seeking some one to tell her again the good news.

The last day but one arrived, and Meg set about the scrubbing and the cleaning of the room heartily, as she had seen her mother do before her father's return. Robin was set upon the highest chair, with baby on his lap, to look on at Meg's exertions, out of the way of the wet flooring, upon which she bestowed so much water, that the occupant of the room below burst out upon the landing, with such a storm of threats and curses as made her light heart beat with terror. When the cleaning of the room was done, she trotted up and down the three flights of stairs with a small can, until she had filled, as full as it would hold, a broken tub, which was to serve as a bath for Robin and baby. It was late in the evening when all was accomplished, and Meg looked around her with a glow of triumph on the clean room and the fresh faces of the children. Very weary she felt, but she opened her Testament, in which she had not had time to give Robin a lesson that day, and she read a verse half aloud to herself.

"Come unto me, all ye that labour and are heavy laden, and I will give you rest."

"I wish I could go to Jesus," sighed little Meg, "for I've worked very hard all day; and he says he'd give me rest. Only I don't know where to go."

She laid her head down on the pillow beside the baby's slumbering face, and almost before it rested there, a deep sleep had come. Perhaps Meg's sigh had gone to Jesus, and it was he who gave her rest; "for so he giveth his beloved sleep."

CHAPTER IV

LITTLE MEG'S TREAT TO HER CHILDREN

ROBIN's birthday dawned brightly, even into the dark deep shadows of Angel Court, and Meg was awakened by the baby's two hands beating upon her still drowsy face, and trying to lift up her closed eyelids with its tiny fingers. She sprang up with a light heart, for father was coming home to-day. For the first time since her mother's death, she dragged the box from under the bed, and with eager hands unlocked the lid. She knew that she dare not cross the court, she and the children, arrayed in the festive finery, without her father to take care of them; for she had seen other children stripped of all their new and showy clothes before they could reach the shelter of the larger streets.

But Meg was resolved that Robin and baby at least should not meet their father in rags. She took out the baby's coat and hood, too small now even for the little head it was to cover, and Robin's blue cap, and brown-holland pinafore. These things she made up into a bundle, looking longingly at her own red frock, and her bonnet with green ribbons; but Meg shook her head at herself admonishingly. It never would do to risk an appearance in such gorgeous attire. The very utmost she could venture upon was to put some half-worn shoes on her own feet and Robin's; for shoes were not in fashion for the children of Angel Court, and the unusual sound of their tread would attract quite as much attention as little Meg dare risk. She dressed her children and set them on the bed, while she put her own rough hair as smooth as she could by a little glass in the lid of the trunk. Her bonnet, which had originally belonged to her mother, had been once of black silk, but it was now brown with years, and the old shawl she pinned over the ragged bodice of her frock was very thin and torn at the edges; but Meg's heart was full of hope, and nothing could drive away the smile from her care-worn face this morning. With the baby in her arms she carefully descended the ladder having put the door-key into the bag round her neck, along with the key of the box and her last half-crown. Then with stealthy steps she stole along under the houses, hushing Robin, who was inclined to make an unnecessary clatter in his shoes; but fortunately the inhabitants of Angel Court were not early risers, and Meg was off in good time, so they reached the outer streets safely, without notice or attack.

Before going down to the docks Meg drew Robin into an empty archway, and there exchanged his ragged cap and pinafore for those she had put up into her bundle. Having dressed the baby also, she sat and looked at them both for a minute in mute admiration and delight. There could not be a prettier boy than Robin in all London, she was sure, with his bright black eyes and curly hair, that twisted so tightly round her fingers. As for the baby, with her shrewd old-womanish face, and the sweet smile which spoke a good deal plainer than words, Meg could scarcely keep from kissing her all the time. How pleased and proud father would be! But when she remembered how she should have to tell him that mother was dead and buried, and none of them would ever see her again, Meg's eyes were blinded with tears, and hiding her face in the baby's neck, she cried, whether for joy or sorrow, she could hardly tell; until Robin broke out into a loud wail of distress and terror, which echoed noisily under the low vault of the archway.

Little Meg roused herself at the sound of Robin's cry, and taking his hand in hers, with the baby upon her arm, she loitered about the entrance to the dockyard, till a good-tempered looking burly man came near to them. Meg planted herself bravely in his way, and looked up wistfully into his red face.

"Please, sir," she said, "could you tell me if father's ship's come in yet?"

"Father's ship!" repeated the man, in a kindly voice. "Why what's the name of father's ship?"

"The Ocean King," said Meg, trembling.

"It's in the river, my little lass," he said, "but it won't be in dock till night. Father can't be at home afore to-morrow morning at the soonest."

"Thank you kindly, sir," answered Meg, her voice faltering with her great joy. Her task *was* ended then. To-morrow she would give up the key of the box with its secret treasure, which she hardly dared to think about, and then she could feel like a child once more. She did feel almost as gay as Robin, who was pattering and stamping proudly along in his shoes, and in the consciousness that it was his birthday. Nobody else had such a thing as a birthday, so far as he knew certainly none of his acquaintances in Angel Court, not even Meg herself, for Meg's birthday was lost in the depth of the ten years which had passed over her head. He scarcely knew what it was, for he could neither see it nor touch it; but he had it, for Meg told him so, and it made him feel glad and proud. It was a bright, warm, sunny autumn day, with enough freshness in the breeze coming off the unseen river to make the air sweet and reviving; for Meg was skirting about the more open streets, without venturing to pass through the closer and dirtier alleys.

"Robbie," she said, after a time, when they had come to a halt upon the steps of a dwelling-house; "Robbie, I'll give you a treat to-day, because it's your birthday. We'll not go home till it's dark; and I'll take you to see Temple Gardens."

"What are Temple Gardens?" demanded Robin, his eyes eager for an answer.

"Oh, you'll see," said Meg, not quite able to explain herself. "I went there once, ever so many years ago, when I was a little girl. You'll like 'em ever so!"

"Do we know the road?" asked Robin, doubtfully.

"I should think so!" replied Meg, "and if we didn't, there's the police. What's the police good for, if they couldn't tell a person like me the road to Temple Gardens? We'll have such a nice day!"

The children trotted along briskly till they reached the broad thorough-fares and handsome shops of the main streets which traverse London, where a constant rush of foot passengers upon the pavement, and of conveyances in the roadway, hurry to and fro from morning to midnight. Poor little Meg stood for a few minutes aghast and stunned, almost fearful of committing herself and her children to the mighty stream; but Robin pulled her on impatiently. He had been once as far as the Mansion House, before the time when their mother's long illness had made them almost prisoners in their lonely attic; and Meg herself had wandered several times as far as the great Church of St. Paul. After the first dread was over, she found a trembling, anxious enjoyment in the sight of the shops, and of the well-dressed people in the streets. At one of the windows she was arrested by a full-size vision of herself, and Robin, and the baby, reflected in a great glass, a hundred times larger than the little square in the box-lid at home. She could not quite keep down a sigh after her own red frock and best bonnet; but she comforted herself quickly with the thought that people would look upon her as the nurse of Robin and baby, sent out to take them a walk.

They did not make very rapid progress, for they stopped to look in at many shop windows, especially where there were baby-clothes for sale, or where there were waxen figures of little boys, life-size, dressed in the newest fashions, with large eyes of glass beads, not unlike Robin's own black ones. The passage of the crossings was also long and perilous. Meg ran first with the baby, and put her down safely on the other side in some corner of a door-way; then, with a sinking and troubled heart, lest any evil person should pick her up, and run away with her as a priceless treasure, she returned for Robin. In this way she got over several crossings, until they reached the bottom of Ludgate Hill, where she stood shivering and doubting for a long time, till she fairly made up her mind to speak to the majestic policeman looking on calmly at the tumult about him.

"Oh, if you please, Mr. Police," said Meg, in a plaintive voice, "I want to get these two little children over to the other side, and I don't know how to do it, except you'd please to hold baby while I take Robbie across."

The policeman looked down from his great height, without bending his stiff neck, upon the childish creature who spoke to him, and Meg's spirit sank with the fear of being ordered back again. But he picked up Robin under his arm, and bidding her keep close beside him, he threaded his way through the throng of carriages. This was the last danger; and now with restored gaiety Meg travelled on with her two children.

By-and-by they turned from the busy Fleet Street under a low archway, and in a minute they were out of the thunder of the streets which had almost

K

drowned their voices, and found themselves in a place so quiet and so calm with a sort of grave hush in the very air, that Robin pressed close to Meg's side, with something of the silent and subdued awe with which he might have entered a church. There were houses here, and courts, but not houses and courts like those from which they had come.

They came upon a fountain in the centre of a small plot of grass and flowers, enclosed within high railings; and Robin uttered a shrill cry of delight, which rang noisily through the quiet court where its waters played in the sunshine. But at last they discovered, with hearts as eagerly throbbing as those of the explorers of some new country, the gardens, the real Temple Gardens! The chrysanthemums were in full blossom, with all their varied tints, delicate and rich, glowing under the brightness of the noontide sun; and Robin and Meg stood still, transfixed and silent, too full of an excess of happiness to speak.

"Oh, Meg, what is it? what is it?" cried Robin at last, with outstretched hands, as if he would fain gather them all into his arms. "Is it gardens, Meg? Is this Temple Gardens?"

Meg could not answer at first, but she held Robin back from the flowers. She did not feel quite at home in this strange, sweet, sunny place; and she peeped in cautiously through the half open iron gate before entering. There were a few other children there, with their nursemaids, but she felt there was some untold difference between her and them.

"Look, Meg," he whispered.

He pointed to a seat not far from them, where sat a lady, in a bright silk dress, and a velvet bonnet with a long rich feather across it. There were two children with her, a girl of Meg's age, and a boy about as big as Robin, dressed like a little Highlander, with a kilt of many colours, and a silver-mounted pouch, and a dirk, which he was brandishing about before his mother, who looked on, laughing fondly and proudly at her boy. Meg gazed too, until she heard Robin sob, and turning quickly to him, she saw the tears rolling quickly down his sorrowful face.

"Nobody laughs to me, Meg," said Robin.

"Oh yes, Robbie, I laugh to you," cried Meg; "and father 'll laugh when he comes home to-morrow; and may be God laughs to us, only we can't see his face."

"I'd like to go home," sobbed Robin; and Meg took her baby upon her tired arm, and turned her steps eastward once more. As they left Temple Gardens, languid and weary, Meg saw the friendly man who had spoken kindly to them that morning at the docks passing by in an empty dray, and meeting her wistful eyes, he pulled up for a minute.

"Halloo, little woman!" he shouted. "Are you going my way?"

He pointed his whip towards St. Paul's, and Meg nodded, for her voice could not have reached him through the din.

"Hoist them children up here, that's a good fellow," he said to a man

who was standing by idle; and in a few seconds more they were riding triumphantly along Fleet Street in such a thrill and flutter of delight as Meg's
heart had never felt before, while Robin forgot his sorrows, and cheered on
the horses with all the power of his shrill voice. The dray put them down at
about half a mile from Angel Court, while it was still broad daylight, and
Robin was no longer tired. Meg changed her last half-crown, and spent six-
pence of it lavishly in the purchase of some meat pies, upon which they
feasted sumptuously, in the shelter of a doorway leading to the back of a
house.

CHAPTER V

LITTLE MEG'S NEIGHBOUR

WHEN their feast was over, the children sauntered on slowly, not
wishing to enter Angel Court till it was dark enough for Robin's
and baby's finery to pass by unseen; but as soon as it was dark
they turned out of the main thoroughfare into the dingy streets more familiar
to them. As they entered the house Meg heard the deep gruff voice of Mr
Grigg calling to her, and she went into his room, trembling, and holding
the baby very tightly in her arms. It was a small room, the same size as their
own attic, and the litter and confusion throughout made it impossible to go
in more than a step or two. Mr. Grigg was seated at a stained wooden table,
upon which stood two large cups, and a black bottle of gin, with a letter
lying near to Mr. Grigg's large and shaking hand. Coming in from the fresh
air of the night, Meg coughed a little with the mingled fumes of gin and
tobacco; but she coughed softly, for fear of giving offence.

"Here's a letter come for your mother, little Meg," said Mr. Grigg, seizing it eagerly. "I'll read it to you, if you like."

"Oh, no, thank you, sir," answered Meg, quickly; "father's coming
home, and he'll read it to-morrow morning. His ship's in the river, and it'll
be in dock to-night for certain. So he'll be home to-morrow."

Upon hearing this news Mr. Grigg thought it best to deliver up the letter
to Meg, but he did it so reluctantly, that she hurried away lest he should
reclaim it. Robin was already half way upstairs, but she soon overtook him,
and a minute afterwards reached their own door. She was about to put the
baby down to take out the key, when, almost without believing her own
eyes, she saw that it was in the lock and that a gleam of firelight shone
through the chinks of the door. Meg lifted the latch with a beating heart,
and looked in before venturing to enter. The fire was lighted, but there
seemed to be no other disturbance or change in the attic since the morning,
except that in her mother's low chair upon the hearth there sat a thin, slight

woman, like her mother, with the head bowed down, and the face hidden in the hands. Meg paused, wonder-stricken and speechless, on the door-sill; but Robin ran forward quickly, with a glad shout of "Mother! mother!"

At the sound of Robin's step and cry the woman lifted up her face. It was a white, thin face, but younger than their mother's though the eyes were red and sunken, as if with many tears, and there was a gloom upon it, as if it had never smiled a happy smile. Meg knew it in an instant as the face of the tenant of the back attic, who had been in jail for six weeks, and her eye searched anxiously the dark corner under the bed, where the box was hidden. It seemed quite safe and untouched; but still Meg's voice was troubled as she spoke.

"I thought I'd locked up all right," she said, stepping into the room, while Robin took refuge behind her, and regarded the stranger closely from his place of safety.

"Ay, it was all right," answered the girl, "only you see my key 'd unlock it; and I felt cold and low coming out o' jail to-day; and I'd no coal, nor bread, nor nothing. So I came in here, and made myself comfortable. Don't you be crusty, little Meg. You'd be the same if you'd been locked up for six weeks. I wish I were dead, I do."

The girl spoke sadly, and dropped her head again upon her hands, while Meg stood in the middle of the floor, not knowing what to do or say. She sat down after a while upon the bedstead, and began taking off the baby's things, pondering deeply all the time what course of action she ought to follow. She could place herself so as to conceal completely the box under the bed; but if the girl's key would unlock her attic door, how was she ever to leave it for a moment in safety? Then the thought flashed across her that father would be at home to-morrow, and she would no longer have to take care of the hidden treasure. In the mean time Robin had stolen up to the stranger's side, and after closely considering her for some moments, he stroked her hand with his own small fingers.

"I thought you were mother, I did," he said. "It's my birthday to-day."

For one instant the girl looked at him with a smile in her sunken eyes, and then she lifted him on to her lap, and laid her face upon his curly head, sobbing bitterly.

"Little Meg," she said, "your mother spoke kind to me once, and now she's dead and gone. I wonder why I wasn't took instead o' her."

Meg's tender heart closed itself no longer against the stranger. She got up from her seat, and crossing the floor to the fireside, she put the baby down by Robin on her lap.

"You didn't ought to go into a person's room without asking leave," she said; "but if you'll hold baby for me, I'll soon get tea. I've got a little real tea left, and father 'll buy some more to-morrow. You mind the children till it's ready."

It was soon ready, and they drank and ate together, with few words. Meg was intent upon getting her weary children to bed as soon as possible, and after it was over she undressed them at once. Before Robin got into bed she addressed the girl hesitatingly.

"Robbie always says his prayers aloud to me," she said; "you won't mind, will you?"

"Go on," answered the girl, with a sob.

"Robbie," said Meg, as he knelt at her knee, with his hands held up between both her hands, "Robbie, it's your birthday to-day; and if I was you, I'd ask God for something more than other days. I'd ask him to bless everybody as well as us, if I was you. If everybody was good, it 'd be so nice."

"Yes, Meg," replied Robin, promptly, closing his black eyes before he began his prayer. "Pray God, bless father on the big sea, and bless me, and Meg, and baby, and take care of us all. Pray God, bless everybody, 'cept the devil. Amen."

But Robin did not get up from his knees. He dropped his head upon Meg's lap, and when she moved he cried, "Stop a minute!" Meg waited patiently until he lifted up his face again, and shutting his eyes very tightly, said, "Pray God, bless everybody, and the devil, and make him a good man. Amen."

"Robbie," said Meg, mournfully, "I don't think the devil can be made good. He doesn't want to be good. If anybody wants to be good, God can make 'em good, anybody in all the world; but he won't if they don't want to."

Robin was already half asleep, and gave little heed to Meg's words. She tucked him snugly into his place beside baby, and stooping over them, kissed both their drowsy faces with a loving and lingering tenderness. Then she turned to the fire, and saw the strange girl there upon her knees before her mother's chair, weeping again in a passion of tears.

CHAPTER VI

LITTLE MEG'S LAST MONEY

"WHAT'S the matter with you?" asked Meg, laying her small rough hand upon the girl's head.

"Oh, Meg, Meg!" she cried, "I do want to be good, and I can't. You don't know how wicked I am; but once I was a good little girl like you. And now I can never, never, never be good again."

"Yes, you can," answered little Meg, "if you ask God."

"You don't know anything about it," she said, pushing away Meg's hand.

"I don't know much," replied Meg, meekly; "but Jesus says in the Bible, that if our fathers 'll give us good things, God 'll much more give good things to anybody as asks for 'em."

"But I'm too bad to ask him," said the girl.

"I don't know what's to be done then," answered Meg. "The Bible says, 'Them that ask him;' and if you're too bad to ask him, I suppose he won't give you any good things."

The girl made no reply, but crouching down upon the hearth at Meg's feet, she sat looking into the fire with the expression of one who is thinking deeply. Meg too was silent for a time, smiling now and then, as she recollected that father would be at home to-morrow.

"I don't know what you're called," said Meg, after a very long silence.

"Oh, they call me Kitty, and Puss, and Madcap, and all sorts o' names," answered the girl, with a deep sigh.

"But that's not your chrissen name?" said Meg.

"No," she replied.

"What does your mother call you?" asked Meg.

For a moment little Meg was terrified, for the girl seized her hands in a strong and painful grasp, and her red eyes flamed with anger; but she loosed her hold gradually, and then, in a choking voice, she said, "Don't you never speak to me about my mother!"

"Have you got any money, Kitty?" inquired Meg, by way of turning the conversation.

"Not a rap," said Kitty, laughing hoarsely.

"I've got two shillings left," continued Meg, "and I'll give you one; only, if you please, you mustn't come into my room again, at least till father's at home. I promised mother not to let anybody at all come here. You'll not be angry will you?"

"No, I'm not angry," said Kitty, gently, "and you must always do what your mother told you, little Meg. She spoke kind to me once, she did. So I'll go away now, dear, and never come in again: but you wouldn't mind me listening at the door when Robbie's saying his prayers, sometimes?"

"No," answered Meg; "and you may listen when I read up loud, if you like. I always read something afore I go to bed, and I'll speak up loud enough for you to hear."

"I'll listen," said Kitty, standing up to go to her own dark, cold attic, and looking round sadly at Meg's tidy room, all ready as it was for her father's arrival. "I suppose you'd not mind me kissing the children afore I go?"

"Oh, no," said Meg, going with her to the bedside, and looking down fondly upon the children's sleeping faces. The baby's pale, small face wore a smile upon it, as did Robin's also, for he was dreaming of the gardens he had visited on his birthday. The girl bent over them, but she drew back without kissing them, and with a sharp painful tone in her voice, she said, "I wish I was dead, I do."

CHAPTER VII

LITTLE MEG'S DISAPPOINTMENT

I F Meg had been up early on Robin's birthday, she was out of bed and about her preparations still earlier the next morning. She had time to go over again most of her brushing and rubbing of the scanty furniture before the children awoke. She reached out all their best clothes, and her own as well, for she did not intend to go down to the docks to meet her father, but thought it would be best to wait at home for his arrival. Her hands were full, and her thoughts also, for some time; and it was not till the nearest clock struck eleven, that she could consider all her preparations completed.

After a long time of waiting and watching Meg resolved to lay the children in bed, dressed as they were, and steal down herself to the docks, under the shelter of the fog, to see if she could learn any news of the Ocean King. She drew the old shawl over her head, which well covered her red frock, and taking off her shoes and stockings—for father would not miss them in the night—she crept unseen and unheard down the dark staircase, and across the swarming, noisy court. The fog was growing thicker every minute, yet she was at no loss to find her way, so familiar it was to her. But when she reached the docks, the darkness of the night, as well as that of the fog, hid from her the presence of her good-natured friend, if indeed he was there. There were strange noises and rough voices to be heard, and from time to time the huge figure of some tall man appeared to her for an instant in the gloom, and vanished again before little Meg could find courage to speak to him. She drew back into a corner, and peered eagerly, with wistful eyes, into the thick yellow mist which hid everything from them, while she listened to the clank of iron cables, and the loud sing-song of the invisible sailors as they righted their vessels. If she could only hear her father's voice among them. She felt sure she would know it among a hundred others, and she was ready to cry aloud the moment it reached her ears—to call "Father" and he would be with her in an instant, and she in his arms, with her own clasped fast about his neck. Oh, if he would but speak out of the darkness! Meg's keen eyes grew dim with tears, and her ears seemed to become dull of hearing, from the very longing to see and hear more clearly. But she rubbed away the tears with her shawl, and pushed the tangled hair away behind her small ears, and with her hands pressed against her heart, to deaden its throbbing, she leaned forward to pierce, if possible, through the thick dark veil which separated her from her father.

She had been there a long time when the thought crossed her, that perhaps after all he had been knocking at the door at home, and trying to open it; waking up the children, and making them cry and scream with terror at finding themselves quite alone. She started up to hurry away; but at that moment a man came close by, and in the extremity of her anxiety Meg stopped him.

"Please," she said, earnestly, "is the Ocean King come in yet?"

"Ay," was the answer. "Came in last night, all right and tight."

Father must be come home then, thought Meg, speeding away swiftly and noiselessly with her bare feet along the streets to Angel Court. She glanced up anxiously to her attic window, which was all in darkness, while the lower windows glimmered with a faint light from within. The landlord's room was full of a clamorous, quarrelling crew of drunkards; and Meg's spirit sank as she thought—suppose father had been up to their attic, and finding it impossible to get in at once, had come down, and began to drink with them. She climbed the stairs quickly, but all was quiet there; and she descended again to hang about the door, and listen, and wait; either to discover if he was there, or to prevent him turning in when he did come. Little Meg's heart was full of a woman's heaviest care and anxiety, as she kept watch in the damp and the gloom of the November night, till even the noisy party within broke up, and went their way, leaving Angel Court to a brief season of quietness.

Meg slept late in the morning, but she was not disturbed by a knock at the door. Robin had crept out of bed and climbed up alone to the window-sill, where fortunately the window was shut and fastened; and the first thing Meg's eyes opened upon was Robin sitting there, in the tumbled clothes in which he had slept all night. The morning passed slowly away in mingled hope and fear; but no step came up the ladder to their door, and Kitty had gone out early in the morning, before Meg was awake. She spent her last shilling in buying some coal and oatmeal; and then, because it was raining heavily, she stationed herself on the topmost step of the stairs, with Robin and baby, waiting with ever-growing dread for the long-delayed coming of her father.

It was growing dark again before any footstep came further than the landing below, and then it was a soft, stealthy, slipshod step, not like the strong and measured tread of a man. It was a woman who climbed the steep ladder, and Meg knew it could be no one else but Kitty. The girl sat down on the top step beside them, and took Robin upon her lap.

"What are you all doing out here, little Meg?" she said, in a low, gentle voice, which Meg could scarcely believe to be the same as that which had sometimes frightened her by its shrill shrieks of drunken merriment.

"We're looking for father," she answered, weariedly. "He's never come yet, and I've spent all my money, and we've got no candles."

"Meg," said Kitty, "I can pay you back the shilling you give me on Tuesday night."

"But you mustn't come into our room, if you do," answered Meg.

"No, no, I'll not come in," said she, pressing a shilling into Meg's hand. "But why hasn't father come home?"

"I don't know," sobbed Meg. "His ship came in the night of Robbie's birthday, that's two days ago; and he's never come yet."

"The ship come in!" repeated Kitty, in a tone of surprise. "What's the name o' the ship, Meg?"

"Father's ship's the Ocean King," said Robin, proudly.

"I'll hunt him up," cried Kitty, rising in haste. "I'll find him, if he's anywhere in London. I know their ways, and where they go to, when they come ashore, little Meg. Oh! I'll hunt him out. You put the children to bed, dear; and then you sit up till I come back, if it's past twelve o'clock. I'll bring him home, alive or dead. Don't cry no more, little Meg."

She called softly up the stairs to say these last words, for she had started off immediately. Meg did as she had told her, and then waited with renewed hope for her return. It was past midnight before Kitty tapped quietly at the door, and she went out to her on the landing. But Kitty was alone, and Meg could hardly stand for the trembling which came upon her.

"Hav'nt you found father?" she asked.

"I've found out where he is," answered Kitty. "He's at the other end of the world, in hospital. He was took bad a coming home—so bad, they was forced to leave him behind them; and he'll work his way back when he's well enough, so Jack says, one o' his mates. He says he may come back soon, or come back late; and that's all he knows about him. What shall you do, little Meg?"

"Mother said I was to be sure to take care of the children till father comes home," she answered, steadying her voice; "and I'll do it, please God. I can ask him to help me, and he will. He'll take care of us."

"He hasn't took care o' me," said Kitty, bitterly.

"May be you hav'nt asked him," said Meg.

Kitty was silent for a minute, and then she spoke in a voice half-choked with sobs.

"It's too late now," she said, "but he'll take care of you, never fear; and oh! I wish he'd let me help Him. I wish I could do something for you, little Meg; for your mother spoke kind to me once, and made me think of my own mother. There, just leave me alone, will you? I'm off to bed now, and you go to bed too. I'll help you all I can."

She pushed Meg back gently into her attic, and closed the door upon her; but Meg heard her crying and moaning aloud in her own room, until she herself fell asleep.

K*

CHAPTER VIII

LITTLE MEG'S RED FROCK IN PAWN

Meg felt very forlorn when she opened her heavy eyelids the next morning. It was certain now that her father could not be home for some time, it might be a long time; and how was she to buy bread for her children and herself? She took down her mother's letter from the end of a shelf which supplied the place of a chimney-piece, and looked at it anxiously; but she dared not ask anybody to read it for her, lest it should contain some mention of the money hidden in the box; and that must be taken care of in every way, because it did not belong to her, or father even, but to one of his mates. She had no friend to go to in all the great city. Once she might have gone to the teacher at the school where she had learned to read a little; but that had been in quite a different part of London, on the other side of the river, and they had moved from it before her father had started on his last voyage. Meg sat thinking and pondering sadly enough, until suddenly, how she did not know, her fears were all taken away, and her childish heart lightened. She called Robin, and bade him kneel down beside her, and folding baby's hands together, she closed her own eyes, and bowed her head, while she asked God for the help he had promised to give.

"Pray God," said little Meg, "you've let mother die, and father be took bad at the other side of the world, and there's nobody to take care of us 'cept you; and Jesus says, if we ask you, you'll give us bread, and everythink we want, just like father and mother. Pray God, do! I'm not a grown-up person yet, and Robin's a very little boy, and baby can't talk or walk at all; but there's nobody else to do anythink for us, and we'll try as hard as we can to be good. Pray God, bless father at the other side of the world, and Robbie, and baby, and me; and bless everybody, for Jesus Christ's sake. Amen."

Meg rose from her knees joyfully, feeling sure that her prayer was heard and would be answered. She went out with her children to lay out the shilling Kitty had returned to her the day before; and when they came in she and Robin sat down to a lesson in reading. The baby was making a pilgrimage of the room from chair to chair, and along the bedstead; but all of a sudden she balanced herself steadily upon her tiny feet, and with a scream of mingled dread and delight, which made Meg and Robin look up quickly, she tottered across the open floor to the place were they were sitting, and hid her face in Meg's lap, quivering with joy and wonder. Meg's gladness was full, except that there was a little feeling of sorrow that neither father nor mother was there to see it.

"Did God see baby walk?" inquired Robin.

"I should think he did!" said Meg, confidently; and her slight sorrow fled away. God could not help loving baby, she felt sure of that, nor Robin; and if he loved them, would he not take care of them himself, and show her how to take care of them, till father was at home? The day passed almost as happily as Robin's birthday; though the rain came down in torrents, and pattered through the roof, falling splash splash into the broken tub, with a sound something like the fountain in Temple Gardens.

But when Kitty's shilling was gone to the last farthing, and not a spoonful of meal remained in the bag, it was not easy to be happy. Robin and baby were both crying for food; and there was no coal to make a fire, nor any candle to give them light during the long dark evenings of November. Kitty was out all day now, and did not get home till late, so Meg had not seen her since the night she had brought the news about her father. But a bright thought came to her, and she wondered at herself for not having thought of it before. She must pawn her best clothes; her red frock and bonnet with green ribbons. There was a natural pang at parting with them, even for a time; but she comforted herself with the idea that father would get them back for her as soon as he returned. She reached them out of the box, feeling carefully, lest she should take any of Robin's or the baby's by mistake in the dark; and then she set off with her valuable bundle, wondering how many shillings she would get for them, and whether she could make the money last till her father came. The pawnbroker's shop was a small, dingy place in Rosemary Lane; and it, and the rooms above it, were as full as they could be with bundles such as poor Meg carried under her old shawl. A single gas-light was flaring away in the window, and a hard-featured, sharp-eyed man was reading a newspaper behind the counter. Meg laid down her bundle timidly, and waited till he had finished reading his paragraph; after which he opened it, spread out the half-worn frock, and held up the bonnet on his fist, regarding them both with a critical and contemptuous eye. Some one else had entered the shop, but Meg was too absorbed and too anxious to take any heed of it. The pawnbroker rolled the frock up scornfully, and gave it a push towards her.

"Tenpence for the two," he said, looking back at his newspaper.

"Oh! if you please," cried little Meg, in an agony of distress, "you must give me more than tenpence. I've got two little children, and no bread, nor coals, nor candles. I couldn't buy scarcely anythink with only tenpence. Indeed, indeed, my red frock's worth a great deal more; it's worth I don't know how many shillings."

"You go home, little Meg," said Kitty's voice behind her, "and I'll bring you three shillings for the frock, and one for the bonnet; four for the two. Mr. Sloman's an old friend o' mine, he is; and he'll oblige you for my sake. There, you run away, and I'll manage this little bit o' business for you."

Meg ran away as she was told, glad enough to leave her business with

Kitty. By and by she heard her coming upstairs, and went out to meet her. Kitty placed four shillings in her hand.

"Meg," she said, "you let me do that sort o' work for you always. They'll cheat you ever so; but I wouldn't, not to save my life, if you'll only trust me. You ask me another time. Is that the way God takes care of you?"

"He does take care of me," answered Meg, with a smile; "or may be you wouldn't have come into the shop just now, and I should have got only tenpence. I suppose that's taking care of me, isn't it?"

"I don't know," said Kitty. "Only let me do that for you when you want it done again."

It was not very long before it wanted to be done again; and then Meg by daylight went through the contents of the box, choosing out those things which could best be spared, but leaving Robin's and baby's fine clothes to the last. She clung to these with a strong desire to save them, lest it should happen that her father came home too poor to redeem them. The packet of money, tied up and sealed, fell at last to the bottom of the almost empty box, and rolled noisily about whenever it was moved, but no thought of taking any of it entered into Meg's head. She was almost afraid of looking at it herself, lest the secret of it being there should get known in Angel Court; and whenever she mentioned it in her prayers, which she did every night, asking God to take care of it, she did not whisper the words, much less speak them aloud, as she did her other requests, but she spoke inwardly only, for fear lest the very walls themselves should hear her. No one came near her attic, except Kitty, and she kept her promise faithfully. Since the four bearers had carried away her mother's coffin, and since the night Kitty came out of jail, the night of Robin's birthday, no stranger's foot had crossed the door-sill.

But November passed, and part of December, and Meg's stock of clothes, such as were of any value at the pawnshop, was almost exhausted. At the end of the year, the term for which her father had paid rent in advance would be over, and Mr. Grigg might turn her and her children out into the streets. What was to be done? How was she to take care of Robin, and baby, and the money belonging to one of father's mates?

CHAPTER IX

LITTLE MEG'S FRIENDS IN NEED

ABOUT the middle of December the first sharp frost set in, and Meg felt herself driven back from this last relief. She had taken the children out as usual, but she had no shoes to put on their feet, and nothing but their thin old rags to clothe them with. Robin's feet were red and blue with cold, like her own; but Meg could not see her own, and did not feel the cold as much for them as for Robin's. His face had lost a little of its roundness and freshness, and his black eyes some of their brightness since his birthday; and poor Meg's heart bled at the sight of him as he trudged along the icy pavement of the streets at her side. There was one cookshop from which warm air and pleasant odours came up through an iron grating, and Meg hurried on to it to feel its grateful warmth; but the shutters of the shop were not taken down, and the cellar window was unclosed. Little Meg turned away sadly, and bent her bare and aching feet homewards, again hushing baby, who wailed a pitiful low wail in her ears. Robin, too, dragged himself painfully along, for he had struck his numbed foot against a piece of iron, and the wound was bleeding a little. They had turned down a short street which they had often passed through before, at the end of which was a small shop displaying in its window a few loaves of bread, and some bottles containing different kinds of sweetmeats, such as they had indulged in sometimes in the palmy days when father was at home. The door was divided in the middle, and the lower half was closed, while the upper stood open, giving a full view of the shop within. Meg's old brown bonnet just rose above the top of the closed half, and her wistful face turned for a moment towards the tempting sight of a whole shelf full of loaves; but she was going on slowly, when a kindly voice hailed her from the dark interior.

"Halloo! little woman!" it shouted. "I haven't set eyes on you this many a day. How's Robbie and baby?"

"They're here, sir, thank you," answered Meg, in a more womanly way than ever, for she felt very low today. "We're only doing middling, thank you, sir."

"Why, father's ship's come in," said her good-natured friend from the docks, coming forward and wiping his lips, as if he had just finished a good meal. "What makes you be doing only middling?"

"Father didn't come home in the ship," replied Meg, her voice faltering a little.

"Come in, and tell us all about it," he said. "Halloo! Mrs. Blossom, just step this way, if you please."

There was a little kitchen at the back of the shop, from which came a very savoury smell of cooking, as the door opened, and a round, fat, rosy-cheeked woman, of about fifty years of age, looked out inquiringly. She came a step or two nearer the door, as Meg's friend beckoned to her with a clasp-knife he held in his hand.

"These little 'uns look cold and hungry, don't they, Mrs. Blossom?" he said. "You smell something as smells uncommon good, don't you?" he asked of Meg, who had sniffed a little, unconsciously.

"Yes, please sir," answered Meg.

"I've ate as much as ever I can eat for to-day," said her friend, "so you

give 'em the rest, Mrs. Blossom, and I'll be off. Only just tell me why father's
not come home in his ship."

"He was took bad on the other side of the world," replied Meg, looking
up tearfully into his good-tempered face, "and they was forced to leave him
behind in a hospital. That's why."

"And what's mother doing?" he asked.

"Mother's dead," she answered.

"Dead!" echoed her friend. "And who's taking care of you young 'uns?"

"There's nobody to take care of us but God," said Meg, simply and
softly.

"Well, I never!" cried Mrs. Blossom, seizing the baby out of Meg's and
clasping it in her own arms. "I never heard anything like that."

"Nor me," said the man, catching up Robin, and bearing him off into
the warm little kitchen, where a saucepan of hot tripe was simmering on
the hob, and a round table, with two plates upon it, was drawn up close to
the fire. He put Robin down on Mrs. Blossom's seat, and lifted Meg into a
large arm-chair he had just quitted.

"I guess you could eat a morsel of tripe," he said, ladling it out in overflowing spoonfuls upon the plates. "Mrs. Blossom, some potatoes, if you
please, and some bread; and do you feed the baby, whilst the little woman
gets her dinner. Now I'm off. Mrs. Blossom, you settle about 'em coming
here again."

He was off, as he said, in an instant. Meg sat in her large arm-chair, grasping a big knife and fork in her small hands, but she could not swallow a
morsel at first, for watching Robin and the baby, who was sucking in
greedily spoonsful of potatoes, soaked in the gravy. Mrs. Blossom urged
her to fall to, and she tried to obey; but her pale face quivered all over, and
letting fall her knife and fork, she hid it in her trembling hands.

"If you please, ma'am, I'm only so glad," said little Meg, as soon as she
could command her voice. "Robbie and baby was so hungry, and I hadn't
got anythink to give 'em."

"I suppose you ain't hungry yourself, neither," observed Mrs. Blossom,
a tear rolling down a little channel between her round cheeks and her nose.

"Oh, but ain't I!" said Meg, recovering herself still more. "I've had
nothink since last night, and then it were only a crust as Kitty gave me."

"Well, dear, fall to, and welcome," answered Mrs. Blossom. "And who's
Kitty?"

"It's a grown-up person as lives in the back attic," answered Meg, after
eating her first mouthful. "She helps me all she can. She's took all my things
to the pawnshop for me, because she can get more money than me. She's
as good as can be to us."

"Are all your things gone to pawn?" inquired Mrs. Blossom.

"I've got baby's cloak and hood left," she replied, mournfully. "He
wouldn't give more than a shilling for 'em, and I thought it wasn't worth

while parting with 'em for that. I tried to keep Robbie's cap and pinafore, that were as good as new, but I was forced to let 'em go. And our shoes, ma'am," added Meg, taking Robin's bare and bleeding foot into her hand: "see what poor Robbie's done to himself."

"Poor little dear!" said Mrs. Blossom, pityingly. "I'll wash his poor little feet for him, when he's finished his dinner. You get on with yours likewise, my love."

Meg was silent for some minutes, busily feasting on the hot tripe, and basking in the agreeable warmth of the cosy room. It was a wonderfully bright little spot for that quarter of London, but the brightness was all inside. Outside, at about three feet from the window, rose a wall so high as to shut out every glimpse of the sky; but within everything was so clean and shining, even to the quarried floor, that it was difficult to believe in the mud and dirt of the streets without. Mrs. Blossom herself looked fresh and comely, like a country-woman; but there was a sad expression on her round face, plain enough to be seen when she was not talking.

"My dear," she said, when Meg laid down her knife and fork, and assured her earnestly that she could eat no more, "what may you be thinking of doing?"

"I don't hardly know," she answered. "I expect father home every day. If I could only get enough for the children, and a crust or two for me, we could get along. But we can't do nothink more, I know."

"You'll be forced to go into the house," said Mrs. Blossom.

"Oh, no, no, no!" cried little Meg, drawing Robin to her, and with a great effort lifting him on to her lap, where he almost eclipsed her. "I couldn't ever do that. We'll get along somehow till father comes home."

"Where is it you live?" inquired Mrs. Blossom.

"Oh, it's not a nice place at all," said Meg, who dreaded having any visitor. "It's along Rosemary Lane, and down a street, and then down another smaller street, and up a court. That's where it is."

Mrs. Blossom sat meditating a few minutes, with the baby on her lap, stretching itself lazily and contentedly before the fire; while Meg, from behind Robin, watched her new friend's face anxiously.

"Well," she said, "you come here again to-morrow, and I'll ask Mr. George what's to be done. That was Mr. George as was here, and he's my lodger. He took you in, and may be he'll agree to do something."

"Thank you, ma'am," said Meg, gratefully. "Please, have you any little children of your own?"

The tears ran faster now down Mrs. Blossom's cheeks, and she was obliged to wipe them away before she could answer.

"I'd a little girl like you," she said, "ten years ago. Such a pretty little girl, so rosy, and bright, and merry, as all the folks round took notice of. She was like the apple of my eye, she was."

"What was she called?" asked Meg, with an eager interest.

"Why, the neighbours called her Posy, because her name was Blossom," said Mrs. Blossom, smiling amidst her tears. "We lived out in the country, and I'd a little shop, and a garden, and kept fowls, and pigs, and eggs; fresh eggs, such as the like are never seen in this part o' London. Posy they called her, and a real posy she was."

Mrs. Blossom paused, and looked sadly down upon the happy baby, shaking her head as if she was sorely grieved at heart.

"And Posy died?" said Meg, softly.

"No, no!" cried Mrs. Blossom. "It 'ud been a hundred times better if she'd died. She grew up bad. I hope you'll never live to grow up bad, little girl. And she ran away from home; and I lost her, her own mother that had nursed her when she was a little baby like this. I'd ha' been thankful to ha' seen her lying dead afore my eyes in her coffin."

"That's bad," said little Meg, in a tone of trouble and tender pity.

"It's nigh upon three years ago," continued Mrs. Blossom, looking down still upon the baby, as if she were telling her; "and I gave up my shop to my son's wife, and come here, thinking may be she'd step in some day or other to buy a loaf o' bread, or something, because I knew she'd come up to London. But she's never so much as passed by the window, leastways when I've been watching, and I'm always watching. I can't do my duty by Mr. George for staring out o' the window."

"Watching for Posy?" said little Meg.

"Ay, watching for Posy," repeated Mrs. Blossom, "and she never goes by."

"Have you asked God to let her go by?" asked Meg.

"Ay, my dear," said Mrs. Blossom. "I ask him every day o' my life."

"Then she's sure to come some day," said Meg, joyfully. "There's no mistake about that, because Jesus says it in the Bible, and he knows all about God. You've asked him, and he'll do it. It's like father coming. I don't know whether he'll come to-day or to-morrow, or when it'll be; but he will come."

"God bless and love you!" cried Mrs. Blossom, suddenly putting baby down in Meg's lap, and clasping all three of them in her arms. "I'll believe it, I will. He's sent you to give me more heart. God love you all!"

CHAPTER X

LITTLE MEG AS CHARWOMAN

MEG and her children did not fail to make their appearance the next morning at Mrs. Blossom's shop, where she welcomed them heartily, and made them comfortable again by the kitchen fire.

When they were well warmed, and had finished some bread, and some coffee which had been kept hot for them, Mrs. Blossom put on a serious business air.

"Mr. George and me have talked you over," she said, "and he's agreed to something. I can't do my duty by him as I should wish, you know why; and I want a little maid to help me."

"Oh, if you please," faltered little Meg, "I couldn't leave our attic. I promised mother I wouldn't go away till father comes home. Don't be angry, please."

"I'm not angry, child," continued Mrs. Blossom. "I only want a little maid to come mornings, and go away nights, like a charwoman."

"Mother used to go charing sometimes," remarked Meg.

"I'm not a rich woman," resumed Mrs. Blossom, "and Mr. George has his old father to keep, as lives down in my own village, and I know him well; so we can't give great wages. I'd give you a half-quartern loaf a day, and Mr. George threepence for the present, while it's winter. Would that suit your views?"

"What could I do with Robbie and baby?" asked Meg, with an air of perplexed thought.

'Couldn't you leave 'em with a neighbour?" suggested Mrs. Blossom.

Meg pondered deeply for a while. Kitty had told her the night before, that she had got some sailor's shirts to sew, and would stay at home to make them. She could trust Robin and the baby with Kitty, and instead of lighting a fire in her own attic, she could give her the coals, and so save her fuel, as part payment for taking charge of the children. Yet Meg felt a little sad at the idea of leaving them for so long a time, and seeing so little of them each day, and she knew they would miss her sorely. But nothing else could be done, and she accepted Mrs. Blossom's offer thankfully.

"You needn't be here afore nine o' the morning," said Mrs. Blossom; "it's too early for Posy to be passing by; and you can go away again as soon as it's dark in the evening. You mustn't get any breakfast, you know, because that's in our bargain; and I'd never grudge you a meal's meat for the children either, bless 'em! They shall come and have a good tea with us sometimes, they shall; specially on Sundays, when Mr. George is at home; and if you'd only got your clothes out o' pawn, we'd all go to church together. But we'll see, we'll see."

Meg entered upon her new duties the next morning, after committing the children, with many lingering kisses and last good-byes, into Kitty's charge, who promised faithfully to be as kind to them as Meg herself. If it had not been for her anxiety with regard to them, she would have enjoyed nothing better than being Mrs. Blossom's little maid. The good woman was so kindly and motherly that she won Meg's whole heart; and to see her sit by the shop-window, knitting a very large long stocking for Mr. George, but with her eyes scanning every woman's face that went by, made her feel full of an intense and childish interest. She began herself to watch for Posy, as her mother described her; and whenever the form of a grown-up girl darkened the doorway, she held her breath to listen if Mrs. Blossom called her by that pet name. Mr. George also was very good to Meg in his bluff way, and bought her a pair of nearly new shoes with his first week's wages, over and above the threepence a day which he paid her. With Mrs. Blossom she held many a conversation about the lost girl, who had grown up wicked, and was therefore worse than dead; and before long Mr. George observed that Meg had done her a world of good.

Christmas day was a great treat to Meg; for though Mr. George went down into the country to see his old father, Mrs. Blossom invited her and the children to come to dinner, and to stay with her till it was the little ones' bed-time. When they sat round the fire in the afternoon, she told them wonderful stories about the country—of its fields, and gardens, and lanes.

"I like gardens," said Robin, "but I don't like lanes."

"Why don't you like lanes?" asked Mrs. Blossom.

"I know lots of lanes," he answered. "There's Rosemary Lane, and it's not nice, nor none of 'em. They ain't nice like Temple Gardens."

"Rosemary Lane!" repeated Mrs. Blossom. "Why, the lanes in the country are nothing like the lanes in London. They're beautiful roads, with tall trees growing all along 'em, and meeting one another overhead; and there are roses and honeysuckle all about the hedges, and birds singing, and the sun shining. Only you don't know anything about roses, and honeysuckles, and birds."

"Are there any angels there?" asked Robin, fastening his glistening eyes upon her intently.

'Well, no," said Mrs. Blossom, "not as I know of."

"Is the devil in the country?" pursued Robin.

"Yes," answered Mrs. Blossom, "I suppose he's there pretty much the same as here. Folks can be wicked anywhere, or else my Posy wouldn't have grown up bad."

Robin asked no more questions, and Mrs. Blossom was glad to talk of something else. It was a very happy day altogether, but it came too quickly to an end. Meg wrapped up her children well before turning out into the cold streets, and Mrs. Blossom gave them a farewell kiss each, with two to Meg, because she was such a comfort to her.

When they reached their own attic, they heard Kitty call to them, and Meg opened her door. She was sitting without any fire, stitching away as for her life at a coarse striped shirt, lighted only by a small farthing candle; but she laid down her task for a minute, and raised her thin pale face, and her eyes half blinded with tears and hard work.

"Where have you been all day, little Meg?" she asked.

"Me and the children have been at Mrs. Blossom's," answered Meg, "because it's Christmas day; and I wish you'd been there as well, Kitty. We'd such a good dinner and tea. She give me a bit of cake to bring home, and you shall have some of it."

"No, no," said Kitty, "it 'ud choke me."

"Oh, it couldn't; it's as nice as nice can be," said Meg. "You must just have a taste of it."

"Did you go talking about that Posy again?" asked Kitty, bending diligently over her work.

"We always talk about her," answered Meg, "every day. Mrs. Blossom's watching for her to go by all day long, you know."

"She'll never go by," said Kitty, shortly.

"Oh, she's certain sure to go by some day," cried Meg. "Mrs. Blossom asks God to let her go by, every day of her life; and He's positive to do it."

"If she's grown up so wicked," argued Kitty, "she didn't ought to go back to her mother, and her such a good woman. God won't send her back to her mother, you'll see."

"But if God sent her back, her mother 'ud never think of her being wicked, she loves her so," said little Meg. "If Robbie were ever so naughty, I'd keep on loving him till he was good again."

"Well, Posy 'll never go home no more," said Kitty; and hot tears fell fast upon her work.

"She will, she will," cried Meg. "I expect her every day, like father. Perhaps they'll both come home to-morrow. I wish you'd ask God to let Posy and father come home to-morrow."

"I'm too bad to ask God for anything," sobbed Kitty.

"Well, I don't know," said Meg, sorrowfully. "You're not bad to me or the children. But I must go to bed now. Let us kiss you afore we go. Mrs. Blossom kissed me twice, and said I was a comfort to her."

Kitty threw down her work, and clasped Meg strongly in her arms, pressing down Meg's head upon her breast, and crying, "Oh, my dear little Meg! My good little Meg!" Then she put them all three gently out of her room, and bade them good-night and God bless them, in a husky and tremulous voice.

CHAPTER XI

LITTLE MEG'S BABY

THE new year came, but Meg's father had not arrived. Kitty was having a mad outburst, as if she had so long controlled herself, that now it was necessary to break out into extra wickedness. She came home late every night, very drunk, and shouting loud snatches of songs, which wakened up the inmates of the lower stories, and drew upon her a storm of oaths. But she continued always good-natured and kind to Meg, and insisted upon having the daily charge of Robin and the baby, though Meg left them in her care with a very troubled and anxious spirit. Things were looking very dark to the poor little woman; but she kept up as brave a heart as she could, waiting from day to day for that long-deferred coming of her father, in which she believed so firmly.

It was a little later than usual one evening, for the days were creeping out since the new year, when Meg climbed wearily up-stairs to Kitty's attic in search of her children, but found that they were not there. Mr. Grigg told her he had seen Kitty take them out with her in the afternoon; and even while he was speaking, Meg saw her staggering and rolling into the court, with the baby fast asleep in her drunken arms. Meg took it from her without a word, and led Robin away up-stairs. Robin's face was flushed, and his hand was very hot; but the baby lay in her arms heavily, without any movement or sign of life, except that the breath came through her parted lips, and her eyelids stirred a little. Meg locked the door of her attic, and laid her baby on the bed, while she lighted the fire and got their tea ready. Robin looked strange, but he chattered away without ceasing, while he watched her set the things in readiness. But the baby would not awake. It lay quite still on Meg's lap, and she poured a little warm tea into its mouth, but it did not swallow it, only slept there with heavy eyelids, and moving neither finger nor foot, in a strange, profound slumber. It was smaller and thinner than when mother died, thought Meg; and she lifted up the lifeless little hand to her lips, half hoping that its eyes would unclose a little more, and that sweet, loving smile, with which it always welcomed her return, would brighten its languid face. But baby was too soundly asleep to smile.

Little Meg sat up all night, with the baby lying on her lap, moaning a little now and then, as its slumbers grew more broken, but never lifting up its eyelids to look into her face and know it. When the morning dawned it was still the same. Could the baby be ill? asked Meg of herself. It did not seem to be in any pain; yet she carried it to the door, and called softly for Kitty to come and look at it; but there was no reply, only from below came up harsh sounds of children screaming and angry women quarrelling. Oaths and threats and shrieks were all the answer Meg's feeble cry received. She sat down again on her mother's low chair before the fire, and made the baby comfortable on her lap; while Robin stood at her knee, looking down pitifully at the tiny, haggard, sleeping face, which Meg's little hand could almost cover. What was she to do? There was no one in Angel Court whom she dare call to her help. Baby might even die, like the greater number of the babies born in that place, whose brief lives ended quickly, as if existence was too terrible a thing in the midst of such din and squalor. At the thought that perhaps baby was going to die, two or three tears of extreme anguish rolled down little Meg's cheeks, and fell upon baby's face; but she could not cry aloud, or weep many tears. She felt herself falling into a stupor of grief and despair when Robin laid his hand upon her arm.

"Why don't you ask God to waken baby?" he asked.

"I don't know whether it 'ud be a good thing," she answered. "Mother said she'd asked him over and over again to let her take baby along with her, and that 'ud be better than staying here. I wish we could all go to heaven; only I don't know whatever father 'ud do if he come home and found us all dead."

"May be God 'll take me and baby," said Robbie, thoughtfully, "and leave you to watch for father."

"I only wish baby had called me Meg once afore she went," cried little Meg.

The baby stirred a little upon her knees, and stretched out its feeble limbs, opening its blue eyes wide and looking up into her face with its sweet smile of welcome. Then the eyelids closed again slowly, and the small features put on a look of heavenly calm and rest. Meg and Robin gazed at the change wonderingly, without speaking; but when after a few minutes Meg laid her hand gently upon the smooth little forehead, the same chill struck to her heart as when she had touched her mother's dead face.

It did not seem possible to little Meg that baby could really be dead. She chafed its puny limbs, as she had seen her mother do, and walked up and down the room singing to it, now loudly, now softly; but no change came upon it, no warmth returned to its death-cold frame, no life to its calm face. She laid it down at length upon the bed, and crossed its thin wee arms upon its breast, and then stretching herself beside it, with her face hidden from the light, little Meg gave herself up to a passion of sorrow.

"If I'd only asked God, for Christ's sake," she cried to herself, "may be he'd have let baby wake, though I don't know whether it's a good thing. But now she's gone to mother, and father 'll come home, and he'll find nobody but me, and Robbie, and the money safe. Oh! I wish I'd asked God."

"Meg," said Robin, after she had worn herself out with sobs and tears, and was lying silently beside baby, "I'm very poorly. I think I'll go to live with the angels, where mother and baby are gone."

Meg started up, and gazed anxiously at Robin. His bright eyes were dimmed, and his face was flushed and heavy; he was stretched on the floor near the fire, in a listless attitude, and did not care to move, when she knelt down beside him, and put her arm under his head. It ached, he said; and it felt burning hot to her touch. Meg's heart stood still for a moment, and then she dropped her tear-stained sorrowful face upon her hands.

"Pray God," she cried, "don't take Robbie away as well as baby. May be it wasn't a good thing for baby to stay, now mother's dead, though I've done everythink I could, and there's been nobody to take care of us but you,

But pray God, do let Robbie stay with me till father comes home. For Jesus Christ's sake. Amen."

Meg rose from her knees, and lifted up Robin as gently as she could, soothing him, and talking fondly to him as she took off his clothes. When that was finished, she laid him on the same bed where the baby was sleeping its last long sleep, with its tiny face still wearing an unspeakable calm; for Robin's little mattress had been sold some time ago. The day was just at an end, that sorrowful day, and a lingering light from the west entered through the attic window, and lit up the white, peaceful features, with the flushed and drowsy face of Robin beside it. Meg felt as if her heart would surely break as she stooped over them, and kissed them both, her lips growing cold as they touched baby's smiling mouth. Then drawing her old shawl over her head, she locked the attic door securely behind her, and ran as fast as her feet could carry her to Mrs. Blossom's house.

"Robbie's very ill," gasped Meg, breathlessly, as she burst into the shop, the shutters of which were already put up, though it was still early in the night, "and I want a doctor for him. Where shall I find a doctor?"

Mrs. Blossom had her bonnet and cloak on, and looked very pale and flurried. When she answered Meg she kept her hand pressed against her heart.

"I'm just a going to one," she said, "the best at this end o' London, Dr. Christie, and you'd better come along with me. He knows me well. Meg. I've seen somebody go by to-day as was like Posy, only pale and thin; but when I ran out, she was gone like a shadow. I'm a going to tell Dr. Christie; he knows all about Posy and me."

But Meg scarcely heard what Mrs. Blossom said. All her thoughts and interest centered in Robin, and she felt impatient of the slow progress of her companion. They seemed to her to be going a long, long way, until they came to better streets and larger houses; and by and by they saw a carriage standing before a door, and a gentleman came out, and got into it hurriedly.

"Why, bless me!" exclaimed Mrs. Blossom, "there's Dr. Christie. Stop him, Meg, stop him!"

Meg needed no urging, but rushed blindly across the street. There was all at once a strange confusion about her, a trampling of horses' feet, and a rattling of wheels, with a sudden terror and pain in herself; and then she knew no more. All was as nothing to her—baby and Robin alone in the attic, and Mrs. Blossom and Posy—all were gone out of her mind and memory. She had thrown herself before the horses' heads, and they had trampled her down under their feet.

When little Meg came to herself again it was broad daylight, and she was lying in a room so bright and cheerful, that she could neither imagine where she was, now how she came there. There was a good fire crackling noisily in the low grate, with a brass guard before it, and over the chimney-piece was a pretty picture of angels flying upwards with a child in their arms. All round the walls there hung other pictures of birds and flowers, coloured gaily, and glittering in gilded frames. Another little bed like the one she lay in stood in the opposite corner, but there was nobody in it, and the place was very quiet. She lay quite still, with a dreamy thought that she was somehow in heaven, until she heard a pleasant voice speaking in the next room, the door of which was open, so that the words came readily to her ears.

"I only wish we knew where the poor little thing comes from," said the voice.

"I'm vexed I don't," answered Mrs. Blossom. "I've asked her more than once, and she's always said it's down a street off Rosemary Lane, and along another street, and up a court. But there's a girl called Kitty living in the back attic, as takes care of the children when Meg's away. She's sure to be taking care o' them now."

In an instant memory came back to little Meg. She recollected bending over Robin and the baby, to kiss them before she came away, and locking the door safely upon them. Oh! what had become of Robbie in the night? She raised herself up in bed, and uttered a very bitter cry, which brought to her quickly Mrs. Blossom, and a strange lady.

"I want Robbie," she cried, "I must get up and go to him directly. It's my Robbie that's ill, and baby's dead. I'm not ill, but Robbie's ill, if he isn't dead, like baby, afore now. Please to let me get up."

"Tell me all about it," said Mrs. Blossom, sitting down on the bed, and taking Meg into her arms. "We're in Dr. Christie's house, and he'll go and see Robin in a minute, he says."

"Baby died yesterday morning," answered Meg, with tearless eyes, for her trouble was too great for tears; "and then Robbie was took ill, and I put them both in bed, and kissed them, and locked the door, and came away for a doctor, and there's been nobody to take care of 'em all night, only God."

Meg's eyes burned no longer, but filled with tears as she thought of God, and she laid her head upon Mrs. Blossom's shoulder, and wept aloud.

"God has taken care of them," said Mrs. Christie, but she could say no more.

"Where is it you live, deary?" asked Mrs. Blossom.

"It's at Angel Court," answered Meg. "But there mustn't nobody go without me. Please to let me get up. I'm not ill."

"You're very much bruised and hurt, my poor child," said Mrs. Christie.

"I must go," pleaded Meg, urgently, "I must get up. I promised mother I'd never let anybody go into our room and they mustn't go without me. They're my children, please. If your little children were ill, you'd go to 'em, wouldn't you? Let me get up this minute."

It was impossible to withstand little Meg's earnestness. Mrs. Blossom dressed her tenderly, though Meg could not quite keep back the groan

which rose to her quivering lips when her bruised arm was moved. A cab
was called, and then Mrs. Blossom and Meg, with Dr. Christie, got into it,
and drove away quickly to Angel Court.

CHAPTER XII

THE END OF LITTLE MEG'S TROUBLE

IT was early in the evening after Meg had gone in search of a doctor, that
Kitty came home, more sober than she had been for several nights, and
very much ashamed of her last outbreak. She sat down on the top of the
stairs, listening for little Meg to read aloud, but she heard only the sobs and
moanings of Robin, who called incessantly for Meg, without getting any
answer. Kitty waited for some time, hearkening for her voice, but after a
while she knocked gently at the door. There was no reply, but after knocking again and again, she heard Robin call out in a frightened tone—

"What's that?" he cried.

"It's me, your own Kitty," she said: "where's little Meg?"

"I don't know," said Robin, "she's gone away, and there's nobody but
me and baby; and baby's asleep, and so cold."

"What are you crying for, Robbie?" asked Kitty.

"I'm crying for everything," said Robin.

"Don't you be frightened, Robbie," she said, soothingly, "Kitty'll stay
outside the door, and sing pretty songs to you, till Meg comes home."

She waited a long time, till the clocks struck twelve, and still Meg did
not come. From time to time Kitty spoke some reassuring words to Robin,
or sang him some little song, she remembered from her own childhood; but
his cries grew more and more distressing, and at length Kitty resolved to
break her promise, and unlock Meg's door once again to move the children
into her own attic.

She lit a candle, and entered the dark room. The fire was gone out, and
Robin sat up on the pillow, his face wet with tears, and his black eyes large
with terror. The baby, which lay beside him, seemed very still, with its
wasted puny hands crossed upon its breast; so quiet and still that Kitty
looked more closely, and held the light nearer to its slumbering face. What
could ail it? What had brought that awful smile upon its tiny face? Kitty
touched it fearfully with the tip of her finger; and then she stood dumb and
motionless before the terrible little corpse.

She partly knew, and partly guessed, what had done this thing. She recollected, but vaguely enough, that one of her companions, who had grown
weary of the little creature's pitiful cry, had promised to quiet it for her, and

how speedily it had fallen off into a profound, unbroken slumber. And there it lay, in the same slumber perhaps. She touched it again; but no, the sleep it slept now was even deeper than that—a sleep so sound that its eyelids would never open again to this world's light, nor its sealed lips ever utter a word of this world's speech. Kitty could scarcely believe it; but she could not bear to stay in that mute, gentle, uncomplaining presence; and she lifted up Robin to carry him into her own room. Oh that God had but called her away when she was an innocent baby like that!

Robin's feverishness was almost gone; and now, wrapped in Kitty's gown and rocked to sleep on her lap, he lay contented and restful, while she sat thinking in the dark, for the candle soon burned itself out, until the solemn grey light of the morning dawned slowly in the east. She had made up her mind now what she would do. There was only one more sin lying before her. She had grown up bad, and broken her mother's heart, and now she had brought this great overwhelming sorrow upon poor little Meg. There was but one end to a sinful life like hers, and the sooner it came the better. She would wait till Meg came home and give up Robin to her, for she would not hurry on to that last crime before Meg was there to take care of him. She saw herself stealing along the streets, down to an old pier she knew of, where boats had ceased to ply, and where no policeman would be near to hinder her, or any one about to rescue her; and then she would fling herself, worthless and wretched as she was, into the rapid river, which had borne so many worthless wretches like her upon its strong current into the land of darkness and death of which she did not dare to think. That was what she would do, saying nothing to any one; and if she could ask anything of God, it would be that her mother might never find out what had become of her.

So Kitty sat with her dark thoughts long after Angel Court had awakened to its ordinary life, its groans, and curses, and sobs; until the sun looked in cheerily upon her and Robin, as it did upon Meg in Mrs. Christie's nursery. She did not care to put him down, for he looked very pretty, and happy, and peaceful in his soft sleep, and whenever she moved he stirred a little, and pouted his lips as if to reproach her. Besides, it was the last time she would hold a child in her arms, and though they ached somewhat, they folded round him fondly. At last she heard a man's step upon the ladder mounting to the attics, and Meg's voice speaking faintly. Could it be that her father was come home at last? Oh! what would their eyes see when they opened that door? Kitty held her breath to listen for the first sound of anguish and amazement; but it was poor little Meg's voice which reached her before any other.

"Robbie! oh, Robbie!" she cried, in a tone of piercing terror, "what has become of my little Robbie?"

"He's safe, he's here, Meg," answered Kitty, starting to her feet, and rushing with him to Meg's attic.

It was no rough, weather-beaten seaman, who was just placing Meg on a chair, as if he had carried her up stairs; but some strange, well-clad gentleman, and behind him stood an elderly woman, who turned sharply round as she heard Kitty's voice.

"Posy!" cried Mrs. Blossom.

No one but her own mother could have known again the bright, merry, rosy girl, whom the neighbours called Posy, in the thin, withered, pallid woman who stood motionless in the middle of the room. Even Meg forgot for a moment her fears for Robin. Dr. Christie had only time to catch him from her failing arms, before she fell down senseless upon the floor at her mother's feet.

"Let me do everything for her," exclaimed Mrs. Blossom, pushing away Dr. Christie; "she's my Posy, I tell you. You wouldn't know her again, but I know her. I'll do everything for her; she's my girl, my little one; she's the apple of my eye."

But it was a very long time before Mrs. Blossom, with Dr. Christie's help, could bring Posy to life again; and then they lifted her into her poor bed, and Dr. Christie left her mother alone with her, and went back to Meg. Robin was ailing very little, he said: but the baby? Yes, the baby must have died even if little Meg had fetched him at once. Nothing could have saved it, and it had suffered no pain, he added tenderly.

"I think I must take you two away from this place," said Dr. Christie.

"Oh, no, no," answered Meg, earnestly; "I must stay till father comes, and I expect him to-day or to-morrow. Please, sir, leave me and Robbie here till he comes."

"Then you must have somebody to take care of you," said Dr. Christie.

"No, please, sir," answered Meg, in a low and cautious voice, "mother give me a secret to keep that I can't tell to nobody, and I promised her I'd never let nobody come into my room till father comes home. I couldn't help you, and Mrs. Blossom, and Kitty coming in this time; but nobody mustn't come in again."

"My little girl," said Dr. Christie, kindly, "I daresay your mother never thought of her secret becoming a great trouble to you. Could you not tell it to me?"

"No," replied Meg, "it's a very great secret; and please, when baby's buried like mother, me and Robbie must go on living here alone till father comes."

"Poor child!" said Dr. Christie, rubbing his eyes, "did you know baby was quite dead?"

"Yes," she answered, "but I didn't ask God to let baby live, because mother said she'd like to take her with her. But I did ask him to make Robin well, and bring back Posy; and now there's nothing for him to do but let father come home. I knew it was all true; it's in the Bible, and if I'm not one of God's own children, it says, 'them that ask him.' So I asked him."

Meg's voice sank, and her head dropped; for now that she was at home again, and Robin was found to be all right, her spirit failed her. Dr. Christie went out upon the landing, and held a consultation with Mrs. Blossom, in which they agreed that for the present, until Meg was well enough to take care of herself, she should be nursed in Kitty's attic, with her own door kept locked, and the key left in her possession. So Dr. Christie carried Meg into the back attic, and laid her upon Kitty's mattress. Kitty was cowering down on the hearth, with her face buried on her knees, and did not look up once through all the noise of Meg's removal; though when her mother told her what they were doing she made a gesture of assent to it. Dr. Christie went away; and Mrs. Blossom, who wanted to buy many things which were sorely needed in the poor attic, put her arm fondly round Kitty's neck.

"Posy," she said, "you wouldn't think to go and leave little Meg alone, if I went out to buy some things, and took Robin with me?"

"No, I'll stop," said Kitty, but without lifting her head. When they were alone together, Meg raised herself as well as she could on the arm that was not hurt, and looked wistfully at Kitty's bowed-down head and crouching form.

"Are you really Posy?" she asked.

"I used to be Posy," answered Kitty, in a very mournful voice.

"Didn't I tell you God would let your mother find you?" said Meg; "it's all come true, every bit of it."

"But God hasn't let baby live," muttered Kitty.

"I never asked him for that," she said, falteringly; "I didn't know as baby was near going to die, and may be it's a better thing for her to go to mother and God. Angel Court ain't a nice place to live in, and she might have growed up bad. But if people do grow up bad," added Meg, in a very tender tone, "God can make 'em good again, if they'd only ask him."

As little Meg spoke, and during the silence which followed, strange memories began to stir in the poor girl's heart, recalled there by some mysterious and Divine power. Words and scenes, forgotten since childhood, came back with wonderful freshness and force. She thought of a poor, guilty, outcast woman, reviled and despised by all, save One, who had compassion even for her, forgave all her sins, stilled the clamour of her accusers, and said, "Thy faith hath saved thee; go in peace." She remembered the time when the records of His infinite love had been repeated by her innocent young lips and pondered in her maiden heart. Like some echo from the distant past she seemed to hear the words, "By thine agony and bloody sweat; by thy cross and passion; by thy precious death and burial, Good Lord, deliver us; O Lamb of God, that takest away the sins of the world, have mercy upon us."

"Oh, Meg! Meg!" cried Kitty, almost crawling to the corner where she lay, and falling down beside her on the floor, with her poor, pale face still hidden from sight, "ask God for me to be made good again."

Little Meg stretched out her unbruised arm, and laid her hand upon Kitty's bended head.

"You must ask him for yourself," she said, after thinking for a minute or two: "I don't know as it 'ud do for me to ask God, if you didn't as well."

"What shall I say, Meg?" asked Kitty.

"If I was you," said Meg, "and had grow'd up wicked, and run away from mother, I'd say, 'Pray God make me a good girl again, and let me be a comfort to mother till she dies; for Jesus Christ's sake. Amen.'"

There was a dead silence in the back attic, except for the near noise and distant din which came from the court below, and the great labyrinth of streets around. Little Meg's eyes shone lovingly and pityingly upon Kitty, who looked up for an instant, and caught their light. Then she dropped her head down upon the mattress, and gave way to a storm of tears and sobs.

"Oh God," she cried, "do have mercy upon me, and make me good again, if it's possible. Help me to be a good girl to mother. God forgive me, for Jesus Christ's sake!"

She sobbed out this prayer over and over again, until her voice fell into a low whisper, which even Meg could not hear; and so she lay upon the floor beside the mattress until her mother came back. Mrs. Blossom's face was pale, but radiant with gladness, and Posy looked at it for the first time fully. Then she gave a great cry of mingled joy and sorrow, and running to her, threw her arms round her neck, and laid her face upon her shoulder.

"God 'll hear me and have mercy upon me," she cried. "I'm going to be your Posy again, mother!"

CHAPTER XIII

LITTLE MEG'S FATHER

THE baby was buried the next morning, after Meg had looked upon it for the last time lying very peacefully and smilingly in its little coffin, and had shed some tears that were full of sorrow yet had no bitterness upon its dead face. Mrs. Blossom took Robin to follow it to the grave, leaving Kitty in charge of little Meg. The front attic door was locked, and the key was under Meg's pillow, not to be used again until she was well enough to turn it herself in the lock. The bag containing the small key of the box, with the unopened letter which had come for her mother, hung always round her neck, and her hand often clasped it tightly as she slept.

Meg was lying very still, with her face turned from the light, following in her thoughts the little coffin that was being carried in turns by Mrs. Blossom and another woman whom she knew, through the noisy streets, when Kitty heard the tread of a man's foot coming up the ladder. It could be no one else but Dr. Christie, she thought; but why then did he stop at the front attic door, and rattle the latch in trying to open it? Kitty looked out, and saw a seafaring man, in worn and shabby sailor's clothing, as if he had just come off a long voyage. His face was brown and weather-beaten; and his eyes, black and bright, were set deep in his head, and looked as if they were used to take long, keen surveys over the glittering sea. He turned sharply round as Kitty opened her door.

"Young woman," he said, "do you know aught of my wife, Peggy Fleming, and her children, who used to live here? Peggy wrote me word she'd moved into the front attic."

"It's father," called little Meg, from her mattresses on the floor; "I'm here, father! Robin and me's left; but mother's dead, and baby. Oh! father, father! You've come home at last!"

Meg's father brushed past Kitty into the room where Meg sat up in bed, her face quivering, and her poor bruised arms stretched out to welcome him. He sat down on the mattress, and took her in his own strong arms, while for a minute or two Meg lay still in them, almost like one dead.

"Oh!" she said at last, with a sigh as if her heart had well nigh broken, "I've took care of Robin and the money, and they're safe. Only baby's dead. But don't you mind much, father; it wasn't a nice place for baby to grow up in."

"Tell me all about it," said Robin Fleming, looking at Kitty, but still holding his little daughter in his arms; and Kitty told him all she knew of her lonely life and troubles up in the solitary attic, which no one had been allowed to enter; and from time to time Meg's father groaned aloud, and kissed Meg's pale and wrinkled forehead fondly. But he asked how it was she never let any of the neighbours, Kitty herself, for instance, stay with her, and help her sometimes.

"I promised mother," whispered Meg in his ear, "never to let anybody come in, for fear they'd find out the box under the bed, and get into it somehow. We was afraid for the money, you know, but it's all safe for your mate, father; and here's the key, and a letter as came for mother after she was dead."

"But this letter's from me to Peggy," said her father, turning it over and over; "leastways it was wrote by the chaplain at the hospital, to tell her what she must do. The money in the box was mine, Meg, no mate's; and I sent her word to take some of it for herself and the children."

"Mother thought it belonged to a mate of your's," said Meg, "and we was the more afeared of it being stole."

"It's my fault," replied Robin Fleming. "I told that to mother for fear she'd waste it, if she knew it were mine. But if I'd only known——"

He could not finish his sentence, but stroked Meg's hair with his large hand, and she felt some hot tears fall from his eyes upon her forehead.

"Don't cry, father," she said, lifting her small feeble hand to his face. "God took care of us, and baby too, though she's dead. There's nothink now that he hasn't done. He's done everythink I asked him."

"Did you ask him to make me a good father?" said Fleming.

"Why, you're always good to us, father," answered Meg, in a tone of loving surprise. "You never beat us much when you get drunk. But Robin and me always say, 'Pray God bless father.' I don't quite know what bless means, but it's something good."

"Ah!" said Fleming, with a deep sigh, "He had blessed me. When I was ill he showed me what a poor sinner I was, and how Jesus Christ came into the world to save sinners, 'of whom I am chief.' Sure I can say that if anybody can. But it says in the Bible, 'He loved'me, and gave himself for me.' Yes, little Meg, he died to save me. I felt it. I believed it. I came to see that. I'd nobody to fly to but Jesus if I wanted to be aught else but a poor, wicked, lost rascal, as got drunk, and was no better than a brute. And so I turned it over and over in my mind, lying abed; and now, please God, I'm a bit more like being a Christian than I was. I reckon that's what bless means, little Meg."

As he spoke the door opened, and Mrs. Blossom came in with Robin. It was twelve months since Robin had seen his father, and now he was shy, and hung back a little behind Mrs. Blossom; but Meg called to him in a joyful voice.

"Come here, little Robbie," she said; "it's father, as we've watched for so long. He's a little bit afeared at first, father, but you'll love him ever so when he knows you."

It was not long before Robin knew his father sufficiently to accept of a seat on his knee, when Meg was put back into bed at Mrs. Blossom's entreaties. Fleming nursed his boy in silence for some time, while now and then a tear glistened in his deep eyes, as he thought over the history of little Meg's sorrows.

"I'm thinking," said Mrs. Blossom, cheerfully, "as this isn't the sort o' place for a widow-man and his children to stop in. I'm just frightened to death o' going up and down the court. I suppose you're not thinking of settling here, Mr. Fleming?"

"No, no," said Fleming, shaking his head; "a decent man couldn't stop here, let alone a Christian."

"Well, then, come home to us till you can turn yourself round," continued Mrs. Blossom, heartily; "me and Mr. George have talked it over, and he says, 'When little Meg's father do come, let 'em all come here: Posy, and the little 'uns and all. You'll have Posy and the little 'uns in your room, and I'll have him in mine. We'll give him some sort o' a shakedown, and sailors don't use to lie soft.' So if you've no objections to raise, it's settled; and if you have, please to raise 'em at once."

Robin Fleming had no objections to raise, but he accepted the cordial invitation thankfully, for he was in haste to get out of the miserable life of Angel Court. He brought the hidden box into the back attic, and opened it before little Meg, taking out of it the packet of forty pounds, and a number of pawn-tickets, which he looked at very sorrowfully. After securing these, he locked up the attic again, and carrying Meg in his arms, he led the way down the stairs, and through the court, followed closely by Mrs. Blossom, Posy, and Robin. The sound of brawling and quarrelling was loud as usual, and the children crawling about the pavement were dirty and squalid as ever; they gathered about Meg and her father, forming themselves into a dirty and ragged procession to accompany them down to the street. Little Meg looked up to the high window of the attic, where she had watched so often and so long for her father's coming; and then she looked round, with eyes full of pity, upon the wretched group about her; and closing her eyelids, her lips moving a little, but without any words which even her father could hear, she said in her heart, "Pray God bless everybody, and make them good."

CHAPTER XIV

LITTLE MEG'S FAREWELL

ABOUT a month after Robin Fleming's return, Dr. Christie paid a visit to Mrs. Blossom's little house. He had been there before, but this was a special visit; and it was evident some important plan had to be decided upon. Dr. Christie came to hear what Mrs. Blossom had to say about it.

"Well, sir," said Mrs. Blossom, "a woman of my years, as always lived in one village all her life till I came to London, it do seem a great move to go across the sea. But as you all think as it 'ud be a good thing for Posy, and as Mr. Fleming do wish little Meg and Robin to go along with us, which are like my own children, and as he's to be in the same ship, I'm not the woman to say No. I'm a good hand at washing and ironing, and sewing, and keeping a little shop, or anything else as turns up; and there's ten years' good work in me yet; by which time little Meg 'll be a stout, grown-up young woman; to say nothing of Posy, who's old enough to get her own living now. I can't say as I like the sea, quite the contrary; but I can put up with it; and Mr. Fleming 'll be there to see as the ship goes all right, and doesn't lose hisself. So I'll be ready by the time the ship's ready."

They were all ready in time, as Mrs. Blossom had promised, for there were not many preparations to be made. Little Meg's red frock was taken out of pawn, with all the other things, and Mrs. Blossom went down to her

native village to visit it for the last time; but Posy shrank from being seen
there by the neighbours again. She, and Meg, and Robin went once more
for a farewell look at Temple Gardens. It was the first time she had been in
the streets since she had gone back to her mother, and she seemed ashamed
and alarmed at every eye that met her's. When they stood looking at the
river, with its swift, cruel current, Posy shivered and trembled until she was
obliged to turn away and sit down on a bench. She was glad, she said, to
get home again, and she would go out no more till the day came when
Mr. George drove them all down to the docks, with the few boxes which
contained their worldly goods.

Dr. Christie and his wife were down at the ship to see them off, and they
kissed Meg tenderly as they bade her farewell. When the last minute was
nearly come, Mr. George took little Meg's small hand in his large one, and
laid the other upon her head.

"Little woman, tell us that verse again," he said, "that verse as you've
always gone and believed in, and acted on."

"That as mother and me heard preached from in the streets?" asked Meg.
Mr. George nodded silently.

"It's quite true," said little Meg, in a tone of perfect confidence, "because
it's in the Bible, and Jesus said it. Besides, God did everythink I asked him.
'If ye then, being evil, know how to give good gifts unto your children:
how much more shall your Father which is in heaven give good things to
them that ask him?' "